Haven Brook Series

'Til Death Do Us Part
The Cradle Will Fall
The Ties That Bind
A Very Haven Christmas
Three Strikes, You're Gone

The Ties That Bind

Samantha Baca

THE TIES THAT BIND

THE TIES THAT BIND

6

One

Grant

The snow was coming down heavy, making it nearly impossible to see more than a couple of feet ahead. I turned my high beams on, knowing that the likelihood of anyone else being out at this time of night during the worst storm Haven Brook had seen in twenty years was unlikely. Hell, I didn't want to be out in it myself. My gloved hand gripped the steering wheel as I slowed down to go through the curve I knew was coming.

Out of nowhere, a pair of headlights blinded me as I rounded the bend. I carefully tried to maneuver the truck to the side to avoid the other car, feeling the exact moment that I hit a patch of ice that sent the truck spinning. There was a loud noise as metal plowed into something solid. A horn blared, cutting into the calm silence of the night.

A few seconds later the truck came to a stop on the side of the hill, the tail end butted up against a thick tree. I put it in park and turned off the engine before I grabbed a flashlight out of the glove box and hopped out. It was pitch black which limited my visibility, even with a flashlight. I stepped carefully as the snow sunk around me with each step, patches of ice just inches below. Luckily, I knew the area and even though I was only in ankle deep snow now, it could be waist high in a matter of minutes.

I made my way toward the side of the road, making sure to stay alert for any oncoming traffic. The sound of the horn was getting closer as I walked toward a clearing on the other side of the two-lane highway.

Plunged head first into an embankment of trees was the red sedan that had almost hit me. I quickly scanned the area with the flashlight as I made my way over, looking for anyone that might have been ejected from the vehicle.

I walked over to the driver's side window and looked in. A woman was face down against the airbag that had been deployed. I quickly moved the flashlight around and glanced in the backseat where I saw a little girl, not much older than my son, sitting in the backseat, crying. My heart raced as I tried to pull the door handle to open it, only to find the doors were locked.

"Can you unlock your door?" I screamed, hoping the little girl could hear me over the horn as I pointed to the lock. She shook her head no as she tried to open it. I let out a frustrated breath as I realized the child lock was probably on since I do the same thing for Liam. I smiled warmly at the girl and hoped that she could see it before I went back to the driver's side door. I knocked loudly on the glass, hoping the woman would come to so I wouldn't have to break it and scare the child.

A few seconds later she slowly lifted her head and looked around as she blinked a few times. Her eyes immediately went to the rearview mirror and I could see her lips move as she talked to the girl. I knocked again on the window, watching as she turned to look at me.

"Can you unlock the doors?" I shouted again, shivering as the wind whipped past me, leaving an icy chill in its place.

She nodded yes and pressed the button. I was relieved when I heard the sound and quickly reached forward to open the door. I had plenty of questions to ask her, including what the hell she was doing out in this weather with a child, but needed to get away from the blaring horn before I completely lost my hearing.

I gave her a few seconds after I opened the door so I didn't startle or overwhelm her. She looked like she was pretty out of it and from the way the front end of her car was wrapped around the tree, I could see why.

"My name is Grant, I'm going to help you guys out of the car and get you into my truck. Can you move?" I asked loudly as I looked between both of them before setting the flashlight on the hood of the car, casting enough light around them without blinding anyone.

"I can move, I'm not hurt," the little girl called back to me as she clutched a stuffed animal against her chest. She was still buckled in which made me hopeful that she didn't have any serious injuries.

"How about you, ma'am? Can you move? Are you hurt?" I looked directly at the woman as I scanned her body to check for any bleeding or signs of injuries.

"I can move, I think." She reached down and pushed the button to release her seatbelt. I grabbed the strap and pushed it to the side when it refused to wind back in place. She turned to look at me, still dazed as if she didn't know what to do.

"Very slowly, I want you to turn to the side and bring your legs out." I glanced around us, checking to make sure everything was still safe before asking them to get out. She nodded as she did what I asked and sat there waiting for me to continue.

"That's great," I said gently. "Now I'm going to reach in and I want you to grab onto my arm with both hands while I help you out. Are you ready?"

She nodded yes and slowly grabbed onto my arm, lifting herself out of the car as I brought my other arm behind to help steady her. She was a little wobbly at first but seemed to regain her balance fairly quickly. When I was confident that she wasn't going to fall, I turned my attention to the little girl.

"Okay honey, now it's your turn. Can you unbuckle your seatbelt while I unlock the door?" She smiled and pressed the button to release it as I heard the door unlock. I was thankful to see that her seatbelt immediately pulled back in and didn't appear to have been damaged in the accident. I opened the door and she scooted forward, taking my hand as she carefully stepped out of the car.

"Watch your step, it's very slick out here," I warned as I held her steady before helping to move her next to the woman.

"My truck is on the other side of the road, not too far away. Do you need anything from the car before we go?"

The woman looked dazed as she stared blankly at me. I ran a hand down the scruff on my face, knowing that we needed to get moving. I grabbed the flashlight from the hood and quickly scanned the car. Aside from a travel pillow and a few duffle bags, there wasn't much in there.

"We don't have anything, just those bags in the backseat. My mom has her purse and her phone up front in the passenger seat," the little girl offered as she shivered. I nodded as I reached in and grabbed the two duffle bags and slung them over my shoulder before walking around to the passenger side of the car. The door was hard to open from the damage of the accident but after a couple of hard pulls, I was able to pry it open enough to get inside. I grabbed the purse and cellphone from the seat and let the door slam shut. I stuffed the phone into my pocket and wrapped the purse over my shoulder along with the duffle bags before getting the flashlight situated.

I walked back around to the driver's side and stood next to them so they could hear me over the horn that was still blaring.

"We need to walk across the highway and over to the other side, do you think you guys can do that?"

I prayed they could, otherwise, this was going to take even longer if I had to carry both of them to the truck in separate trips. They both nodded and the little girl reached up and grabbed the woman's hand, forcing her out of her daze.

"Come on, mom, we need to walk across the street to get to the truck." Her voice was small but there was the maturity of a little girl who had to grow up way too quickly. It hit a little too close to home when I thought of Liam and how he grew up faster than he should have after his mom died.

The woman smiled and nodded before turning her head to look at me. The flashlight caught her features just right, casting a warm glow on her golden-brown hair. She was incredibly gorgeous, even with trickles of blood-stained on her head. I shook my head and forced myself to focus as I glanced toward the highway. It was one thing to get myself across an icy, snow-packed highway, knowing how to walk in this weather. It was another to get a woman and a child across safely, assuming that they didn't know how to walk in it given that they were severely underdressed for the weather to begin with.

"Alright, we better get going," I huffed as I drew in a cold breath of air. "What's your name, sweetie?" I asked, looking down at the little girl who was still holding the woman's hand.

"I'm Annie, this is my mom, Lacey." She looked up at her nervously, the way a child does when they get in trouble for giving too much information to a stranger.

"That's a pretty name." I smiled to try to put them both at ease. "Okay, we're going to walk very carefully up this small hill and onto the freeway. The snow has started to pack which will help keep us from having to walk on ice, but that doesn't mean that you won't still hit a patch. I want you to be very careful and take one step at a time. Make sure your foot is planted and secure before taking the next step, okay?"

They both nodded and slowly started walking toward me. We walked alongside each other and I was relieved that it was going faster than I thought. We reached the highway, which was empty, and made it across quickly without any problems. I could see the truck not too far off in the distance and was happy that we could finally get inside and warm up. I clicked the button to unlock the doors as we got closer. I shined the light toward the back, making sure there wasn't any damage that would keep us from getting out of there. More snow had fallen and had already covered up the footprints from where I had been earlier which meant that the storm was coming quickly and we needed to get moving before we were stranded for the night.

I opened the back door and helped Annie get in, making sure she was buckled in before reaching under the seat and pulling out a couple of blankets. I handed one to her as she smiled and grabbed it, quickly wrapping it tightly around herself as she shivered. I sat the duffle bags on the floor below the seat next to her and closed the door before walking around to the passenger door and helping Lacey inside. Once she was settled in, I handed her the other blanket and waited until she had pulled it around herself before putting on her seatbelt. I pulled the phone out of my pocket and handed it to her along with the purse before shutting the door and making my way around to climb in.

I stuck the key in the ignition and turned it, disappointed when it refused to start. I saw the look on Lacey's face from the corner of my eye as worry lines formed across her brow. I clenched my jaw and tried again, relieved when I heard it sputter a few times before it finally started. I made sure the four-wheel-drive was still turned on before slowly putting it in drive and easing up the side of the hill. Thank the Lord that it wasn't a steep hill. I couldn't deal with anything else tonight and was already frozen to the bone from being out in the cold for so long. I cranked up the heat and made sure the vents were aimed toward the back so Annie would get warm.

The drive back to my house wouldn't take long but I had no idea where they were planning to stay. If they hadn't made a reservation they were going to be screwed with everything already being booked for New Year's Eve. Haven Brook was far from a big city but they threw one of the best New Year's Eve parties and all of the neighboring small towns came in to celebrate which meant booming business for the two hotels that were still open.

"Where do you want me to take you?" I asked, keeping my eyes on the road to make sure there weren't any more close calls for the night.

"Um, if there's a hotel nearby, that would be great." Her voice was soft and had the loving tone that you would hear from a mother. It had been hard to hear her earlier with the horn blaring in my ears.

"Do you have a reservation?" I quickly glanced at her before focusing on the road again.

She shook her head no and looked out the window as she pulled the sleeve of her sweater over her hand and covered her mouth nervously.

"Okay, do you have anyone you could stay with?" I was trying to figure out what she was doing here in the first place, my mind completely boggled that she would attempt to drive through this storm without stopping to let it pass. This was just the beginning of it and according to the news, it was about to get really bad, really quick.

"I don't know anyone here, we were just passing through. I didn't expect for us to need to stay the night." Her tone changed slightly and I heard an edge to it.

I don't know what came over me but I looked in the rearview mirror into the eyes of a scared little girl and found myself doing the unthinkable.

"You can stay with me." I gripped the steering wheel tighter than necessary and stared at the road in front of me while trying to fight off the feelings of regret that were already starting to blossom.

Two

Lacey

I stared out the window into the darkness as the truck slowed down once we were in town. Subtly, I cast a glance at the stranger beside me, wondering what I was going to do with his offer for us to stay with him. I anxiously ran my tongue back and forth along the roof of my mouth as I tried to think through what options I had left.

My car was totaled, I was stuck in a small town with no place to stay, in the middle of a freaking blizzard. I shivered at the thought of what would have happened if he hadn't come to save us. Tears started to fill my eyes as I quickly blinked them away, pushing aside the images that had been haunting me for months. As much as I hated the thought of staying the night at some man's house that I didn't know, I hated the thought of what would happen if we didn't find somewhere to lay low for the night. I had no idea where I was but I could definitely tell that it was a small town, and you don't just show up in one and expect not to be the talk of it by morning.

I looked around as we turned left and started heading through a neighborhood of cozy-looking houses. Each one was slightly different than the other but overall they looked the same. A smile played across my lips as I imagined little kids playing in the street as their parents visited with the neighbors while they sat on the front porches drinking lemonade. That was always the life I thought I would have but it's funny the curveballs that were thrown at me instead.

A few minutes later the truck slowly eased into a driveway and I glanced back to see Annie had already fallen asleep. The truck crept forward as the garage door opened and I was thankful that I wouldn't have to try to carry her inside in the snow. The garage door closed quietly behind us as he turned off the engine and turned to smile at me.

He was a very attractive man, relatively clean-cut aside from the scruff on his face from missing a couple of days of shaving. In the dim light of the garage, I could see the slightest hint of blue in his eyes and had to reassure myself that serial killers were often good looking guys and not to let my guard down. Okay, so maybe I wasn't actually worried that he might be a serial killer. It was more likely that I was guarded because I couldn't remember the last time a man was genuinely nice to me without wanting something in return. I smiled back nervously as my fingers fumbled around, working to undo the seatbelt when he opened the door and got out, closing it softly behind him to keep from waking Annie. Once I had my seatbelt undone, I quietly opened the door, surprised to see him on the other side as he helped me out.

"Thanks, Gra—" I paused, completely embarrassed that I had already forgotten his name. I knew it started with a G but now that I was trying to use it, I couldn't remember it for the life of me. Was it Graham? Garth? Gonad? I wrinkled my nose and shook my head, knowing I must be delirious if I was considering that was his name.

I heard him chuckle as he tried to look away, a dimple making its way next to the smile that pulled across his face. He coughed to clear his laughter before looking back at me with a forced stoic expression on his face.

"I'm so sorry," I whispered as I felt the heat travel up my neck to my face. He let a small laugh out as he held up his hand to stop me from saying anything more.

"No worries, it's Grant," he laughed as he looked past me to the back seat. "Do you want me to carry her in for you?"

"Oh no, you don't have to do that. I'll get her, but thank you." I took a few steps back and quietly opened the door before reaching in and leaning across her to undo her seatbelt. Her puppy was clutched to her chest forcing a lump in my throat every time I saw how much she cherished the worn-out stuffed animal. I gently pulled it from her arms so I could pick her up, grabbing it once I had a good hold on her. I smiled as Grant turned and walked in front of me, opening the door as he stepped to the side to let me through.

I heard his footsteps beside me as he reached over and flipped on the light switch in the kitchen, casting enough light for us to see without it waking up Annie. The house already felt cozy and welcoming which was a nice feeling given everything that we had been through in the past 24 hours. He quickly showed me the kitchen and asked that we help ourselves to anything in the fridge before leading me around the corner into the living room. There was a long hallway that separated the two rooms with a staircase at the end.

I shifted my weight to try to adjust for Annie's weight when Grant noticed and pulled his brows together. The tour of the house wrapped up quickly as he cleared some books and a video game controller from the couch so I could set Annie down. He apologized several times, mostly muttering under his breath, about not having a spare room to offer us. The couch was big enough for Annie to sleep comfortably, and there was an oversized recliner in the corner that I could take. Honestly, I was happy to not have to sleep in the car as I had planned.

"This is perfect, thank you so much," I said quietly as I laid Annie down on the couch and pulled the blanket from the truck up over her. She looked so small and fragile while she was sleeping and I had to remind myself that she was only 8 and not the 14-year-old she sometimes acted like. She was growing up too fast, and unfortunately, life was forcing her to leave a part of her childhood behind with the hand she was dealt.

"I'll go grab your stuff from the truck and bring it in for you." His eyes shifted to Annie laying on the couch and I could see a look of concern on his face.

"Maybe we should get her to a hospital, have her checked out," he said warily with his hands on his hips. I looked down and looked at her as a flood of emotions swept over me as I had been wondering the same thing since we fled.

"She's fine, she just needs some rest." I swallowed hard and lifted my eyes, pinning him with a look that I hoped would shift his focus from her to me.

"You guys were in a pretty bad accident, you should go see a doctor and have them run tests."

"Trust me, I see this kind of stuff all the time. We're okay." I smiled the smile I was used to wearing every day for two months as I lied and told everyone I was okay.

"Are you a doctor?" He crossed his arms over his chest and studied me with intense curiosity.

"No, I'm not a doctor," I snapped and crossed my arms to match his. I was exhausted and not in the mood to deal with whatever this was. Perhaps he had good intentions and was simply asking a question, but part of me knew that there was more to it than that. There was judgment lingering in the air between us that I had been dealing with from men in my life for as long as I could remember. The constant feeling of needing to explain myself before they took my word to be good enough.

"Exactly— you need to get to the hospital and—"

"I'm a trauma nurse and I see stuff like this every day in the ER. I've been doing this for 5 years and know the signs and symptoms of what to watch for. There is no need for us to risk our lives by going out in this storm for them to tell you the same thing I'm telling you now." My tone was firm as I stood my ground, trembling on the inside as a quick burst of adrenaline shot through me. It was the truth though, I had been watching Annie from the moment we got into his truck, looking for any signs that I should be concerned with.

"Fine, it's your call. I'll be back with your stuff in a few minutes." He turned and walked out the door to the garage, leaving me in silence and alone with my thoughts. When he came back with the duffle bags, he set them down and mumbled goodnight as he stalked off down the hall and upstairs where I heard a door close behind him. I pushed the bags to the side with my foot so they were out of the way before I leaned down to adjust Annie on the couch.

I looked down, her beautiful face was angelic with her brown hair fanned out on the pillow, her skin a soft ivory color. I reached out and gently touched the bruise that was fading on her cheek before I wiped away the tear that slid down my face. I pulled in a deep breath and forced myself to release it slowly, the way I had learned to do it during my therapy sessions. This wasn't the time or the place for a breakdown so I tucked the blanket into the back of the couch and placed a soft kiss on her forehead before climbing into the recliner and closing my eyes. It was strange but for the first time in months, I felt oddly safe and for once, I slept peacefully.

Three

Grant

The house was eerily quiet when I woke up, sending me into a panic when I didn't hear Liam's cartoons blaring from the living room, the tell-tell sign it was Sunday. As suddenly as the fear washed over me, it evaporated just the same when I remembered that he had stayed the night with my mom after I had to run out of town to help a friend fix their furnace before the storm hit.

I rolled out of bed and stretched, my back and neck super achy and sore as I remembered the impact I felt when my truck hit the tree. I ran a hand over my shoulder as I slowly rolled my neck a few times until I heard the pop that provided the relief I was looking for. I pulled the curtain back and looked outside, confirming that at least 12 inches of new snow had fallen since we got home last night.

We. The word hit me like a ton of bricks, forcing back all of the thoughts and feelings I struggled with last night as I tried to fall asleep. I pulled a hoodie over my head and worked my jaw back and forth as I pictured the beautiful woman and her daughter that were still downstairs. In my house. I let out a heavy sigh before grabbing my cell phone and shoving it into the pocket of my sweatpants.

Quietly, I went downstairs, hoping I wouldn't wake them as the stairs softly creaked beneath my weight. I paused outside the living room and glanced in to see both were still sound asleep. Annie's arms were stretched out above her head as she slept sprawled out on the couch, while Lacey was curled up into a ball in the recliner with a throw blanket barely covering her.

I shook my head as I walked into the kitchen, disappointed in myself for not being a better host, and making sure they had things they might need— like blankets. That was where Renee really shined, she was the perfect host and always thought of the little details that would make someone feel welcomed and comfortable. She was the better half of me and some days I was furious that she was taken from me and I was left with the qualities that I hated the most about myself.

Luckily, Annie still had the blanket covering her that I had given her in the truck. The blanket Lacey was using was one of Liam's old blankets that he had outgrown years ago but refused to part with. He insisted on keeping it in the living room for when he wanted to stay up late watching movies, which was every single weekend since Thanksgiving break. School would be starting up again soon once winter break was over and would put a damper on how often we were able to do that.

I walked lightly through the kitchen and started a pot of coffee, not knowing if Lacey was a coffee drinker. Trying to be a better host, I decided to make a full pot and hope that she was so that I wouldn't feel inclined to drink the entire pot by myself. I stood by the sink and watched as the snow fell peacefully while the aroma filled the room and floated down the hallway.

My head whipped around as I heard footsteps behind me as Lacey walked in and joined me. There were dark circles under her eyes which made me wonder if she had slept any last night. Her brown hair was piled loosely on her head, slightly messy from sleeping in the chair. Or at least trying to. She covered her mouth as she yawned and tried to look away. When she finished, she turned back toward me and smiled shyly as if she felt as uncomfortable about being there as I felt having her there.

"Coffee?" I offered as I held up an empty mug out for her. Her long fingers reached out and grabbed it, a warm smile on her face as she pulled it to her chest and waited for me to finish pouring my cup. I walked around to the other side of the island and opened the fridge to grab the creamer as she poured.

I slid the bottle along the countertop to her but she subtly shook her head no as she lifted her mug and took a sip. My eyebrows rose in surprise given that she didn't strike me as the kind of woman who drank her coffee piping hot and black.

"You like your coffee black," I said attempting to make small talk as I nodded in approval and took a sip, suddenly feeling like less of a man for adding creamer to mine.

"Just like my soul," she teased and lowered the mug. I stopped to look at her in the light, finally able to see what she looked like now that she wasn't hidden in the darkness. Her eyes were a beautiful hazel-green color which left me staring harder than I intended as I tried to figure out if they were more green or brown. I looked away to keep from making her uncomfortable and walked to the open space between the kitchen and living room to check on Annie.

It was more out of habit from doing it with Liam than anything but as I looked at Annie, my stomach dropped when I saw a rather decent sized bruise on her cheek. I wondered how I missed it last night but remembered that I didn't get to see her in the light much either. The parental instincts in me kicked in and before I knew it my temper was flaring as I turned around and locked eyes with Lacey.

"How did she get the bruise on her cheek?" I nodded toward Annie, trying to keep any anger or judgment out of my voice.

"It must have been from the accident. She always has a handful of toys in the backseat with her, something must have hit her during the impact." She looked away nervously and something pulled deep in my gut that told me she was full of shit.

"Really?" I tilted my head and studied her, waiting for her to give in and tell me the truth. "You think she has a bruise on her cheek from an accident that barely happened less than eight hours ago?" Something was off, I could feel it. I didn't want to scare her off by accusing her of anything, but I also couldn't just turn the other way if this little girl was in danger and being abused.

She watched me cautiously as I continued to watch her with the same intensity.

"Look, I don't know you. I don't know where you came from. I don't know what your story is. But I do know that that little girl isn't going anywhere until I know what happened to her. A child her age shouldn't have a bruise that big on her face. I can't in good conscience turn my head and look the other way if she's in trouble which means I have no choice but to get Child Protective Services involved." My tone was firm and steady as I walked over and stood in the doorway, blocking her from leaving the kitchen as she set her coffee cup down and started toward the living room. I needed her to talk to me, to reassure me that I wasn't crazy for thinking that she might have caused the bruise on Annie's face.

"You can't be serious," she scoffed. "I told you, it was from the car accident. I already have bruises from it, see?" She tilted her head back to show me her neck. Black marks were starting to cover her skin from the impact of her flying into the steering wheel and having the airbag hit beneath her face.

"Most of your bruises can be explained by the car accident, not all of them." I gave her a knowing look and watched as she looked down and avoided eye contact. My stomach started to twist in knots as I read the truth in what she wasn't saying.

"There's a handful of bruises along your throat that are not from the accident. And they look like they're a few days old. So, what's going on?" I took a step back and leaned against the doorway. I didn't want to have to call the cops on her but there was absolutely no way that I was going to turn my head and look the other way when I had a little girl sleeping on my couch with a decent sized bruise on her face that I was now pretty sure it had something to do with her mom. If she wasn't responsible for it, why not just tell me what happened? She seemed to be working rather hard to keep it a secret and that made me very suspicious.

She glanced behind me to check on her daughter before looking at me. There was a look of worry on her face that I wanted to associate with being a concerned parent, but everything was still too foggy to see clearly.

"Lacey, what happened to Annie?" My tone was softer as I hoped she would give in and talk to me, allow me to help her with whatever was happening.

"I can't get into it, okay? But she's safe with me. I promise you that." She started to tap her foot impatiently as I saw her look past me again.

"That's not good enough for me to just look the other way and let you leave once this storm passes. I need to know that she's not in danger."

A look of panic flashed across her face, her eyes darting up to meet mine, as I said the word I didn't want to say. Danger. Something was wrong.

My anger and frustration were starting to build as I pushed off from the wall and took two strides toward her, catching her off guard as I stood face to face with her.

"I'm not going to keep asking, damn it! I'm a man of little patience and

if there is something or someone that you're running from — I need
to know about it. Now!" I growled as I caught a glimpse of fear in her
eyes before she pulled her shoulders back and pushed her chest out to
make herself look taller next to me. I immediately felt the impact of my
reaction and knew that I had just forced her even further away. I let out a
heavy sigh and waited for the tongue lashing she was about to give me.

"You don't know me. You have no idea who I am or what I'm going
through. So why don't you deflate your ego and stop acting like some
big, badass guy who's going to make me do something I don't want
to?" She stared at me as she spoke, each word crisp with anger. "I
appreciate you sheltering us from the storm, but your help ends there.
It would be better for everyone if we kept our distance and respected
each other's boundaries." She glared at me as she pushed past me and
walked away, sitting down on the floor in front of where Annie was
still sleeping on the couch.

I blew out the frustrated breath I had been holding as I turned and
walked upstairs, needing some space from this infuriating woman.
Whether she wanted my help or not, she was going to get it.

Four

Lacey

I leaned back against the couch, making sure I didn't wake Annie, and closed my eyes as my head rested on the cushion. For once I wanted to just stop everything and take a moment to breathe. To think. To process everything that had happened in the last two months when my world was first turned upside down while everything was still crashing around me.

I tried to focus on my breathing, pulling in slow, cleansing breaths, and forcing out the frustration and irritation that Grant had just created. Maybe his name should be Gonad, given how he had acted when he didn't get his way. I don't know if he was just a naturally entitled person or if something had happened in his life that made him think that the world owed him something, but I wasn't in the mood to deal with his bullshit. I had plenty of problems of my own, including figuring out how to get another car so we could get the hell out of town as soon as possible.

My anxiety started to rise as I thought about the accident and the storm last night, suddenly feeling more grateful that he had been there when he was. I realized as I started to calm down that my anger wasn't actually with him- he hadn't done anything wrong other than push a little too hard to find out what had happened to Annie. I couldn't blame him though, as a mother I would have been just as concerned if I had met a random woman with a child that had the kind of bruise on her face that Annie had. My anger was with myself for allowing everything to happen that had happened, and worst of all – for letting

Annie get caught up in the middle of it.

My breathing started to level out as I tried to remember what had happened, how I lost control of the car so quickly. I wasn't a reckless driver, and having grown up in Colorado, I was used to this type of weather. I relaxed as I let my mind wander, not focusing on anything in particular as I felt my body give in, needing to rest. I sunk further and let Annie's light snores lull me to sleep.

"Get your hands off of her, now!" I screamed as I watched in horror, my hands desperately reaching out to try to grab her and pull her back. His eyes were black, the anger and hatred in them masked by the smell of stale beer on his breath.

"You don't tell me what to do!" His voice boomed through the room, rattling the picture frames on the wall behind him.

I lunged forward and grabbed Annie, pulling her away from him. I immediately noticed the red marks around her arm from how hard he had been holding her. In an instant, rage surged through me as I looked from her back to him. As quickly as I could, I pushed her behind me before I pulled my arm back and swung, hearing the shattering sound as I felt my fist make contact with his cheek. His head whipped back before he shook it off and turned to face me.

I stood in front of Annie, blocking her the best that I could while waiting for him to strike. Flashbacks of my childhood came flooding through and I was thankful for the reminder of what he was capable of. My chest heaved, trying to plan out our next move while knowing that I only had a few seconds. I slightly turned my head to the side so Annie could hear me without taking my eyes off of him.

"Run, Annie, go! Now! Don't look back, run to the car, and get inside!" I yelled loud enough for her to hear me. I felt her fingers tremble as she let go of the back of my shirt and took off running. There wasn't much room with stuff scattered everywhere, but she ran as I told her to. I watched as his eyes shifted to her, the anger prominent again before he kicked the coffee table out of the way to try to get to her.

I jumped in front of him, shielding her body from his reach when I heard a commotion behind me. As we crashed to the floor, I looked over and saw that Annie had fallen, catching her cheek on the end of the coffee table that had been kicked into her path at the last second. She looked at me, eyes wide with fear.
"Run!" My voice screeched through the room as I saw her lip tremble

before she got up, grabbed her stuffed puppy, and ran out of the house. The door slammed behind her, reassuring me that she was safe. "You stupid bitch!" He grunted as his hands wrapped tightly around my throat. I dug my nails in and clawed as hard as I could, trying to get him off of me. "If you're going to live under my roof, you're going to do as I say!"

I tried to turn my head, desperate for a breath as he pushed down harder on my throat. The smell of the beer on his breath was another reminder of my childhood which forced a memory of my mother laying on the floor in this same position. I swore that I would never have the same tragic fate when I watched the life drain from her face as she cried when she saw me watching.

It took everything I had in me to just let go and allow him to think that he had won. He was over three hundred pounds and stronger than me. There was no way of fighting him or getting out from under the weight of his drunk body. I said a quick prayer for Annie as I closed my eyes and let my body relax. I held my breath for what felt like an eternity as I waited for him to notice I wasn't fighting anymore. He chuckled as he rolled off of me, leaving me for dead.

"Annie, you get your ass back here right now!" he yelled, walking toward the front door. Pushing through the lack of oxygen that hadn't yet been replaced, I forced myself to get up. I could hear him down the hallway, opening and closing the doors as he looked for her. As he rounded the corner he saw me standing by the front door with a baseball bat in my hand.

His face started to change as a cruel smile pulled across his face, his laugh starting to rise out of his chest. I swung the bat as hard as I could, knocking him to the ground. I didn't wait to see if he had gotten up before I sprinted out the front door and ran to the shed behind the house. I swung the door open and frantically looked around, straining to listen for the sound of the front door. My eyes wildly searched the shelf in front of me before finding what I needed.

I ran back to the house as quickly as I could, glancing at the car to see Annie's head in the backseat. I picked up the pace and ran the last few steps before swinging the front door open and expecting to see him standing on the other side. A small gasp escaped my throat as I looked down and saw him lying face down in a puddle of blood. My hand trembled as I unscrewed the top of the gas can and started to shake it back and forth, allowing it to soak into the carpet. I let out a shaky breath as I glanced at his body lying lifeless on the floor before striking a match and letting it fall. Within seconds I watched the flames spread, the heat engulfing me.

I sprung forward, gasping for air as I woke up from the nightmare. My eyes frantically scanned the room, confused as I tried to figure out where I was. Voices quietly floated in from the kitchen and I blew out a ragged breath as I started to remember. I held my hand to my chest, trying to calm myself as I turned to check on Annie when I felt her moving behind me. Her eyes softly fluttered open, looking around before spotting me as she smiled.

"Good morning, mommy," her little voice whispered.

"Good morning, princess. How did you sleep?" I turned around and faced her, taking a moment to look her over again.

"Good but I'm kind of sore. My neck hurts." She winced as she reached up to touch it and I saw a burn on her shoulder by her neck from where the seatbelt had been.

"I'm sorry baby, I'll see if I have some Tylenol. How do you feel otherwise?"

"I'm good, you don't have to worry about me, mommy." She smiled and pulled her puppy into her chest as she squeezed it.

"Okay, good. Well, let me find you some Tylenol, and then I'll see about getting us a ride to go get some breakfast." I softly patted her shoulder as I stood up at the same time Grant walked in with a little boy behind him that looked just like him. I quickly realized that I knew nothing about him and wondered if there was a wife he was hiding along with the child that had magically appeared.

"Good morning, ladies, this is my son, Liam." He stepped to the side and pulled him under his arm as the boy tried to wrestle his way out from his dad's embrace.

"Daaadddd," he groaned as a blush crept up his neck. "You're embarrassing me."

"Sorry, my bad," he joked and held his hands up in the air, letting go. I smiled at the interaction, surprised to see this playful side of him.

"I'm Lacey, and this is my daughter, Annie," I said, nodding to the couch as she sat up and waved. Liam smiled and waved back which got a giggle out of Annie.

"My dad made pancakes for breakfast, do you want to come eat then we can watch cartoons?" Liam asked Annie.

I felt my heart skip a beat as the anxiety started to work its way through me again.

"Sure!" Annie exclaimed excitedly as she jumped off the couch. I quickly reached out and gently grabbed her, pulling her back to me.

"Thank you for the offer, that's very sweet. I'm actually going to find a ride and then we'll be out of your hair before you know it." I smiled as I wrapped my arms around Annie, feeling the warmth of her back from being wrapped in the blanket, against my stomach.

"I hate to break it to you— you're not getting a ride. No one is going out in this weather today unless they have to." Grant leaned against the doorframe and nodded toward the window behind me. I squinted my eyes to see through the sheer curtains, dread filling me when I saw the amount of snow that had fallen. He was right, no one was going out in this.

"I made plenty of breakfast for everyone, let's go eat before it gets cold." He cocked an eyebrow as he looked at me, a silent plea for me not to fight him on this. I let my shoulders fall as I nodded and looked out the window again. There were worse things that could happen than to have breakfast with an incredibly good looking stranger and his son.

We followed them into the kitchen and I guided Annie to a chair at the table as they sat down on the opposite side. After she was situated, I picked up the plate in front of her and eyed the options that had been set out on the table. I must have been in a deep sleep because I completely missed him making bacon, eggs, sausage, pancakes, and hash browns. Everything smelled delicious as my stomach growled in anticipation.

Soon everyone had their plates and were busy eating when I caught Grant looking at Annie and subtly shaking his head before looking down to take a bite. I knew how it had to look, to see a child with a bruise like that on her face. There was no way that I could tell him what had really happened, not until it was safe. And honestly, there was no way to know if we would ever be safe.

"How was your slumber party at Nana's?" Grant asked Liam in between bites, a feeling of relief washing over me that he had redirected his attention.

"It was fun, we stayed up late watching movies and eating junk food." His smile spread across his face, revealing a missing tooth up top.

"How's that any different than what you do here?" Grant laughed as he tore off a small piece of bacon and tossed it into his mouth.

"Nana lets me watch the movies you won't let me watch," Liam said dramatically, forcing a giggle out of me as I watched Grant's shocked expression.

"Oh really?"

"Na, not really. But Nana is a lot more fun. She doesn't snore as loud as you do when you guys fall asleep in the middle of the movie."

"I don't snore." Grant lifted his glass and took a drink as he playfully stared at Liam and challenged him to disagree. Liam smirked as he turned and looked directly at me.

"He snores. Like a bear. I'm surprised you didn't hear him last night."

I laughed and turned my head to keep from choking on my bite.

"I was too tired to notice," I teased, briefly looking away from Liam to Grant. He arched an eyebrow as he smiled, the dimple making another appearance.

"So what was Wyatt doing at Nana's this morning?" Grant asked, turning his attention back to Liam as the flirty smile I saw a second ago started to vanish.

"He wanted to check on her to make sure the heater was working."

"How did he get volunteered to bring you home? I was planning to come get you at eight."

"I asked, he agreed." Liam shrugged his shoulders as he shoved a bite of pancake into his mouth. "Besides, his girlfriend lives down the street so it was practically on his way anyways."

Grant laughed as he shook his head and took a sip of coffee. It was interesting to see the dynamic between him and his son but it left me curious as to what their story was. Neither of them had mentioned his mom so I kept my mouth shut and gave them the same respect for their privacy that I prayed Grant would give me.

After everyone was done eating, the kids asked permission to go watch cartoons in the living room. As they cleared out of the room, I worked on piling the dirty dishes on the table to take to the sink. Grant walked up beside me and grabbed the other pile I had made before turning and carrying them to sink.

"You don't have to clean up, you can go sit with the kids and relax if you want to," he said over his shoulder as he set the dishes on the counter and turned on the water in the sink.

"I'm not leaving you to do the dishes after you cooked breakfast for everyone," I scoffed as I carried the other pile over and set them next to his.

"Why not?" He pulled his brows together in confusion.

"Because that's rude!" I turned and leaned back against the counter so I could see his face. "If you would scoot out of the way, I can wash those for you." I pushed my lips together into an awkward duck-kissy face pose and hoped it would make me look cute enough to get my way.

"I'm not washing all of these," he said matter-of-factly as he rinsed each plate and set it on the other side. "I'm just rinsing them, that's what the dishwasher is for." He nodded to the side so I leaned forward and looked at it.

"Okay," I said, pushing off from the counter. "You rinse, I'll load." I walked over and opened the dishwasher, pulling the bottom rack out when his hand reached out and stopped me.

"Thank you, but it's fine. I'll load it."

I let out a loud, frustrated sigh as I crossed my arms over my chest and glared at him.

"What's your problem?" I demanded.

"I don't have a problem. I like to do things a certain way and you're a guest in my house. Guests don't do chores." He shrugged as he turned his head back to focus on rinsing the rest of the dishes.

"Do you not think that I'm capable of loading a dishwasher?"

"I don't know what you're capable of or not. What I do know is that I will do the cleaning. If you want to hang out and talk, that's fine. You can start by explaining what happened last night." He reached over to turn off the water before drying his hands and tossing the towel on the counter as he turned around to look at me.

We stood staring at each other for what felt like minutes before I heard Liam call for him to come fix the internet that had gone out again. His shoulders fell slightly as he pursed his lips as he debated whether to say whatever he was going to say before he left. I let out a shaky breath as I felt the air in the room change once he was gone. I said a silent prayer that this storm would pass as quickly as it came so I could get the hell out of here before things got too complicated. I quickly loaded the dishwasher with the dishes from the sink, feeling somewhat satisfied that he didn't get his way. As childish as it seemed, this guy pushed every button I had and I found it getting progressively harder not to push his.

Five

Grant

The day went by at a slow pace, perfect for a lazy Sunday. After I got the internet restarted for Liam, I went back into the kitchen to find that Lacey had finished loading the dishwasher and started it as she acted nonchalant, drinking coffee while watching the snow fall outside. While it had irritated me that she didn't listen when I had asked her not to do the dishes, I found that I wasn't as angry as I thought I would be.

Control was a major issue for me and had been ever since Renee died and sent my life spinning out of control. How are you supposed to feel in control of anything when your world shatters around you and you have to pick up the pieces before they fall because a child is depending on you? After losing Renee I made sure that I was constantly in control of everything, even the tiniest details. Not just for me, but for Liam. It was a very delicate balance that needed constant attention to keep everything from falling apart.

I glanced across the room at Lacey who was curled up in the recliner with her legs tucked under her while she watched the kids play a video game that Annie had chosen. I hadn't seen Liam play this game in months, but he lit up the moment Annie asked if they could play it and insisted that he knew all of the tricks to help them beat the bad guy. Lacey's face was pointed at the tv which made it look like she was watching it but the worry in her eyes gave her away. She was somewhere else completely, worrying about something that she refused to talk to me about.

I had gone back and forth over things in my head all morning as I cooked breakfast, sneaking a quick look into the living room as they slept, trying to figure out what she could be hiding. Who she could be running from. The problem-solver in me wanted to do just that-solve the problem. Whatever it was, I could help her fix it. But when I put myself in her shoes, I remembered how reluctant I was to accept anyone's help after Renee died so I didn't blame her for not wanting to talk to a stranger about her problems.

The thing that kept eating away at me was the bruise on Annie's face. I had seen plenty of bruises in my lifetime, growing up as a middle child with two brothers, as well as being a P.E. teacher for elementary school kids. The bruise that Annie had on her cheek was long and didn't match what I expected to see if someone had hit her. It almost looked like she had run into something, or possibly had something hit her. I considered Lacey's explanation that a toy had flown up and hit her during the accident but it looked like it had been there a little bit longer than that.

My attention was redirected when I heard clapping and a giggle from Annie as Liam slammed his controller down on the couch next to him before getting up to do a victory dance. The image on the screen showed a bad guy laying on the ground with stars circling his head, confirming that they had defeated the big boss that they had been talking about for the past hour. I glanced at the time on my phone, debating whether I should be the tough dad and stick with cutting Liam off for the day since he had already been playing for a few hours, or if I should make an exception and let him play a little bit longer given we had company and I didn't have anything else to entertain them with. Besides, it was New Year's Eve, why not let them go out with a bang on the last day of the year.

I felt my phone vibrate and looked down to see Chase's name on the screen. I slid my finger across the screen to unlock it as I lifted myself off the floor and walked into the kitchen to answer it.

"Hey, what's up?" I said as I refilled my cup of coffee and took a sip.

"Just wanted to check in to see what you and Liam were up to tonight and if you guys wanted to hang out and ring in the new year together?"

I glanced back into the living room as I thought about it. While it would be good to see them and celebrate New Years together like we always did, it felt weird to tell him that we had unexpected guests staying with us. I could make something up to avoid having to tell anyone, but I knew that Liam had been looking forward to seeing them tonight. There wasn't much that he looked forward to these days so I couldn't bring myself to take this away from him. As I was about to speak, I saw Lacey coming toward me, her eyes locked on mine as she froze in her tracks when she noticed I was on the phone. I nodded and waved for her to come in as I turned around in my seat so I could focus on the conversation instead of what she was doing.

"Yeah, we can still hang out and celebrate the new year. Did you guys want to come here or is it too hard to take Rylee out in this storm?" I tried to keep my voice low so Lacey wouldn't hear but it was nearly impossible as the room was completely silent aside from the sound the water made as it filled her glass.

"We can go there if that works for you guys, the storm isn't too bad and we only live ten minutes away."

"Sounds good. Have you talked to Noah and Jade to see if they're coming too?" I asked, glancing at Lacey out of the corner of my eye as she filled a second glass with water.

"Not yet, I'll call him when we hang up and let him know the plan."

"Okay," I sighed, taking in a deep breath. "Oh, and Chase?"

"Yeah?"

"We have company tonight, just so you guys know." I gritted my teeth as I said it, noticing the moment Lacey's body tightened in response as she heard it.

"You do? Who?" There was genuine curiosity in his voice as he asked it which meant that he was going to give me shit about this and read more into it than what it was.

"A woman named Lacey and her daughter, Annie. They were in a car accident last night and are stranded due to the weather, so they're staying with us since all of the hotels are booked." I ran a hand through my hair and leaned back against the chair.

"Grant Fucking Walker has a woman in his house? No fucking way!"

I rolled my eyes and looked out the window as I listened to Chase laughing his ass off on the other line.

"Just be here by 8," I snapped and hung up the phone. I set it on the table in front of me as I slowly turned to look at Lacey. She still had her back to me as she wiped down the counter. I watched as she lifted the towel to put it back on the hook above the sink, her fingers trembling as she did. When she turned around holding both glasses of water, there was a look of worry on her face.

"I'm sorry, I wasn't trying to eavesdrop on your phone call but I couldn't help but overhear your plans for tonight. Annie and I will find somewhere to go and will be out of your hair in no time." She smiled like she was embarrassed as she started to walk out of the room.

"Lacey," I said before she could leave, feeling relieved when she stopped and turned around. Her eyes looked up and met mine. "I really hope that you and Annie will feel comfortable hanging out with my family tonight, we would love to celebrate the new year with you."

A smile quickly washed across her face before she looked away. When she looked back, her face was back to the solemn expression she had been wearing all day.

"Thank you, but we don't want to be in the way." She offered a tight smile as she waited to make sure I was done before she turned to leave.

"You won't be in the way, it's just a laid back group of people, hanging out and celebrating the new year. They'll be here around 8."

"Okay. Thank you." She licked her lips nervously before turning and walking into the living room. I watched as she handed a glass of water to Annie and took a drink out of her own. I could hear the excitement in Annie's voice when she asked her mom if they were really staying with us for a New Year's Eve party. Lacey subtly looked up at me before answering her, nodding as Annie set her glass on the coffee table before reaching up to wrap her arms around her mom's neck as she hugged her. I felt a pull deep in my chest that I hadn't felt in a long time as I watched the kids smile and laugh with Lacey in the other room.

<u>Six</u>

Lacey

It was after seven when we finished dinner and I convinced Grant to let me help with cleaning up. The day had been surprisingly relaxing, which was great given that my body felt like it had been run over by a truck and needed the rest. I had it in my mind that we wouldn't stay long and that I could get us back on the road sooner than later, but when Grant confirmed that the roads in and out of Haven Brook were closed due to the storm, I knew we were stuck for a little while longer.

I was thankful that I had thought enough in advance to pack the duffle bags for Annie and me with the things we would need if we ever had to leave at the last minute. There was a full week's worth of clothes for each of us, as well as a few sentimental items that I made sure to pack. For days, I stared at the duffle bags, praying that I had packed them for nothing; praying that my instincts weren't right and that my mind wasn't playing terrible tricks on me.

I stepped out of the shower and wrapped the towel tightly around my body, shivering from the cold tile under my bare feet. Grant had insisted that Annie and I move our stuff up to Liam's room and use the guest bathroom since we would be staying a few days, at minimum. While Liam seemed happy to give up his room to us, he groaned when he joked about how he wasn't going to get any sleep with how loud his dad snores.

Annie had already taken a quick shower and was sitting anxiously on the floor while I finished mine. I knew she was excited to go downstairs and help get things set up for the party, which I still felt terrible about crashing. My nerves had been fried all day, wondering if Annie was old enough to remember what today was. It was killing me inside and I hoped that she was too little to know that today would have been mine and her father's tenth wedding anniversary. We did a big celebration every year, partly to celebrate the new year, but mostly to celebrate each other.

I got ready quickly while Annie played in the room, pulling my hair up in the front so it was out of my face. My fingers trembled as they worked the bobby pins into place, forcing a cute little bump up in the front as I straightened the pieces that hung to the side of it, framing my face. I didn't have anyone to get dolled up for but I also didn't have the heart to go through with breaking that tradition this year. Things were hard enough already, I wasn't ready to deal with picking up the pieces of my heart when it shattered at the thought that I wouldn't have anyone to celebrate with tonight. No one to make a toast with about how great the new year would be and no one to kiss at the stroke of midnight.

I rubbed my lips together, watching as the red lipstick coated each lip perfectly. I stepped back and ran a hand down the front of my cream-colored sweater dress, wondering what Derek would have thought when he saw me in it. The warmth of a tear trickled down my cheek as I bit my lip to keep from crying. I sucked in a deep breath and forced it out, determined to pull myself together as I spun my wedding ring around nervously on my finger. I heard Liam call for Annie, asking her to come look at the decorations he had found. She quickly peeked in the bathroom, begging me to let her go. I sighed and nodded yes, knowing that I would be down there in a few minutes myself. I didn't like having her away from me, but I was able to hear everything downstairs clearly which made me feel more at ease.

It was 7:30 by the time I finished getting ready and made my way downstairs. I turned the corner to go into the kitchen at the same time Grant was coming out and crashed into him. I braced myself against this broad chest, feeling the solid muscles beneath my fingertips. I felt his hands on my hips as he tried to steady both of us, the warmth of them sending a chill through my body. My eyes fluttered open as I slowly looked up, taking in his blue eyes as he looked down at me.

"You okay?" he asked quietly, his voice scratching in the back of his throat while his hands still held onto me.

"Yeah, I'm good." I parted my lips to speak but the words caught in my throat as I watched his eyes wander down my body, a look of lust on his face. My body felt like it was on fire under his gaze, paralyzing me in place as he took his time soaking in every tiny detail.

"Hey, Dad, can we hang up some streamers for decoration?" Liam called from the kitchen, breaking his focus. His head snapped up as he listened before agreeing to let Liam do what he wanted. Slowly he pulled his hands away from my body and clenched his fists at his sides as he appeared to struggle with not reaching out and touching me again. I tucked a strand of hair behind my ear, more out of nervous habit than anything.

"You look nice," he said as stepped to the side to let Liam pass by as he ran upstairs to get the supplies he needed.

"Thank you." I smiled as I ran a hand over my stomach, suddenly feeling nervous and self-conscious that I was probably the only one who was going to be dressed up. Maybe this was a big mistake after all. My palms started sweating as I fought the urge to run upstairs, crawl in a corner, and cry. I could feel the anxiety building as my bottom lip started to tremble, knowing that I was about to lose any control that I had left.

"Hey, what's wrong?" His eyes were sympathetic as he studied me.

"Nothing, I'm just a little anxious about crashing your party and meeting your friends. And I'm pretty sure that I'm way overdressed. I should go change," I rambled as I quickly turned to go back upstairs. His hand reached out and gently grabbed my elbow, holding me in place as he took a step forward.

"I'm sorry that you're feeling anxious, but I promise they are really cool people and you'll feel like part of the gang in no time. Plus, they're family, not friends. That means that we don't pretend to be anything or worry about anyone judging us. You're safe here."

I knew that his words were meant to put me at ease with being around new people but the moment that he said I was safe, I knew that I was far from it. The hours had passed by slowly and with each minute I knew the chances of him getting closer and finding us were increasing.

"Thanks, I'm just going to change real quick." I forced a smile and was about to walk away when I saw Annie come around the corner. Her eyes lit up when she saw me, running over to wrap her arms around my waist. Grant smiled warmly as he stepped back to let her in.

"Mama, you look so pretty! I knew it would be like all of the other

New Year's where you get dressed up and we have a party!" Her eyes were wide with excitement and I watched in sadness the moment that everything clicked into place for her. Her eyes filled with tears as she looked up at me. "It's not like the other parties, is it mama?"

I shook my head as I held my breath and fought back the tears.

"No, baby, it's not," I whispered.

Annie held onto my waist and hugged me tightly as she turned her head to look at Grant.

"Mommy and daddy always had a big party and played kissy-face all night while we celebrated the new year. But daddy can't be here for this party."

Her face fell and she tucked her head into my stomach as I rubbed her back. Grant looked up at me as a tear slid down my cheek. I bit the inside of my cheek to keep from crumbling to the floor and falling apart.

"I've got the streamers, Annie do you want to help me put them up?" Liam asked as he bounced down the stairs, completely unaware of what had happened. She looked up at me for approval.

"Go ahead, baby. Go have fun and make everything look really pretty," I said as my voice cracked. She smiled and let go as she walked with Liam to go hang the decorations in the living room. When they were out of sight I let out the breath that I had been holding. I forced a tight smile at Grant before I turned and walked away. I could hear him say my name as I went upstairs, not having the strength to talk about what happened.

<u>Seven</u>

Grant

The night was turning out to be an easygoing, relaxing get-together as I had hoped for. Lacey had been quiet the majority of the night so I tried to give her space and not force her to talk about what happened. I was pleasantly surprised that she hadn't changed her dress after all. I didn't know the full story behind what had happened between her and Annie earlier but I could tell that it meant a lot to Lacey for her to get dressed up tonight and continue with a tradition that she had with her husband. Part of me wondered if things had gone sour between them and that's who Lacey was running from, while the other part of me recognized the unmistakable grief that someone has when they've lost someone close to them: a spouse.

Everyone was gathered around in the living room, spread out between the couch and the floor while the kids played with Rylee who had just started to walk. I glanced over at my brother and saw the adoring look he was giving his wife, Mia, and felt a bit jealous of the life they had together. I was happy for them, that wasn't the problem. It was that they represented everything that I would never have – a constant companion to share their life with and grow old together as they made new memories with the family they created.

"So, what's the plan for Ry's birthday?" Noah asked, interrupting my thoughts. He was sitting in the recliner with Jade on his lap as she twirled a stray piece of hair around her finger. It was a nervous habit she tried to break but hadn't. I watched as her blonde hair wrapped tightly around her finger before she would unwind it and start over again. I looked away before I got lost in the hypnotizing trance.

"We're just doing something small, cake and ice cream with the family, next Saturday at our house," Chase said as he pulled Mia closer to him on the couch.

"What? It's her first birthday— you're not going all out for it?" Noah teased, trying to get a rise out of Chase. They were best friends who gave each other shit like brothers.

"I'm too tired for a big party," Mia sighed before her eyes went wide with panic. She chewed her bottom lip as she looked up at Chase who was chuckling and shaking his head.

"You might as well tell them," he said quietly in her ear, loud enough that we could hear. I laughed as Liam's head quickly turned in their direction, excited to hear that someone had a secret.

"Tell us what?" His voice was higher than normal with excitement.

Mia studied Chase's face as he slowly nodded yes and planted a kiss on her forehead.

"Okay, um," she hesitated. "Rylee is going to be a big sister!" She smiled as Chase rubbed a hand over her belly, a small bump showing against the thin fabric of the dress she was wearing. I shifted my attention to Liam, watching as the emotions flashed across his face before he got up and went over to hug them. I felt eyes on me as I looked over and watched Lacey as she took everything in. The look on my face must have spoken some secret words that only she could understand as she gave me an empathetic smile before looking over at Liam. I hadn't told her about Renee but she wasn't stupid and had to have noticed that there wasn't a woman in his life given that we hadn't talked about one.

The room got noisy as everyone said congratulations and got settled again. I looked over at Jade and Noah, wondering how she was taking the news of Mia being pregnant. I knew that finding out that Chase and Mia were having another baby was hard for Liam and I, knowing that we would never know what it felt like to have another child on the way. I could only imagine what Jade was feeling, hearing that her best friend was pregnant again, less than a year after Jade had lost a baby.

Noah leaned forward and whispered something in Jade's ear as he gently rubbed his hands up and down her arms. I couldn't hear what he was saying but I watched as Jade listened, a smile pulling tightly across her face as she nodded. She shrugged her shoulders and leaned her head back against his chest. He smiled broadly as he looked around the room, waiting for the right time to get everyone's attention. "Jade and I have a little announcement we would like to make as well," he said as his voice boomed through the room. Everyone got quiet and turned to look at them. "We've decided to move the wedding up to March, instead of September."

"Didn't want to do it in the heat after all?" Chase asked, chuckling as if he knew he was right. Noah and Jade had been engaged for 9 months and couldn't agree on when to get married. Noah and Jade looked at each other, a smirk on his face as she rolled her eyes. As she looked back at everyone in the room, she smiled and took a deep breath.

"We've moved it to March because we're having a baby in June," she said slowly as she forced it out in one long-winded breath as she placed a hand on her stomach.

Mia's hand clasped over her mouth as her eyes filled with tears. The room was quiet as everyone took in the news, my attention shifting back to Liam again. He tried to keep the hurt off his face as he forced a smile and came over to hug Noah and Jade. Everyone was up and moving, giving hugs and pats on the back, while I stayed sitting on the floor. Everyone's lives were changing and moving forward while we were frozen in place.

The night went by at a fast pace after that. While the women sat and talked about due dates and cravings, the guys retreated to the kitchen to drink beer and bullshit. I was relieved that Lacey had jumped into the conversation with the girls, knowing that Mia and Jade were two of the nicest women I had ever known. The clock wound down and soon it was time to ring in the new year. We all gathered around in the living room as I turned the TV on and found a channel to watch the ball drop.

"Mama, can I kiss Liam at midnight or is that not okay?" Annie asked Lacey, catching her off guard. Lacey looked at me with panic on her face, unsure of what to do. I shrugged my shoulders because the hell if I knew what to do.

"I think a kiss on the cheek would be fine if it's okay with Liam, and his dad," Lacey replied cautiously, allowing me to veto her decision.

"That's fine with me, buddy," I said, smiling at Liam as he looked up at me.

"Yay! And you and Mr. Grant can kiss too!" Annie exclaimed excitedly.

Lacey and I looked at each other nervously before she shifted her attention back to Annie.

"No, honey, we're not going to kiss," she said softly, gently reaching out and brushing a thumb across the girl's cheek.

"Why not? You can have a friend's kiss, like me and Liam. Otherwise, you will be the only two who don't kiss at New Year's and that's bad luck, mama." She looked up at Lacey with sadness in her eyes.

"I would be honored to share a good luck, friends' kiss with you," I said softly, pulling Lacey's attention back to me as Annie squealed. She studied my face, a concern on hers that I couldn't quite read. The countdown on the TV started as everyone yelled out the numbers together.

"Seventeen!"
"Sixteen!"
"Fifteen!"

"We don't have to if it makes you uncomfortable," I offered, trying to read what she was thinking.

"No, it's okay," she sighed and pulled her shoulders back.

"Ten!"
"Nine!"
"Eight!"

"Are you sure?" I stepped closer, my fingers itching to touch her as my mind screamed for me to stop.

"Five!"
"Four!"
"Three!"
"Two!"

I reached out and wrapped an arm behind her waist as I gently lowered my lips to hers. I could feel the warmth as she let out a shaky breath, her lips gently parting as she kissed me back. Her lips were soft and suddenly I felt the need to kiss her deeper, to feel her kiss me back. Her hand wrapped around my neck as her fingers gently ran through my hair. I wanted to pull away but the pull to her was stronger. My lips pressed harder against hers, excitement flooding through me when she pressed hers into mine and parted her lips to allow my tongue access. I softly licked her lips as I eagerly wanted to explore.

"I don't think friends are supposed to kiss like that," Liam said sarcastically as he walked off with Annie. Lacey and I stepped apart as she quickly brought her hand to her mouth, replacing where my lips had just been. I wanted to say something to her, to apologize for crossing the line, but when I went to open my mouth she was already gone and rushing upstairs.

Everyone left soon after I declined their offers to help with the clean-up. I had wanted to talk to Liam privately, to make sure he was okay, but he was already asleep in my bed by the time I got up there. I felt restless with an excess amount of energy running through me. Knowing I wasn't going to get any sleep anytime soon, I walked downstairs to watch tv for a bit. As I made my way down, I noticed a light on in the bathroom at the end of the hall. Lacey and Annie had gone to bed earlier so I figured someone had left the light on by accident. As I reached to open the door I stopped when I heard crying on the other side. I knocked softly, trying not to startle whoever was on the other side.

A few seconds later I heard the lock turn and the door opened. Lacey stood in front of me wearing a T-shirt and a pair of sweatpants, her hair tossed up in a messy ponytail, with streaks of mascara running down her face. Her nose was red and her cheeks were splotchy from crying. I didn't say anything because I didn't know what to say. The kiss had messed with my head ever since it happened and I was still struggling to figure out how I felt about it. I reached a hand out to her and was surprised when she took it. She stepped out slowly, her body shaking as she started crying again. I wrapped her in my arms and held her. A few minutes later she had calmed down enough to walk with me to the couch. We sat in silence for a few minutes as she sniffled and tried to catch her breath.

"Lacey, I'm really sorry about the kiss earlier. I didn't mean to overstep, and I'm so sorry that it happened." I looked over at her, my face etched with shame.

"The kiss was fine," she pulled in a deep breath, "that's not why I'm... crying..." Her shoulders fell as she started crying again.

"Okay. Do you want to talk about it?" I offered, placing a hand on her knee.

She shook her head as pulled a worn-out tissue out of her pocket and wiped at her face before blowing her nose.

"I'm sorry, I don't mean to be such a mess. Tonight was har…hard… harder than I thought." Her voice rose as she struggled to get the words out before she started crying again. I reached over and placed the palm of my hand on her back, gently patting her like I do when Liam gets upset.

"You don't have anything to be sorry about."

She nodded her head and sucked in a ragged deep breath as she turned to look at me.

"Tonight was supposed to be… my ten-year… anniversary," she said in one long-winded breath. "My husband… was killed…three months ago… in a car accident." Her eyes closed as she said it, her shoulders falling as her body shook the harder she cried. She leaned forward and let her head fall forward as she allowed the grief to take over. I closed my eyes and took a deep breath, trying to think of something to say that could help her feel better but I knew that there wasn't anything that I could say. You don't ever feel better after losing the love of your life.

"I'm so sorry, Lacey," I whispered loud enough for her to hear me as I continued to pat her back.

"I thought I would be okay tonight, I thought I could do it." She turned to look at me, her eyes a darker green than I had ever seen. There was so much sadness in her eyes that I couldn't tell if I was seeing her grief or my own reflected in hers.

"It's hard to know what situations are going to be hard, sometimes they just take you by surprise. That's the unfortunate thing about death, it doesn't care whether our hearts can handle it."

Her eyes searched my face as she listened to my words and I could tell that she knew there was a deeper meaning behind them. Instinctively, I moved my hand away and rubbed at the scruff that was getting thicker on my jawline.

"Liam's mom?" she asked quietly. I nodded, unsure of whether I was ready to talk about this. I took a deep breath as my leg started to bounce nervously. She had opened up to me about something personal and painful, I could try to do the same.

"My wife, Renee. She lost her battle with cancer almost four years ago."

38

"I'm sorry for your loss," she said as she reached over and squeezed my hand.

I nodded as I tried to blink past the tears that were threatening to come out. I hadn't cried since the day that Renee died and I wasn't going to start again now.

THE TIES THAT BIND

Eight

Lacey

"Seven. Eight. Nine. Ten. Ready or not, here I come." His voice was low as he spoke the words that should have sounded like a game. I could hear it in his tone that this was going to be anything but fun. I quietly slid back further, trying to keep my skin from sticking to the wood floor beneath me as I hid under the bed.

Mom was at work and dad had been drinking all afternoon which only made him more furious when she called to say she had to work late. It was the last straw for him in his drunken stupor, making him even more irritable than when he was sober. I knew today was going to be a bad day when I walked into the kitchen to fix a bowl of cereal and dad had mom pinned to the wall by her throat again.

His footsteps were heavy, the floor shifting beneath his weight as he walked toward the bed. I pinched my eyes shut and held my breath, praying that he was too drunk to find me. I crossed my fingers and tucked my teddy bear under my arm as I waited it out. Just a few more minutes and he would get frustrated and leave.

My lungs burned as I continued to hold my breath, not willing to risk making any sound that might lead him directly to me. Panic started to rush through me as I worried about passing out, or worse, dying, with no air. Everything around me went silent and I couldn't tell if it was from the pressure in my ears, or if I had lucked out and he had left. I slowly let out the breath, forcing myself to be calm so I wouldn't suck in another one and

give away my hiding spot. As the air slowly left my body I felt a hand wrap around my ankle, yanking me out from under the bed.
"Found you," he growled as his eyes turned black as night.

I sprung forward on the bed, clutching my chest as I gasped for air. I quickly looked around the room, looking for him before I recognized the collection of action figures on the shelf beside me and remembered where I was. I glanced down and sighed, relieved that I hadn't woken Annie up.

It wasn't unusual for me to have bad dreams, they had haunted me the majority of my life and always resulted in me waking up, gasping for air. My problem was that I had a hard time figuring out if they were real memories from my childhood or if they were terrible, made up situations that my brain decided to conjure up, just to torture me. Almost all of my nightmares involved my father and I had a hard time knowing what was true and what wasn't.

I shook my head to clear the thoughts as I quietly got out of bed and checked my phone. My stomach dropped when I looked down and saw 3 missed calls from my dad. I had been anxiously waiting for them to come, knowing that he would be pissed about what happened. My dad wasn't one to forgive and forget. He was the ultimate revenge seeker, making sure those who wronged him paid for whatever they did. And I wasn't going to be an exception. The past few days I had held onto the hope that he hadn't called because he hadn't survived but fate seemed determined to prove that evil never dies.

It was still early in the morning and technically it wouldn't hurt to try to sleep some more but my body was too used to getting up this early to go in for my shifts at the hospital. Besides, there was no way I could try to rest now after knowing that my father was actively trying to reach me. There was nothing planned for today, and as I looked outside and saw more snow falling, I knew we would be with Grant for at least one more day. If this storm was as bad as the last one, it would mean that the roads into Haven Brook would be closed a little bit longer, giving us some more time to figure out what to do and where to go. Letting Annie sleep, I tucked my phone into my pocket and crept downstairs, making sure not to wake anyone else up.

As I walked into the kitchen I was surprised to see Grant sitting at the table, drinking a cup of coffee and reading a newspaper. I smiled as I walked in, still feeling somewhat awkward around him after falling apart on New Year's Eve. Several days had passed and yet we hadn't spoken of my breakdown or the kiss.

My lips still tingled every time I thought of the way his had felt against them. I ran a finger over them as I poured a cup of coffee, completely lost in thought. My daydreams had quickly started to shift, leading us to doing more than just kissing, which was an incredibly odd feeling for me. There was a tremendous amount of guilt that weighed on me when I remembered that Derek hadn't been gone 3 months yet, and I was already fantasizing about another man. But the way that Grant made me feel, it was completely different than Derek had ever made me feel.

Things with Derek were great but after we had Annie, things started to fizzle out, just like everyone warns you they will when you have kids. We tried to keep the spark between us but between busy work schedules, very little sleep, and a newborn that needed constant attention, things just started to fall by the wayside. I kept telling myself that things would get better, we would find our way back to each other, but we didn't. We were like best friends who decided to have a baby together. Nothing more and nothing less. I had realized that part of why I loved getting dressed up every year for New Year's Eve was because it was the only time that he was focused on me again. He made me feel beautiful and sexy, but most importantly, I felt wanted.

I was still rubbing my fingers across my lips when I heard the sound of the coffee spilling over, out of my cup. I snapped out of my trance and looked down as I quickly set the pot on the warmer, stepping away before the scalding hot liquid dripped off the counter and onto the floor.

"Shit!" I hissed, frustrated that I hadn't been paying attention. Grant looked up and set his newspaper down before rushing over to help. He grabbed the roll of paper towels off of the counter behind me and reached around to start blotting the counter to keep the coffee from dripping off. My breath hitched as I felt the warmth of his body behind me as he worked quickly to clean up the coffee. I was frozen in place, desperate to clean up my mess, but afraid to move and allow my body to have any more contact with his. A few seconds, later he was still reaching around me, adding more paper towels to the pile on the counter as they soaked up the coffee.

"Are you okay? Did you get burned?" His voice was quiet in my ear as his chest slightly brushed against my back. I had to force myself to remember to breathe so I didn't pass out. Unable to speak, I nodded my head slowly, embarrassed that he had to come to my rescue, yet again.

"Why don't you go sit down and I'll clean this up and bring you your coffee? You look a little frazzled this morning." He gently placed his hand on my lower back, guiding me over to the table. I sat down, thankful that I didn't have to worry about my knees giving out. I wasn't usually the kind of girl who was so physically impacted by an attractive man. For whatever reason, he was having a huge effect on me which meant that we needed to leave and soon.

I watched as he cleaned up the mess, his T-shirt pulling tight across his toned body as he reached forward to wipe up the rest of the coffee. A few minutes later, he threw the last paper towel in the trash and walked over, sitting down across from me at the table. He gently slid my coffee over, eyeing me carefully to make sure I didn't spill it again.

I felt my cheeks flush as I looked away, embarrassed, wrapping the cup in my hands. I pretended to be interested in the snow that had started to fall outside so I could avoid having to look at his disheveled bed hair that had me wanting to run my fingers through it.

"So, what has you all worked up this morning?" He arched an eyebrow and lifted his cup to take a sip. I licked my lips before slowly turning to look at him. Even though I knew it would be hard to look at him and keep the emotions off of my face, I knew it would make it even harder if I avoided him. It would make me look like I was avoiding him, which I was.

"Nothing," I lied. "Bad dreams, that's all." I shrugged as if it was nothing and took a sip, trying to keep myself distracted from the look he was giving me. It was a look that was calling me on my bullshit and challenging me to tell the truth. I had barely started processing the fact that my dad was alive and well, likely soon to be hunting me down. How was I supposed to explain that to him? Of course I was worked up between the random slew of thoughts working through my mind.

"Interesting," he replied casually as he picked up the newspaper and went back to reading it. I pulled my neck back and looked at him, confused about what that was supposed to mean. He didn't say anything that should offend me, but it was HOW he said it that had my temper starting to flare.

"What's that supposed to mean?" I leaned forward and narrowed my eyes at him, waiting for him to lower the newspaper so he could see the glare I was giving him.

"Nothing." He shrugged as he turned the page, seemingly uninterested in the conversation.

"Really?" I let out a loud sigh and crossed my arms over my chest as I leaned back against the chair and stared at him. For a moment I envisioned myself having some sort of superhero powers where I could burn a hole through his stupid newspaper with the amount of heat that was radiating from my glare. As if sensing my frustration, he folded the newspaper and set it down before folding his hands in front of him on the table. He met my glare, not backing down, or looking even the slightest bit bothered by it.

"I find it interesting that you're going with the bad dream excuse when I sat here and watched you run your fingers across your lips while you were lost in some sort of erotic fantasy while spilling coffee all over the counter." He quirked an eyebrow and challenged me to counter what he was saying.

I felt the color drain from my face as his eyes stayed focused on me.

"I wasn't lost in an erotic fantasy," I whispered, looking away.

"Are you sure?" He pulled his bottom lip in between his teeth as he watched my reaction. My heart was racing as my palms started to sweat. I wasn't willing to admit there was a fantasy to myself, let alone to him.

"Yeah, I'm sure." I looked up and met his look, watching as the blue darkened around his pupils.

"Okay, if that's how you want to play this," he said as he stood up and slid his chair under the table. I held my breath, waiting for him to turn and walk away. Instead, he took a step closer and leaned down, locking me in place as one hand held onto the back of my chair and the other planted firmly on the table. He leaned in close enough that I could feel the heat of his breath on my neck as he started to speak.

"Call me crazy, but I thought maybe you were thinking about the kiss we shared the other night. The one we keep avoiding talking about." He paused for a second, letting out a heavy breath that tickled my skin. "And yeah, I would call it an erotic fantasy because fuck if I haven't ever been that turned on by a single kiss."

He straightened and stood next to me, pausing to grab his coffee before he walked away. As he was about to walk out of the room, he turned and looked at me over his shoulder.

"Don't worry, it's fucking with my head too. But that doesn't make it any less real."

I heard him make his way upstairs and a few minutes later the shower was turned on as the sound of running water filled the silence in the kitchen. I was completely stunned by what he had said before he left, especially since I wasn't the only one who had been turned on by that kiss. Butterflies fluttered through my stomach as I briefly entertained the thought of something happening between us. But as quickly as the thought entered my mind, the grief and guilt came rushing back with it.

We moved around each other in silence the rest of the morning as I got ready and he made breakfast once the kids were up. It was the last week of winter break before school started again and I felt anxious about not being able to send Annie to school. I never thought I would actually go through with leaving, so the last minute decision didn't give a lot of time for planning. Even though I daydreamed about us leaving, I only ever focused on the getting far enough away part. I had only thought of getting us to a place that was safe.

My mind raced through all of the worst-case scenarios while I chewed on a piece of bacon and the kids talked about building a snowman. I could feel Grant's eyes on me again but I purposely avoided him as long as I could. After breakfast was done, the kids ran off to the fenced-in backyard to build a snowman.

I glanced out the window so many times to check on Annie that I heard Grant sigh as he slammed his fists down on the counter, pulling my attention away from her. My hand flung up to my chest in surprise, as I tried to figure out what he was so mad about.

"What is going on? And I want the truth, Lacey."

The look on his face was more frustration than anger, but either way, I hated that I was the reason it was there.

"Nothing is going on, I don't know what you're talking about." I walked past him and went to the sink, turned on the water, and started rinsing the pile of dishes on the counter.

I heard his footsteps come up behind me as he reached forward, his chest rock hard and solid against my back, and turned off the water. I let my wet hands rest against the edge of the sink, refusing to turn around and look at him.

"Then why do you keep looking outside every 30 seconds, like someone is going to come take Annie?" His voice was low in my ear.

My shoulders slumped and I let my head hang down as I closed my eyes. I wasn't ready to talk about what happened and yet I was running out of options to keep avoiding it.

"Lacey, I'm going to ask again. What's going on?" His voice was calmer this time as he sounded like he was struggling to control it.

"Nothing," I snapped, whipping around to face him. I pulled in a deep breath and looked at him. "But I do need to get a few things from the store today, I'll check to see if there are any vacancies at the hotel now that the storm has passed through."

He clenched his jaw as he stepped back, allowing me some room to move.

"My keys are on the table by the door, take my truck, and go grab what you need." He shook his head as he walked out of the room. I let out a shaky breath before going outside to ask Annie to go to the store with me. After several moans and groans from her about wanting to play, I gave up and decided to trust Grant when he offered to watch her while I went to the store. I reached into my pocket to silence my cell phone without bothering to check the caller ID as I grabbed his keys and went out through the garage. I hopped into the truck and waited for the door to finish opening before I pulled out and made my way to the only store in town.

THE TIES THAT BIND

Nine

Grant

Lacey had been gone a few hours when the kids decided to come in and warm up. Annie was feeling tired and asked if she could go upstairs to lay down for a little while. After she left, Liam and I sat in the living room, watching a movie we had seen a hundred times. I watched as his face lit up every time the family was together and instantly felt bad that he didn't have that kind of childhood. I had been wanting to talk to him about how he felt about the new babies that were going to be joining our family soon, but we hadn't had much alone time and I didn't want to have that conversation with him in front of anyone else. I reached over and turned the volume down a little as I turned toward him on the couch.

"Hey, I've been meaning to ask you— how do you feel about all of the recent baby news?"

He looked over at me nervously, unsure of what to say. He shrugged and looked back at the tv.

"It's great, they're all going to be really happy with new babies."

"Liam, how do YOU feel about it? It's okay to be honest with me, you know that. There are no right or wrong answers."

"I don't know," he grumbled, irritated that he was having to talk to me about this. "I guess I'm fine with it, I'll have more cousins to play with. But really, I haven't thought about it that much."

"No? Why not?" I narrowed my eyes, knowing there was something else he wasn't telling me.

"I've been busy with other stuff," he said nonchalantly.

I arched a brow at him, wondering what he had been up to.

"You're on winter break and haven't left the house in a week- what could you possibly be busy with?" I asked with a chuckle.

"Protecting Annie." He turned to look at me as my stomach dropped.

"Protecting Annie from what?" I asked cautiously.

"From the monster that's coming for her."

For a moment I felt a bit of relief and wondered if Annie had nightmares like Lacey.

"Have you talked to her to tell her that monsters aren't real?" I pried softly.

"Yeah, but then I realized that she wasn't talking about fake monsters. She was talking about a real one."

My blood pressure started to rise as I realized that my son knew what was going on and hadn't bothered to tell me. If Lacey wasn't willing to talk to me, maybe I could get it out of Liam and prove to her that I could protect her against whatever monster was after them.

"Who is the real monster?" I asked sternly, forcing his attention back to me.

"She said she's not allowed to tell me, her mom said that if they talk about him, he'll find them. She was really scared after they ran away because there was so much fire in the house so she doesn't want him to know where they are because he'll try to take her mama away like he did her daddy." He paused for a moment as he thought about something. "But I think his name might be Bill."

"Why do you think that?"

"Because when we were playing outside earlier, she was using her stuffed puppy to fight off the bad guy and she kept saying- die, Bill, die! Then she said she didn't feel well and wanted to go to sleep."

I took in the information he had given me as I heard the garage door open, knowing that Lacey was back. I smiled and patted his knee as I got up, chuckling when I saw him reach for the remote to turn his movie back up after I left. I opened the door to the garage at the same time Lacey was reaching for it, forcing her to stumble in, directly into my arms.

She had shopping bags hanging from both arms and was wearing a new beanie that I hadn't seen before. She blew out a breath, forcing the stray piece of hair out of her face as she tried to regain her balance. I carefully slid the majority of the bags off of her arms and carried them into the kitchen, setting them on the table as she walked in behind me.

She pulled her gloves off as she glanced into the living room, looking for Annie. With concern on her face, she asked, "Where's Annie?"

"She said she was tired and asked to lay down, maybe 30 minutes ago," I replied as I helped her with the other bags.

"Was she okay?"

"I believe so, Liam said that she had said she wasn't feeling well. But in all fairness, he just told me that two minutes before you got here."

"Maybe I should go check on her," she said as she pulled her coat off and hung it on the back of the chair.

"Yeah, probably a good idea." I stayed watching her, unsure of whether I should tell her what Liam had told me. While I wanted to talk to her and get the truth, I didn't want Liam to know that I had ratted him out. I also needed to think through what he told me and decipher what was true, and what was being embellished by a child's imagination. A few awkward seconds passed without us saying anything before she turned and went upstairs to check on Annie.

I left her bags on the table since I didn't want to be disrespectful and go through the things she bought. Fifteen minutes later, she came into the kitchen with a look of concern etched on her face. I turned away from the stove, studying her as she shuffled through the bags on the counter.

"Everything okay?" I asked casually as I turned back to the stove and pushed the rest of the spaghetti noodles down into the boiling water.

"Yeah," she sighed. "I'm looking for my phone." She threw her hands up in the air as she stared at the bags with frustration. I dried my hands on the towel and flung it over my shoulder as I walked over to help her. I looked between the bags, seeing plenty of clothes and a few toys for Annie amongst a few bags of food. I watched her out of the corner of my eye as she started rummaging through the bags again, looking flustered.

I reached forward and grabbed the first bag I found, pulling items aside as I felt around for her phone. My fingers slid across something silky. Against my better judgment, I lifted a black, silk thong out of the bag, letting it hang off my finger as I studied it. I could feel the blood rush from my head, down to my groin, as I imagined Lacey wearing them. I slowly looked toward her at the same time she looked over, her skin turning red as she saw the underwear in my hand. We stayed staring at the underwear for what felt like minutes before I heard footsteps approaching the kitchen. Quickly, I shoved the panties back into the bag and pushed it down, trying to keep them hidden.

"Mommy, my head hurts," Annie whined from the doorway. I smiled at her and walked back to the stove, tending to the noodles before glancing over my shoulder to see if she needed help.

"I'm sorry, baby, I was looking for my phone, then I was going to get your Tylenol." Lacey sighed and stopped going through the bags to look at Annie.

"You left your phone on the dresser in the room. It keeps vibrating and beeping."

"No honey, mommy got a new phone today. That's the one I'm looking for." There was a worried look on Lacey's face as she said, pausing momentarily to look at Annie after she said that it had been vibrating. I turned around and kept my back turned to them, giving them as much privacy as I could while I wondered why she had gotten a new phone. There were a lot of unanswered questions that were making me doubt everything that I thought I knew about her.

"So, do I have to memorize this number now too?" Annie asked, sitting down at the table.

"No honey, this is just a temporary phone. You don't have to worry about any of that."

I felt Lacey's eyes on me as she said it. There was no way that I was going to be able to keep skirting around everything and acting like nothing was going on.

"Hey, Grant, do you have a thermometer?" Lacey asked as she held her hand to Annie's forehead.

"Yeah, let me grab it real quick." I set the fork on the counter as I walked over to the cabinet where I kept all of the medical stuff.

"Mommy, I don't feel well," Annie said right before she threw up all over the floor.

I rushed over and handed Lacey the thermometer before hurrying back to the sink and wetting a paper towel to give to Annie. Lacey took it and quickly cleaned Annie up before scanning her forehead with the thermometer. Her brows pulled together as she read the temperature, then scanned her again a few times just to be sure.

"What's she at?" I asked, knowing that Annie was running a fever higher than Lacey was comfortable with.

"103.5," she said warily.

"Do you want to try to get her to the hospital?" I knew that another storm was supposed to come through soon but I didn't doubt my ability to get her to the hospital if needed.

"I can watch her here for a little bit, see if I can get it to break or at least keep it from climbing. This came on pretty quickly so I'm not sure what we're looking at yet."

"What can I do to help?" I asked, hoping that she would let me.

"I don't want her too far from me, do you think she can rest on the couch?"

"Absolutely," I assured her as I worked with Liam to get everything cleaned up and set blankets and pillows out for her to lay down on. After Lacey got some Tylenol in her, she brought her in and laid her on the couch, tucking her in as she quickly went back to sleep.

I quickly cleaned up the kitchen while Lacey was checking on Annie, making sure there was nothing else for her to worry about. I finished the spaghetti and threw some garlic bread in the oven while I waited for Liam to wash up for dinner. Lacey cleared her bags from the table and set them in the living room before coming back to the kitchen.

"Dinner's ready," I said as she walked in. I nodded to the table where I had set out the spaghetti, salad, and bread. She smiled softly and looked up at me.

"Thank you," her voice was quiet but sincere.

"Don't thank me yet, it's spaghetti sauce from a jar," I joked.

"I'm sure it's delicious," she laughed as she took a seat. "But I meant thank you for helping me earlier. For watching Annie while I went to the store and for helping me with her being sick."

"It's no biggie." I shrugged my shoulders and smiled as I grabbed the Parmesan cheese shaker from the fridge and closed it. I could hear Liam in the bathroom washing his hands and knew I had a few minutes before he came in for dinner.

"So, who's Bill?" I asked as I sat down across from her. I watched as the color drained from her face as if she had just seen a ghost. She opened her mouth to say something at the same time Liam walked in and sat down. Her mouth quickly snapped shut as she excused herself and walked away.

Ten

Lacey

I felt bad for running off and not joining the guys for dinner but when Grant said Bill's name, my blood went ice cold and I had to get away. I had no idea what had happened while I was out at the store or what Annie might have told them. She was too little to really understand what was happening to begin with so I had to assume that anything she might have said could have been exaggerated, making things look worse than they were.

I leaned back against the couch after gently scanning her forehead again to check her fever. She was still at 103 which made me nervous that it wasn't dropping with the Tylenol. I had been applying cold washcloths to her head as well but even those weren't working. She was restless in her sleep, fighting some invisible demon that I couldn't help her with. I hated that she was sick, but I hated even more that I felt so helpless, not knowing how to help her. Usually, I would see when Annie was coming down with something and I could try to manage it head-on. This came out of nowhere and I was stumped, already feeling out of sorts with everything else going on.

An hour later I heard Liam go upstairs, the shower turning on a few minutes later. Grant quietly came into the living room holding a bowl of spaghetti with a piece of garlic bread laying on top. He smiled softly as he extended the bowl to me and said nothing. My stomach chose the worst time to growl, confirming that I was starving as I reached forward and took the bowl from him.

"Thank you," I said softly, trying to keep from disturbing Annie. He nodded in response before looking at Annie and raising his eyebrows to ask about her.

"Still the same," I sighed as I glanced back at her. "I'm sorry, I was hoping to have already booked a hotel when I got back from the store so we would be out of your hair. I'll call soon and see if there are any vacancies."

"Lacey, you don't need to do that. You and Annie are fine here. Besides, it's not fair to her to try to move her around when she's this sick and needs rest. Just stay here, it's not a problem."

I smiled and let my shoulders relax as I twirled the noodles around my fork before taking a bite. Even though he said this was just sauce from a jar, it was still the best spaghetti I had eaten in a long time. I closed my eyes as I savored the flavor, allowing it to explode on my tongue. I shoved another bite into my mouth, quietly moaning as I did, lost in the delicious food before me. When I slowly opened my eyes, I found Grant sitting in the recliner, watching me intensely with his hands firmly gripping the end of the armrests. Subconsciously, I wiped my mouth with my finger, drawing more attention to my lips. I was about to look away when I heard footsteps approaching.

"I'm going to bed, Dad," Liam whispered as he waved to us before turning around and heading back upstairs.

"He's a good kid," I said softly, hoping to change the subject to anything other than the spaghetti foreplay we were just engaged in as I set the bowl on the coffee table beside me.

"Yeah, he really is."

"So, what all did Annie have to say earlier?" I asked knowing that we needed to talk about the elephant in the room. He pulled his eyebrows together in confusion as he had no idea what I was talking about.

"About Bill. What did she tell you?"

He leaned forward and blew out a heavy sigh.

"Annie didn't tell me anything. Liam did," he admitted.

"How did Liam know about him? How did this conversation even start?" I knew that Annie and Liam were spending a lot of time together playing but I didn't know that she was confiding our secrets in him as well.

"I had asked him how he felt about everyone having a new baby and he mentioned that he hadn't been focused on it too much because he was protecting Annie." His eyes searched mine as he said it, waiting for my facial expressions to give away my emotional reaction. I swallowed hard and looked away. I didn't want to ask the next question but I knew that I had to.

"Did he say what he's protecting her from?" I closed my eyes as I said it, bracing myself for what would come next. As I opened my eyes, I saw him nod yes and I felt the air rush out of my body. There was no way that we could stay here any longer now that he knew what I had done.

"He said that Annie is afraid of a monster named Bill."

Our eyes locked as my head whipped up at the sound of the name.

"I'm sorry, I didn't mean to put you in this position. We'll be gone by morning." I pulled in a deep breath, forcing the air back into my lungs as I sat a little taller and tried to pretend that I was stronger than I looked.

"Lacey, I still don't know what's happening, but I want to. I really, really, want to. I wish you would trust me enough to let me help you with whatever it is that you're running from."

"I can't tell you what happened, Grant. Can you please just trust me that I can handle this?" I begged as I glanced back at Annie.

"Do you really think that you can handle it? I'm not trying to be a dick but whatever it is seems to be pretty bad, and I know that when things get that bad, they are harder to handle on your own."

I looked down and nervously spun my wedding ring around my finger as I debated whether to tell him. I had felt alone for so long that it felt odd to have someone who not only wanted to be there for me, but they were begging me to let them help me. It was making my head cloudy and for a moment, I decided to give in and allow myself to trust again.

"Bill is my father." I looked up and saw the look on his face after I said it. He subtly nodded for me to go on. "After my husband died, I didn't have a choice but to move back home and live with him until I could get on my feet again. I was working full time and 12-hour shifts meant that I wasn't home when I needed to get Annie to and from school. Or to get dinner on the table. I was so used to Derek picking up the slack and the teamwork that made everything run so smoothly between us. When he died, the first thing that I thought was – how am I going to do this on my own?" I let out a ragged breath as my fingers trembled in response.

"So I moved back home with my father because I didn't have any other options. I was so overwhelmed with grief. Having our lives completely uprooted and changed in one day (or overnight), I subconsciously blocked out everything from my childhood. Those are the terrible memories turned nightmares that still haunt me."

Grant's eyes never left mine as he listened quietly to every word that I said.

"My dad was a bad man. IS a bad man. A raging alcoholic with a passion for beating women when they don't do as he says. I watched him beat my mom every day growing up until the day he killed her. I was seven when it happened and I can still remember every single detail about that day. When the cops showed up, he told them that she had fallen and hit her head on the edge of the counter. I didn't want to lie to them but he had already promised me that they would take me away if I told them the truth and that they would put me in a home with people who would do worse things. I was used to my dad beating me as it was, I couldn't imagine living somewhere where someone else would treat me worse than that. So, I lied and pretended that I didn't know what had happened. No one gives that much credit to a child that age so they didn't bother pressing me for more information."

"Shortly after I had moved back, I noticed he had started drinking again. Derek and I didn't visit him often and he had only met Annie a handful of times. We lived in Montana and he was still back in Colorado, so distance was a good excuse not to visit. When Derek died, he made an effort to come to the funeral to show his support. He was sober for once and had told me that he had been sober for fifteen years. I was at my absolute worst- a widow with a young child and no one to turn to. When he wanted to act like a dad and show me the kind of love that I had always wanted, I jumped at the opportunity. He made it sound so perfect when he talked about how he was going to help me with Annie and be the grandpa she deserved."

I felt movement behind me and turned to look at Annie. She was still asleep but restless as she turned over and tried to get comfortable. I continued talking, lowering my voice as I scooted closer to Grant so he could still hear me.

"We hadn't been there long when I started noticing that he was drinking. Not just a drink here and there- he was drunk all day long. It started bringing back old childhood memories so I started to panic, wondering if I had made a big mistake moving back home and subjecting my daughter to this environment." I let out a breath and took a moment to collect myself before I continued.

"One day he was pissed because I had burned dinner. But the problem was that he thought I was my mom. He started yelling and calling me by her name before he tried to attack me. Annie saw it and cowered in the corner, terrified. When he saw her, he thought she was me. Somehow he was transported back in time in his drunken stupor that he thought it was my mother he was beating and his daughter who was watching. After that he started to get obsessed with Annie – not in a gross way—but in a 'frustrated that she didn't love him like she should love a grandfather' kind of way. His drinking was out of control. I was terrified to leave the house and have Annie there by herself."

I watched as Grant's jaw moved back and forth as he listened, anger and irritation evident on his face.

"So I decided we needed to leave. I packed a few bags and hid them in my car, just in case. One afternoon, he was hellbent on picking a fight and I didn't have it in me. He pinned me to the wall by my throat and told me all of the hateful things he had wanted to say since I was a child. This time he knew who I was and he knew who Annie was. I gasped for air as Annie came up and hit him in the back with the baseball bat that he keeps by the front door. It was enough for him to drop me and for me to catch my breath, but I knew that it was the breaking point that I needed to force us to get out of there. Long story short, there was a scuffle and I was trying to get Annie out. I told her to run and as she did, he kicked the coffee table and shot it out toward her, tripping her and causing her to fall and hit her face on the edge of it. That's how she got the bruise. Annie was able to get out and go to the car like I asked her to."

My lip trembled as I struggled to keep going, to confess the sin I had committed.

"He tried to go after Annie so I lunged forward and knocked him to the ground. It didn't take long until he was on top of me and trying to choke me. I was already pretty weak from the other attacks so I knew I wasn't going to be able to fight him off. Instead, I laid there and played dead. He got up a few minutes later and went looking for Annie. Knowing that I didn't have any other choice, I grabbed the baseball bat and hit him in the head with it, hard enough to knock him to the floor." A single tear slid down my cheek as Grant's thumb gently reached over and wiped it away. "I ran to the shed and grabbed a can of gasoline and a pack of matches. When I went back into the house I was relieved to see him still lying there. I was furious with him for so many things that I didn't think about it as I poured the gas all over the carpet and lit a match. The house was engulfed in flames by the time I got to the car with Annie. Once I saw that she was safe and he wasn't around, I threw the car in drive and sped off. I got the hell out of there and didn't look back."

He continued to listen, complete empathy on his face as he took in the words that felt like razors coming out of my mouth.

"The past few days I had been hopeful that he had died in the fire. That he hadn't come to and been able to get out in time. I hadn't heard from him so what else could I think?" A sob escaped my throat as I tried to force myself to keep going. "But then this morning I had 3 missed calls from him and they haven't stopped since then. I haven't listened to all of the voicemails yet, but the ones I did listen to were pretty detailed in how he wanted to make me pay for what I did."

I closed my eyes as more tears slid down my face. Nightmares of what I had done haunted me every night since it happened but in each dream, I knew where he was. I knew that I had won and that he would never be able to hurt us again. I shook my head to try to get rid of the images as I buried my head in my hands and cried silently, the way I learned to cry after Derek died. Grant reached forward and gently pulled me, bringing me up to sit with him as he wrapped his arms around me and held me as we rocked gently.

"Is that where you were coming from the night of the accident?" he asked quietly. I shook my head yes.

"Where does your dad live?"

"Easterville, it's a small town a few hours away from here."

"I've heard of it but I've never been there."

"You're not missing out on anything," I joked between muffled sobs.

"You're a very brave woman, Lacey," he said as he softly placed a finger under my chin and turned my face to look at him.

"I'm not brave. I'm stupid. I never should have moved in with him, and I never should have left without making sure he couldn't come after us."

"You're safe here, I promise you that. I will not let anything happen to either of you." His tone was soft as he held me tighter when he said it.

"Thank you, I appreciate that. But we can't stay here. He'll find us. And if he finds us, he'll kill us." I felt the sharp breath that Grant took when he heard my words and knew that we needed to leave before things got even more complicated than they already were.

<u>Eleven</u>

Grant

The next couple of days were rough as Annie got worse before she got better. I tried staying out of Lacey's way and minding my own business, but as a father, it was hard to look the other way when it was so obvious that Annie needed medical attention. Lacey grew as frustrated with me as I was with her which created this thick tension around us.

I had tried to talk to her about what she had told me about her father the other night but she constantly avoided it and would instantly change the subject. She was, by far, the most infuriating woman I had ever met. Sexy as hell—but she had a way of getting under my skin without trying. It was Friday night and Liam and I had planned to do pizza and a few movies to wrap up the end of his winter break before he started back to school on Monday. As I went by his room, I glanced in and saw Lacey packing their duffle bags with the clean laundry she had just pulled out of the dryer.

"What are you doing?" I asked as I leaned against the doorway and folded my arms over my chest.

"Packing," she sighed, not bothering to look at me.

"Where are you going?" I knew my tone had changed and the frustration was evident but I didn't give a damn.

"I was able to book a room at the inn down the street for a few nights."

She folded a pair of sweatpants and shoved them down into the bag

that was already packed to the brim. I blew out a frustrated breath and ran a hand through my hair.

"What's this all about? Really?" I asked as calmly as I could.

"We've been here a week, it's time for us to get out of your hair and let you get back to your lives."

I pushed off from the wall and walked over, putting my hand over the top of the bag so she couldn't stuff anything else inside.

"Did I ask you to go? Have I insinuated that you and Annie haven't been welcome here or that it's been an inconvenience for us?"

"No," she sighed and turned to look at me, dropping the shirt in her hand onto the bed. "But that doesn't mean that we should outstay our welcome. This was never in the plan…"

"You admitted yourself that there was no plan other than getting out of that house and finding somewhere to go that was safe. If you ask me— you've accomplished that plan."

She eyed me cautiously as if she was waiting for me to change my mind and tell her to get her things and get packing.

"Do you have a new plan? Any idea where you're going to go? How you're going to get by until you get settled in? You said it yourself that you moved in with your dad because you needed help getting back on your feet after Derek died. What makes you think that you're going to get on your feet by leaving and running off on your own again?" I knew my words probably sounded harsh but I needed her to think things through and to realize that she didn't have anything set up for her and Annie. It was completely reckless to just take off and not have any idea where they were going or what she was going to do. Who was going to look after Annie while she worked? There were so many things that I was worried about and it completely surprised me that Lacey wasn't concerned about anything other than getting out of my house.

"No, but that's not the point. You didn't ask for any of this, Grant. It's not fair to you that we came storming in and completely shifted everything in your life." Her face fell when she said it, realizing what she was saying. She closed her eyes and shook her head before looking back at me. "I'm sorry, I didn't mean for it to come out that way," she apologized.

"It's fine. The truth is that we do know what it's like to have everything shift and have our lives turned upside down. It's not fair, but at least this time it brought two new people into our lives instead of taking someone away." I smiled sympathetically, hoping to ease some of the discomfort I could still see on her face.

"I don't know what to do. What am I supposed to do?" She threw her hands up in the air and plopped down on the bed. The look in her eyes told me that she was genuinely asking.

"What do you want to do?"

"I want to stop running and find somewhere safe for Annie to grow up. Somewhere that doesn't remind her of everything that she's lost. Somewhere we can just slow down for a bit and not always be rushing for something." She let out a heavy sigh as her shoulders slumped, the stress of the week starting to show in how tired she looked.

"Then stay here and let me help you," I offered. My pulse started racing as I panicked about what I was saying. I knew deep down that I meant it, I really wanted to help her. But this was all new territory for me and I was terrified that I wouldn't know how to handle it. The thought of living with a woman and her child, permanently, scared the shit out of me. Knowing that she had nowhere else to go and was safer here with me, where I could protect them, was the only thing that kept me from turning around and leaving a giant hole in the wall as I burst through it like the Kool-Aid man.

She nervously chewed her bottom lip as she thought about it.

"We need to agree on certain conditions first," she said and I tried not to roll my eyes as I chuckled. Of course, this damn woman would have conditions.

"Okay, let's hear them." I took a step back and spread my feet apart as I crossed my arms over my chest and stared at her.

"First- there won't be any more of you catering to us. We will help with the chores around the house, including cooking and cleaning." She arched an eyebrow and waited before I rolled my eyes and nodded yes.

"Second- I will start contributing to the monthly bills including paying rent and splitting the cost of the utilities. I have some money still saved up from selling the house in Montana, however, I plan to start looking for a job immediately."

I clenched my jaw as I listened. There was no way in hell that I was going to let her pay half of the bills that I was already used to paying. That money should be set aside for an emergency, or a college fund for Annie. She was out of her mind if she thought I was going to take it. I stayed quiet and let her continue before I countered with my own conditions.

"Third- I know that there may be times when you will need to look after Annie for me, and maybe I can help watch Liam for you. Can we please agree to be respectful of each other's parenting styles and not undo everything that we have in place? Change can be hard for kids so it's important that you and I stay united on this one." She looked at me with a desperation in her eyes that said this wasn't the first time she's had to have this conversation with someone.

"What else?" I asked, unsure of whether she had more conditions. She pursed her lips and squinted her eyes as she looked at the wall, concentrating, before turning back to look at me and smiling.

"That's it I think. But of course, there's always the standing option to modify or add any additional conditions later on as we see fit," she said playfully with a smirk on her face.

"Fair enough," I chuckled. "Okay, here's my counter to your conditions. I will try to budge and let you help out with some of the chores. Since you're a better cook, maybe you can do more of the cooking and I'll do all of the cleaning?" I laughed as she frowned and folded her arms over her chest.

"Okay, fine. We'll consider keeping it 50/50. For now. Second- you will not pay half of the bills or utilities. I've been paying them just fine on my own, so while I appreciate the offer, I respectfully decline. Save that money and use it for an emergency fund, or keep it for Annie if she wants to go to college." I took a deep breath and let my arms relax as I looked at her. "Third- I will never question your parenting with Annie, nor would I ever try to undo anything that you've done. I can't imagine how I would feel if someone did that to me, so I won't do that to you."

She smiled and mouthed thank you as if it was something special that I was doing for her.

"I have some conditions of my own when you're ready." I winked and waited for her blush to finish creeping up her fair skin.

"Let's hear them," she said and scooted back on the bed.

"First, this isn't a temporary thing. You and Annie will stay with me for as long as you need until you're ready to go. It can be a few months or it can be a few years- I don't care. But for the love of God, please stop trying to book a hotel room. You're driving me crazy with that. If you book another room- it better be because you want some alone time and have something special planned for yourself." I paused when I noticed the blush creeping her cheeks again. I licked my lips, wondering what could possibly be going through her mind that would have her reacting this way.

"While we're on the topic of you and Annie living here, I think we need to discuss making this place more functional. You can't keep sleeping in this tiny ass bed with Annie, and I can't keep getting kicked in the ribs by Liam every time he thinks I'm going to snore," I joked.

"Okay, what do you suggest?"

"I want to go shopping and if you're okay with it, I suggest converting Liam's room to a space that he and Annie can share. I know it's a small room, but I think if we get creative enough, we can make it work."

I watched as panic rushed across her face as she listened.

"Grant, no, there's no need to do that."

"Lacey, you agreed to stay with me and to let me help you get on your feet. So yeah, there is a need. Annie needs to be able to feel like she has a home, she can't live out of that duffel bag forever."

She rubbed her lips together and tapped her foot on the carpet. I could tell that this was hard for her to accept and I wanted to make it as easy for her as possible.

"Trust me, it will be fun and Annie will love getting to pick out her own bed and dresser," I said calmly, hoping to ease some of her anxiety. "I'll help Liam clean up his room and we'll pack up some of the stuff he doesn't play with anymore and move it up to the attic. There's plenty of room in here for two standard beds and two dressers. They can share the space in the closet, and I'll add another bar along the lower half, giving them more room."

"Fine," she said reluctantly. "Annie can share a room with Liam. I'll sleep on the couch and keep my stuff out of the way."

My eyebrows shot up high on my forehead as I heard what she was planning. Did she really think that she was going to live here and sleep on the couch every night?

"Yeah, I don't think so. You'll move into my room with me." I felt my breath hitch as I said it. It was a huge leap for me but I kept reminding myself that it wasn't anything romantic, it was simply a living arrangement that revolved around a house that was now too small for the four people who were trying to live in it.

"There's no way that I can do that. It wouldn't be appropriate, what would the kids think?" she shrieked, eyes wide in horror.

"They'll think that we're trying to make everyone as comfortable as possible with our new living situation in a small house. My room is plenty big enough, and if it makes you feel more comfortable, I can get rid of my bed and we can get two full-sized beds instead." I waited anxiously for her to respond.

She finally let out the breath she was holding and looked me in the eyes, holding my stare.

"So I get stuck with the snorer?"

I watched as the smile spread across her face before she erupted in laughter, falling back on the pillows as I reached forward and playfully swatted her leg.

"Just for that, you don't get a separate bed," I teased, secretly hoping that she wouldn't want to go through with separate beds after all. It would be strange having a woman in my bed again, and I knew it would be hard to get used to, but I honestly really loved my bed and wasn't ready to part with it.

"Alright, I think we agree on all conditions, however, I do have one more." She stood up and stepped close enough to me that I could smell the vanilla from her shower gel. "I get to buy the furniture for Annie, and if Liam gets excited that she's getting new furniture, then I'll buy him new stuff too."

Before I could open my mouth to protest she lifted a finger and placed it on my lips.

"I would be spending this money either way once I found a place for Annie and me to live. I won't argue this with you so please stop acting like a damn cock in a hen house and just agree to this." She pinned me with a look that made me want to do everything she asked and more.

"Fine," I sighed and shrugged my shoulders.

"Good, I'm glad we have that situated." She smiled smugly.

"You're impossible, you know that?" I stepped a fraction of a hair closer, my eyes searching hers for any indication that she wasn't feeling as hot and bothered as I was by being this close to each other. Her lips slightly parted as she leaned forward, gently reaching out and holding onto my shoulder as she leaned in close to my ear.

"So I've been told," she whispered as she pulled back and walked away, allowing her hand to drop and brush across my stomach in the process.

There was no doubt about it—this woman was going to be the death of me.

Twelve

Lacey

Saturday morning came quickly as we got up early to get a head start on shopping before Grant and Liam had to go to Rylee's first birthday party that afternoon. We sat down with the kids at breakfast and explained the new living situation, including them sharing a room. I was relieved when they both had grins stretching from ear to ear as they excitedly talked about their plans for their new room. Grant and I sat back and listened, both in awe of how well they got along. Almost like brother and sister.

It killed me that Annie didn't have any siblings to share these experiences with, so it was bittersweet that she had Liam and he had her. Both of them were dealt a real shitty card in life with losing a parent and I could relate to how lonely it could be as an only child. I always wanted to give Annie a sibling but Derek and I had the hardest time conceiving her that I knew it would be harder to try to have another one. You have to want to have sex in order to get pregnant and Derek was rarely in the mood after we had Annie.

We cleaned up and hopped in the truck for the first time as a make-shift family of four. I smiled as I sat in the passenger seat and glanced behind me to see Annie and Liam sitting next to each other, excitement on their faces as we made our way to the store. Excitement flooded through me as I imagined this being our new life, going places together as a family, then I remembered that it wasn't really like that. It was a living arrangement that was as temporary as we wanted it to be.

Once inside the store, the kids ran ahead to the back of the store so they could start checking out the bed options for Annie. Liam had confirmed that he didn't want a new bed, he loved the one he had. Grant had recently purchased him a new bed when they moved out of his mother's house, shortly after Renee had passed. It was the first big purchase they had made after being on their own and was special to both of them.

I pushed a shopping cart alongside Grant as we followed the kids, knowing that I needed to get more stuff for Annie than just furniture. If we were going to actually live there, she needed more of her own stuff. Including some toys and new clothes for school. I had no idea what the plan was for her going to school and figured now was as good of a time as any to ask Grant about Liam's school.

"Hey, I was wondering, do you think Annie would be able to start school on Monday with Liam? Or am I way too late to get her registered?" I worried my lip in between my teeth as I realized how much there was to get done.

"I'm sure they can get her in. I'll make a call later and talk to the principal, let her know what's going on."

"You know the principal that well that you can just call them up and ask for a favor?" I asked suspiciously.

"Yeah, I know the principal that well. She's an old friend, and she happens to be my boss."

"You work at the school?" I turned my head to look at him as we rounded a corner and almost caught up to the kids.

"Yeah, I teach P.E." He shrugged as he walked over to where the kids were standing and looking at a white daybed with pink roses that ran along the arch of the frame.

"I can't believe I didn't know what you did," I said more to myself than to him. "I'm sorry, I feel so rude that I didn't think to ask before."

"Well it hasn't really come up in conversation," he laughed as he turned to look at me. "I'll call Mary and ask her if you can go by Monday morning to get Annie registered. We can grab some basic supplies today too, that way she'll have everything she needs."

His smile was so sweet and genuine that I found myself smiling back and honestly believing that everything would work out.

Hundreds of dollars later the shopping cart was filled to the top with new clothes and school supplies for Annie, along with the new furniture she had picked out that was in the cart that Grant was pushing. I reached down and checked my cell phone, making sure we were doing okay on time so they didn't miss the party. There were a few things that I had wanted to look at getting for myself but didn't want to tie up anyone's day longer than needed. As I was about to slide my cell phone back into my pocket, I felt it vibrate with a new call. Trying to be as discrete as possible, I glanced at the caller ID and felt relieved when it wasn't my dad. I could feel Grant's eyes watching me as I debated whether to answer the call or not.

"I need to take this call real quick," I said quietly, so only Grant could hear me. He nodded as he pushed the cart the other way, taking the kids with him to go look around, giving me some privacy. I sucked in a deep breath as I slid my finger across the screen to answer it.

"Hey," I said in a half-whisper as my voice started to break.

"Lacey Ann Holbrook – where the hell are you and are you and Annie okay?!"

I pulled the phone back from my ear to get away from the loud shriek that greeted me on the other side.

"Are you by yourself?" I asked as my voice evened out some as I turned my cart and wandered down the lotion and body wash aisle. Kayce was my cousin and best friend growing up, the only person that I've ever been close with, and knew all of the dark secrets of my family, never judging me for any of it.

"Yes, I am by myself. I just got back into town and heard about the fire from my mom," she sighed heavily. "Tell me the truth Lacey, are you guys okay? Are you safe?"

"We are okay and we are safe. But I can't tell you where we're at and I can't talk about what happened," I explained knowing that she would already know and understand why. I looked around at the different body washes and grabbed one with a tropical-looking label on it. Hawaiian Paradise. I smiled softly as I let myself fantasize about how wonderful that sounded as I tossed a bottle of it into my cart.

"Okay, that's all I need to know. I won't ask for details, I know better."

"Thank you, I appreciate that," I said as I slowly moved the cart forward and tossed in a few more items including some mud face masks and a couple of bath bombs. I wasn't even sure that Grant had a bathtub in his house, the only bathrooms I had been in were either a half bath or was limited to a walk-in shower. I shrugged and left them in the cart as I kept walking.

"You know, if you would have moved in with me you wouldn't have had to worry about this in the first place, you know?" she teased, forcing a smile across my face.

"Oh please, Kayce, you barely even fit in your studio apartment! There's no way that Annie and I would have fit there," I laughed and shook my head at the thought. "Plus, you're never home anymore, living the glamorous life of constantly being on the road with the hottest rock star on the west coast. How's that going by the way?" I asked, hoping to change the subject.

I suddenly remembered a few other things that I needed so I turned and headed in that direction, making sure that I stayed mindful of the time so I didn't make Grant and Liam late for the birthday party.

"It's okay I guess. I don't see him much when I travel with him so I don't know why I go anymore. They're constantly practicing or having band only meetings so I just end up sitting alone in the hotel or I go sightseeing on my own. It's getting kind of boring."

"That sucks," I said as I listened and shopped at the same time. "I guess it's never as glamorous as it seems, is it?"

"Not at all. I just got back this morning and decided to stay here and skip the next few stops they were going on. I'm tired and really wanted to just be home for a while. But then I got back and found out about you and Annie which made me feel terrible that I wasn't here to begin with."

"Honestly, there wasn't anything that you could have done. If you were there it would have just put you in danger and I would never want that."

"I know, but I hate that now you're on the run and I might not ever get to see you guys again."

"If I didn't run, you most likely wouldn't see us again anyways," I said softly as a somber tone fell between us.

"I know. For what it's worth, I wish you had been dealt a better card in life than having Bill as a father."

"Me too, kiddo, me too."

Kayce was only two years younger than me but I always felt like her big sister growing up. I settled down at an early age, got married, and had a baby all before I was 21. She just turned 25 and was traveling with her rock star boyfriend, seeing the world with very few responsibilities to tie her down. Her last big expense was the dragon tattoo she got on her back as a birthday present to herself after coloring her hair bright pink. She worked as a mechanic in Easterville which didn't pay much but kept her afloat with what she wanted to do with her life.

A few minutes later we said our goodbyes as I spotted Grant and started making my way toward them. Kayce promised to keep in touch and to let me know if she heard anything more about my dad. She hadn't bothered trying to get any information on him before she called so she knew as much about his whereabouts as I did. I felt a tad bit uneasy that I was talking to her, knowing that he could go after her at any time, trying to get information out of her. I pulled my cart up alongside Grant's and smiled as the kids came up beside him.

"I think we're all set. We can go check out so we have time to get everything home in time for you and Liam to get over to the birthday party," I said as I started to turn my cart toward the check-out line. Grant's brows pulled together as he adjusted his cart to follow mine.

"You're not coming with us?" he asked with a hint of disappointment in his tone.

"Why would we? It's your family." I was genuinely confused as to why he would assume that we were going.

"So? You've met everyone. You spent hours talking to them on New Year's Eve. They expect that you and Annie will be there with us today."

I watched as Annie's face turned up to look at me, her brown curls bouncing down her back.

"Can we go, mommy? Pllleeeasssee?" she whined as she held her hands together and begged me. I glanced at Grant out of the corner of my eye and saw the smirk on his face knowing that I wouldn't be able to say no to her.

"Okay, fine. We'll go," I sighed, shooting a glare his way. "But we need to get her a present and a card before we go."

"You can share ours," Grant offered before I shot him down with another look.

"We are not showing up to a birthday party without a card and a gift of our own," I warned as I turned my cart around, almost knocking myself and the cart over as it struggled with the weight in it. I heard Grant laugh behind me as I made my way back to the toy section.

The day felt long as we rushed home and unloaded everything from the truck into the living room before packing up Rylee's gifts and rushing out of the house again. Thankfully they only lived a few minutes away so we weren't as late as I had expected we would be. Grant held the door open as Liam rushed in, letting Annie and I go in next. I could feel my palms start to sweat as I looked around and instantly felt out of place with Grant's family. There were a few people that I knew but a handful of people that I hadn't met yet. Curious eyes started making their way toward us as I heard a few whispers of people asking who we were.

A few seconds later I smiled as I saw Mia come rushing over, quickly grabbing me and pulling me in for a hug. Grant wasn't lying when he said that she was one of the nicest people he knew.

"Lacey! I'm so glad that you and Annie could make it today!" she said excitedly as she pulled back and smiled at me before looking down to say hi to Annie. "I can take that," she offered as she reached for the gift bag and set it on the table behind us before leading me off to meet everyone else.

Everyone was just as friendly as Mia and apparently super curious about why Grant was there with a woman. Were they dating? Did they know each other long? Was it true that she was living with him? I tried to ignore the whispers as I made my way to the kitchen to see if I could help out with anything while Annie ran off with Liam to go play with Rylee.

The kitchen was tied into the living room as it all flowed into one which didn't really allow for a place to hide, which was what I was needing. I found Jade by the sink with her back turned toward everyone as she sliced a tomato and set it to the side. She grabbed another one and went to slice it when her hand slipped and I watched in slow motion as the knife went directly into her hand. A slew of curse words came flying out of her mouth as the knife fell to the sink before she quickly turned and held her hand away from the food as blood starting trickling down her hand. In an instant Noah was by her side, grabbing a paper towel and wrapping her hand as it quickly turned bright red from the blood.

"Are you okay?" Mia asked panicky as she came rushing over to see what had happened.

"Yeah, I missed and cut myself instead of the damn tomato," Jade grunted as Noah tried to hold the paper towel that was now soaked in blood against her hand. I could tell by the look of it that she was going to need help to get the bleeding under control.

"I can help with that," I offered, feeling my cheeks heat as everyone stopped and turned to look at me. "I'm a trauma nurse in the ER," I explained.

A few minutes later I helped Jade sit down, making sure the toilet seat lid was down first, and waited for Mia to bring the first aid kit they had. I smiled as I took it from her, watching as Jade held her hand over the sink as it continued to bleed.

"Will I need stitches?" Jade asked, looking up at me.

"I'm not sure yet, but hopefully not. I'll see what I can do to stop the bleeding first."

"Noah is going to give me crap about this," she muttered under her breath as Mia watched from the doorway. I opened the first aid kit that Mia had brought and prayed that it had the supplies I would need. I was relieved when I looked inside and found a decent supply of bandages and tape. Quickly I set the items that I needed out on the counter beside the sink and gently reached over to check on Jade's hand.

"Why's that?" I asked as I slowly pulled the paper towel away, being careful to not go too fast and risk opening the wound again. I took a closer look and was pleased to see that the bleeding had started to slow down which was a good sign.

"Because he's scared of everything. He would wrap me in bubble wrap and lock me in the house if he thought it would keep me safe." She rolled her eyes and shook her head as she and Mia shared a private look in the mirror.

"Some men get like that when their partner is pregnant," I laughed and quickly worked to get the paper towel off before it started bleeding heavily again.

"Yeah, I'm sure. He's just afraid because this is our miracle baby." She looked up and locked eyes with me as I glanced at her.

"Miracle baby?" I tilted my head to the side to glance at her before I turned my attention back to focus on getting a new bandage in place.

"I lost a baby, almost a year ago." There was a sadness in her voice that broke my heart. That was a loss that I was familiar with as well, even though nobody knew. Not even Derek.

"I'm so sorry for your loss." I smiled down at her as I continued to wrap another bandage around her hand, just to make sure.

"Thank you. I was around 8 weeks when it happened, but I didn't know that I was pregnant. We didn't think that I would or *could* get pregnant again, so this one was a big surprise."

"That's wonderful, how far along are you?" I asked as I cut the tape and gently pushed it down to make sure it was going to hold. I gathered up the supplies and started putting them back in the kit.

"I'll be 14 weeks tomorrow. Mia and I are basically having twins, she's 13 weeks as of yesterday." They smiled at each other in the mirror and I felt a sting of jealousy as I admired their friendship and this wonderful journey that they would get to share together.

"Alright, I think you're all set," I said as I stepped back and looked down at her hand. "We'll keep an eye on it just to make sure it doesn't start bleeding again, but I don't think you're going to need stitches."

I smiled as she thanked me before I ducked out of the room and went to find Grant. I walked down the hallway with my head down, not paying attention when I almost crashed into someone. I quickly looked up and saw a younger version of Grant smiling down at me.

"I'm so sorry," I said as I tried to excuse myself, turning awkwardly so I was walking backwards to the living room behind me.

"So you must be the hot new girl who's shacking up with my brother?" He said as he stepped to the side band watched me. I stopped in my tracks, unsure of what to say as I felt Grant come up behind me. I didn't have to hear his voice to know he was there. My body told me by the tingles that radiated through it every time he was around.

"Really, Wyatt?" he sighed as he placed his hand on my lower back possessively.

"What?" He shrugged. "She is hot, they weren't lying."

I felt my body turn fifty shades of red from embarrassment before the thought hit me that someone had been talking about me and it had gotten back to Grant's brother. And if someone knew that I was new in town, that meant that I wasn't going to be able to lay low after all. I looked up at Grant with worry on my face as I thought about amending our conditions and getting the hell out of town.

Thirteen

Grant

Lacey was quiet on the ride back from Chase's house and the kids were worn out in the back. I knew that it had been a long, overwhelming day for everyone, but something was different with Lacey and I couldn't quite put my finger on it. Part of me wondered if it was the phone call she had taken while we were at the store. As I pulled into the garage, I saw Annie and Liam undo their seatbelts, excited to go inside and get everything set up for their new room. I glanced at Lacey and saw the exhaustion on her face and knew everything would have to wait until tomorrow.

"Hey dad, can we go build Annie's bed so we can sleep in our new room together tonight?" Liam asked excitedly as he waited behind me as I opened the door into the house.

"It's late, son, and there's a lot that goes into building furniture. How about we do it first thing in the morning instead?" I offered, hoping he wouldn't be too disappointed.

"Yeah, I guess that's fine." He patted me on the back before saying goodnight to Lacey and Annie and running upstairs to get ready for bed. I was relieved that I didn't need to bug him to do it tonight.

"I'm tired too, mama," Annie said as she tugged at Lacey's sweater.

"Okay, honey, why don't you go get ready for bed too. I'll be up in

just a minute." Lacey ran her hand through Annie's hair, pushing it out
of her eyes before she ran upstairs to do as her mom asked.
I waited a few seconds until the kids were upstairs before talking to
Lacey about what was bothering her. She looked exhausted so I didn't
want to keep her up too long, but I wanted to make sure she wasn't
going to have another hotel room booked by morning. She slid out of
her jacket and hung it over the back of the chair in the kitchen before
turning to look at me.

"I think I'm going to head upstairs and call it a night too," she said
with a tired smile as she tried to fight off a yawn.

"Real quick, before you go," I reached out and gently grabbed her
arm, pulling her back into the kitchen before she walked away. "I just
wanted to make sure you're okay. You seemed upset when Wyatt was
talking to you. Which I get, he tends to have that effect on people," I
joked, hoping to lighten the mood.

"I'm okay, just nervous that Wyatt heard about me staying with you
through the grapevine. I was hoping to find someplace where we could
lay low but I know that's almost impossible in small towns."

"I get it, I really do. But I wouldn't worry too much about what Wyatt
knows. If there's a new woman anywhere in a 50-foot radius he can
find her. I swear he's going to get himself in trouble someday with all
of the women he messes around with," I chuckled. "We used to think
that Noah was bad until he settled down with Jade. After that, Wyatt
took his place and has been unstoppable ever since."

"Maybe he just needs to find a girl who can settle him down, as Jade
did with Noah," she teased.

"I don't think there's a single girl in Haven Brook that can tame him.
He needs someone who won't put up with his shit and will put him in
his place."

"Sounds like a challenge for my cousin, Kayce, they don't call her a
man-eater for nothing." She laughed and I could hear that it was forced
nervous laughter.

"You sure you're okay? Am I going to wake up to you packing to go to
the hotel again in the morning?"

"No," she laughed. "We made a deal, I'll stick to it. Besides, I'm too
tired to call and make a reservation."

I laughed at her joke, earning a cute smile from her in return. We said goodnight as she wandered upstairs. My mind had been busy all day as I struggled to figure out what all of these changes meant. Earlier at the birthday party, while Lacey was helping Jade with her cut, my mom cornered me to ask about Lacey and whether we were a thing. Everyone was thinking the same thing, drawing the same conclusions, but no one wanted to ask me about it.

Part of me wondered what life would be like if Lacey and Annie stayed with us forever. Would we continue to feel like the family we felt like earlier when we were at the store? Would we continue to share meals together and ask about each other's days? Everything felt so simple now, I wondered what it would be like the longer we went on pretending this was something it wasn't. I gave up trying to clear my head and went upstairs to try to get some rest, relieved that tonight would hopefully be the last night of getting kicked in my ribs every time I started to snore. If the kids thought they were excited about the new room arrangements, they had no idea how excited I was about it.

Fourteen

Lacey

I cowered in the corner of the room, under the kitchen table as I watched my dad stand over my mom, his knuckles white from how hard his hands were wrapped around her throat. She looked panicked as she tried to move out from underneath him, her arms swinging in the air as she tried to make contact with him. I could see her losing the battle, I could see the life draining from her body. In the last few seconds, her head turned toward me and her eyes locked onto mine. There was nothing but love and sadness behind them as I watched her fade away.

I screamed inside, desperate to help her. Desperate to bring her back to life. I knew that if I made any noise, I would be next. My dad grunted as he stood up and kicked her, grabbing his open beer off the counter and stumbled into the living room. I wrapped my arms around my knees as I stared at her and cried silently, wishing for one last hug. One last moment to tell her how much I loved her. I closed my eyes and pictured us sitting outside on a blanket, having a picnic while we looked up at the sky and made up stories about the images we found in the shapes of the cloud.

All of that was gone now. I was all by myself, left to learn how to protect myself from the only person I had left. The person who was supposed to love me but had constantly told my mom that she should have had the abortion when he told her to. My life would never be the same and I knew that. He had robbed me of everything that I had ever wanted and needed. To be loved.

I felt the wetness on my face as the tears slid down my cheeks, slowly waking me from the nightmare. I was desperate to wake up, to escape from the memory, but my mind and body were too exhausted to let me. Off in the distance, I could hear voices. Faint voices that sounded familiar. I struggled to listen as my dream shifted to one of Derek. It was the day of our wedding, the first time I had really been happy since before my mom died. I remembered smiling as I watched all of the guests start to arrive from the room where I was getting ready. Then came the moment of dread when I saw my father get out of his car and walk into the church as if he belonged there.

The voices got louder, an urgency to them. A fear. He wasn't supposed to be there. He wasn't invited. Panic filled me as I recognized the voice. It was Annie's voice. None of this made sense, Annie wasn't at our wedding. So who was she talking to? I felt my blood run cold when I realized that I wasn't hearing her in my dream, she was talking to someone right beside me. My eyelids felt heavy as I desperately tried to open them, forcing my body to wake up. There was a male's voice that I could hear now too but it sounded further away. I pushed harder, wishing someone would shake me and make my body do what I needed it to.

"I'll see you later, grandpa," Annie's voice was soft as my eyes blinked rapidly as I woke up. A movement from the corner of my eye forced my head to whip in the direction of the door as I saw a shadow move in the hallway. I quickly glanced at Annie as she rolled over and curled into her stuffed puppy before she let out a breath confirming she was asleep.

My body was shaking as I replayed her words over and over in my head as I slowly got out of bed and looked for something to use as a weapon. Liam's room was filled with toys but none of which looked like a promising weapon to use against someone lurking in the shadows. Knowing that I didn't have much time, I reached down and grabbed the first thing that my hand came in contact with while keeping an eye on the door.

I slowly crept down the hallway and tiptoed along the edge of each stair, trying to keep them from creaking beneath my weight. I could feel the cold metal in my hand as I tightened my grip around it before turning toward the kitchen. As I rounded the corner I saw a shadow at the sink and my heart skipped a beat. I raised my hand, ready to do harm, as they turned around.

A shirtless Grant eyed me suspiciously as I lowered my arm and brought my hand to my chest, trying to catch my breath.

"What the hell are you doing in here? You scared the shit out of me!" I quietly exclaimed, trying to not wake the kids up.

"I'm getting a drink of water…" He stepped closer and narrowed his eyes as he tried to figure out what I was holding in my hand. "What exactly are you doing?"

"I was having a bad dream, and then Annie started talking in her sleep which freaked me out. Right after she said it, I saw a shadow in the hallway and I came to investigate," I explained with a shrug of my shoulders.

"So instead of coming to get me, you decided to come sneak up on a possible burglar, and use this as your weapon?" he asked as he reached out and took it from me. "What is this?" He pulled his eyebrows together as he looked back and forth between me and it.

I had to stifle a laugh when I saw him holding the cosmetics case that I had picked up at the store earlier. It had an assortment of makeup brushes and other beauty tools inside, but I had liked it because of the sleek, metal case that it came in. I pulled my mouth into a thin line to keep from laughing as I answered him with the most serious tone I could find.

"It's a cosmetic case," I said, squaring my shoulders and tilting my chin up toward him. He arched an eyebrow and turned to look at it, studying it intensely.

"Okay… so what exactly were you planning to do? Pin them down and give them a hideous makeover? Pluck their eyebrows until they begged you to stop?"

I narrowed my eyes at him as I heard the laughter he was trying to keep out of his voice.

"I'll have you know that there are sharp scissors in there… And I know how to use them." I pursed my lips as we continued to have a stare down.

He nodded his head as if he was giving me the benefit of the doubt before he turned away and slid the lock on the side, opening the case and revealing the contents. He chuckled as he pulled out the smallest pair of grooming scissors I had ever seen.

"You're right, I wouldn't want to be caught alone in a dark alley with you if you were packing these bad boys," he said as he turned to cough to hide the laughter that was getting harder to suppress.

"You are such an ass." I rolled my eyes and held out my hand. "Give me those before you hurt yourself."

He laughed and closed the case, handing it back to me as our hands briefly touched each other. I let out a heavy sigh, thankful for the comedic relief- as brief as it was. My mind had already gone back to the nightmare and the fact that I had heard Annie talking to someone while I was trying to wake up. I felt a shiver jolt through me and wrapped my arms around myself to stop it.

"What did Annie say in her sleep that you freaked you out so bad?" he asked with genuine sincerity.

"I'll see you later, grandpa." I cringed as the words slipped off my tongue and watched as his body tensed when he heard it.

"Okay, yeah, that would freak me out too. Does she know that he's been calling?"

I nodded my head no, unsure of what else to say. My mind was already playing tricks on me so it was hard to tell what was part of the dream and what was a reality, but I was almost certain that she had said it. It bothered me even more that I actually felt like someone else had been in the room. The hair on my arms had stood on end while my heart practically raced out of my chest. There weren't many times that my body had that kind of reaction except when my father was around.

"So what are you going to do now?" Grant shifted his weight and shoved his hands into his pockets. I glanced behind him to the clock on the stove. It was three o'clock in the morning and way too early to be awake on a Sunday, yet I couldn't bring myself to go back up to the room and try to sleep in there again. But at the same time, what kind of mother would I be to leave my daughter alone in a room where I felt there could be some sort of a threat? Grant studied me as I worked my jaw back and forth, sorting through the options.

"Do you want to sleep on the couch and I can sleep in the hallway outside of Annie's room?"

I pulled my head back and looked at him. There was no way that I was going to let him sleep in the hallway.

"That's not necessary, thank you. I just need a cold glass of water and then I'll go back up and try to get some sleep with Annie."

"You know as well as I do that you're not going to sleep if you go back up there. And you need some sleep. How about I go up and check on both kids -- make sure everything looks fine and check to make sure no one is up there. Then I'll come down and sleep in the living room with you. If anyone is getting in or out of this house, we would hear and see them from the living room."

I licked my lips as I considered it. He had a good point. There was no exit upstairs and very few places that anyone could hide. I wasn't convinced that anyone had been in the house but I also couldn't relax knowing that someone could get into the house. With what Annie said on top of Wyatt knowing I was here and staying with Grant, I was on high alert. I agreed to his suggestion and worked on getting the pillows and blankets ready for us while he went back upstairs to check on the kids. A few minutes later, I could hear the soft sound as his bare feet padded across the tile floor, relieved to see he had put a shirt on while he was up there.

"Do you want the couch or the chair?" I asked as I stood in between both, holding up a blanket.

"Whichever you don't want is fine with me."

"I want you to have the more comfortable option," I countered and shifted my weight as I watched him.

"Let's be honest- neither of them are that comfortable," he said with a chuckle. I smiled, knowing he was right about that.

After a few minutes it was apparent that neither of us could decide, nor were we relaxed enough to fall asleep anytime soon. At Grant's suggestion, we curled up under blankets and sat next to each other on the couch as we watched reruns on tv. The anxiety I had been feeling since I woke up from the nightmare started to ease as I felt my body gravitate toward his. The warmth of it was so welcoming and relaxing that I found myself leaning against him as he wrapped an arm around me and held me. Soon our breathing had fallen in sync, just as quickly as our heartbeats did. With every breath we took together, I could feel our bodies melting into each other as we peacefully drifted to sleep.

There were plenty of things that I had tried to control in my life. Having our children wake up to find us asleep in each other's arms wasn't one of them.

"How could you, dad?!"

Liam's voice startled us awake, the look of anger on his face evident as he stormed off and slammed the door upstairs. I saw Grant lean his head back as he closed his eyes before I scooted over so he could get up. He pulled the blanket off and tossed it next to me on the couch as he went upstairs to talk to Liam. I shook my head, disappointed that we had let this happen. This wasn't the message that either of us wanted to send to the kids. As I glanced to the side, I saw Annie sitting at the kitchen table, looking at me with tears in her eyes.

Fifteen

Grant

I took the stairs two at a time, trying to catch up to Liam as he stormed off. There was zero intention of having Lacey in my arms last night, let alone falling asleep with her still cuddled up to my chest. I let out a quick breath of air as I climbed the last step, making my way to Liam's room as the door slammed shut in my face. I gritted my teeth, reminding myself to try not to lose my temper. He was upset by what he had seen, and rightfully so. Still, we were going to have a quick conversation about his rude behavior after we finished talking about the problem at hand.

I clenched my jaw as I knocked on his door, trying to bring my blood pressure down quickly before walking into the hot zone that was waiting for me on the other side. After a few seconds of complete silence, I knocked again.

"Go away! I don't want to talk to you!" he screamed from the other side, reigniting the flame of my temper. I rolled my neck back quickly as I tried to alleviate as much tension as possible before I turned the knob and opened the door. I saw him sitting on the edge of his bed, arms folded as he glared at me with his head lowered while he pouted.

"When I knock on your door," I pointed to it now standing wide open behind me. "It's out of respect. You're getting older and I would like to be able to treat you like a man." I spoke slowly with a firm tone. I waited for him to look up and make eye contact with me before continuing. His blue eyes that matched mine looked up, tears forming in the corners.

"However, if I'm going to treat you with respect, I expect it from you in return. Slamming your door in my face and telling me to go away— that's far from being respectful. Part of being a grown-up and acting like a man is knowing how to handle situations when you're upset and angry. So we'll keep working on that, okay?" I eased up some and noticed when his shoulders started to drop some once he calmed down. Renee had always joked that he was my mini-me, in every way possible. Little did she know just how true that was. I watched as he struggled with his emotions while waiting for me to continue with the lecture.

"Are you ready to talk about what happened downstairs and why you're so upset with me?" I asked cautiously, not at all prepared to have this conversation with him. He looked away and exhaled heavily through his nose as I watched his temper start to swell again.

"Liam..."

"It's not fair!" he shouted so loud that it startled both of us. I walked into the room and sat down on the beanbag chair that was so worn out it could explode at any minute. I took a slow breath in, hoping he would see me do it and do the same.

"What's not fair?" I tilted my head slightly to the side, catching his eye as he tried to look past me.

"That you're trying to replace mom. Lacey is nice but she's not my mom and she's never going to be."

His words tore through me like a knife, cutting deeper than I ever imagined they would. I had thought about this conversation plenty of times in the past four years, but I never thought it would be a reality. That was the main reason that I had never bothered with trying to date after Renee. Not only was I unsure whether my heart could handle it, but I was also absolutely positive that Liam's couldn't.

"Son, Lacey isn't trying to be your mom. No one— I repeat— NO ONE will ever replace your mom. The love you have for her will never change. Okay?"

He nodded forcefully as his jaw stayed clenched.

"Nothing is going on between me and Lacey. She had a bad dream last night and I offered to hang out on the couch with her while we watched TV until she could go back to sleep. It's no different than what we do when you have a bad dream," I explained, his face softening a little as I said it.

"I know that it had to be hard for you to see me with someone other than your mom, and I'm sorry. I really am. But Liam, at some point, there may be another woman in my life. Another woman in OUR lives. And I hope that you will always know that she will never replace what your mom meant to either of us and that you'll give her a chance to be part of our lives."

My heart felt like it was breaking as I talked to Liam about this. Thoughts of Renee filled my head while thoughts of Lacey tried to join in. There was a clash between the two, making me increasingly uncomfortable as I tried to sort out how I felt about both. Guilt weighed heavily on me as I thought about what I was saying to Liam and I wondered if he knew I was lying about Lacey as much as I knew I was. My head wanted to say the words that I knew my son needed to hear but my heart wanted to say the words that neither of us could handle. I was starting to move on.

After a lengthy talk with Liam, I felt mentally and emotionally exhausted as I wandered back downstairs to check on Lacey and Liam jumped in the shower. As I walked into the living room I found Lacey sitting on the couch with Annie laying her head in her lap, fresh tears on her face. When Lacey looked up at me, I could see it on her face that they had a similar talk. I ran a hand down my face, feeling the rough scruff on my jawline as I turned and made my way into the kitchen to make breakfast. I started to question whether it had been the right call to have Lacey and Annie move in with us after all.

An hour and two fresh-smelling kids later, we were sitting down at the table for a late breakfast. Thankfully, the day was still early but it definitely did not start out how I had planned. Nor was I looking forward to the awkward silence that filled the room as we ate in silence. I hadn't had a chance to talk to Lacey by ourselves since everything had happened this morning but I could see it on her face that she hated how uncomfortable things were, the tension thickening as the minutes ticked by. Unable to take it anymore, I slammed my fork down on the table, startling everyone, including myself. I hadn't meant to be so dramatic about it but I had gotten so caught up in everything in my head that I didn't realize just how worked up I was.

I felt my cheeks flush with heat as everyone turned to look at me, Lacey's eyes wide with horror as if I had finally lost my shit. If she only knew. I struggled as I tried to think about what I was going to say now that I was on the spot.

"Okay, I think we all need to talk about what happened this morning so we can clear the air and make sure there are no misunderstandings," I said cautiously, watching Lacey to make sure she was okay with where I was going with this. She pulled her lips into a thin line and nodded as she glanced between the kids. I gave her a curt nod in agreement as I looked at Annie and Liam, their faces blank and expressionless as they waited for me to say something important. I cleared my throat and leaned back in my seat, unsure of how to start.

"Liam and I have already talked, and I know that Lacey, your mom, has talked with you as well. However, if we're all going to live here together, we need to talk about this as a family." I felt my throat tighten as I said the word, panic on my face as I looked to Lacey for help. She smiled warmly as her eyes softened, a look of encouragement on her face. I didn't want to send the wrong message by calling us a family, especially given everything that had already upset the kids. But I also didn't want them to think of this as anything other than that. I wanted Annie and Lacey to feel welcomed and at home with Liam and me, which meant that we were going to treat each other like family.

"I know that it surprised you guys this morning when you found Lacey and me asleep together on the couch. As we've explained to both of you, nothing happened other than we were watching tv and fell asleep. There are no intentions of me trying to be Annie's dad or Lacey trying to be Liam's mom, so please know that even though we will be a family, we are NOT trying to replace the parents that you guys lost. Okay?" I looked between both of them as they nodded their heads in agreement before picking up their forks and resuming their breakfast. I sighed a breath of relief that everything already started to feel a little better, the air a little easier to breathe.

I leaned forward, resting my arms on the table as I cut into my pancake with the fork. I popped the bite into my mouth and started chewing when Annie blindsided me with a question that I didn't see coming.

"Are you going to do it with my mom?" Her little voice was filled with innocence as she looked up at me with a giant smile stretched across her face. Her hand was lifted in the air, holding her fork in limbo as she waited for me to respond. I could feel the moment the pancake hit the back of my throat as I sucked in a breath of air, forcing it to get lodged. The syrup burned as it tried to make its way down past the piece of pancake that stayed stuck in place. I forcefully coughed a few times, trying to dislodge it as Lacey started to get up to help. I waved her off as I continued to cough, reaching for my water to take a drink.

I could see the blush on Lacey's neck as it crept up to her cheeks while she leaned over and whispered something in Annie's ear. She sat up straight and gave me an apologetic smile as she waited for confirmation that I was okay and not about to suffer a sticky death by pancake. I took another drink of water, relieved when I felt the lump move down my throat. Annie waited for me to swallow before she spoke, probably learning the hard way not to say anything while I had food in my mouth.

"I'm sorry for what I asked," she said as she shrugged. "I just thought that maybe you were going to do it with my mom since she's so pretty and all of the boys back home wanted to do it with her too."

Lacey and I exchanged a look as I arched a brow in question. She looked mortified as she ran a hand down her face.

"Annie, what exactly are you talking about? What do you mean by 'do it'?" Lacey asked, turning to look directly at Annie.

"You know, the hugs and hand-holding. All of the gross stuff that boys like to do. Then you guys can write each other secret notes about how you have the butterflies and make eyes at each other like they do in the movies," she explained as she pushed her food around on the plate with her fork. Lacey and I exchanged a look of relief as we listened and I was thankful not to have another uncomfortable conversation.

"Honey, that's called dating. When a boy and girl like each other, they start dating. Then someday, when they're ready, they might decide to get married. Like your daddy and I did, and like Liam's mommy and daddy did." Lacey smiled as she brushed a piece of hair out of Annie's face as she talked to her.

"Okay, that makes sense," Annie said before pulling her brows in together before she pinned me with a serious look. "So, why don't you want to date my mommy?"

My eyes darted up to Lacey's, desperate for help with how to answer that question but not finding any. No matter what I said, I was bound to be the bad guy with at least one person. If I lied and said that I didn't want to date Lacey then I risked hurting her and Annie's feelings. If I admitted that I might be interested in dating Lacey then I would risk breaking the promises that I gave to Liam this morning when I assured him that nothing was going on between us and that I wouldn't start dating again before I talked to him about it first.

"That's not an appropriate question to ask someone, especially an adult," Lacey scolded calmly as her posture stiffened. "Dating isn't something that Grant or I would take lightly, as we explained to you guys this morning when we had our separate talks. Dating when you have children is a lot different than regular dating and it's not a decision that we can make lightly. Not only do we have to decide if we are ready to date, but we also have to decide whether you guys are ready for us to date. There are a lot of things that have to be considered, but rest assured that neither of you have to worry about any of this because Grant and I are not dating."

I stayed quiet as I watched Lacey talk to the kids, both their attention focused on her. I hated that we had to have this conversation with the kids before we were able to talk about it ourselves. We had made it very clear to the kids that we weren't interested in dating anyone, especially not each other, so we both felt a strong pressure to stick with what we said. The problem was that I didn't know if either of us actually meant it.

We spent the rest of the day working on getting the room converted for the kids as well as getting Lacey set up in my room. By seven o'clock we had shifted gears to get the kids ready for their first day back at school tomorrow. Lacey was reluctant to believe that they would let Annie start tomorrow since she wasn't registered yet, but agreed to get her stuff ready anyways. It was after nine o'clock when we made our way to the bedroom, awkward chemistry sparking between us as we tried to figure out how to be in the same small space with each other.

I had cleared out the nightstand on the other side of the bed, thankful that I had bought all new furniture when Liam and I moved into this house so I didn't have feelings of guilt with letting Lacey use something that had belonged to Renee. She went to the bathroom to get ready for bed while I quickly changed in the walk-in closet. It had been a while since I had lived with a woman so I forgot how long they took to get ready for anything.

Fifteen minutes later, Lacey came out of the attached master bathroom with her hair loosely piled in a messy bun on her head while her face looked like something out of a sci-fi or horror movie. I pulled a pillow up to my face and hid behind it as I tried to stifle a laugh while she climbed into bed next to me. I could sense her irritation as she swatted at the pillow, pulling it down to force me to look at her.

"What's so funny?" she asked with a hint of annoyance in her voice, her face rigid as she waited to see if I was making fun of her.

"Nothing," I mumbled as I laughed harder, trying to hide behind the pillow again before she grabbed it and threw it across the room.

"It's just a face mask, don't be such a child," she scoffed as she rolled her eyes and pulled the pillow down behind her as she tried to get comfortable.

"That is a mask indeed," I joked, getting a side-eyed glare from her in return. She ignored me as she reached over and pulled open the bottom drawer of the nightstand and grabbed a pair of socks. They were low-cut with cartoon penguins on them. My eyes slowly moved from her feet up to her masked face as she slid them on, oblivious to the additional jokes that threatened to come spewing out of my mouth.

I licked my lips as I tried to find something else to focus on without any luck. After she slipped her socks on she adjusted the pant legs of her pajama bottoms and leaned against the padded headboard and closed her eyes. I took the opportunity to lean in and really get a look at the mask. It was a thin white paper looking mask with a gooey film underneath that was holding it in place. There were holes cut out for her eyes, nostrils, and mouth, but everything else was covered by this thin white paper. I tried to remember if Renee had ever been into this sort of stuff but nothing came to mind. I definitely would have remembered laughing at this if she had whipped one out and acted like it was nothing. I was still staring at the mask when I saw one of Lacey's eyes open and glare at me as she let out a heavy sigh.

"Are you still obsessed with my mask?" she asked dryly.

"I'm sorry, I still can't get over it," I laughed.

"You're so immature," she muttered as she closed her eyes again. "Not all of us have the skin of some twenty-year-old without a care in the world, some of us have to actually work to have nice skin and not look like we're pushing eighty."

"You act like you're so ancient," I said with sarcasm. "How old are you anyway? Twenty-one? Twenty-two?"

"A real gentleman never asks a woman her age," she teased as she opened her eyes and climbed out of bed. "Now if you'll excuse me, this old lady has to go deal with her mask."

I watched as she strutted to the bathroom and closed the door behind her. I laced my hands behind my head and laid down, knowing tonight was going to be a long night. A few minutes later Lacey made her way back to the bed, her face still moist from washing the goo off of her face. She climbed into bed and reached over to open the top drawer of her nightstand. I shook my head as I saw the giant jar of earplugs that she took out and opened, pulling two from the container and sitting them on her lap. She silently put the lid back on and set the container back in the drawer before closing it.

"Earplugs? Seriously?," I asked with a smug smile knowing what she was insinuating.

"What? I need my beauty rest and I'm not about to let some loud, cranky, grizzly bear keep me up all night with their snoring." She shrugged her shoulders as she pushed them into her ears and smiled before rolling over and facing the opposite way. I shook my head and turned onto my side as I tried to remember why I ever agreed to this arrangement in the first place. Despite the creepy face mask and childish socks, the bulge in my sweatpants reminded me exactly why I had come up with this crazy idea.

Sixteen

Lacey

I tapped my foot nervously as I sat in the cold metal chair outside of the Principal's office, waiting for her to come in. Grant leaned against the wall opposite of me, arms casually folded over his chest as I glanced at the long-sleeved t-shirt and jogger track pants he was wearing. I pulled at the hem of my dress pants, suddenly self-conscious about getting dressed up to meet with her, even after he assured me that it was a casual meeting. It was simply to get Annie registered for school, not a job interview.

Which was another thing that was weighing heavily on my mind. I needed to get busy looking for a job as soon as I was done getting Annie set up at school. While I had loved the busy life of the ER at the hospital, so much had changed these past few months that I suddenly felt dread about going back to the same hours and being away from Annie for long. It had barely been a little over a week since I had taken off from my father's house but in that time I was forced to slow down. There was nowhere to go and nothing to do which was an odd feeling for me. The problem was that I was starting to like the easy-going, laid-back environment that I felt at Grant's house and I could see that Annie was enjoying it too. Going back to the hospital would mean that we would have to say good-bye to all of that.

I forced out a steady breath as I looked to the side and watched Annie talking to Liam before the bell rang for him to go to class. The clock hanging on the brick wall across from me showed that there were only a few minutes left before classes would start. As if on cue, I heard the quick clicking on the tile floor as a beautiful woman wearing six-inch heels came walking toward us. Her long blond hair hung loosely down her back, swaying gently with each step as her hips threatened to hypnotize me. Her lips were painted a soft pink color that enhanced the fullness of them the closer she got. Baby blue eyes looked down at me and lit up as she reached a hand out for me to shake once she got to me.

"Hi! You must be Lacey!" Her hand was soft and warm, yet her grip was firm. She reminded me of the type of woman who has had to fight hard to get to where she is in her career and therefore she's used to having to make herself not only seen but heard.

"Hi, it's nice to meet you, Ms. Anderson." I smiled as we continued to shake hands. "This is my daughter, Annie." I nodded down as Annie turned to look at us after hearing her name. The bell rang, sending Liam off to his class as the principal showed us into her office. I was surprised when Grant didn't take off as well, assuming he had a class he needed to get to.

"You can call me Beth," she said as she rounded the oversized desk that took up the majority of the office and hung her purse on the coat rack behind her. I settled down into one of the plush leather chairs across from her and scooted Annie over toward me to allow Grant to take a seat. He shook his head no as he stood off in the corner and pressed his lips into a thin line. There was a glance that was exchanged between the two of them and it made me wonder if there was a history there. I wouldn't be surprised given that she was a beautiful woman who looked to be around his age. I tried to shake the thoughts from my head as I turned my attention back to her as she began asking Annie about the last school she attended.

I watched as she quickly typed, entering all of the information into the computer in front of her. A few minutes later she smiled as she reached behind her to grab the paper she had printed and handed it to Annie.

"This is the paperwork that you'll need to give to your teacher this morning when you get to class. Mr. Walker can show you to the classroom as well as give you a quick tour of the school." She looked at Grant and he nodded before she turned her attention back to me as Annie stood up and followed Grant out of the room. "Our school is fairly small so she should be able to find everything pretty easily. And we have a lot of helpful students here that can always show her around if she forgets." Her voice was calm as she reassured me.

I adjusted in my seat, unsure of what to do next. I had expected this process to be a lot lengthier and more tedious like it was when I first registered her in Montana. Granted her school in Montana was a lot bigger than this one, both of us getting lost several times just trying to find the office. I felt better that she was going to be in a smaller school and prayed that she would make friends and quickly and easily. Beth turned her attention back to the computer and I let out the breath I had been holding when I realized that we weren't finished after all.

"Okay, I have all of Annie's information in the system so we could go ahead and send her to class right away, but I still need to collect her personal information, as well as yours." She looked away from the computer for a quick second to flash me her perfectly straight, white teeth, before looking back at the computer.

I started to feel my heart race as I realized that I hadn't asked Grant about using his personal information, even though we were living together so it would be assumed that I would use it. But who did I list as an emergency contact? What if there was an emergency? Worse- what if my dad found us and came to the school to get Annie? Would they allow her to leave with him because this is such a small town? I felt my face go white as a ghost as I stared at her, wondering if it was too late to pull Annie out of class and take off running again. How was I going to be able to go to work every day and not be able to keep an eye on her?

A few minutes passed by as I answered her questions in a zombie-like fashion, giving her Grant's address which was met with raised eyebrows as she politely entered the information in without asking any questions. I decided to give her both of my cell phone numbers since I hadn't gotten around to canceling my old phone number just yet. In a way, I felt reluctant to because every time I saw a missed call- or ten- from my dad, it reassured me that he didn't know where we were based on the hateful things he said in each voicemail. Keeping the phone on was my new safety net that I hadn't known I would need. I tapped my fingers nervously against my leg, feeling the silky fabric of the trousers as it brushed against my thigh. I had purchased these to wear to Derek's funeral and forced myself to put them on today. For some reason, it had felt like we were going to have to audition to get Annie into the school and I felt like the more presentable I looked, the less they would be able to see what a hot mess I was.

Beth was still entering information in the computer when Grant came back in and leaned against the doorway.

"Hey, I was trying to show Annie where Nurse Lorna's office is but the room was locked and the lights were off. Is she not coming in today?" he asked as she slowly turned around and looked at him with a disappointed frown on her face.

"No, unfortunately, she decided to put in her notice. This morning. That's why I was so frazzled trying to get in this morning. Not only is it the first day back after winter break, but now we don't have a school nurse. So, I really pray that all of the ice that is covering the playground doesn't result in anyone needing a nurse since I still need to find one."

I felt Grant's eyes move toward me, knowing what he was going to do before he did it. I swallowed hard as I heard him start to speak.

"Well, that's actually funny because Lacey here is looking for a job," he paused and looked between me and Beth. "And she was a trauma nurse back home."

Beth's eyes went wide as she turned and smiled, a look of pure excitement on her flawless face.

"I know it is several steps down from the ER, but would you be interested?" she asked cautiously.

I took a shaky breath and glanced at Grant who was nodding for me to consider it. This would fix the problem that I had with being away from Annie, as well as allow me to work the same time she was in school. I wouldn't have to try to find a hospital or clinic to work in which would be nice as well, however I would have to look into what was needed for me to transition to a school nurse with the Colorado Board of Nursing. With Grant letting us live there without paying any bills, it wouldn't matter what the pay was since I would be able to put money aside for when we were ready to move out on our own while still having enough to contribute to groceries and other random expenses. I tried to keep my excitement to a minimum as I turned to look at Beth and nodded yes.

"Thank you, I would be very interested," I said as I felt the excitement course through me. I couldn't believe it, it felt like all of my unanswered prayers were coming true.

Grant left the room to go check in on a few students who were supposed to be getting things ready for his class, leaving us to finish my new hire paperwork. She expected that everything would be final in a few days, pending the background check and making sure my license covered me before she could officially offer me the job and allow me to start working. I was giddy as I walked out of her office and took myself on a quick tour of the school as I tried to process that this would now be my new work.

The sky was clear with a sun that promised more warmth than it actually provided. I stepped outside, feeling the sharp sting of the icy chill that bit at my skin. I ran my hands up and down my arms as I spotted Grant and made my way over to him. He smiled and waved before he jogged over to keep me from having to walk across the field.

The way his body moved so fluidly as he ran made me think of all of the other things it could probably do as well. My mind was exhausted from the lack of sleep I had last night while my body was on constant alert any time he was around. We had talked a few times about whether it was a good idea for us to share a bed after getting the kids situated in their room. In the end, we both agreed that we could be adults and understood that it was just sleep- nothing more- so we let the issue rest as we struggled to get comfortable last night.

I tried my best to keep things as friendly as possible but the truth was that I had been anxiously obsessing over sleeping next to him since we talked about it before the shopping trip. I even went the extra mile to buy as many non-sexy things as I could think of to keep me from getting any other ideas as we got ready for bed. I put on the hideous face mask that took forever before I could get it to stay in place because I kept laughing at how ridiculous it looked. Then there were the childish pajamas and socks that I had grabbed as well because honestly, who feels sexy with pink fuzzy penguin socks? Apparently, I do, as I imagined him pulling them off my feet with his teeth before he did unimaginable things to me.

I sucked in a deep breath as I forced the thoughts from my head right before he reached me. He was slightly out of breath but it was nothing compared to what I would look like if I had tried to run across the field in freezing cold temperatures that turned your breath to ice the moment it left your mouth.

"Hey, did you get the job?" he asked with a huge smile on his face that stretched perfectly across as tiny wrinkles appeared just beneath the corners of his eyes.

"I did, thank you," I said with a warm smile. "Well, technically it's pending a background check so I can't start until then, but that should come back clean." I laughed as I said it, imagining that it sounded as odd to him as it did to me when I heard it. I wanted to smack myself in the head and see if I could knock some intelligence back into my brain.

"That's awesome, congratulations. Why don't we do a celebratory dinner tonight?" he offered as he glanced over his shoulder to check on the few students that were arranging supplies in the field as the bell rang. I didn't want to keep him from work any longer than I already had.

"That sounds great." I nodded enthusiastically because I was actually feeling pretty on top of the world right now and couldn't remember when the last time was that someone had offered to have a celebratory dinner for me. Not even Derek made the effort and there had been plenty of things that we could have celebrated. The thought made me sad, threatening to damper my mood if I didn't shift my thoughts quickly.

"Okay, well, I'll be back this afternoon to pick Annie up." I smiled and turned to walk away when I felt his hand reach out and gently grab my arm.

"You do know that I work here and will be bringing Liam home as well, right?" he asked as he raised a brow.

"Yeah…" I narrowed my eyes at him, trying to figure out where he was going with this.

"I figured I could bring Annie home since Liam and I are going to the same place." He stared at me as if I was dense, not getting the obvious fact that he had just pointed out. While I understood that it would be easier, it felt nerve-wracking not to get her myself.

"Yeah, I know that you work here and will be bringing Liam home anyways. It just feels weird not to be here to pick her up from her first day of school."

I felt nervous as I watched his face change, relieved when it softened after he got where I was coming from. He nodded sympathetically and gave me a quick pat on the shoulder.

"I'll see you this afternoon. Her class will let out by this field and the parents wait over there." He pointed in the direction of a small parking lot that was gated-in before he smiled, waved, and jogged back over to where the students had begun setting things up. I gave a small wave, knowing he wouldn't see it, as I turned to walk away. My phone vibrated in my pocket against my thigh as I pulled it out to see Kayce's name on the caller ID. I smiled as I slid my finger across to answer it.

"Hey, did you miss me already?" I asked with a smile.

"Bill is gone! My dad said that he talked to him briefly at the gas station before he flew out of the parking lot and sped off toward the highway." Her voice was filled with panic, sending shivers down my spine.

"When did he talk to him?" I froze in place as I waited.

"This morning, like maybe an hour ago?"

"Which direction is he headed?" I asked as I looked around.

"He didn't say, he just said that he was going to go fix what needed fixing."

I ran a hand down my face as I stood paralyzed with fear, wondering where he was. The highway that went through Easterville only went two directions- north and south which left a 50/50 chance that he was already on his way to find me.

Seventeen

Grant

I looked for Annie while lightly jogging through the mass of first graders swarming out of their classrooms as the bell rang. My goal was to catch up to her before she made it to the parking lot to meet Lacey so I could ask her about the celebratory dinner that I had been planning all day. Lacey and I had text each other throughout the day, random stuff here and there, but mainly it was just Lacey second-guessing her decision to go home and relax while Annie was at school. I could tell that being away from her today was hard with everything they had been through, so I wanted to make tonight extra special for her.

A few minutes later I spotted the pink ribbon wrapped around her ponytail as she skipped alongside another little girl, their arms linked together. I smiled, thrilled that she had already made a friend, as I caught up to them.

"Hey, Annie," I said softly so I didn't startle her but loud enough that she could hear me over the sound of the other kids as they laughed and talked around us.

"Hi!" She looked up and smiled when she heard my voice. We were getting close to the parent pickup area and I knew I needed to talk fast if I wanted to talk to her before she got to Lacey. I also needed to find Liam and make sure he wasn't off playing with his friends as he usually was.

"I have a quick question for you." I stopped and quickly pulled her to the side to let the other kids pass, glancing up to make sure Lacey hadn't spotted us yet. Her head was down as she looked at something on her phone, a few quick glances every few seconds as she looked for Annie but didn't spot us.

"Sure, what's up?" she asked as she stopped and looked at me.

"What's your mom's favorite food?"

She jutted her chin forward as she tapped it with her finger, giving it some thought. Finally, her face lit up as she answered me.

"Pizza!"

Her smile was contagious and I found myself smiling back at her while wondering if she was telling the truth or if this was really *Annie's* favorite food.

"Is that your mom's favorite, or is that your favorite?" I asked playfully as her eyes danced wildly with excitement.

"It's momma's favorite AND my favorite! Except I only like pepperoni, mommy puts gross stuff on her pizza."

I chuckled as I listened, making note of what they liked.

"What does your mom like that's so gross?" I started making a mental list of the possibilities. Anchovies. Onions. Tomatoes. Who knew what Lacey would like that Annie thought was disgusting.

"Ugh, it's too gross to even say." She held a hand to her forehead as if the thought of it alone was too much and she might pass out. I also made a note to find out if she had been enrolled in the drama class because she definitely needed to be.

"Lay it on me." I spread my arms out to the side, making sure not to accidentally knock any of the other kids in the side of the head as they passed by.

"Are you sure you can handle it?" She eyed me suspiciously as she folded her arms over her chest, looking like a mini version of Lacey. I nodded and quickly looked past her to find her mom scanning the crowd of kids, fixated on finding Annie. We were running out of time and I needed her to spill it.

"Okay, you asked," she sighed. "It's pineapple and sausage."

I bit the inside of my cheek to keep from laughing as I quickly patted her back and thanked her for letting me know before I pointed in her mom's direction and sent her on her way. A few minutes later, I found Liam and we all made our way to the truck. The inside of the cab was noisy on the quick drive home as the kids excitedly talked about their first day of school. Lacey had turned sideways in her seat so she could face them as she listened and asked questions.

Once we were home, the kids eagerly ran upstairs to go work on their homework, leaving Lacey and me downstairs by ourselves. I wasn't sure if it was the excitement of having Annie at his school or their new room arrangement but I had never once seen Liam excited to do homework. After we got home and everyone was situated, it was already after 4:30. I wanted to get a headstart on dinner since I knew I wanted to get a pizza from Paul's Pizza. It was hands down the best pizza in Haven Brook and guaranteed to have a wait tonight since it was the first day back to school. Most families were trying to get back in the groove of things which meant no time to cook.

I told Lacey that I was heading out to go grab dinner without telling her where I was going or what I was getting. I wanted it to be a surprise and I prayed that Annie didn't lead me down the wrong path with a pineapple and sausage pizza. Worst case scenario— I would eat it because there wasn't much that I wouldn't eat but I didn't want to look like an ass if I got it wrong. I quickly glanced at the parking lot, finding a space, before jumping out and heading inside.

The bell chimed above me as I opened the door and walked in, waiting in a short line. Almost all of the tables were filled with people either sitting down to eat or waiting on their own to-go order. I quickly scanned the room as I made my way to the end of the line, chuckling when I spotted Noah and Chase sitting at one of the tables in the corner of the room. I walked over and clapped a hand on Chase's shoulder, startling him as they both turned around to see who was there.

"Looks like this is the place to be tonight," I joked as I gave Noah a quick pat on the shoulder before stepping to the side so a waiter could pass by to deliver a pizza to the table behind us.

"Cravings," they both said in unison before laughing and shaking their heads. I laughed along with them, remembering how I had practically lived here when Renee was pregnant with Liam.

"I think this place and SlowMo's are the go-to place for all pregnant women," I said as my eyes shifted over to a woman in line, rubbing a hand over her pregnant belly while she stood on her tiptoes to get a glance at the pizza options through the window by the register.

"That's because those are the only decent places to eat in Haven Brook," Noah snorted.

"Oh really? What about The Vine?" Chase wadded up the napkin he had been tearing apart in front of him and threw it at Noah's head, barely missing him.

I leaned my head back and laughed as the realization crossed Noah's face that he hadn't included their own brewery as an option, even though he ate there more than anyone I knew. I glanced at the line as a few more people had come in and knew that I needed to get in line soon or I would be stuck waiting forever.

"Alright, I'm going to go place my order. Try not to kill each other before the ladies get their food," I teased with a smile.

"You and Liam doing back to school pizza night?" Chase tilted his head up to look at me. I debated on what to say because I didn't want it to come off as something bigger than it was but I also knew that it was a small town and people were already talking about us living together. Now that Lacey had taken the job at the school, it felt more real that they would be there with us for a while. I sucked in a deep breath and held it, knowing it was better for them to find out from me than to hear it from someone else in the gossip mill.

"Actually, we're having a celebratory dinner tonight. Lacey accepted a job as the school nurse and she and Annie will be living with Liam and I for the foreseeable future." I felt my hands tremble as the words rushed out of my mouth in one long-winded sentence. There was a quick glance that was almost easy to miss between the two of them before they turned their attention back to me.

"Awesome, tell Lacey we said congratulations," Noah said as his attention shifted briefly to the waitress that was carrying a pizza box in our direction.

"Yeah, same here. Tell her that Mia and I are happy that she found a job so quickly. It'll be nice to have her around."

I looked between the two of them, waiting for one of them to say something about how crazy and reckless and irresponsible this all was but there was nothing. No hidden messages or tongue-in-cheek replies. No judgmental looks on their faces. Both of them looked unphased as if I had just told them the score of the football game.

"Okay— you guys are freaking me out— you don't have anything to say about me having a woman and her daughter living with us when we've barely known them a week?" I studied their faces as I waited for it to come. The what-in-the-hell-is-wrong-with-you lecture that had to be brewing in their heads. Finally, I saw Chase's chest rise and fall as he looked at Noah, his lips pulled into a thin line as he rapped his knuckles on the table before turning to look at me.

"I'm going to be honest with you because I feel like that's what you're asking from us," he started and I clenched my jaw waiting for it.

"Grant, I'm not going to sit here and lecture you on what you do or don't do in your life. You're a grown man who has had to figure out a lot of really hard things on your own and I don't doubt your ability to figure this out as well. There's nothing that you should feel ashamed of by having Lacey and Annie stay with you. While we don't know what's happening in their personal life, we can tell that she needs help. And it's okay to do that for her." He stood up and faced me, his eyes softening as he started to speak again.

"You're my little brother, I know you very well and can read you like a book. So I'm going to answer the questions that you won't allow yourself to think about right now. Yes, it's okay. No, she wouldn't be upset. And it only matters what your heart wants for you and Liam."

I stared at him with a puzzled look on my face, completely unsure of what the fuck he was talking about. I shook my head and looked to Noah, hoping he could shed some light on the cryptic message Chase had just given me. I watched as the corners of Noah's lips pulled up into a smile as he stood up and set his cell phone down on top of the pizza box that had been delivered.

"It's okay to move on and be happy. No, Renee wouldn't be upset. And it only matters what your heart wants for you and Liam in regards to you questioning whether you could have a relationship with Lacey, and your worries about what everyone will think." Noah's voice was gentle as he said the words that ripped my heart open and forced me to take a ragged deep breath. I felt Chase's hand on my shoulder and turned my head to look at him.

"We're here if you need us," Chase offered as another waitress came over and handed him a box of pizza before swiping the number card from the table and heading to the back. "And it's okay to not know how to handle this. Sometimes the best things in life are those that scare us the most."

I thought about their words as they said goodbye and left, leaving me alone in line to order a sausage and pineapple pizza that now felt more significant than before.

Eighteen

Lacey

The first week working at Annie's school flew by before I knew it. I was thankful for how quickly the background check had been completed and that I was able to start right away. Knowing that my dad had left Easterville on Monday had me uneasy all week that he could show up in Haven Brook at any time. Grant and I had talked Monday night after the kids had gone to sleep and I filled him in on my conversations with Kayce and the update on my dad. We both agreed that we would have to remain extra aware for a little while longer since no one knew what direction he had gone.

The problem with not knowing which direction he went in was that there were so many small towns in between Easterville and Haven Brook, that he could be in any of them. Or he could have gone the opposite way and be headed to Denver. Five days sounded like a lot of time when Easterville was only five hours away, but each small town had another one, off in the distance. It was a cluster of small towns separated by tiny patches of absolutely nothing.

I waited for the bell to ring, dismissing school for the day. The kids seemed way too excited for the weekend given that they had only been back for a week. I packed up my stuff and slid my purse onto my shoulder, bumping my phone from the desk as it fell to the floor. I picked it up, bile rising in my throat as I saw that the fall had accidentally answered an incoming call that I hadn't heard. My fingers trembled as I slowly lifted the phone to my ear and listened.

There was complete silence on the other end as I let out the breath that I had been holding. I was about to pull the phone away and hang up, wondering if maybe he hadn't realized he called me— there were plenty of drunk dialing incidents in the past. As I started to pull the phone away I heard his voice, paralyzing me with fear.

"Hello, Lacey."

I closed my eyes and stayed silent as the warm tears started to slide down my face.

"Did you really think you could get far without me finding you?"

I pulled my bottom lip in between my teeth and tasted the saltiness from the tears. I tried to steady my shaky breaths as I listened to him talk.

"I'm your father—I will *ALWAYS* find you. Didn't you learn that the hard way as a little girl?" I recognized the menacing tone in his voice and knew that he hadn't been drinking. Yet. "I always won at hide and seek and I have a feeling you're not under the bed this time."

I opened my eyes as I heard movement at my door. Grant leaned against the doorframe casually before noticing the look on my face. I put a finger to my lips to ask him to stay quiet as I watched concern wash over his face. He rushed over and stood next to me. I could feel the warmth of his hand on my lower back as I kept the phone pressed to my ear.

"You don't have to talk, you know I like the thrill of the hunt. It's even better when I can feel how scared you are." He let out a heavy breath as if he was bored. "And Lacey— you should be terrified."

The words hit me hard as I heard him hang up. I looked up at Grant, unable to speak as I tried to process what just happened. My fingers were still trembling as I lowered the phone to my chest, my heart hammering against it.

"Are you okay?" he asked gently, his hand still resting on my back.

"Yeah, just a little shook up." I tried to force a smile but my body refused. There wasn't an ounce of happiness that could be found inside me right now. Grant nodded his head slowly before glancing up at the clock hanging on the wall above my desk.

"We need to go get the kids, they're going to be waiting at the parent pick up for us."

"Okay," I said breathlessly, "let's get going."

I tried to force the phone call out of my head as we walked quickly to meet Annie and Liam. The walk felt long in the bitter cold but wasn't nearly long enough to allow me the time to pull myself together. Annie looked up at me, the smile on her face vanishing almost immediately.

"Mama, what's wrong?" she asked as she ran over and wrapped her arms around my waist. My eyes darted over to Grant, pleading with him to help me figure out what to say to her. She didn't know about any of the other phone calls and now wasn't the time to tell her about them.

"There was a mouse in your mama's office," Grant said, looking down at Annie. "It scared your mom but we were able to catch it and set it free. She's just a little shook up about it."

I smiled at Grant as I let out a shaky breath before looking down at Annie. Her face turned up to look at me, a hint of a smile pulling at her lips.

"Mama, mice don't hurt you," she explained as she tried to hold her laughter in. "They're cute and cuddly, like Mr. Jelly in our class. Ms. Phillips said that not all mice are pets, but we got really lucky that Mr. Jelly wanted to be our class pet. Maybe that one wanted to be your pet?"

She looked up at me with the innocence of a child and I felt my heart skip a beat. She was so sweet and kindhearted that she would never think of hurting an innocent animal, let alone a rodent, so it never occurred to her that someone wouldn't want one as a pet. I brushed a stray strand of hair out of her face and tucked it behind her ear.

"Well, you know, they don't really let me have pets in my office because I have to take care of kiddos who don't feel well. I wouldn't have time to take care of a pet. But Grant made sure that he found the best home for the little guy, that's why we were a few minutes late." I watched as she smiled up at Grant with an approving nod. "Alright, it's freezing out here, let's get in the truck before we all turn into popsicles!"

I tickled her sides as she ran off toward the truck, Liam right beside her. I could hear Grant's footsteps as he walked next to me in silence.

"Thank you," I whispered loud enough for him to hear me as the kids opened the back doors and hopped up into the truck. He winked as he glanced at me before walking to the driver's side to get in.

"Hey dad, can I go to Nana's house early tonight?" Liam asked after we were on the road heading home. Grant looked at Liam in the rearview mirror before casting a glance at me.

"Did you already ask Nana?"

"Yeah, she said I could come over right after school and that Annie can come too."

I tried to keep from whipping my head around to look in the backseat, afraid of the look I would see on Annie's face when I said no. I didn't know anything about Liam going to his grandma's house but I wasn't comfortable with letting Annie tag along.

"That wasn't your place to ask, Liam," Grant scolded as he shot me a quick apologetic look.

"I know," he muttered from the back seat. "I'm sorry, I wasn't trying to be disrespectful but I didn't want to leave Annie out. She's kinda like my little sister now, I just thought maybe she could stay the night at Nana's with me."

I caught myself looking over my shoulder to find Liam shrugging his shoulders in defeat as he looked out the window. There was a look of excitement on Annie's face, happy to be included without me having to force someone to do it. Back home she didn't have many friends so her friendship with Liam had been really important to her because it was genuine and I hadn't intervened in any of it. I had watched them together the past few weeks and the longer we stayed there, the closer they got. My heart nearly burst several times when I had overheard him call her his sister and I cried actual tears when Grant told me that he threatened everyone at school that they better not mess with her.

I couldn't remember the last time that Annie had a sleepover somewhere or even the last time that she and I had been apart longer than a few hours while I was at work. I shifted in my seat as I wondered if maybe I needed to give her some space and let her be herself. Even with the fear that my dad could show up at any time, I knew that I couldn't hide her forever. Every day that passed brought about a greater risk of him finding us but I couldn't force her into a life of constant fear. My childhood wasn't hers to repeat.

I watched as we took a turn onto another street, heading the opposite direction of the house. I was relieved when we stopped in front of a small house a few minutes later, realizing that we weren't that far from

Grant's house after all. He put the truck in park and slowly turned off the engine as the kids unbuckled their seat belts and jumped out, running up the short lawn to the front porch before Liam knocked excitedly on the door.

"I'm sorry about that, he had good intentions but didn't bother to ask me about it first," Grant said as he wrapped his arms around the steering wheel and leaned against it, nodding at Liam as the front door opened and a woman with gray hair stood on the other side smiling.

"It's okay, I was just caught off guard by it. I know Annie will be excited about it but I don't want her to impose on your mother's time with Liam."

"Trust me, my mom loves kids and she would love to have Annie stay with them if you're okay with it."

I looked nervously from the house back to him as my hands fidgeted in my lap. I couldn't tell who this was a bigger step for: me or Annie. Could I do this? Was I really able to allow my daughter to stay the night with a complete stranger? Although I had known Liam from the time we had been living together, the only thing I knew about Grant's mom was that everyone loved and adored her. She was widowed at a young age when Grant was a junior in high school and never remarried.

My head whipped up to look at Grant as I felt his hand softly reach over and touch mine.

"Why don't we go inside and hang out for a bit, then you can decide what you feel comfortable doing?"

I nodded in agreement, thankful that he had such a sound and well thought out plan in mind. It couldn't hurt anything to go inside and get a feel for everything before I made a decision that was eating away at me. I worried that it would be the wrong one regardless of what it was.

A few minutes later I was wiping my feet on the doormat outside before walking into a cozy little house. I was surprised to find that everything was rather organized with very little clutter. The walls were painted a soft cream color with picture frames hung neatly down the hallway. The kitchen and living room were one big area, separated by a half wall that extended into the living room to create an island that was used as the dining table. There were two oversized couches that looked like they had pull out beds inside nestled in the corner pointed at the tv that was mounted above the fireplace.

I smiled as I looked around, noticing that the majority of the time here was spent in the living room and not the kitchen. The space could have easily been divided between the two and an actual table and chairs could have been set up, but instead, the area was taken up by the couches and a few end tables in between. We walked into the living room to find Nana sitting on one couch, while Liam and Annie sat on the other.

"Come on in, we'll make some room," she said as she patted the couch and Liam jumped over to sit next to her. Grant smiled at me as he led the way, sitting on the other side of Liam, leaving the other couch for me and Annie.

I sat down next to Annie and smiled as I took in the kind-looking woman across from me. Many times over the years, I had wondered what my mother would have looked like as she grew older. She was gorgeous with long, curly, brown hair, and beautiful green eyes. Whenever I closed my eyes and pictured her it was always the framed picture that I keep with me of her when she first met my dad. She looked so young and carefree, not a worry in the world. That's the way I've always tried to remember her because the images of her covered in bruises and blood still broke my heart to this day.

I pushed the thoughts out of my head and listened as Liam told Nana all about his school day. Her brown eyes lit up with excitement every time his voice got a little louder and she would quietly clap her hands together as he told her about his accomplishments for the day. She lifted a hand to tuck a piece of hair behind her ear, a faded gold wedding ring glistening in the sunbeam that filtered through the sheer curtains behind us. A knot formed in my stomach as I glanced down and touched mine, wondering if I would someday be her age, still wearing the promise of a love that had died.

"How was your day today, Annie?" she asked as she turned her body to face Annie, giving her her undivided attention. I looked at Annie and watched as her eyes lit up the same way as Liam's when she talked about school and the science experiment they did in class. She giggled as she talked about how the teacher cussed on accident when she accidentally tipped over the jar of liquid she needed but was quickly saved when another student rushed up to help her. Thankfully, according to Annie, it was just water and no one had to worry about turning into a zombie from the spilled liquid.

We stayed talking for half an hour, the kids still filled with excitement as they talked to Nana about everything they could think of. After they ran out of steam, Liam asked if they could go play in the spare room which was now the grandkid room and not just his room anymore. I laughed when he joked about how he used to be the baby until everyone started having real babies. He had the same dry humor as his dad, with a bit more sarcasm.

As the kids ran off down the hallway I started to feel anxious again about the thought of leaving Annie here. My fingers tapped nervously on my thigh as I stared off into the distance, absentmindedly, as Grant talked to his mom about his younger brother. I had only met him once but had heard plenty of stories in the two weeks that I had been there to know that he was definitely the wild child of the bunch. I was so lost in thought that I hadn't paid attention when Grant asked me a question. I heard my name again, snapping me out of my trance as I looked up and found them both looking at me.

"I'm sorry, what?" I asked softly, looking to Grant for help. He chuckled and tried to hide his smile behind his hand.

"Did you give it any more thought about having Annie stay over tonight?"

I felt the color drain from my face as my eyes darted over to his mom. The second that we made eye contact I immediately started to feel myself relax. There was something about her that felt so calming and I found myself being pulled in by it.

"Grant, why don't you go check the fridge for me and make sure I have plenty of chocolate milk for tonight?" She subtly nodded to the kitchen as he got up and left. I let out a shaky breath and folded my hands together in my lap as I looked at her.

"I know that you don't know me, dear, and honestly I would be more worried if you weren't nervous about leaving your child with me." She smiled warmly before continuing. "I won't pressure you either way, I respect your decision as a parent to do what you think is the right thing for your child. But please know that Annie will never be an imposition to us and she's welcome here anytime."

I nodded and returned her smile, still unsure of what to do.

"It's hard," I said quietly as I looked from her to the hallway that led to where Annie was.

"I know." She sighed and leaned back against the cushion, pulling a throw pillow into her lap as she rested her hands on top of it.

"Does it ever get any easier?" I asked with a small laugh, already knowing the answer.

"Nope. My oldest is 28 and the youngest is 24. They still keep me on my toes and I worry about them constantly. Even when there's nothing to actually worry about, I still worry. It's what we learn to do when we're unexpectedly forced to be a single parent. You push through and do things because you have to, but there's never any time to just stop and think things through. Sometimes I wish that I had taken a moment to just stop and be their mom." Her lips pulled into a thin line as tears started to cloud her eyes.

"What do you mean?" My voice was soft and gentle.

"I was always the caretaker, rushing around to make sure dinner was made and chores were done. There was always a list of things that I had to get to, things that needed my attention. But rarely did I ever stop and just be their mom. I didn't take the time to check in to see how school was going or to find out what happened with the girl they liked. Sure, I knew some of it, but it was only on the surface. I kept such a tight grip on everything, terrified that if I let up even a *tad*, that I would lose control and everything would be taken from me. I had already lost so much, I couldn't stand the thought of losing anything else."

I could hear as her voice broke at the end and knew that this was hard for her to talk about. I pulled in a deep breath and held it, hoping it would give me the courage I needed to say what I needed to say.

"I can understand that. I lost my husband three months ago in a car accident. He was rushing home because I was overwhelmed with trying to get Annie fed before I had to go back to work to cover a night shift. He was speeding and the rain was coming down hard. They said that he lost control and was killed on impact. Thankfully no one else was involved, but unfortunately for me, I will always remember it as it being my fault. If I wasn't the one who was freaking out about having things done a certain way then he wouldn't have had to rush. If I would have been able to just sit back and not try to control everything then my husband would still be here. My daughter would still have her father and I wouldn't have put her life in danger by living with my dad."

The words were out of my mouth before I could stop them, my hand quickly reaching to try to cover up what I had said. I watched in horror, waiting for her reaction as my stomach dropped. Her expression remained calm and neutral as she thought about what to say.

"That's a heavy burden to carry," she said sympathetically. I could feel the sting as the tears prickled at my eyes. I blinked quickly, trying to force them away. "But honey, you can't go on thinking that it was your fault. I know that's hard to do, trust me, but you need to let go of that guilt. It'll eat you alive if you let it."

I nodded as we turned to see Grant walk back into the room. It was silly to think that he hadn't heard the conversation given that the space was barely separated by a half wall, but it still felt nice to feel like I had some privacy to get to know his mom better.

"We should probably get going," he said as he glanced between us. "Do you want me to go get Annie?" He arched an eyebrow as he asked cautiously.

I looked at his mom and felt that same level of comfort that I had felt earlier and knew that Annie would be safe here. I straightened in my seat and forced the tiny bit of confidence that had started to blossom to come out.

"I think Annie will enjoy having a sleepover here tonight," I said as steady as I could. "I'll leave my cell phone number with you in case there are any problems, you can call--"

She held her hand up to stop me as she leaned forward and locked eyes with me.

"She won't be any problem at all, and I promise that I will call if she needs anything. Even if it's just because she misses you. I know it's hard to let them go, but I promise that she's in great hands."

I let out the breath I had been holding and forced my shoulders to relax.

"And for what it's worth, I'm a retired nurse and used to be an avid hunter, always bringing home more kills than my husband. So, as the kids would say, I'm not afraid to pop a cap in someone's ass if they try to mess with my family, and Annie is family. She will be safe here, I promise you that."

I held in the laugh that threatened to come out as I pictured her as a pistol-wielding grandma, popping caps into someone's ass. We said our goodbyes as I hugged Annie a little longer than normal. My nerves were shot to hell as I walked out the door, glancing over my shoulder to see the huge smile spread across her face. It may have been torture for me to leave her but I could tell that she was already in heaven.

Nineteen

Grant

"Beer or wine?" I asked Lacey as we drove toward the store to grab stuff for dinner. I could tell that she was still struggling with leaving Annie, as well as the added tension she was still feeling from the phone call she had this afternoon at school.

"Either is fine with me," she sighed as I pulled into a parking spot and put the truck in park. "Maybe wine so I can stick a straw in it and call it a day."

I tried not to laugh as she climbed out of the truck and closed the door, shoving her hands into the pockets of her coat as she shivered against the icy wind. I was relieved when she bought new winter clothes last weekend for her and Annie.

We walked into General Bob's and I grabbed a handheld shopping cart, knowing we weren't getting that much. I walked with Lacey over to the deli section, waiting for her to browse the options in the case while the elderly woman on the other side smiled and waited patiently for us. I watched as Lacey's eyes wandered over the variety of food, stopping and fixating on the fried chicken before moving back over to the salad bar options. I could see her struggling with whether to go for the fried food or to try to stick with a healthier option.

"What are you thinking?" I asked, nodding to the case as I pulled her attention away from the chicken.

"Um, I don't know. The salad looks good?" she said as if she questioned whether it really did. I arched an eyebrow at her and waited as I saw the hint of a blush creep up her cheeks. She rolled her eyes and sighed dramatically before turning to the woman and smiling.

"Fine," she said to me, turning to narrow her eyes at me quickly before returning her attention to the woman who was waiting. "I would like the two-piece — no, make that the three-piece, fried chicken meal please."

The woman smiled as she slid the door open and grabbed a pair of steel tongs, getting ready to grab the chicken.

"Wait! Just two pieces, sorry." Lacey reached up on her tiptoes to make sure the woman could hear her as she stopped with her hand mid-air, afraid to pull out a piece of chicken until Lacey made up her mind.

"Are you sure? Just two pieces?" she asked as the tongs remained suspended in the air.

Lacey worked her jaw back and forth as she tried to force herself to decide. It was like watching someone make the biggest decision of their life and I was worried that if I didn't step in soon, we were going to be the woman behind the counter's age by the time she decided.

"We'll take a full bucket, mixed, please," I said as I stepped forward, bringing her attention to me. She nodded and leaned forward as she started piling the chicken into a bucket. I looked at Lacey and lowered my voice some as I said, "The thighs are really thick but the breasts are better, plumper and juicier."

I watched as her cheeks flushed bright red and her hazel eyes nearly bulged out of her head. She looked at me as if she couldn't believe I had just said what I said. I let out a low laugh as I reached forward and grabbed the bucket of chicken that was being handed to me. "The fried chicken," I chuckled as it clicked in her head what I had been talking about.

We ordered a few sides before making our way back to the liquor department to grab a bottle of wine. I wasn't a big wine drinker so I left it to Lacey to pick one while I perused the dessert options. There wasn't much, most of the good stuff was usually gone by mid-morning since it was baked fresh daily. I found a box of fudge brownies that looked promising and tossed them in the cart, hoping that Lacey had a sweet tooth and liked chocolate.

After we got home I worked on opening the bottle of Riesling while she worked on getting dinner set up for us. She offered to set the table but I thought she might relax more if we had dinner in the living room. In an effort to keep Liam from acting like a complete barbarian when company was around we had recently started eating at the kitchen table again, but most nights when it was just us, we would plop down on the couch and use the coffee table.

I poured two glasses of wine and carried them to the living room, setting them down on the table next to the boxes of food. Everything smelled delicious and was making my mouth water as I tried to remember the last time that I had eaten fried chicken from the deli at General Bob's. I had tried to be better about cooking for us, but when I didn't we were usually at my mom's house or we spent a lot of time eating at The Vine.

We sat down on the couch and looked nervously between each other, trying to decide who was going to go first.

"You first," we both said at the same time, laughing at how predictable it was.

I shook my head as I smiled and slid the box of chicken over to Lacey while I began to scoop mashed potatoes onto my plate. A few minutes later both of us had full plates and were digging in. I watched as Lacey ate her chicken, closing her eyes as she took a bite and let the flavor melt on her tongue. It reminded me of the night that I made spaghetti and I thought she was going to have an orgasm from that damn sauce. That had been a hard image to get out of my head this week, and now I was watching her tilt her head as she brought a drumstick to her mouth, slowly opening it as she closed her eyes and bit down.

This woman was like some sort of food erotica, making everything she ate look sexier than it should be. I shifted on the couch, pulling at my pants to try to allow some room for the erection that was growing underneath as I thought about how I wished my dick was that drumstick. She brought a finger to her mouth and wiped as she licked her lips. I quickly finished my bite before I could choke and grabbed my glass of wine, taking a long drink.

For the remainder of the meal, I tried to keep my attention focused on the food and not choking to death as she continued to moan little moans with each bite she took. Fuck if I wasn't suddenly jealous of the spoon that kept going into her mouth. A few minutes later she pushed her plate away and leaned back against the couch, resting her hands on her stomach.

"Oh my goodness, I am so full," she laughed and looked at her plate before turning to look at me.

"See, it's better that we got the bucket. You would've been disappointed if you would've stuck with your 2-piece meal." I nodded toward her plate with the evidence that she had eaten three pieces after all. She started to blush a little as she looked away and I instantly felt bad for embarrassing her. I hadn't meant to insinuate that she ate too much. Hell, I was impressed with how much she was able to eat given how petite she was.

"Well, you had me at juicy breasts and thick thighs," she teased as she licked her lips and I knew she was getting back at me for embarrassing her at the deli.

"That's usually what gets me into trouble." My eyes locked onto hers, challenging her to look away. She arched an eyebrow as she pulled her bottom lip in between her teeth.

"Hmm, I would say that you're the one that's trouble." Her eyes slowly traveled from my eyes down my body as they lingered on the obvious bulge in my pants. I watched as her breathing changed the longer she stared, the way her eyes suddenly became hooded. The urge to reach over and grab her, to pull her onto my lap and show her just how hard I was, was quickly extinguished when she suddenly took a deep breath and stood up. She loaded her arms with the plates and trash from the table before rushing off to the kitchen. I leaned back against the couch for a second and closed my eyes. I was playing with fire and I knew it. But everything about Lacey made me want to light a match and watch it burn if it meant that we gave in to this sexual tension that was radiating between us.

I stood up and took the last of the boxes into the kitchen, setting them on the counter next to the ones she had already brought in. Her head was down as she nervously scrubbed the plate in the sink.

"We have a dishwasher you know?" I asked, hoping to sound playful and not like the overly- aroused teenager that she had seen a few minutes ago.

"Oh yeah, I know. But it's just these two, figured might as well wash them since we don't have a full load." She glanced up at me and forced a smile before returning her attention to the plate that was probably now the cleanest that it had ever been.

I laughed as I walked over and opened the dishwasher, looking inside to find it full of dirty dishes from this morning and last night. Her head turned to the side, a smile pulling at her lips as she realized she was caught in a lie.

"I would really hate to see what you consider a full load," I teased before I realized the sexual tone that it was laced with. It felt like no matter how hard we tried, we couldn't escape the tension that kept building between us. She opened her mouth to respond before thinking twice about it and snapping it shut. I ran a hand down my face as I tried to figure out what to do next since everything that came out of my mouth was some sort of plea for her to have sex with me.

"So, um, what did you want to do tonight? It's your first night of being kid-free," I said trying to change the tone.

"Uh, don't remind me," she sighed as she turned off the water and dried her hands on the towel next to the sink. The look on my face must have come across as insulted because she immediately looked worried and rushed to correct what she had said.

"I didn't mean any disrespect by that, I know that you and Liam have your separate time from each other often and I think that's great. I just, I don't know. I guess I feel bad and guilty that I have time away from her? It's weird but it makes me feel like a bad mom for wanting some downtime to myself. She's a wonderful kid and I love spending time with her, but-"

I held my hand up to stop her as I watched her panic about what she was starting to feel.

"But it's okay to have time to yourself, just like it's okay for her to have time for herself. That doesn't make you a bad mom, Lacey. That just makes you a mom. The guilt mixed in with the inability to know what to do with yourself without a kid around is what parenting is all about. Except they don't tell you about it in any of those what to expect books."

I felt some of the tension ease as I saw her smile, a genuine smile, when she realized that she wasn't the only one who felt that way.

"So what's on your list for your alone time?" I asked, trying to get a feel for what she wanted. As much as I wanted to spend time with her, I would gladly back off and give her the time to herself if she asked.

"I don't know, I wasn't prepared for this," she laughed. "What do you do with your downtime?"

"Usually I soak in a hot bubble bath while drinking wine and reading celebrity gossip magazines. Then I slap on a hideous face mask and devour boxes of chocolate while finishing off the bottle of wine." I shrugged as if it was an everyday thing and watched as she rolled her eyes and started to laugh. She stepped closer and pointed a finger at me, poking me in the chest as she pretended to glare at me.

"You and those damn masks," she teased as she kept poking my chest. "You know it wouldn't hurt you to wear one. You have a dry patch of skin right here..."

Her voice trailed off as she lightly ran her finger across my forehead and down my nose. I sucked in a breath at the contact, the feel of her body so close to mine that I could smell the tropical scent of her new body wash. My eyes fluttered closed as she continued to softly run her finger across my skin, heightening every sense to the fullest. I opened my eyes and reached up, grabbing her hand and pulling it down as a look of fear crossed her face.

I tried to hold back but the electricity between us was too much for me to fight. I let go of her hand as I reached forward and gently grabbed her face, leaning forward as my lips lightly landed on hers. I wanted to kiss her harder, devour her, but I knew that I needed to go slow. For both of us. I hadn't been with another woman since Renee and I assumed she hadn't been with another man since her husband. I didn't even know if she wanted this.

Softly, I moved my lips against hers, feeling the soft breath that she let out before her lips responded. A quiet moan escaped her throat and shot straight to my dick, making me desperate for more. Her hands reached up as her fingers wound their way through my hair as our mouths worked quickly over each other. I felt her lips part as she welcomed my tongue to explore her sweet little mouth. Our breathing quickly became more ragged, our hands darting over each other's body in an attempt to fulfill the desires that were quickly building between us.

Then as suddenly as it started, it all ended. Lacey pulled away, covering her mouth with her hand as she paced back and forth, her eyes wide with shock. I stepped back and lowered my head, feeling ashamed for making a move before checking to see how she felt about it.

"Lacey, I'm so sorry, I didn't mean to-"

"No- don't apologize," she held her hand up to stop me. "I don't know what that was, that's not like me. But you didn't do anything wrong."

"I didn't mean to take advantage of you, I should have checked first," I spoke slowly, with caution to keep from making things any worse.

"I liked it…" She tilted her head at me in confusion, which was fitting because I was just as confused by her statement as she was.

"Okay?..."

"Why did I like it so much? What was that?" She started to pace again and I could tell that she was asking herself, not me. "I was married for ten years. TEN YEARS— and I never felt that level of heat!"

She ran her hands up the front of her body and shivered as if it was a reminder of what she had just felt.

"Ten years of love and marriage but never that kind of rush, that feeling of being wanted. Like I seriously feel like if we would have kept going, that I would be bent over the kitchen table while we go at it- that's how hot and bothered I got just from kissing you."

She let out a sharp breath as she looked from the table to me then back to the table. I tried to control myself but I couldn't keep from looking at the table too, hoping to get half of the visual she was getting every time she looked over at it and blushed.

"I loved my husband, I really did. With my whole heart. He was my first love. My only love. And now it feels like I'm betraying him and going against everything I promised him with our wedding vows because I'm feeling so insanely attracted to you right now and I want to have really dirty, really kinky, kitchen sex!"

I tried to turn my head to the side to keep from laughing. Her eyes got big again as she stared at me before reaching over and playfully swatted at my arm.

"Grant! This isn't funny, what am I supposed to do?"

There was a hint of laughter in her voice as she started to calm down, realizing how worked up she had gotten about it. I gently reached my hand out and was relieved when she took it. I sat on the edge of the table and pulled her close to me, holding her in my arms while I looked into her eyes.

"Lacey, there is nothing that I want to do more than have kinky kitchen sex with you, right here on this table. But there is no rush. It's whenever YOU are ready. Okay?" I raised my eyebrows and watched as she closed her eyes and nodded.

"What you're feeling is completely normal, and honestly, it feels weird for me too. As much as I want to fuck you sideways on this table, I can't stop feeling guilty that I'm cheating on my wife. Just because they're gone, it doesn't mean that we stopped loving them or caring about them. It's okay for us to still feel the weight of the grief that we carry, just like it's okay for us to decide when we're ready to move on. It doesn't mean that we leave them behind, we just learn a new way to move forward without the guilt."

I wiped the tears that started to roll down her cheeks and pulled her close to me before she could see the ones that were rolling down mine. Thirty minutes later and an empty bottle of wine, we decided to find something to entertain ourselves with that wouldn't end up being sexual. Watching movies while we were cuddled on the couch was out of the question.

"Monopoly?" She pulled her brows down and frowned at the game in my hand.

"What? It's a family-friendly game. Look— there's a family playing it in the picture on the back." I turned it around to show her.

"Fine," she sighed. "But don't be mad when I take all of your money and leave you bankrupt." She pursed her lips and gave me a smug smile as she sat down on the floor, clearing the empty wine bottle from the table so I could set the game down.

"Sounds like a typical woman," I muttered as I set it down and walked to the kitchen to grab the new bottle of wine we had opened. She reached out and playfully swatted at my leg when I came back, sitting down next to her after I refilled our glasses.

"I heard your snarky little comment before you left," she teased as she opened the box and started to unpack the game pieces.

"Good, I said it loud enough." I winked and ducked as she playfully tossed the lid to the game at my head.

"Oooh, Mr. Big Shot over here, running his mouth. Why don't you put your money where your mouth is?" She narrowed her eyes as she offered her challenge.

"You're on, but I don't think you're going to like the stakes, especially since I'm gonna whoop your ass."

"Why? What are they? Strip Monopoly?"

My eyes went wide as she said it, her cheeks flushing in response when she realized that wasn't what I had been thinking.

"I was going to have you do all of my chores but I think I like where you were going with this better." I leaned back on my hands and studied her as she tried to talk her way out of it.

"No, that's not what I meant— I just assumed that was what you would come up with—you know? Like it's a guy thing?" Her voice went up and got squeaky as she started to talk faster. "I wasn't the one trying to start strip Monopoly— I just assumed—"

"Lacey?"

"Yeah?"

"Stop rambling and get the money dealt so we can play strip Monopoly." I smiled and licked my lips as I watched her consider the proposal.

"Fine. But we play by my rules," she said, squaring her shoulders.

"Okay, lay them on me." I leaned forward and took a look at the game pieces on the board, looking for the car.

"If you land on my property, you take off a piece of clothing and vice versa. If one of us goes to jail, we take off two pieces of clothing. When we pass go, we can add 1 piece back on."

"Sounds fair," I said as I hopped up and ran into the kitchen to grab the brownies. I came back and plopped down on the floor next to her, smiling as I set the box between us. She looked down and her eyes came alive as she spotted the dessert.

Forty-five minutes later and we were fully invested in the most intense, competitive game of Monopoly I had ever played. We were both buying as many properties as we could every chance we had. Lacey was doing rather well, only missing her shoes, socks, and her shirt, while I had landed in jail twice already and had yet to pass go. Needless to say that I was feeling the heat as I held the dice in my hands while sitting in my boxers. I had one roll and needed to avoid landing on any of her property, as well as going to jail. If I could roll a five I would be in the clear and on my own property.

I took a deep breath and closed my eyes as I rolled, relieved when I opened them and saw a two and a three on the dice as they came to a stop. I jerked my hand in the air in celebration while Lacey ignored it and rolled the dice. I was out of money and almost out of clothes so it was pointless to tell her it was her turn. She moved the hat around the board, landing on the Community Chest. The board had been good to her so far but I was hoping that her luck would soon run out.

Her face fell as she looked at the card in her hand that was sending her straight to jail. She looked up at me as she lowered the card to the table as she worked her mouth side to side.

"Well, I'm getting tired so I guess we can go ahead and call the game. We can call you the winner if you want, given you've already lost so much," she teased as she nodded toward the pile of clothes off in the corner by the fireplace.

"Nope, I don't think so." I shook my head and leaned forward to pick up the card. I set it in front of her and smiled the cockiest smile I had. She was right where I wanted her and I wasn't about to pass on this opportunity. I sat back and rubbed my hands back and forth in excitement as I watched her pretend to glare at me.

"I believe that card says 'Go To Jail' which according to YOUR rules means that you lose 2 pieces of clothing... and you only have 3 left. So Lacey, what do I get to see first? Top or bottom?" My voice was getting a little husky from the arousal that was coursing through me as I waited to see what she was going to take off.

She pulled her shoulders back and took a deep breath, exhaling slowly. Her eyes looked up and met mine, a nervousness behind them.

"I hate you right now," she said smugly as she stood up and started to pull her pants down over her hips, letting them fall to her feet. She stood before me wearing nothing but a black lace bra with black cotton boy short panties.

"These were your rules sweetheart," I replied with a wink. "But I have to admit that strip Monopoly might be my new favorite game."

Her fingers slid down and hooked into the top of her panties, starting to lower them before she stopped. A sexy smirk started to cross her face as she reached up and slowly slid one strap of her bra down her arm. She held the top in place with one hand while she worked the

strap down the other. My eyes watched hungrily as her hand reached around the back to unclasp the bra when she stopped again.
I looked up and found her eyes focused on me as she slowly slid her hands back down over her stomach, skimming over the top of her panties as she ran the palm along the thin fabric that covered her. She kept eye contact with me as she continued to run her hand over herself, slowly moving it under the top of her panties. My dick was uncomfortably tight as it throbbed in my boxer briefs, desperate for a release as I watched her fingers move inside of her under her panties.

"So, which one do you want me to take off? Bra? Or panties?" Her voice was barely above a whisper as she kept touching herself while I watched, the thin lace of her bra shifting slightly with every movement as it threatened to slip off of her.

"Both," I growled as I got up and stood next to her. I wanted to touch her, to strip her of her clothes but I needed to know that she was ready this time.

She pulled her hand out and gently pushed her panties down, letting them fall to the floor as she stepped out of them. I sucked in a breath as I watched her reach up and unclasp her bra, letting it fall to the floor next. She was completely naked and unbelievably beautiful with the perfect curves that I couldn't wait to run my hands over. I reached down and slid my boxers off, chuckling as I heard her gasp when she saw how hard I was. I reached down and grabbed it, slowly pumping my fist around it as she watched.

I had never touched myself in front of a woman before and was worried that I was going to come in seconds with how arousing it was to have her watching me the way she was. Her fingers trembled as she reached down and ran a finger in a lazy circle around the head. I closed my eyes and groaned as my head fell backward.

Her hand ran over my mine, gently pushing it away as she took over touching me. Her hand was much smaller than mine, making my dick look even bigger in her delicate hand as it jerked back and forth over my long shaft. She watched me intently as she increased her pressure, nearly sending me over the edge. I reached down and softly held her hand in place, needing her to stop before I came all over her.

"Lacey— are you sure you want to do this?" I asked breathlessly, eager for her to answer.

"Yes," she whispered before reaching up and wrapping her hands around my neck, pulling me in as she kissed me. This kiss was

different than before. Instead of soft and gentle, it was urgent and needy as her lips crushed down against mine.
I wrapped my hands around her waist, letting them slowly move down over her ass, feeling the soft skin beneath my fingers as I dug my fingers into the round globes. I reached down and lifted her, feeling the warmth of her pussy as her legs wrapped around my waist. Her breasts were soft and full as she pushed herself against me, as desperate to feel me as I was to feel her.

I walked the short distance to the kitchen and stopped in front of the table. She broke away for a quick second to glance at the table before she started giggling.

"You're not serious!" she shrieked excitedly as I set her down on top of it.

"You bet your ass I am," I growled as I slowly pushed her back so she would lay on her back. My eyes slowly trailed her body as she slid back to keep from falling off, her hands sensually rubbing over her hard nipples. "Now lay back so I can see how good you taste."

Her eyes widened with shock as she propped up on her elbows.

"You already had dinner," she teased playfully.

"Yup, and now I'm having dessert." I liked my lips and waited for her to lay down so I could run my tongue inside of her and confirm that she tasted as delicious as I imagined.

"That's why you bought brownies," she said, nodding to the living room where we had left them.

"You're right. I'll be right back." I smiled and rushed off, hearing her giggle as she laid naked on the kitchen table. I bent down and grabbed the brownies then hurried back to the kitchen.

"Alright, lay back and let me enjoy my dessert," I instructed as she watched me open the box. She laid back and adjusted herself before leaning her head to the side to watch me. I pulled a fudge brownie out and set the rest on the chair beside me. I ran a finger along the top, pulling some of the fudge off before extending my finger to her. She lifted her head off the table as she pulled my finger into her mouth, sucking the fudge off with such an intensity that it made me wonder what it would feel like to have her do that to my cock.

I slowly pulled my finger out as she laid her head back down on the table. My first instinct was to ignore all of the foreplay and just fuck her, right then and there. But I wanted to take my time with her and show her how much I wanted to be with her. Something told me that she needed me to take my time with her because no one else ever had.

Focused on teasing her as much as possible, I carefully placed small pieces of the brownie along her body, starting at her breasts and ending at the sweet spot that I couldn't wait to get to. I leaned down, careful not to smash the brownie underneath me, as I licked up the first piece in between her breast while gently caressing both breasts in my hands. I could hear a soft moan as her back slightly arched off the table, urging me to continue. My tongue leisurely trailed across one nipple, pulling it into my mouth and sucking before moving over to the other.

Her fingers wrapped around my head, running through my hair as her body responded beneath me. I slowly moved along the trail of brownies, licking up each one as I worked my way down her stomach. There was one piece left and I was anxious to devour it. I looked up and watched her as I let my tongue trail over her flushed skin, licking up the last piece of brownie before dipping down and flicking it over her clit.

She gasped as she nearly shot off the table, her legs falling to the side, allowing me direct access. I spread her legs as I dropped to my knees and licked up the wetness that was waiting for me. My tongue focused on her clit, circling the overly sensitive area while I slid a finger inside of her. She bucked beneath me as she moaned, quickly rotating her pussy around my face to get the friction that she needed. I pushed my fingers in and out of her, amazed at how wet she was as I thought about how good she was going to feel with my cock buried deep inside of her.

I focused on her breathing, knowing she was getting close as I fucked her harder with two fingers and sucked her clit. Her orgasm was fast and intense as her walls tighten around my fingers with each spasm that shook through her. Once she was done, I slowly pulled my fingers out and stood up, seeing the most beautiful woman looking completely satisfied, sprawled out on my kitchen table.

"I want more," she whispered as she bit her lip and reached forward to pull me on top of her. I wasn't sure that the table was sturdy enough to hold our weight but several thrusts later it was still standing as I came inside of her.

I felt slightly embarrassed about how fast I came but she didn't seem to mind when I offered a do-over upstairs in the bedroom. While things seemed fine between us on the surface, I couldn't help but wonder if there wasn't a ticking time bomb of grief lying just beneath the surface, ready to explode at any second.

Twenty

Lacey

My body was sore in the most wonderful way when I woke up the next morning. I don't know if it was the bottles of wine that we drank or the fact that I didn't have any responsibilities for the first time in eight years, but last night I had totally let go and surprised myself with how bold I was with Grant. The initial kiss in the kitchen had thrown me off and I wasn't sure how I felt about it, but as the night went on everything felt so right between us. So easy and comfortable, almost like how things used to be between Derek and me when we first started dating.

I used to believe that the chemistry was still there for us, that if we had the chance to rekindle that spark it would surely ignite a fire. But after Annie was born it felt like that spark was almost non-existent. I finally realized last night that I had been making excuses all of these years about why Derek and I hadn't been romantic with each other and blamed it on being exhausted and too busy with work and having a child. But the truth was that we had fallen out of love and never stopped long enough to realize it.

Sure I still loved him, nothing would ever change that. But the kind of love I had for him wasn't the same as the love I could feel myself having for Grant which terrified me. With Derek, we were a team. We shared chores and responsibilities with Annie but it didn't go much deeper than that. In the few weeks that I had lived with Grant, things fell so easily into place for us with the kids. Neither of us overstepped and I didn't have to worry about asking him to watch her for a few minutes so I could run to the store or go take a shower. As weird as it was, we all sort of just fell naturally into this perfect, little, blended

family that worked together to keep everything running and each of us checking in to make sure everyone was happy.

I rolled over, surprised to find that Grant was already out of bed since we didn't have the kids this morning. Maybe it was my silly girlish expectations from watching too many romcoms, but I had pictured us waking up together, cuddling as we thought about the wonderful night we shared. Then it hit me that we hadn't bothered to talk about what last night was and I had no idea what he was wanting out of this. We had both promised the kids that nothing would happen between us unless we talked to them first. Needless to say, we had already broken that promise, however, we still owed it to ourselves and each other to talk about it before they got back and things got awkward.

I got up and slid on the pair of sweatpants and T-shirt that had been tossed to the floor when we came up here last night for round two. I didn't know what time the kids were coming back so I wanted to make sure we had time to talk before then since it was already after eight. I made my way down the stairs and paused for a minute as I heard Grant on the phone. I didn't want to eavesdrop but couldn't easily make it back up the stairs without them creaking underneath me which left me stuck in place in the middle of the stairs. I was in the processing of trying to turn around so I could attempt to quietly sneak back up the stairs when I heard Grant's voice getting louder as he came around the corner out of the kitchen.

He stopped mid-step and looked at me with surprised humor on his face while he mumbled something into the phone before covering the mouth piece with his hand.

"What are you doing?" he asked quietly as he tried to keep from laughing at my awkward position. I was bent over, ass up, as I hung on to the banister beside me to keep from falling. I had quickly panicked when I heard him and my instincts— as stupid as they were— were to try to crawl up the stairs because that would be faster and less awkward.

"I didn't want to eavesdrop," I whispered loud enough for him to hear as I shrugged in explanation.

"So you're crawling up the stairs so I can't see you?" The smile quickly spread across his face as he tried to focus on his phone call. He nodded toward the living room as he walked that way and sat on the couch. I stood up and walked down the stairs as I tried to pretend like I wasn't a complete dork this morning.

"I don't see why that would be a problem, but let me ask her real quick," he moved the mouthpiece part of the phone behind his face so he could talk to me. "It's my mom, she wanted to see if the kids could stay with her for the rest of the weekend. They started a massive puzzle last night and the kids are excited to see if they can finish it by tomorrow. She said she can bring them back around dinner time on Sunday so they have time to get back into the routine for school."

It took me a few seconds to process the question as I was struggling with how much I already missed Annie but I couldn't remember the last time she had this much fun with someone her age. I shut my eyes and took a deep breath as I tried to let go of all of the insecurities that I was feeling. When I opened them I found Grant looking at me with empathy on his face.

"Yeah, that sounds fun. I'm sure Annie will have a great time," I said as my voice betrayed me and cracked, revealing the true emotion behind my words. I forced a smile as I stood up and walked into the kitchen, not bothering to listen as Grant talked to his mom.

I stood at the coffee pot with shaky hands, trying to pull myself together. It was only a few days, it wasn't like I was going to lose Annie forever. We had always been close but after Derek died I felt like there was a deeper bond between us and part of me was terrified to let go of her because I didn't want to risk losing it. Tears started to run down my face faster than I could wipe them away. I heard footsteps behind me and quickly turned my head away to keep him from seeing me cry. I felt his hand softly touch my lower back, bringing immediate comfort with it.

"Lacey?" he asked quietly.

"Yeah?" I whispered, reluctant to turn around and face him.

"Annie's on the phone and wanted to say hi. I think she's missing her mom a little bit this morning."

I turned around to look at him and found a soft smile on his face as he handed me his cell phone before leaning forward and gently kissing my forehead. I took the phone and waited until I heard him walk away before I sucked in another deep breath and tried to keep the emotion out of my voice.

"Hey, princess! How's my sweet girl this morning?" I said excitedly, wishing I could hug her and see her beautiful face.
"Hi, mommy! I'm good! We stayed up late last night building a 5000 piece puzzle mama! It's HUMONGOUS! I've never seen one this big, but Miss Sue said that we can stay with her all weekend and help her finish it."

I could hear the excitement rushing through the phone as she talked and closed my eyes as I pictured her precious face lit up with happiness. In the background, I could hear Grant's mom telling her to call her Nana instead of Miss Connie and laughed when I heard her joke about how it made her feel ancient to be called Miss in general. Annie giggled and apologized to Nana before reassuring her that she wasn't ancient. A few seconds later she was back on the line talking to me before she got distracted by Liam showing her something. I laughed as I realized how silly I was being for worrying about her when she was clearly having a wonderful time. We said goodbye and she promised to call me tonight with an update on the puzzle and her day.

I hung up the phone and went looking for Grant to give it back to him when I heard a knock at the door. I froze in place, unsure of what to do. I had no idea if he was expecting anyone but I was pretty sure he wasn't. And in the few weeks that I had been staying there, it wasn't common for people to just drop in unannounced. I glanced down the hallway and saw the bathroom door closed as someone knocked again. Whoever it was apparently came by for a reason so I tucked Grant's phone into my pocket and walked to the door, reaching up on my tiptoes to look through the peephole before opening it.

I rolled my eyes when all I could see was the back of someone's head as they turned facing the street instead of the door. I slowly turned the doorknob and opened the door, feeling relieved when the person turned around and I recognized it was Grant's youngest brother, Wyatt. I offered a smile as I pulled the door open further and stepped to the side so he could come in.

"Hi," I said, hoping it didn't sound as awkward as it felt. He smiled a crooked smile that I imagined melted women's panties as often as Grant claimed when he was telling me that his brother had taken on the new role of the town playboy after Noah settled down with Jade.

"Mornin," he replied, his voice a tad bit deeper than I had remembered from the last time I had talked to him, though it was too brief to really remember much. He stood in the entryway and shoved his hands in his jeans as he looked around for Grant.

"He should be out in just a minute," I explained as I glanced past him to the bathroom. "Do you want some coffee?" I silently prayed that he did so I would have an excuse to walk away and make myself busy doing something other than standing awkwardly with the brother of the man I slept with less than 12 hours ago.

"That'd be great, thank you."

I smiled as warmly as I could, trying to force the corners of my lips to pull up enough to keep it from looking creepy. I slipped past him and darted into the kitchen as I heard the bathroom door open. I could hear Grant's footsteps coming down the hall as I grabbed another coffee mug out of the cabinet and set it on the counter before filling three cups from the fresh pot Grant had recently made.

"Hey, what's up man?" Grant asked as he walked into the living room. I listened as his voice moved around the small room and could tell that he was by the couch now. I guessed that Wyatt was already in there and sitting down when Grant realized he was there. I topped off the last cup then set the pot back on the warmer, debating whether or not to start a new pot. I had no idea how long Wyatt would be here and whether they would want another cup. Deciding against it, I grabbed the creamer out of the fridge and fixed Grant's coffee the way he liked it.

I didn't want to look like I was trying to play hostess in a house that wasn't technically mine, even though I was living there, but at the same time, I didn't want to be rude when I had offered to get Wyatt coffee. I carried their cups of coffee into the living room and set them on the coffee table as they both smiled and looked up at me.

"Do you want cream or sugar?" I asked Wyatt, hoping to get out of their hair as quickly as possible. It felt strange being there and I couldn't imagine that whatever brought Wyatt over this early on a Saturday morning was something that he wanted to discuss with his brother while I sat in the corner and listened.

"No thank you, this is fine." He picked up the cup and slightly lifted it in the air as a thank you before taking a sip.

"Sounds good, I'll let you guys be so you can talk." I turned to walk away when Wyatt spoke.

"Actually, I'm here to talk to you." He lowered his cup and set it on the coffee table as he shifted on the couch to turn to face me.

"Me?" I asked confusedly as I pulled my brows together.

"Yeah, I ran into a guy named Bill…"

His eyes locked onto mine and I felt the color drain from my face as I stared at him in disbelief. A shiver ripped through my body leaving an icy chill behind.

"What are you talking about?" Grant asked, taking over the conversation. Wyatt turned his head and looked at him, a seriousness on his face that resembled Grant when I first met him and he saw the bruise on Annie's cheek.

"I was out of town for work this week and decided to stay the night in Eastern Point because another storm was supposed to roll through and I didn't want to risk getting stranded. There's a little bar there that the locals hang out at, it's kinda like the town gossip mill – anyways, I was having dinner when some crazed looking man approached me, asking if I had seen his missing daughter and granddaughter." Wyatt paused and turned his attention from Grant back to me. "He showed me a picture of the three of them together and expressed how concerned he was because his drug addict daughter fled town and kidnapped his granddaughter that he has full custody of after her father recently passed away."

I covered my mouth with my hand, my fingers trembling as I listened. I was comforted knowing that he wasn't in Haven Brook yet, but it was still unsettling to know that he was close. I vaguely remembered seeing the signs for the exit to Eastern Point on my way to town but in my frenzied state to get away, I had no idea where along the road I had seen them before I had the accident.

"Son of a bitch," Grant muttered under his breath and dropped his head into his hands as he leaned forward on the couch.

"So I came by to find out what the fuck is going on," he shifted his attention from me back to Grant. "And what the fuck you got yourself into."

His words stung me as he spit them out and I realized that he was right. I had absentmindedly drug Grant and Liam into this mess, not worrying about how it could impact them if my dad showed up here. My stomach dropped when I thought about the danger I had put them in, knowing there was no easy way out of it now.

"What did you say?" Grant asked him as he looked up and locked eyes with him.

"I told him that I wasn't from around there, that I was just passing through for work. He didn't ask anything else after that and I didn't tell him anything more."

"Good, that's good," Grant said as he nodded his head. His eyes wandered over to mine and I felt the anxiety start to rise inside of me as I thought about how things would have to end before they could even start.

"You're not going to run, Lacey. We've already talked about this," he said gently, keeping his eyes on me. I could feel the intensity of the look from Wyatt but kept my eyes on Grant. This was all too much to deal with.

"I have to," I whispered. "I have to go before it's too late."

"No, you don't. You can stay here and I'll protect you and Annie, just like I promised."

"I can't put you and Liam in that kind of danger. Anyone I talk to is at risk when it comes to the people he will go through to get to me. You. Liam. Your mom. Mia. Jade. The list is getting really long, really quick. I can't let him hurt anyone else. I have to go."

Wyatt sat on the couch, taking in our conversation without saying anything. I knew that once I was gone they would talk about this and I prayed that Grant would remember that I never wanted to bring any harm to any of them.

"Look, I don't need to know the details of what's happening, I just need to know one thing—are you in trouble?" Wyatt looked directly at me as he asked the question that I couldn't answer. The tears started to run down my cheeks as I closed my eyes and shook my head. This was like a living nightmare that I would never be able to wake up from.

"That's all I needed to know." Wyatt stood up and walked around the end of the coffee table to where I was standing. My eyes fluttered open when I saw his tall frame standing in front of me.

"My brother doesn't let people in easily and yet he's let you in. I know for a fact that he hasn't been with another woman since Renee, so whatever this is—it's important to him. You're important to him. And that means that you're important to me now too. I agree with Grant, you don't need to leave. You should stay here where we can all work to protect you. I know what he looks like and I can easily find out if someone new pops up in town, asking around." His tone was gentle

despite his deep voice. When I looked up at him I no longer saw a man who intimidated me, I saw a man who was being genuine and sincere.

"Thank you," I whispered, unable to say anything more. He smiled and nodded before turning away to talk to Grant who had now stood up and was standing next to us.

"It's probably a good idea to let Chase and Noah know what's going on so they can keep an eye on any new people hanging out around The Vine. The more of us who know what's going on and who to look for, the easier it will be to know when he's here." Wyatt explained to Grant who nodded in agreement.

"Do you really think he's going to come this way?" I asked with hopeful desperation in my voice. Wyatt nodded his head as he worked his jaw back and forth.

"Eastern Point is only a few hours away and I overheard him say that he's made it through all of the other towns between Easterville and Eastern Point. He's stopping in each one but he hasn't changed direction so I think it's inevitable. And there aren't that many other towns between here and Eastern Point so I think it'll be sooner than later."

I felt my body go numb as the words between Wyatt and Grant floated around me, my mind unable to process what they were saying. A few minutes later, I smiled as Wyatt waved goodbye and Grant walked him to the door. I sat down on the couch and stared off into space as I thought about what all of this meant. My mind raced as I thought about the possibilities of everything that Wyatt had suggested. Would we really know that he was here before he found me first? Would he show up at The Vine and tip off Noah and Chase before he lurked around town in the shadows, trying to find me on his own? Was he still drinking while he was going from town to town looking for us, or had I pissed him off enough to sober him up enough to plan things out? The couch shifted as Grant sat down next to me and placed a hand on my thigh, pulling me from my hopeless trance.

"You okay?" he asked quietly.

"I don't know, honestly. That's a lot to take in." I let out a heavy sigh and turned to look at him.

"I know, I'm sorry that it wasn't better news."

"Yeah, finding out that my dad is going town to town, asking people about his drug-addicted daughter who kidnapped his grandchild isn't the best news to get."

The problem with being new to a small town was that you were automatically considered suspicious by the locals. Add that to another new person coming through town, spreading terrible rumors and making you out to be some sort of monster and people would turn on you in a hurry. Which meant that if he talked to anyone in town before he talked to Chase or Noah, they would immediately freak out and point him in my direction because they would fear that it was true.

"No one in town is going to believe that, Lacey," he tried to reassure me.

"No one actually knows me. They'll freak out and think they're doing the best thing by pointing him in my direction because there's a child involved and they wouldn't want to risk her being in danger," I countered.

"People here are smart, they know that if you're staying with me, that you're not a bad person. This town has known my family for so long that they know that we are good people who only hang out with good people. You're going to be fine here, I promise."

"How does Wyatt know that we had sex?" I asked without realizing I was shifting gears and changing the topic.

"What are you talking about?" he asked confused with an eyebrow arched.

"He said that he knew for a fact that you haven't been with anyone since Renee, and that I must be important if you were with me. I'm paraphrasing but that was the gist of it."

Grant sighed and rolled his head back, stretching his neck. He ran a hand down his face then turned to look at me.

"Wyatt was the one person that I was the closest to when Renee was sick and going through her treatments. She thought it would be funny to make Wyatt agree that he would try to get me laid after she was gone so I wouldn't turn into a bitter, lonely, unhappy old man. He joked and asked her how she knew that I wouldn't go find someone on my own and she said 'because I know him too well'. The day he gets laid will be the day you show up at his house and another woman answers the door with a look of pure satisfaction on her face. If she looks pissed off -- they haven't had sex yet." He chuckled as he said it and watched for my reaction as I felt the blush creep up my neck.

"Well, I guess I should have answered the door pissed off then, huh? Protect your secret a little while longer," I teased.

"Eh, I kinda like the thought that you had a look of pure satisfaction on your face instead. Besides, it wasn't going to be long before people started to assume anyways." He shrugged as if it was no big deal.

"So, how do you feel about what happened? We never got around to talking about what all of this means and what we would want or expect from it," I asked cautiously as I eased into the topic.

He let out a slow, steady deep breath as he took a minute to think before answering me.

"Honestly, I don't know. I thought that this would be some crystal clear turning point, that I would have these signs that would tell me what to do and how to feel, but I have nothing."

"Do you regret what happened?" My tone was harder as I braced myself for his response and the high likelihood of rejection.

"Do I regret making you come four times? No. Do I regret eating fudge brownie off of your naked body while I slipped my fingers inside of you? No. Do I regret how good it felt to be so deep inside of you as you rode me on the stairs last night because we couldn't wait to make it to the bed? No. I don't regret a single thing about what happened between us last night, Lacey, and I hope that you don't either."

I felt the goofiest smile spread across my face as I bumped my shoulder against his, feeling the same giddiness from last night flow through my body at the memories of all the dirty stuff we did.

"I don't regret any of it either," I admitted, looking down at the wedding ring on my finger. "I feel kind of guilty though."

"Why is that?" He leaned back against the couch and pulled me closer to him. I let the warmth of his body flow through mine as I thought about how to say it.

"Because I never felt that way with my husband and in a way, it feels like I cheated on him. I think if sex with you would have been similar to what I had with him, I wouldn't feel as guilty about it. But it was better. A LOT better, and that makes me feel really guilty."

"I get it, that makes sense."

I swallowed hard and tried to force the new tears away.

" I felt guilty too," he confessed quietly. "Guilty for still being here, enjoying life, and having mind-blowing sex with another woman when my wife wasn't given a chance to live her life. She was always so focused on being the best mother to Liam and the best wife for me that she rarely did anything for herself. I realized recently that I didn't even know what she liked before she passed. She didn't take the time to do anything for herself and I was too selfish working at a job that sucked everything out of me that I didn't do anything for her either. I took her for granted and now she's gone." His voice cracked and I could feel the tension in his body as he tried to hold it together.

I twisted around and looked up at him as I pressed my hand to his cheek. I didn't say anything because I knew there were no words to say that would ease the pain he was feeling.

"It's okay to not be okay, Grant. Even if it's just once when no one else is around. It's okay to break down and allow yourself to feel whatever you need to and let out everything you've been holding in," I said quietly as I held his face in my hand. His eyes filled with tears as he tried to look away before I pulled his chin back in my direction and held his gaze. "It's okay, I promise."

His eyes closed as the tears started to run down his face. I gently wrapped my arms around him, just enough to comfort him without making him uncomfortable. His body trembled beneath me as he sobbed harder, trying to catch his breath. I didn't bother to wipe away the tears that ran down my cheeks as I shared in his grief with him.

"I didn't tell her that I loved her enough, she didn't know how much she meant to me," he choked out between sobs. "I should have made love to her every day and cherished every minute with her but I didn't. I didn't appreciate the time we had together when we still had it and now I'm stuck with this ache so deep inside of my chest that I feel the walls caving in as I struggle to take a breath." His words were scattered between sobs but still made perfect sense because it was exactly how I had felt after Derek died.

"I know, I know," I softly whispered in his ear as I continue to hold him.

"No one ever understands—it eats you alive to have to deal with this on top of everything else, all by yourself."

"I understand," I cleared my throat and spoke a little bit louder so he could hear me. "Losing someone we love is always hard, but losing someone that we thought we would be with forever—there's no grief that compares to that. The loss of someone that we shared all of our deepest, darkest secrets with and made plans with for the future. The loss of someone that spoke so deeply to our soul that a part of us died with them, yet we are forced to try to carry on as if we are whole. There's different grief that we feel when we lose a spouse and that grief is so consuming because it carries over into every single aspect of our lives. It's hard and no one should have to experience this."

He pulled back and looked at me, tears stained on his beautiful face as he looked deep into my eyes.

"That's why you can't leave, Lacey. You have to stay and let me protect you because there is no way that I can live through losing another woman that I care so deeply about. I couldn't save Renee, but I can save you. Please, don't make me go through this pain again, Lacey, I don't think I could survive it a second time." His voice cracked as his eyes pleaded with me and in that instant, I felt the shift that rocked my world as I knew it.

Twenty One

Grant

It was dumb of me to break down with Lacey this morning and I had been kicking myself for it ever since. After four years I thought I had finally learned to deal with the pain of losing Renee and was starting to move on, then out of nowhere, this beautiful woman comes crashing into my world and changes everything as I've known it. Talking to Wyatt this morning opened my eyes to how real the threat of Lacey's father was. He wasn't just a bad man that Lacey talked about from her childhood, he was really the crazed lunatic that was going town to town, making up terrible lies to find her and Annie. My stomach knotted when I heard that he was in Eastern Point, knowing that he could be in Haven Brook by lunchtime.

There weren't many towns along the way which meant that Haven Brook was likely his next stop. I was feeling thankful and relieved that the kids were with my mom through tomorrow night so I could have a little more uninterrupted time to think about what to do when he got here. I hoped that he would stop by The Vine or SlowMo's as they were the only places to pop in and talk to the locals, but who knew what his plans would be. We assumed that he had just stopped in Eastern Point and immediately began asking around but I had to consider whether he was calculating and scoping out the town before he started asking.

Lacey had told me that he was a raging alcoholic but the information that Wyatt had given us led me to believe that he may actually be sober right now, which was even more alarming than if he was in his regular drunken state. I wanted to talk to Lacey about it but she was immediately guarded on the subject after Wyatt left and I didn't want to further upset her. Or at least I hoped that was what had upset her and that it wasn't my out of the blue confession that I had serious feelings for her after a few weeks.

I opened the fridge and looked inside, my stomach growling as I searched for something to make for us for lunch. There were very few options sitting on the shelves and I wasn't in the mood for any of them. I closed the door and walked into the living room, finding Lacey sitting on the couch, staring at the blank tv.

"Everything alright?" If she needed space to think through things I didn't want to be up her ass or hovering over her.

"Yeah, I'm just still trying to process everything and figure out what to do when my dad gets here. Part of me is still screaming for me to go grab Annie and run, get as far away as we can, as fast as we can..." Her voice trailed off as her thoughts shifted to something else that left a saddened expression on her face.

"But?"

She waited a moment before speaking, her hazel eyes looking up at me as she contemplated whether to say what she was thinking.

"But part of me is terrified of leaving and never feeling this way again."

My heart skipped a beat as I slowly sat down on the edge of the couch and waited for her to say the words that I needed to hear her say.

"Feel like what?"

She closed her eyes and pulled in a long, slow breath before letting it out and pulling in another.

"Like I could be falling in love with you. Like I already love Liam like a son. Like I feel like we could all be a happy little family and have the happily ever after that both of us have already been robbed of once."

The smile pulled across my face before I could stop it, the ache of it one of the best feelings I've had in a long time.

"I feel like we could be really happy together too, Lacey. And I know that it's only been a few weeks and this feels totally crazy—but I'm not ready to lose you. Not even if it means that you had to run and you take Annie with you. I don't want that to happen and I'm really scared that you're going to keep considering it."

"But don't you get why I have to do it?" her voice pleaded with me to understand what her heart was trying to say. I subtly shook my head no because no matter how hard I tried, I would never understand her wanting to leave us if she thought that she might be falling in love with me and wanted to have a family together.

"I love you enough to leave. I love Liam enough to disappear and shield him from having another funeral to go to. I love you both enough to spare you the void that you're going to feel when this ends too soon because I can't stop the man who's trying to kill me. And he's not going to stop, Grant. I've seen what he can do and I know what's coming."

I sighed in frustration and ran a hand down my face. I needed her to know that there wasn't a single thing that I wouldn't do for her. When I said I would protect them, I meant it. Even if I had to use my own body as a shield to keep them safe. I had already learned by now that when her mind was set, it was set. The way she clenched her jaw told me that this wasn't a conversation that was going to go anywhere because she had already made up her mind. The only thing left to do was try to buy some time and pray that I could change her mind once her mood changed.

"Okay, how about we put a pin in this conversation for now and grab something for lunch?" I said as I stood up, hoping to change the conversation as well as the energy in the room. There was a sudden burst of energy shooting through me that made me feel desperate to get out of the house.

"Sure, what do you want and I can go make it?" She stood up and stretched before reaching up and pulling her hair into a ponytail. We both took some time this morning to get ready, even though we hadn't planned to go anywhere. As cute as she looked in her yoga pants and t-shirt, I was suddenly itching to get her out of the house and do something other than obsessing about the threat that was heavy in the air between us.

"Actually, I want to get out of the house for a bit. You okay with that?" I raised an eyebrow and waited, hoping she would say yes.

"Will Annie be okay while we're gone?" she asked nervously as she chewed on her bottom lip.

"Yeah, I'll call my mom and let her know that we're going out for a bit, and if you want, I'll ask Wyatt to go hang out there for a bit, just to be sure they're covered if they need anything."

"Okay, that sounds good. Do I need to change?" She looked down at what she was wearing before looking up at me.

"Maybe go put on something a little bit warmer and I'll pack a few things into the truck before we go."

"Are you going to tell me where we're going?" She narrowed her eyes at me suspiciously.

"Nope, now go change so we can get going," I said over my shoulder as I walked into the kitchen to pack a few things to load into the truck.

Thirty minutes later we had stopped to grab a quick sandwich and were back on the road as we headed toward Lakeview. It was a small town just outside of Haven Brook with a beautiful lake that we all used to hang out at when I was growing up. Before Renee died, we used to bring Liam trout fishing but neither of us could bring ourselves to come out here after she passed. It was a sacred memory that would forever be stored in my heart. I slowly pulled the truck around the bend, avoiding the north side of the lake where I used to go with Renee.

The lake was empty, which wasn't surprising given that it was still frozen and no one bothered to come out here in the middle of January. Something had clicked inside of me earlier and I wanted to bring Lacey here to clear her head the way I used to be able to come here and think after my dad died. There's something about the quiet calmness of the lake that really lets you do some intense soul searching. And one thing that I've learned over the years is that it's hard to do any soul searching as a single parent because you rarely get a free moment to even think for yourself, let alone get lost in thought. There may not be much that I could offer Lacey to change her mind about leaving, but at least I could offer her a chance to clear her head and make peace with the decisions she needed to make.

I put the truck in park as we stared ahead at the lake covered in thick layers of ice. The sun struggled to break free from the clouds which left it feeling a bit somber. I was about to reconsider everything and turn around to leave when Lacey let out an easy sigh and scooted forward to rest her arms on the dashboard as she stared out the window.

"This is gorgeous," she whispered.

"I was hoping you would like it," I said, feeling calmer about bringing her here.

"I love it, it's so peaceful and quiet."

"I used to come here a lot after my dad died to clear my head and try to figure things out." I felt her eyes on me as she slightly turned her head and looked at me. "Everything at home was always loud and chaotic after he died, everyone was angry about something and my mom was always super stressed out. I would sneak out and drive out here, then just sit and stare at the lake for hours. It was like it was magical, forcing all of the thoughts to the surface that I couldn't bring myself to think about at home. I would leave feeling calmer than when I first got here, and head home, ready to handle the chaos. It didn't solve any of my problems, but it definitely helped me to be able to handle them better."

"Is that why you brought me here? So I can feel calm and clear my head so I can reconsider whether I should leave?"

"No," I chuckled, loving that she was quick to call me on what she thought was some bullshit. "I brought you here because you deserve to have some downtime and peace in your life. A moment to just stop and breathe. Not have to worry about anyone or anything." I looked over at her and found her smiling at me. "Plus, we have full service out here and we're only forty-five minutes from home so we can get back quickly if we need to." I pulled my phone out and held it up for her to see, just in case she didn't believe me.

"You're too much," she joked as she leaned back against the seat and laughed. "So, what is the plan now that we're here?"

"Well, the plan is that there isn't a plan. We have lunch and no kids, so the possibilities are endless," I said as I patted the brown paper bag sitting between us on the console as I wiggled my eyebrows.

"In that case, I vote for eating. I'm starving." She licked her lips as her eyes traveled down to the bag. Something about the look on her face sent my dick into overdrive as I imagined her lips on me. As she leaned forward to reach for the bag, her t-shirt shifted, allowing me the perfect glimpse at her full breasts that were sitting heavily in a black lace bra. I swallowed hard as I tried to redirect my thoughts but I couldn't. My dick was harder than flying a kite with no wind.

"Keep looking at me that way and no one is eating lunch," she warned quietly under her breath as she grabbed the bag and looked inside. She pulled one sandwich out and turned it around to find the writing on it to see which one was hers. Her fingers grazed the side of it as she ran her hand down the length of it, intentionally fucking with my head. She casually passed me the sub sandwich and reached in to grab hers. A few seconds later she had fished out the bags of chips and napkins that were at the bottom.

I carefully unwrapped the top of it, making sure to keep the rest of it covered so I wouldn't make a mess. They had the best meatball sub in town, however, it was also the messiest sub and I didn't feel like wearing half of it. I went to take a bite when I saw Lacey set hers down on the dashboard and turn in her seat. There was a look of desire on her face, mixed in with a sexy smirk as she pulled her bottom lip in between her teeth.

I held the sandwich in the air as I watched her slowly lean across the middle console as she reached down with one hand and unzipped my jeans. I could feel the blood rushing through my ears as dirty thoughts raced through my mind of what she was about to do. She glanced up at me and smiled as her fingers slowly reached inside my boxers and pulled my dick out. She giggled when she felt how hard it was as I closed my eyes and leaned my head back, enjoying the feel of her hand on my cock.

I could feel her shift beside me as she got herself situated over the console. As I slowly opened my eyes I found her watching me with hooded eyes as she stretched across the seat, her ass in the air as she slowly lowered her mouth to my throbbing dick. Her tongue gently ran along the head, making me desperate to push her head down so I could feel her mouth wrapped around me. My breathing quickened as her tongue slowly ran up one side and down the other while her fingers reached down and ran across my balls. I shifted in my seat, the sensation almost too much when she stopped and looked up at me.

"Why don't you focus on your meatballs, and I'll focus on mine," she whispered as she nodded toward the sandwich in my hand. I was so horny and worked up that I was about ready to throw the sandwich out the window and bury my dick inside of her. She gave me a pointed look as she looked at the sandwich, then back to me, before lowering her head and pulling me to the back of her throat. My breath hitched as I jolted forward, instinctively reaching out with my free hand to hold her head in place as she bobbed up and down. I was seconds away from coming when she slowed down and pulled me out, slowly running her tongue along the sides of my cock.

I took a deep breath as I brought the sandwich to my mouth and took a bite. I had never had a woman ask me to eat a fucking sandwich while she gave me head, but here I was, eating a fucking sandwich while her brown hair flowed down her back, moving like water as she gave me the best blow job in my life. I devoured the sandwich quickly, ready to be done so I could move on to Lacey. I tossed the dirty wrapper into the back seat, thankful that I had leather seats, even though at the moment I couldn't care less about what they were.

She took one hand and brushed her hair out of her face as she slowly looked up at me, my dick still filling her mouth as she sucked me in even further. We locked eyes and never broke contact as she worked her mouth over me, sucking while working my shaft with her hand. I felt the pressure building, ready to explode at any moment.

"I'm about to come," I warned in a moan as her mouth sucked me even harder. "Now, Lacey, I'm gonna come…"

She began moving her head up and down quicker than before, creating the perfect pace as I felt the moment my orgasm pulsed through me and down her throat. A few spasms later and my body was completely relaxed as I leaned my head against the headrest and tried to catch my breath. She gently kissed the head before scooting back to her side of the truck and grabbing her sandwich.

"Man, I'm really hungry now," she teased as she leaned back and unwrapped the turkey sandwich, taking a big bite as she looked coyly at me before giggling.

Fifteen minutes later and Lacey had finished her food while my body recovered from the very unexpected but wonderful surprise. We got out of the truck and walked toward the lake, feeling the bitter chill from the water once we were only a few feet away. It was beautiful year-round but I quickly realized that beautiful didn't mean it was worth freezing my balls off to be next to it. I shivered as a gust of wind whipped through us, blowing through Lacey's hair and leaving a sweet scent behind. My body started drifting in that direction, desperate to be closer to the scent that had become almost like a drug to me.

Lacey's eyes were soft as she stared out at the lake, ignoring the cold while she was lost in thought. I could see her body trembling but didn't want to interrupt whatever was going through her mind by asking if she wanted to go back to the truck. Instead, I unzipped my hoodie and pulled it off before wrapping it around her shoulders. It was cold as fuck but I would rather that she be warm and have this time to decompress than to be warm myself. She smiled warmly as she pulled it tighter around her before she looked back toward the lake.

I decided to give her some space and walked back to the truck, remembering that I had packed a few things before we left including a heavier jacket. I opened the door and reached behind my seat to grab my jacket when I saw a new text message and a missed call on my cell phone that was sitting in the drink holder in front of the middle console. I glanced over at Lacey before picking it up and seeing that both were from Wyatt.

I opened the text message first and rolled my eyes when all it said was: call me. I closed the message and went to the voicemail, listening to it before calling him back. The message was quick, asking me to call him back as soon as I got it. There was something different in his voice but I couldn't figure out what it was. I looked at the time of the missed call and messages then glanced at the current time. It had only been ten minutes so not too terrible. I grabbed the jacket from the backseat and pulled it on, then pressed send to call Wyatt back. The phone didn't even get through one full ring before he answered and I realized what I had heard in his voice. Fear.

"What's up?" I asked, still watching Lacey as she leaned against a tree and gazed out to the water.

"Lacey's dad is here," he blurted out quickly in one anxious breath.

"Here, where?" I immediately started to panic, wondering if he meant that Bill was at my mom's house, which is where Wyatt was supposed to be while Lacey and I were at the lake.

"Sorry, he's in Haven Brook. Not at mom's," he explained quickly. "Didn't mean to panic you, but either way—the fucker is here and Chase said that he's already asking around about Lacey and Annie."

"Fuck," I muttered as I ran a hand along the back of my neck, squeezing it to relieve some of the mounting tension.

"I'm here at mom's and she's aware of everything that's going on. Noah offered to come by and help but Jade wasn't feeling well so I told him to stay with her."

"Does anyone know that the kids are at mom's?"

"I have no idea, it's a small town. I could take a shit and someone would know what color it was without me telling them."

I cringed at the analogy and rolled my eyes at how direct he was, though I wasn't surprised given this was who he was all the time.

"Okay, I'll tell Lacey and we'll head back to town," I said as I started walking to where she was.

"Do you think that's a good idea?" he asked, stopping me in my tracks.

"Why wouldn't it be?" I pinched the bridge of my nose in frustration that the problem was here in front of my face and I had no idea how to handle it.

"Because he's here asking about her but doesn't know that she's actually here. If you come back, there's a chance that he will see her. If you stay out of town for a little while longer and the kids stay here with mom and me, there's a chance that Chase can convince him that she's not here and he'll keep moving."

I took in a deep breath and held it for a minute before forcing it out when I realized that he was right. Wyatt might be known as the town's playboy with no desire for responsibility, but for those of us who really knew him, he was one of the most reasonable, logical, problem solvers that I had ever met. He was right and as much as I knew that Lacey would hate the idea of being away from Annie during this ordeal, there weren't any better options to choose from.

"Okay, you're right. I'll talk to Lacey and let her know what's going on. Are you staying at mom's from here on out?"

"Yeah, I told the kids we would have a slumber party tonight so they didn't think anything odd was happening. Liam seemed a little suspicious but he went along with it once he saw how excited Annie was. Where are you guys planning to stay so I know more or less where to find you?"

"We're at the lake in Lakeview, I'll check around and see if I can find us someplace to stay for the night and let you know. Keep me posted if anything happens—and I mean ANYTHING. I'll keep my phone on me and the volume turned up."

"Sounds good, stay safe," he said before hanging up.

I glanced at Lacey as I hung up the phone and made sure the ringer was on and turned up. She looked so peaceful that I didn't want to have to go give her the bad news and ruin the wonderful time we were having. While it wasn't a complete shock that he was here and in town, it still felt like a jolt to know it was really happening. Wyatt's words kept playing over and over in my ear, *stay safe,* like a bad omen.

I slid my phone into my pocket as I quietly walked over to where she was standing, trying not to interrupt. She kept her gaze on the water but her body shifted slightly to where I was now standing beside her.

"He's here," she said without any emotion in her voice. I swallowed hard, trying to force air past the lump that was forming in my throat when I heard the tone in her voice. The sound of defeat for a battle that hadn't even started.

"How did you know?" I asked quietly, staring out at the water hoping it would bring the same feeling of peace to me that it was offering her.

"Because today was too good to be true, and my friend, all good things must come to an end." She pulled in a deep breath as she turned and looked at me, fresh tears in her eyes.

"I'm so sorry," I said as I reached over and lightly wiped a tear away.

"We knew it was coming. Now we just have to figure out what to do to keep Annie safe." She squared her shoulders, ignoring the shiver that coursed through her body with the gust of wind. "So, what's the plan?"

"Wyatt is at my mom's house and he'll be there to help watch the kids. They are both aware that Bill is in town. Chase was the first to spot him and talked to him before he called to let Wyatt know since he knew we were out of town and that Wyatt would be with the kids. Everyone is alert and aware, it's just a waiting game now. I don't know if he'll stick around long and keep asking around, but Wyatt suggested that we stay out of town for now and hope that he leaves and moves on to the next town."

"I can't leave Annie there alone while he's in town. If he finds her…" Her eyes widened with panic as she stared at me in disbelief at what I was suggesting.

"I know it's scary, but I really think it's the best option. There's a good possibility that no one knows the kids are with my mom, which means he won't know where to go looking for her if he thinks she's in Haven

Brook. If we go back now, we have a very strong chance of him seeing you and knowing you're there. I won't tell you what to do. If you want to go back to be with Annie, I'll figure out a way to try to sneak us back without anyone seeing you."

She looked away from me and back out to the water as she thought about it, a series of emotions flashing across her face. One final shake of her head then she turned back to me with a determined look on her face.

"I need to go back, Grant. She's my daughter and it's my job to protect her."

I hated the idea of trying to get Lacey back to town without her being seen. The last thing we needed was for one of the locals to see us driving by then run into Bill and tell him that they just saw her. If she stayed out of town it was likely that no one would remember where they had seen her last. Even if they told him that she was living with me, we wouldn't be home when he went there looking for her. There was a huge risk with what we were about to do. I nodded my head as we walked back to the truck and climbed in, the doors slamming shut and shattering the peace that we were now leaving behind us.

THE TIES THAT BIND

Twenty Two

Lacey

My fingers tapped nervously against my knee as I stared out the window on the drive back to Haven Brook. I had been going back and forth on whether this was the right thing to do or if I was being selfish and putting Annie in even more danger by not listening to Grant and staying away. My body felt like it was flooded with adrenaline, ready to run at any moment. Grant's hand reached over the console and gently squeezed mine, a tight smile on his face as he glanced at me before turning his attention back to the road.

"So, I have a question for you," he said, pulling my attention away from obsessing over getting back to Annie.

"Sure, what's up?" I shifted in my seat to face him, making sure his hand stayed resting on my thigh as we continued to hold hands.

"Not that I'm complaining – at all—but what was that about earlier? With the blow job?" He cast a quick glance at me before focusing on the empty stretch of highway we were on. I was relieved that he was focused on the road so he couldn't see the blush that was heating my face.

"I knew that you wanted to make today special for me and to help me relax, but I also knew how hard it was for you to go back to the lake so I wanted to take your mind off of everything. In hindsight, now I worry that it was completely disrespectful and in poor taste to give you a blow job at the lake that you used to go to with your wife and son." I let my head fall back against the headrest and closed my eyes while

realizing what a huge mistake that had been. "I'm so sorry Grant, I wasn't trying to ruin the lake for you."

He let out a laugh which startled me as I opened my eyes and turned to look at him. His face was lit up with happiness as the smile pulled tight across his face, looking completely carefree.

"You don't have to worry about that but thank you," he laughed and looked out the window.

"Why not? I don't get it, what's so funny?"

"It's nothing, I'm sorry. It's just that growing up here, everyone knew that Lakeview Lake was where you went if you wanted to sneak off and have sex. It almost feels sacrilegious to go there with a girl and not get some action. Where do you think Liam was conceived?"

I burst out laughing as I covered my mouth with my hand, shaking my head as I looked at him. I playfully pulled my hand out from under his and swatted at his chest.

"Grant Walker! You took me to the sex lake?! What kind of woman do you think I am?" I pretended to be insulted as he chuckled.

"The kind of woman who lets me lick brownies from her pussy as I eat her out on the family dinner table," he joked as he winked at me. My cheeks were on fire from the heat running through them as I remembered last night and the brownie incident.

"You're a dirty, dirty man Mr. Walker," I teased playfully.

"That I am," he wiggled his eyebrows suggestively. "But you like it when I talk dirty to you so I guess that makes you my dirty, dirty girl."

"So it would seem," I laughed, noticing the sign confirming that we were now entering the town of Haven Brook as Grant took the exit that would lead back to his house. I sucked in a breath and looked around, wondering if I should try to duck down in my seat and hide to avoid having anyone see me.

"It'll be okay," Grant assured me as he took an immediate right and took a dirt road that I had never been down before.

"Where are we going?" I asked as I leaned forward and looked around, concerned that even though I was trying to avoid being seen, I would feel better if I were able to spot Bill and know his exact location.

"This road will take us the back way to my house. The locals use it on occasion but for the most part, it's usually empty. This way no one will see us driving through town and we can decrease the chance of anyone even knowing we were here."

I nodded my head and leaned back against the seat, trying to force myself to relax even though I knew it was pointless. Grant's phone started to ring, startling me with the sound as it got louder as he fished it out of his pocket.

"It's Chase," he said as he slid his finger across the screen to answer it, pushing the speakerphone button before setting it in the cup console between us. "Hey, what's up?"

"Just wanted to let you know that Bill just left The Vine. I tried to keep him here as long as I could but he was getting antsy when it started to die down and there was no one else for him to talk to. Just wanted to give you a heads up, I don't know where he's going from here."

"Thanks for the update," Grant said, looking at me to see if there was anything I wanted to say.

"Was he drinking?" I asked loud enough for Chase to hear me.

"Only water," he confirmed before covering the phone to yell to someone else to clear the table in the back.

I could feel my anxiety start to build when I knew that he was actually sober and probably had been from the minute he started looking for me. I was used to dealing with drunk Bill but I had never had to deal with sober, pissed off Bill.

"Let us know if you hear anything. We just got back into town now, I'm on the back road heading to my house." Grant said, filling the silence while I was unable to speak.

"I thought you guys were going to stay out of town for a day or two until he left?" Chase asked confused.

I bit the inside of my cheek, hearing the concern in Chase's voice about why we hadn't stayed away like everyone had discussed. Apparently, I was the only one who had thought it would be a good idea to come back, and now I was seriously questioning that decision.

"Lacey didn't want to be away from Annie," Grant explained softly.

"I get it, I wouldn't be able to stay away if I thought Rylee was in trouble. We do what we have to do as parents to keep our kids safe and there's nothing wrong with that." Chase replied, making me feel better that not everyone was judging me for coming back.

"Are the kids going to stay with mom tonight or are you picking them up?" Chase asked as Grant turned down another side road and houses started to pass by my window. Most of them looked familiar and I was pretty sure we were only a few blocks away.

"I'm not sure, we haven't talked about it yet," Grant said, turning his attention toward me. "What do you want to do?"

I tried to weigh the options but it all came back around to me needing to know that Annie was safe and I couldn't trust that she was unless I could see her.

"I want to pick Annie up and take her home so I can keep an eye on her and make sure she's safe."

"Okay, I'll call my mom real quick and let her know the change of plans," Grant confirmed as he slowly turned the corner and waited before pulling onto his street. I knew that he was being cautious, making sure that no one was around watching us but it still sent a chill up my spine.

"Sounds good, Noah and I are both free if you guys need anything. Just call."

I smiled as we hung up the call with Chase and pulled up to the garage. Grant put the truck in park but didn't turn it off as he thought about what to do.

"Do you want to go with me to my mom's to get the kids or do you want to wait here to make sure everything is okay? We can go inside and check the house, then if everything is fine, I can run and pick up the kids and bring them back while you wait here for us."

His idea made a lot of sense and seemed like the most practical option that we had. Instead of both of us going to his mom's and coming back with the kids to a house that may or may not be safe, it seemed better to split up and confirm the house was safe before we brought them back. A few minutes later we made our way through the house, feeling somewhat silly as we worked as a team to clear each room, looking in closets and under beds as if there was a real-life boogeyman just waiting to jump out and scare us.

I said bye to him and planted a quick kiss on his lips before he darted out the door and hopped in his truck to go to his mom's. Even though I had planned to spend some time this weekend talking about us and what this new relationship meant to both of us, that never happened and I didn't want to get in the habit of kissing him in front of the kids before we could talk about it. I tried to make a mental note to talk to him about it tonight so we could make sure we were all on the same page before we slipped in front of the kids.

Fifteen minutes had passed while I was upstairs unpacking the things I had taken with me earlier for the lake. I heard the front door open and close, smiling when I knew that I was going to see Annie's beautiful face in just a few minutes. I waited anxiously to hear the sound of her footsteps as she came bouncing up the stairs looking for me, or the sound of her sweet voice as she called for me. I stopped for a second and listened, wondering if I had imagined hearing the front door close as it was eerily quiet downstairs for having Grant and two rambunctious kids come back.

The silence was deafening as the pounding in my ears got louder from my blood pressure rising quickly. Something was wrong, I just knew it. Annie was never this quiet, what if something happened to her? I tossed the hoodie I had been wearing that Grant wrapped around me earlier on the bed and softly crept downstairs. I glanced around in each room looking for a sign that someone was there, not seeing anything. My heart was racing as I opened the closet door in the hallway, waiting for someone to jump out and get me.

A few minutes later I rolled my eyes for having imagined hearing the door when clearly no one was there. I checked my phone to see a text message from Grant that they were packing up the kid's stuff and would be back in a few minutes. I pushed my phone back down into my pocket and made my way back upstairs, forcing myself to finish unpacking instead of worrying about checking each of the rooms again. I had checked things thoroughly while I was downstairs so the likelihood that anyone could have quietly snuck up the stairs while I wasn't looking was slim. I was being overly paranoid and needed to calm down before Annie got back and started to worry.

I quickly hung up the hoodie and my sweater from today, closing the closet door behind me. As I turned around, my heart stopped beating as I clutched a hand to my chest.

"Hello, Lacey," he growled, standing in the doorway, blocking my only way out. My eyes frantically searched the room, looking for anything that could be used as a weapon as he stepped closer. A few seconds later I heard the front door open and the sound of happy children rushing in, filling the silence between us.

"Mama, where are you?" Annie called excitedly as I heard her footsteps already running up the stairs.

Bill quickly stepped to the side, the baseball bat that I had used to knock him out before gripped tightly in his right hand. I watched in terror as I heard Annie coming up the stairs, no idea of what was about to happen as Bill hid inside the room waiting for her.

"Annie, go back downstairs, I'll be right there," I called to her quickly, as loud as I could hoping that Grant would hear the fear in my voice and know that something was wrong.

My stomach dropped as I saw her run toward the bedroom, pure happiness on her face to see me. I must have looked like I had seen a ghost because she immediately stopped and fear filled her eyes but it was too late. I watched in horror as Bill reached out to the side and grabbed her, pulling her into him as he locked one arm around her neck, holding her small body against his so she couldn't move. Her beloved stuffed puppy fell to the floor by her feet before Bill kicked it out of the way. My heart filled with sadness as her eyes watched it tumble across the room, the only thing that had brought her real comfort in the past few months was now out of reach.

"Let her go," I warned, moving closer. He raised the bat and smirked as he swung it, barely missing Annie's head by a fraction of an inch. I gasped as she closed her eyes and started to cry. Where was Grant?? I was too afraid to take my eyes off of him to try to search for something to use as a weapon.

"She's just a child," I pleaded as I watched on helplessly. Annie looked up and her eyes met mine. There was a look in them that I had never seen before as she gave me a subtle nod before lifting her foot and smashing it down as hard as she could on his. He quickly released his hold on her as he pulled his foot away, letting out a slew of curse words in the process. Annie spun around and jabbed her elbow into his nose before bringing her knee up and kicking him in the balls. Everything happened so fast that I could barely believe my eyes as I watched him crumple over in pain.

"Come on, mom, we have to go!" she screamed at me before reaching down and grabbing her puppy. Her small hand grabbed mine as she pulled me away and we ran down the hallway to the stairs. I let go of Annie's hand and smiled when she turned to look at me.

"Run fast and go find Grant," I commanded as we both started to rush down the stairs. She was almost to the bottom when I felt strong arms grab me from behind and tackle me, pulling me back up the stairs. My eyes went wide with fear when I felt Bill's arm wrapped tightly against my waist as he drug me up to my feet. Annie stopped at the bottom and spun around to look for me when she saw what was happening. Bill reached into his pocket and pulled out a lighter and a piece of cloth that reeked of gasoline. His eyes danced wildly as he let me go and pushed me to the side so I couldn't get past him as he lit the cloth on fire and watched it fall over the rail to the ground in the living room.

Within seconds a fire had started in the carpet, spreading quickly as Annie looked back and forth between the fire and me, terrified. I pushed as hard as I could to try to get past Bill, unable to move him out of the way as I watched the fire growing quickly. Within seconds I saw Grant and Liam come running in as the back door in the kitchen slammed shut. Grant's face was etched in fear as he saw the fire before looking up to find me pinned to the wall with Bill's hands wrapped tightly around my throat.

"Since you like to start fires and all, I thought you would enjoy this one. We can watch your fake little family burn together," he sneered in my ear as he held me in place. I turned my head the best I could and made eye contact with Grant. Unable to speak, I mouthed the words I needed him to hear.

Take care of my baby.

Twenty Three

Grant

I quickly dashed over and grabbed Annie, picking her up by her waist as she clutched her stuffed animal to her chest and screamed for Lacey. Within seconds I had both kids outside as the fire continued to spread throughout the living room.

"Run to Nana's house and tell her to call for help. Go!" I screamed at Liam as his eyes fearfully watched the house go up in flames. "Take Annie and run to Nana's!"

He snapped out of his daze and nodded as he reached down and grabbed her hand, pulling her with him as they took off running for my mom's house. I hated sending them off on their own but it was the safest thing I could do right now. I needed to get them away from the house while I went back in to save Lacey. I quickly looked over my shoulder to make sure they were still running the direction they needed to before I turned and ran into the house.

As soon as I ran through the door I was immediately engulfed in heat from the fire that was now crawling up the curtains and dancing across the ceiling. It wouldn't take long for the fire to go through the ceiling and spread to the rooms upstairs where Lacey was. I pulled my jacket up and brought it over my nose and mouth, trying to shield it from the smoke as I ran and took the stairs two at a time. It was already starting to get smokey upstairs, making it hard to see more than a few feet in front of me.

I heard a loud crash coming from the bedroom and took off in that direction. There were loud grunts as Lacey and Bill struggled though I couldn't see where they were through all of the smoke. I tried to move quickly, pushing my way through until I could figure out where they were. A few seconds later I heard a loud thud followed by a body dropping to the floor. My heart was racing as I tried to find Lacey and get her out of there.

The heat was quickly spreading through the bedroom as I saw the smoke thickening and further clouding my view. I knew better than to try to call for her and risk inhaling the smoke but I was starting to feel helpless and desperate.

"Lacey!!" I screamed, hoping she would hear me and point me in the right direction to find her.

I kept walking, my hand in front of me as I tried to figure out what was in front of me, praying that I would reach her soon. There was very little time left if we were going to get out before the fire trapped us. I could hear the sound of footsteps pounding on the floor near me and turned to see Wyatt as he crouched down beside me. We looked at each other before he nodded and went the opposite way while I crawled across the floor trying to find her. As I got lower, I was able to see a little better and felt my heart skip a beat when I looked straight ahead and saw Lacey's hand covered in blood as it laid lifelessly on the floor in front of the bed.

I raced over to her, letting go of my jacket as I was forced to take in a deep breath to catch my breath. Her face was bloody and swollen, her body unresponsive.

"She's over here!" I yelled, praying that Wyatt could hear me. I had no idea where Bill was but I didn't give a fuck at that moment. My only concern was Lacey and getting her out of there. Within a few minutes, Wyatt was by my side.

"We need to get her out of here, quickly," I said as I stood up and tried to pick her up. I felt the tightness in my lungs as I took a breath, the lack of oxygen more noticeable as the smoke filled the room. Wyatt went to the other end and picked up her feet as I lifted under her arms and we carefully carried her back down the stairs. The fire was already spreading, climbing up each baluster as it reached the top of the handrail. We walked quickly, making sure we were careful not to drop her, while also making sure we got out of the way before the fire decided to take over the stairs.

A few more steps and we were down the stairs and almost to the doorway when I glanced up and saw a tall shadowy figure at the top of the stairs. I nodded to Wyatt who quickly looked behind him and turned back around. We needed to move faster. In the distance, I could hear the sirens as help was on the way. As we walked the last few steps to the door I watched as Bill made his way down the stairs, grabbing onto the wall as he coughed and struggled to breathe.

The front door was still open which made it easier for us to rush Lacey outside and lay her down in the snow-covered grass. She was still unconscious and I feared that I might have been too late after all. I reached under her jaw and felt her neck, trying to find a pulse but couldn't. My mind was racing as I tried to remember everything that I knew about CPR and prayed that I would remember what I needed to do. I bent down and listened to see if I could hear her breathing. Nothing. I was starting to panic when I saw Bill coming out of the doorway, heading straight for us.

There was no way that I was going to let Lacey die this way so I bent down and blew two breaths into her mouth before finding the spot to start compressions. He would have to kill me and pry my dead body off of hers before I would let him hurt her again. Wyatt watched on as I continued to do CPR, oblivious to the fact that danger was quickly upon us. I tried to focus on Lacey as I felt the weight of every step Bill took as he stalked toward us. My eyes stayed focused on him as he got closer, redirecting Wyatt's attention as he turned around and sprung to his feet.

I lowered my head to do two more breaths as I heard the scuffle as Wyatt started to wrestle Bill away from us. There was a loud thud as the two rolled around on the ground, Wyatt swinging as hard as he could to keep Bill off of him. I glanced up and watched as everything happened in slow motion in front of me.

Bill had rolled out from underneath Wyatt and was now hovering over him as Wyatt clutched his side and tried to breathe through the pain of the last blow to his ribs. Bill's hand reached behind his back and pulled out a knife, bringing it around and stabbing it straight into Wyatt's chest. I gasped as I watched the blood quickly turn the snow red beneath my baby brother's body. The sirens were closer but I couldn't focus on any of that right now. I had to quickly decide who's life I was going to save- my brother's or the woman I loved.

Twenty Four

Grant

"I hate this fucking hospital," I muttered as Chase sat on one side of me and Noah sat on the other. The emergency room waiting area had quickly started to fill up as my family came in for an update on Wyatt and Lacey. I glanced off to the side where my mom sat in the corner with Liam and Annie, trying to keep them calm and distracted from what was happening. I didn't want the kids to be there and I would have done anything to keep them from being there but after I was brought in for smoke inhalation monitoring, there weren't many options since my mom was stressed with having two out of three of her children in the hospital.

"I know, brother, I know," Chase said as he wrapped an arm around my shoulders and gave me a quick hug. My feet tapped anxiously on the floor as I waited for an update.

My mind kept replaying everything that happened, even after it felt like I had told the same story a hundred times already. Between giving statements to the police, the doctors, and my family, it felt like the story was on repeat but the problem was that I didn't know how it ended which kept me anxious. After the adrenaline wore off some, I was able to process everything that happened after the stabbing and the CPR I tried to do on Lacey. From what the police told me, they were already there when it had happened and they had seen everything. Apparently, in a state of shock, I blocked out the rest.

From what I was told, the police and paramedics were there immediately as they took over working on Lacey and got Wyatt into the ambulance and rushed him to the hospital. I don't remember any of it, other than hearing a loud sound, which I was told was a gunshot. After Bill refused to drop the knife and charged at a police officer, they shot him. It was a non-lethal shot and he was currently in surgery. No one had told me anything about Lacey or her condition since we got here which was starting to piss me off. They would only give updates to immediate family, which she didn't have aside from her minor child who didn't need to hear the details of what happened, and a father who was in surgery and tried to murder her.

I stood up and started pacing the hallway, hoping that someone would tell us something soon. Off in the distance, I heard Annie talking and turned around to see her on a cell phone. I pulled my brows together in confusion as I looked at my mom who shrugged her shoulders. I walked over and squatted down in front of Annie, smiling as she smiled back at me.

"Whose phone is that, sweetheart?" I asked gently, not wanting her to feel like she was in trouble.

"It's mommy's," she said happily as I heard a female voice on the other line.

"Where did you get her phone?"

"I borrowed it," she said sadly and tucked her chin to her chest in embarrassment. "I wanted to have a phone to call mommy while I was at school in case I needed her. I didn't tell her that I took her new phone."

"It's okay sweetie, I'm sure she wouldn't mind," I reassured her. "Who are you talking to?"

"It's mommy's cousin, Kayce." She smiled and handed me the phone.

"Thank you," I whispered as I took the phone and stood up, needing to give my legs a break from being in a crouching position for so long. "Hi, I know that you don't know me, but—"

"You're Grant, the single father with the heart of gold and temper of an ox," a feminine voice said on the other line.

"I am. And you must be the wild cousin, Kayce," I joked as we both chuckled.

"How is she?" she asked, a worried tone to her voice.

"I don't know, they won't give me any details because I'm not family." I ran a hand down my face and turned back to the receptionist station, hoping someone would soon be coming over to give us an update.

"What happened? Annie said that Bill was there and that she was calling me because she was going to need to come live with me when her mommy went to heaven to be with her daddy."

I heard the crack in her voice as I struggled to keep the tears in my eyes from overflowing. I looked down at Annie and wondered how she could be so strong and brave when she knew that her world might be changing forever. Was she so used to the grief of losing a parent that it didn't bother her the way it would most people? Or was she simply in shock like the rest of us and refusing to believe it?

I quickly explained everything to Kayce and gave her a minute as I heard her crying on the other line.

"I'm so sorry that I wasn't there to protect her," she whispered.

"I keep saying the same thing. Even though I was there, I didn't get to her before he could and I feel like it's my fault that she's in this hospital, fighting for her life."

"I'm going to pack up a few things and then I'll drive down there. This is my cell phone number, will you keep me updated as you know anything?"

"Absolutely," I said as I spotted a doctor come out of the double doors from the emergency room and started walking our way. I quickly wrapped up the phone call and made sure she had my cell phone number so she could call as soon as she got to town. I held my breath and waited as the doctor glanced down at the clipboard in his hand before looking up at the waiting room full of anxious people.

"Family of Wyatt Walker?" he called out.

I reached down and offered my mom a hand to help her stand up, not sure that she was going to be able to hold herself up if there was bad news. We walked a few steps toward him as Chase came over from the other side. He nodded and offered a tight smile before he started talking.

"Wyatt suffered substantial damage from the knife wound, however after several procedures, we were able to stop the bleeding. The angle that the knife entered his chest barely missed the heart which is probably the only thing that saved his life. At this point we're waiting for him to come out of recovery, then we can further assess him. A nurse will be out later to let you know when he can start having visitors after he's been moved to a room in the ICU."

We all breathed a sigh of relief and thanked the doctor for the update as he made his way back to the emergency room. I was thankful that Wyatt was going to be okay, even if he had a long road ahead of him. We were a strong family and we could help him through this. I sat down and ran my hands down my jeans as my palms started to sweat again, wishing there was something on Lacey.

I looked outside and saw the sun starting to set, casting an orange glow across the wall which reminded me of the flames that spread quickly up the walls of my house. It hadn't even occurred to me until now that in addition to everything else, Liam and I now had nowhere to live. I didn't even know if the house was still standing, but needless to say, it wasn't safe to go into any time soon. I had been so caught up in everything else that I hadn't had a chance to talk to Liam and see how he was doing with everything.

Chase and Noah took off to go grab food for everyone and bring it back which left me alone with my mom and the kids after everyone else finally went home after we had an update on Wyatt. It was calm and quiet in the empty room, the sound deafening as I thought about how to talk to both kids about what had happened today. They were off in the corner, sitting on the floor while they played a game of Uno. Mia had been kind enough earlier to swing by with a handful of things to keep the kids entertained after she had been unsuccessful in getting them to go back to her house so she could watch them for us.

I walked over and sat down between them, smiling as I watched them play. I loved the relationship that they had with each other, a special sibling type of love that I had with my brothers. A few minutes later, their game was over and they laughed when Annie won, again.

"Do you want to play, dad?" Liam asked as he collected the cards in a pile and shuffled them.

"No thanks, bud. But I do want to talk to you guys about what happened today," I said carefully, glancing up at my mom who was pretending to read the book in her hand that had been on the same page for ten minutes now.

"Okay," they both said, neither of them showing any sort of emotion about it. Liam set the cards down between them as they both turned to look at me and waited for me to start talking.

"I know that today was very scary with the fire and everything that happened with Bill," I started, looking between both of them. "Do you guys have any questions or want to talk about anything that happened today?"

They both stared at me in silence before looking at each other as some secret passed between them.

"I have a question," Liam said, turning to face me. I nodded for him to ask and waited.

"I know that I didn't want you and Lacey to date when I first thought you guys might like each other, but that was only because I didn't want to get attached and lose another person like I lost mom. I know that she isn't my mom, but I didn't want to get close to her and then lose her. But now that she might not make it," he glanced nervously at Annie before looking back at me, "I don't want Annie to have to move away with her mom's cousin. Can Annie live with us and we can protect her since her mom and dad will both be in heaven?" His eyes filled with tears as they pleaded with me.

"It doesn't really work that way, son," I said as I tried to swallow past the lump in my throat.

"But Dad, I promised her that I would protect her. If her mom goes to heaven, who will protect her if I'm not there? She shouldn't have to keep losing everyone she loves, that's not fair!" he shouted as the tears started rolling down his face. "I don't want Lacey to die, that's not fair either!" He stood up and balled his fist.

I grabbed him and pulled him to my chest as I wrapped my arms around him while his body trembled as he cried.

"I know it's not fair, but we have to stay positive and keep praying that the doctors will make Lacey better, okay?"

"Why does it even matter? They couldn't fix mom, they're not going to fix her either. I'll never know what it's like to have a mom in my life because God doesn't want to give me one. I try to be a good kid but maybe I'm not doing something right and it makes him mad so he keeps taking the people I love from me." His words shattered my heart into a million pieces as the warm tears slid down my face. I hugged him even tighter, not having the words to say what he needed to hear. My mom set her book down on the chair beside her and folded her hands in her lap.

"Come here, Liam, Nana wants to talk to you for a minute," she said as she smiled and patted the empty chair on the other side of her. I eased up on the tight hold that I had around him as he stepped to the side and sat down, looking straight ahead instead of at my mom.

"Life has been extremely hard for you my sweet boy, and I'm so sorry that you've had to go through so many challenges in the short time you've been on this earth. But that doesn't mean that you've done anything wrong. Sometimes we are dealt really bad hands in life but it's up to us to decide what to do with them. We all experience loss and some of us experience more than others. That doesn't mean that we've done anything wrong or that we deserve bad things. That means that everyone that comes into our lives plays a role and teaches us something. For example, your mom was taken from us way too soon, however, she taught you how to love with all of your heart and I will always be thankful for that. Your dad has taught you how to be strong and to do what's right. And Annie, she's taught you how to be brave."

She smiled as she looked over at Annie who smiled back at her.

"We have to take each experience in life- the good and the bad- and decide what to do with it. It's easy to play the victim and complain about the things that we don't like but that also means that we take for granted the special things that come our way as well. We don't know what's going to happen with Lacey but either way, I can see that she's made a very special impression on you and that you have sincere feelings about her. It's okay to allow yourself to love her like a mother because I can see that she loves you like a son. And both of you know that no one would ever replace your mom. She will always hold a very special place in your heart that no one can replace."

"Thanks, Nana, sometimes I forget how smart you are," Liam said, getting a full smile from my mom in return. She wrapped an arm around his shoulders and pulled him close to her, kissing the top of his head.

"So does this mean that I will live with you if my mommy goes to heaven with my daddy? Or will I have to move away again? I don't like moving," Annie said as her voice trailed off.

"Let's not worry about that right now, okay sweet girl?" I said as I reached over and pulled her over to me, giving her the biggest hug that I could without hurting her.

"Where are we going to live now that the fire burned down our house?" Liam asked as he looked between me and my mother.

"You guys will all come stay with me again until we get everything figured out. Besides, we still have that massive puzzle to finish building," my mom said with a smile as she looked between both kids before looking up at me. I was thankful for everything she had ever done for me growing up but now that I was an adult and having to deal with things on my own, I was even more grateful for her.

A nurse came through the double doors with a solemn look on her face as she walked in our direction. My heart stopped as I held my breath and waited.

"Family of Lacey Holbrook?" she asked as she looked from me to Annie, her eyes saddening when she saw her.

"That's my mommy!" Annie exclaimed as she jumped up and ran over. I climbed to my feet and took the few steps toward her, putting my hand protectively on Annie's shoulder to stop her.

"We're not family but I'm all she has besides her daughter," I looked down at Annie. "She's living with me and we're dating," I explained, regretting that this was how the kids were going to find out about us officially dating.

"I think it would be best if you came with me so we can talk in private," she said, forcing her lips into a thin line when the smile refused to go any further. I nodded and quietly asked Annie to go sit with my mom as I sucked in a deep breath and followed the nurse through the double doors. In all of the times that I had been to this hospital, the only time I had been taken to a private area for an update was when I received the news about Renee. I followed her down the long, empty hallway, stopping briefly as she opened a door and waited for me to go inside. I took a few steps in and turned to face her.

"I'm so sorry," she started as my world shattered around me, drowning out her voice as she continued to talk.

Twenty Five

Lacey

Everything around me was white and peaceful as I walked—no floated—around, trying to figure out where to go. It wasn't like there were any signs or a check-in desk that had an angelic receptionist waiting to greet me. I tried to take a deep breath, surprised by my inability to do so. Everything felt odd, different. There was no pain or anxiety, but there was also no other feeling or emotion at the moment either.

I kept floating about, drifting along the perfect white clouds, looking around as I wondered if this was my new eternity. I had to admit that it was nice and all, but I could imagine that I would get bored with this real fast.

"Hello??" I called out, my voice sounding sweeter than usual.

There was no answer so I kept floating until I came to an area where the colors started to change. The white was thinning out and suddenly I was floating through somewhere that looked very familiar. It was a happy place, I could feel it in my bones as I waited for my memories to catch up to me. A few minutes later more details started to appear and suddenly I was back at home, in Montana. Derek was in his office, while Annie and I were in the living room playing before dinner. I remembered this night, it was one of the best nights we had shared as a family.

I smiled as I watched Annie and I sneak into his office carrying a tray of cookies and a glass of milk. He had been overly stressed with work and we wanted to do something nice for him. I watched as his face lit up, completely surprised by the gesture as he spun his chair around and picked Annie up, wrapping her in a big hug. He looked up at me, a sad smile on his face that I didn't remember being there before, then reached to the side to close his laptop.

I had remembered this night so clearly, everything playing over and over again in my head on how we had been so happy and so in love, then everything was taken so quickly from us. But as I watched it now, I noticed that the happiness I remembered before wasn't really there. I was happy and Annie was happy, but Derek wasn't. I stared at him, trying to figure out the emotion that was heavy on his face that he tried to hide behind the forced smile and then recognized it from the way my mom looked growing up. Desperation.

I shook my head, unable to process what I was seeing as I continued to float by. The scene changed again and this time I felt dread as I saw the night sky covered in rain, the darkness of the night more ominous than ever. I watched as Derek left his office, glancing down at his cell phone and closing his eyes in frustration. He had been working late and just received a text from me, asking him to come home to take care of Annie so I could go in to work. We were struggling with our finances but I had no idea he was this stressed out.

I watched as he got into the car and sat down, texting me back before putting his phone into the cup holder. He started the engine and slowly reversed as he turned on the windshield wipers to clear the rain that was coming down harder. I could feel myself panicking as I watched him shift the car to drive, never putting his seatbelt on like he always did. He drove out of the parking lot and onto the main street before getting on the highway. Derek was always a cautious driver so it shocked me when I saw the speedometer quickly moving as he pressed his foot to the gas, the car going 90 mph as the rain splattered against the windshield quicker than he could clear it.

There were no other cars around as he pressed harder on the gas, forcing the car to 100 mph. Then out of nowhere, he started talking and everything went silent as I heard his final words.

"Lacey, I'm so sorry to do this to you. I don't have any other choice. I'm drowning here, literally and figuratively, so I need to set you free. Take care of our Annie and make sure she always knows how much I love my little puppy." Tears rolled down his face as he jerked the steering wheel to the right, forcing the car to spiral out of control as it hydroplaned and flew over the side of the embankment. My hand flew to my chest as I watched in horror, seeing how my husband's life had ended.

Suddenly, I felt a presence beside me and looked up to find Derek next to me, decked out in white, floating as he looked down at the scene of the accident with me. I stared at him as I tried to find the words to say to him.

"That was one hell of an accident, but I hope you know that I didn't suffer. I mean, I was suffering a lot before it happened, but I didn't suffer when it happened. It was instant," he explained, looking over at me.

"Why the hell did you do that?" I demanded, completely shocked that he was even there and I was talking to him. Okay, maybe it was more that I was shocked that I was the one who was there and talking to him.

"We were going under fast, I couldn't get us caught up on bills. We were about to lose the house, my business was going under. There wasn't anything I could do to save us. So I took the only way out and knew that you would be okay without me, that there would be enough in the life insurance policy to take care of you and Annie."

"Why didn't you talk to me first? We could have figured this out another way, Derek," I said still completely pissed at him. "And what insurance policy?"

"That was the only way, trust me. And you have to look deeper, you'll find it if you look hard enough." He started to fade away, leaving me frustrated as I begged for him to come back and finish talking to me.

I looked back down at the accident and shook my head, needing to get away from it. I floated along, praying that the next stop would be more peaceful than the last. It didn't feel like I was actually in heaven yet but I definitely wasn't alive and talking to my dead husband while being shown the truth about what happened. It seemed to be some sort of weird parallel universe that I was starting to feel desperate to get out of.

As I kept floating, I suddenly smelled the heavenly scent of fresh-baked apple pie and smiled, remembering the days when my mom would bake one with me after school. We had an apple tree out front and she always loved to collect the apples before the birds could get them, then we'd go inside and bake a pie. She would make two and let me sneak a few bites out of the secret one before my dad got home, then we would serve the other one after dinner. I loved our secret pie and enjoyed the afternoons when we would sit outside and read books on a blanket under the tree while eating it before dinner.

I floated faster, glancing around the kitchen from my childhood, relieved when I saw my mom bent over, reaching into the oven to pull out a pie. She turned around and I gasped, her face as beautiful as I remembered, frozen in time. As a child, I remembered her face bright with happiness but now that I really got a look at her and had experienced my own traumas, I saw the pain beneath the smile. Her eyes were tired and her body looked frail and weak as she turned to grab the plates from the cabinet and a row of bruises showed beneath her shirt as it lifted.

"You better get in here before the pie gets cold," she said over her shoulder before turning to smile at me.

"Hey mama, it's me, Lacey," I said as I floated in and stood on the other side of the table.

"I know who you are, sweetheart." She smiled and set the plates on the table that was now between us.

"You can see me? Like I can see you? And we can hear each other?" I asked, completely confused by what was going on. This was all a crazy, surreal dream. It had to be.

"Of course I can, silly girl. I've been watching you for years, I just didn't think I would get a chance to talk to you so soon," she said worriedly.

"I didn't think I would get to talk to you this soon either," I admitted as I shrugged. "Does this mean that I'm dead?"

She looked me over and gave me a quick shake of the head.

"Nope, not dead. Not yet."

"Well, then how am I here and talking to you?"

"Our imagination is a very powerful thing, I've always told you that," she said as she grabbed a knife and started to cut into the pie.

"You're telling me," I sighed. "So what do I do now? Just keep wandering around, talking to dead people?"

"I suppose that's up to you, you're the only one who can know what your heart truly wants."

"It's not that easy."

"Why not?" she asked, setting the knife on the table next to the pie.

"Because, I'm stuck here, in this world, or whatever it is."

"So what do you want?" She tilted her head to the side and smiled as if she already knew what I was going to say.

"I want Annie. And Grant. And Liam. I want to live and not be in fear of dad. I want to get past the guilt I feel over Derek's death. I want to be happy and live a life you would have been proud of."

"Then what are you waiting for?" she asked as she reached over and shoved me in my chest.

"What the hell was that for?!"

"Clear!" She shoved me again, harder. I watched as she started to change before me. The last thing I saw before everything went bright white was her hand reaching out and shoving me one last time, harder this time as she yelled *clear* and I fell backward.

Twenty Six

Grant- 2 Weeks Later

"What kind of Valentine's Day cards do you want to get, Annie?" my mom asked as she shuffled around the kitchen, getting breakfast ready for the kids. I glanced behind me as I reached into the fridge and saw the sad look on her face when she considered the question.

"I don't think I want to do Valentine's Day cards this year," she said quietly as she sat down.

"Why not?" I asked gently as I grabbed the gallon of milk and closed the fridge. Her sweet eyes looked up at me with the same sadness I had seen for the past two weeks since Lacey was taken to the hospital.

"Because it's a day of love and I don't feel like being lovey when I'm still so sad."

"I get it," I sighed and my shoulders fell. "And it's okay to be sad, sweetheart."

Liam wrapped an arm around her shoulders and walked her over to the couch where they sat down and watched cartoons while we finished making breakfast.

"Poor thing," my mom whispered only loud enough for me to hear. "This has to be so hard for her. First her dad, now her mom."

I nodded my head in agreement, unable to say anything about what had happened. These past few weeks had been difficult and trying with everything going on all at once. From losing the house to Lacey and Wyatt being in the hospital, it was all too much and my recent focus had been on getting the kids and I settled in at my mom's house while the insurance company worked the claim on mine. There were so many questions about what we would do next— would we knock down the rest of the house that was barely standing and rebuild? Would we walk away and find somewhere new to live? And the question that ate at me daily was whether Annie would keep living with us or move five hours away to live with Lacey's cousin Kayce.

"I heard that Wyatt might be over later today, he's slowly trying to get around on his own again," my mom said, continuing on in a one-sided conversation which she was pretty used to these days since I had become the worst company to have around.

"I'm happy to hear that he's doing better, seems his recovery is moving along at the right pace," I offered, trying to force myself to engage.

My cell phone started to ring, startling both of us the way it did anytime it rang lately. It seemed we were always waiting for a call with bad news to come. The other shoe to drop. I glanced down and saw the phone number for the hospital displayed on the screen and blew out a breath. I caught my mom's eye, a worried look on her face as we nodded at each other and I stepped outside to take the phone call.

"Hello?" I answered, trying to brace myself. I hadn't heard anything in over a week so I was on pins and needles that this was the call I had been dreading would come.

"Grant Walker?" a woman asked.

"Yes, that's me."

"My name is Marie and I'm calling from Haven Brook hospital, we have an update for you on Lacey Holbrook."

I sucked in a deep breath, allowing the cold air to burn through my lungs.

"Yes?"

"She's awake."

Twenty Seven

Lacey

I listened as the doctor talked, glancing over his shoulder every few minutes to check to see if Grant or Annie were coming. I was so anxious to see them and wrap my arms around Annie in the biggest hug ever, never letting her go. The doctor explained the multiple operations I had undergone as well as the blood transfusion I needed after everything was said and done. I nodded along, trying to take in everything while my mind wandered to more important things. Like my family.

"Do you have any questions for me?" he asked as he set my chart down on the counter behind him and folded his hands in his lap, pulling the crisp, white coat tight across his shoulders.

"Honestly, I have no idea. That's a lot to take in and for a minute there, I thought I died. I had this crazy dream where I was walking around in this white cloudy area and I got to see and talk to my dead husband and mother," I laughed, brushing it off as being as ridiculous as it sounded. His face looked grim as he pulled his lips into a thin line. "What is it?" I asked, concerned.

"There were a few times that we did lose you, and after the last one, we weren't sure that we were going to get you back. You gave us quite a scare."

I tried to process what he was saying but it seemed so unreal. I had heard of people having similar near-death experiences but I never would have believed they were real had I not had one myself. Part of me still believed that it was just a dream that was playing tricks on my mind, but the other part needed to believe it was real so I could finally have the answers that I was looking for. I wasn't ready to give up so easily on the idea that easy that my dead husband had offered me some insight into his final days just yet.

"Well, if you don't have any questions for me, then I'll be on my way. Your nurse can page me if anything comes up." He stood up and grabbed my chart from the counter.

"Do you know when I will be able to go home?" I asked.

"Given everything that you've been through, I would like to monitor you for another 24-48 hours, just to make sure you're in the clear. After that, we can talk about discharging you if you're ready."

"Sounds good, thank you," I said as he started to walk out the door. "Sorry," I squealed as I held my hand up for him to stop. "Will someone let my family know they can come back to see me now? I'm sure they're tired of sitting in the waiting room." I smiled warmly as I thought about seeing Annie.

"I'm sorry, there isn't anyone in the waiting room," he said gently as he walked back into the room and stood next to my bed. My face fell with disappointment as I looked up at him and tilted my head to the side. Why would they leave?

"No one?" I asked as my brows pulled together in confusion. He shook his head no.

"Why? Did someone force them to leave?" None of this made any sense. Grant and I were doing well before everything happened, wouldn't he be worried about me enough to stay? And did he take my daughter away from me as well? Then I realized that I had no idea what happened to Bill and whether Annie and Grant were even okay. Panic flooded through me as I tried to remember everything that happened and couldn't. How did I get out of the house? Did Annie make it out? Did everyone die in the fire except me? The monitor next to my bed started to beep loudly causing concern to flash across his face as he stepped closer.

"Everything is alright but I need you to try to calm down for me, okay?" He sat back down where he had been a few minutes ago and scooted his chair closer to me.

"Lacey, do you remember anything about what happened and why you're in the hospital?" he asked as he studied my face.

"I remember my father attacking me. He had me pinned to the wall by my throat and then I started to lose consciousness but not before he threw me to the floor and punched me repeatedly." I turned my head away and lowered my voice, embarrassed to be saying the words out loud.

"What happened after that?"

"I don't know, everything started to get foggy. I couldn't breathe, there was a lot of smoke in the room. Then I guess I passed out."

He nodded quickly and rubbed his lips back and forth together.

"Did my family die in the fire?" I asked, the words mixing with the bile that was rising in my throat.

"There was one casualty, yes." His eyes softened and he waited for me to take another breath as the alarms on the monitor started beeping again. I looked at him with tears in my eyes, begging him to tell me without making me ask.

"Your father did not survive his injuries. I'm so sorry. There were complications from the gunshot wound as well as respiratory distress from the smoke inhalation. We did everything we could but we weren't able to save him."

I covered my mouth with my hand as a loud sob escaped and my body started to tremble. *Gunshot wound?!?*

"But the rest…?"

"They're fine," he assured me with a smile.

"Then why aren't they here? I want to see my daughter, please," I begged.

"They stayed here for a while, actually longer than I've ever seen a family stick around. But after the first week, we asked them to go home and try to get the kids back to some level of normal."

"First week?" I pulled my head back in shock and frowned.

"Lacey, do you remember me telling you that you've been here for two weeks and that you've been in a coma until now?" He tilted his head to the side and waited to see if anything clicked as I remembered him telling me. I felt my cheeks blush as I got embarrassed that I didn't remember because I hadn't been paying attention. I was too distracted with thoughts of Annie.

"I'm so sorry, I wasn't paying very good attention earlier. My mind was preoccupied with seeing my daughter."

"I completely understand, I'll make sure the nurse calls Mr. Walker and asks that he bring her to see you. Try to rest and take it easy, your body has been through a lot in two weeks."

He smiled and walked out the door leaving me feeling overwhelmed with the massive amount of information he had just given me. There were still a thousand other details that I needed to know about what happened but right now, I was only focused on one thing. Seeing Annie.

Twenty Eight

Grant

"Come on guys, let's go!" I called through the house as I stood at the front door, ready to leave and get to the hospital to see Lacey. I didn't know anything other than that she was awake. After two weeks of agonizing over everything that happened and beating myself up on all of the things I should have done differently, she was finally awake.

I was an intense combination of excited and anxious, feeling like I might jump out of my skin at any moment. I had already called Kayce and given her the update as the kids worked on getting ready to go. Annie wanted to take the special cards she had been making for Lacey with us and Liam offered to help her get them together. It was adorable and so heart-warming but also slightly irritating that we were taking even longer to get out of the house and to the hospital. I had waited for this moment for what felt like forever and I didn't want to wait any longer.

I had no idea what we were supposed to expect with Lacey as I made sure the kids were buckled in before smiling at my mom in the passenger seat as I flew out of the driveway and made my way to the hospital as if our lives depended on it. These past few weeks had been devastating and heart-wrenching on all of us, so maybe our lives did depend on it. Maybe we all needed to see her and know she was okay so we could start to feel okay again ourselves.

A few minutes later the truck slid into a parking space and everyone climbed out, excitement radiating off of all of us. I prayed that Lacey was going to be the same as she was before the attack but I had to prepare myself that she might not be. I had vivid flashbacks of coming to this very hospital to see Renee, expecting to see the woman I knew and loved, but instead, I saw the shell of that woman as cancer ate away at every tiny bit of her that was left. I pushed the thoughts out of my head as I headed for the receptionist's desk and asked what room Lacey was in.

The long hallway through the ICU was empty and eerily quiet as we walked quickly to the room number the nurse had given me. I knocked gently on the door before opening it and stepping inside. I held my hand back and asked the kids to stay put for a second so I could make sure it was okay for them to go in. I had no idea what to expect since she was still in the ICU and wanted to be prepared before the kids were possibly blindsided. I walked a few steps in and gently pulled the curtain to the side to find Lacey leaning back against the pillow with her eyes closed. She looked beautiful, even with the faded bruises on her face and the ones on her neck that made my stomach knot. I took a few more steps toward her, trying to be quiet as I debated whether we should let her rest and come back later.

Her eyes fluttered open and her face lit up as she saw me. She struggled to push herself up into a seated position as I rushed over to help her.

"You're here," she whispered happily, looking up at me as if I were a figment of her imagination. I gently reached over and brushed my thumb against her cheek.

"There's nowhere else in the world I would rather be," I said as I smiled down at her. "I have someone else who is dying to see you."

I planted a quick kiss on her forehead before scurrying off to get my mom and the kids. I pulled the curtain back and stood to the side before I opened the door and waited for Annie to come in. I could hear Liam and my mom coaxing her to go in, my heart breaking for her knowing how scared she was of what she would find on the other side. A few seconds later, her head popped in around the corner and her eyes went wide when she saw Lacey.

"Mommy!!" she cried as she ran across the room and went to the side of the bed where Lacey was reaching over, arms wide open as she waited to hug Annie. I wiped a tear away as I saw them hold each other, Lacey's own rushing down her face as she held her daughter as tight as she could.

"I was so scared, mommy, I didn't want to lose you," Annie cried as she held onto Lacey.

I wrapped an arm around Liam's shoulders as we stayed off to the side with my mom, giving the girls some time together.

"I know, princess, I'm so sorry you had to go through that. But I'm okay, baby." Lacey rubbed her hand up and down Annie's back, pulling the IV in her hand in the process. I saw the moment she flinched as it pulled against the tape and remembered that we still didn't know how Lacey was feeling. Having been in a coma for two weeks, there were a lot of unknowns that the doctors had been waiting on before they could confirm if she would be able to go back to her normal self. Who knew what normal would be at this point?

Annie pulled back and sat on the edge of Lacey's bed, clutching her stuffed puppy to her chest.

"I tried not to be scared, but then daddy came to visit me in a dream, and he told me that you had talked to him recently and you were mad at him. He didn't know if you were going to have to stay in heaven with him, but he wanted me to know that he would still watch over me. So I felt better knowing that I had both Daddy and Grant, to watch over me. I really missed you though."

Lacey's face fell as she listened to Annie and I wondered if it had upset her to hear about Annie's dream. I had known about it from when she first told me the next morning, but maybe it bothered Lacey because it was her ex-husband and she knew how hard it was for Annie to lose her father.

"Did daddy say anything else to you in the dream?" she asked quietly.

"He mentioned that you were going to be looking for something and that was it. It didn't really make sense," Annie shrugged and Lacey nodded before glancing up at me.

"Hey, Liam," Lacey said with a smile as she looked down and caught his eye. I patted his shoulder and smiled when he rushed over to go see Lacey. Annie scooted over on the bed and left a space for Liam to reach up and get a hug from Lacey. It warmed my heart to see how much they loved each other. My mom sniffled next to me as she tried to wipe her tears away with the back of her hand. I reached over and wrapped my arm around her, pulling her in for a hug as I said a quick thank you that we were all in this room together, crying tears of happiness.

A little while later my mom had taken the kids down to the cafeteria for ice cream to give Lacey and me some time to talk. I had offered to go and let her get some rest but she quickly rejected that idea and told me that she didn't want to be away from any of us, ever again. She leaned against the pillows that I had fluffed and tucked behind her as I went over everything that had happened. She had a few questions but overall she seemed to be taking everything in and processing it.

I watched as the tears filled her eyes when I told her about Wyatt and smiled when she laughed after I told her that he hit on every nurse who tried to take care of him that they eventually had to rotate in all of the male nurses until he was discharged. We talked about her father and the complications during surgery but I had a hard time figuring out how she felt about the news that he had died. She sucked in a deep breath and held it as I talked, slowly blowing it out when I told her that the police would be in touch with her soon to discuss the next steps.

"So, did the house burn completely down?" she asked quietly as her fingers ran along the vein in my hand as I cuddled up next to her in the hospital bed.

"It's not *completely* down, but it's not safe to enter at this point. There's no telling when the rest of it will collapse."

"Grant, I am so sorry," she sighed heavily and looked up at me. "I am responsible for all of this and I feel terrible about it! I got your brother stabbed, your house burned down—literally everything is my fault."

She dropped her head and looked down in shame before I gently pressed my finger under her chin and lifted it.

"Lacey, none of this was your fault. You can't take the blame for anything that happened. And everyone is okay, you're safe, and you never have to live in fear of your dad again." I smiled and watched as her face changed like she was trying to recall something.

"What is it?" I asked, pulling to the side to see her better.

"Nothing," she said, still lost in thought. A few seconds later she turned to look at me and asked, "Did my dad die right away?"

I paused for a minute before answering her, wondering why she was asking. But if it helped her to move on by knowing all of the details, I didn't see what it would hurt to give them to her.

"No, he didn't die right away. He was actually in recovery, then had some complications and was rushed back to surgery. That was when he passed."

"Where was I when it was happening?"

"Um, gosh, I don't know," I drug a hand through my hair as I tried to remember the timeline of everything that had happened over the past few weeks. "Let me think about it for a minute."

I closed my eyes and tried to remember the details of everything then suddenly it came rushing back to me.

"You were in surgery and they were having a hard time stabilizing you. I know for a fact because I remember begging God to spare your life and let you live. I asked if he had to take one, that he make the right choice and take the one who didn't deserve to be here anymore."

Her shoulders fell and she looked away from me.

"Why do you ask?" I pushed, hoping to get her talking about whatever was weighing on her mind.

"It's nothing, it's silly more than anything," she paused and looked at me, unsure of whether to tell me. "I had this crazy, intense dream that I got to talk to Derek and my mom. She asked what I wanted and I told her that I wanted my family—you, Annie, and Liam and that I didn't want to live in fear of my father anymore. Next thing I knew she was shoving me in my chest and shouting clear as the dream ended."

I felt a chill run up my spine and tried to shake it off.

"Maybe it wasn't a dream, maybe it was you getting a chance to talk to her?"

"Maybe," she shrugged. "I talked to Derek as well, and if it wasn't a dream, then I saw how he died and everything that led up to it."

"You mean the accident?" I asked as I pulled her closer to me when I saw her shiver.

"Yeah, except in my dream, it wasn't an accident. He purposely crashed his car and killed himself so Annie and I would be taken care of with the insurance policy he had."

"That's intense," I whispered, running my hand up and down her arm as she laid her head on my chest and talked.

"Very." She let out a heavy sigh and sunk deeper into my side.

"But if it wasn't just a dream, if it was real—then I have to accept the fact that my husband didn't die on accident. He told me in my dream that he was drowning and that everything was about to go under. We were going to lose the house, he was going to lose his business—there wasn't anything he could other than kill himself to set us free. I could feel his pain and truly saw it in my dream which is a total mind game compared to how I remember him before he died. How am I supposed to know what the truth is? How will I ever know whether my husband died by accident or if he purposely killed himself to try to protect me and Annie?" Her voice started to rise as panic started to take hold.

"I don't know that there ever will be a way to know what the truth is," I offered as I looked down at her and met her gaze. "But if he did do it to make sure that you guys would be taken care of with the life insurance policy, then I guess you have to see that as being pretty selfless and brave. To love someone so much that you would make the ultimate sacrifice to make sure they were okay, that's a lot of love, Lacey."

"But there wasn't a life insurance policy, or at least if there was, I know nothing about it."

"Is there someone you can ask about it? Like whoever handled his estate?" I asked, remembering how overwhelming everything had been when Renee died, even after we had purposely taken the time to set everything up to make it easier.

"His brother was supposed to handle everything but I couldn't deal with it when it happened so I asked him to just do what he needed to and didn't ask any questions. He mentioned that he needed our bank account number, but I just figured it was so he could pay for expenses, like the burial."

"Have you checked that bank account, Lacey?" I asked softly, watching as it hit her. She brought a hand to her mouth and covered it as she shook her head.

"No, I haven't. Honestly, I didn't think much about it because I knew the balance in our account was high from selling the house so I didn't have to bother with logging in to check the account." She turned to look up at me, tears in her eyes again. "I'm so stupid, I should have checked and I shouldn't have ignored all of the phone calls from his brother after the funeral. I was in so much pain that I couldn't talk to any of his family, it was just too much at the time."

"Well, once we get you home, we'll check on everything and I can help you get in touch with his brother to make sure everything is wrapped up."

"Where is home?" she asked as she turned her head up to look at me.

"Right now, the kids and I have been living with my mother. But now that you're back, I wanted to talk to you about what you would like to do—assuming we are past the phase of you still trying to sneak out and book a hotel?" I teased as she blushed and giggled.

"We can either buy a new house once the insurance wraps up the claim or we can build a house together. Something that we both want, something for *our* family."

She lifted her finger to her mouth and tapped it a few times as she thought about it.

"I think I want to build a house with you, Mr. Walker. Something big and beautiful for our perfectly blended family."

She lightly reached up and pressed her lips to mine, offering me the sweetest kiss that I've ever had.

Epilogue

Grant- Eight Months Later

"Don't just sit there, rip them open!" I taunted as the kids sat in front of the Christmas tree in their matching pajamas. Lacey had picked out matching family pajamas for us to wear as a family for our first Christmas together in our new house. She was curled up in my lap as we rocked gently in my chair, watching the kids look at their presents as they decided which to open first.

We had decided to live with my mom while we knocked down the old house and built a brand new one. Everyone had a say in what they wanted with the new house and we tried to make sure we could accommodate all of them. Annie had wanted room in the backyard for a swing set and Liam had wanted a treehouse, which was rather impossible given that there were no trees in the backyard. So we compromised and got a giant swing set that came with a built-in treehouse that seemed to please everyone for the time being.

Lacey had asked for an oversized tub and larger master bathroom than we had before, which was fine by me as long as she agreed to part with those god-awful face masks. She wiggled her feet with excitement as Liam opened a gift from her and I rolled my eyes at the socks she was wearing, red with a giant cartoon penguin right smack in the center of her foot. I wanted to build a shop in the back, a place that I could work on projects and build things but after we added in the stuff for the kids, there wasn't much room back there for an additional structure.

THE TIES THAT BIND

As the contractors were building the house, I had come by to check in and see how things were going when I realized there was a huge mistake in the framing they had done compared to the blueprints we had given them. Everything else was perfect with a large kitchen and dining room area downstairs with an open concept that flowed into the living room so Lacey could keep an eye on the kids while she was cooking. Down the hall toward the extra bathroom, there was an additional room that we hadn't talked about.

I asked to see the blueprints and was surprised when they handed me a copy I hadn't seen before. At the back of the house, where we had agreed everything would end, was a new room that Lacey had added and labeled "man cave". The room spread the entire length of the house and was larger than I had talked about with my original idea. The room was separated into smaller spaces including a home theater that we could all enjoy on our weekly movie night, as well as a separate office that was just mine.

I had rushed back to my mom's house and pulled Lacey to the side, asking if she knew about the new plans. Which in hindsight was rather stupid, given that she was the one who had given them to the contractor to replace the original one. She smiled warmly as she heard the excitement in my voice, my mind still completely blown that she would do such a thoughtful thing for me.

The additional room had been way out of budget, but then I found that there were other amenities that we had decided to skip because of cost, that Lacey had gone back and added in without telling me. My heart was bursting at the seam as I realized how much she wanted to give us everything we had ever wanted in our house. While I tried to be logical and rational, she thought it was time to live a little on the wild side and splurge a little.

After she was discharged we had looked at her bank accounts and spoke to Derek's brother who had confirmed that he did have a life insurance policy in place but that he hadn't been able to file a claim until Lacey was ready because they required her signature. The process was rather quick after that and Lacey felt oddly at peace with everything she had learned from his brother who had to handle things after he passed. It seemed no one really knew the real Derek until after he was gone. Maybe that was true about all of us?

Lacey had put the bulk of the money into savings and used some of it to pay for the extra things she wanted for the house, as well as buying new furniture. The kids enjoyed their quick shopping spree as they picked out stuff for their own bedrooms, no longer having to share one. Lacey had insisted on an extra bedroom which seemed odd given she had given me an office downstairs as well as the massive backyard set up for the kids. When I asked her about it, she simply said, "you never know when we might need it."

The kids continued to shriek as they opened their presents, excitement filling the room and making my heart full and happy. I had already talked to the kids about it and they knew my plan but my palms started to sweat as I patted my pocket of my joggers to make sure the ring was still there. Liam looked up at me and raised his eyebrows, looking for the clue that we had agreed would be the signal that I was about to do it. I winked and his face lit up as he looked over at Annie and winked. Lacey smiled and looked between the kids, curious about their sudden odd behavior. She turned to look at me with a puzzled expression on her face before Liam called her name and pulled her attention away from me.

"Lacey, can you come help me open this? I really want to check it out," Liam said, looking past her as he made eye contact with me and attempted another wink. I chuckled as I watched how terrible he was with being subtle as Lacey climbed off my lap and glanced back at me.

"Sure, kiddo, what do you got?"

I waited until she was bent over by Liam, looking down at whatever random toy he was pretending to need help with. I sucked in a deep breath and pulled the ring out of my pocket, smiling at Annie as she watched, her face lit up with a huge smile. I dropped down to one knee and waited for Lacey to turn around.

"Never mind, I think I got it," Liam said with another wink to me.

Lacey stood up and put her hands on her hips as she looked between the kids.

"Okay, what's going on?" she asked before she turned around and spotted me. A small gasp escaped her throat as she clutched a hand to her chest. "Grant?" her voice trailed off.

"Lacey, I have loved you through so much already that I can't imagine spending a single minute apart from you. I want to spend the rest of our lives together, eating fried chicken and playing Monopoly, as we grow old together and watch our children grow up. Will you do me the honor of being my wife?" I held up the ring and watched the tears roll down her face as a faint blush flushed her cheeks, knowing she knew damn well what I was talking about with fried chicken and Monopoly.

"Yes!" she cried and gave me her hand. Mine slightly trembled as she watched me slide the ring onto her finger. I quickly stood up and wrapped her in my arms, swinging her around as she giggled and held onto me.

Thirty minutes later we had all finished opening our presents from each other as we sat in a giant pile of torn-up wrapping paper. I pulled Lacey over to me and wrapped my arm around her as I looked at the beautiful children we now shared.

"Did everyone get what they wanted for Christmas?" I asked, watching their angelic faces in the glow of the lights from the tree.

"Yeah, thank you guys so much, I can't wait to start playing with all of this," Liam said excitedly. Annie looked down at the worn-out puppy in her lap and nervously played with its ear.

"Annie, was there something you wanted for Christmas that you didn't get?" I asked gently, trying to think back to the list that Lacey and I had worked off together when we did our shopping. If there was something she wanted that she didn't get, it must not have been on the list she had given to us to give to Santa. Lacey tilted her head and waited for Annie to answer.

"No, I got everything I asked for," she said with disappointment heavy in her voice.

"But was there something that you *wanted* that you didn't get?" Lacey coaxed, pulling Annie's attention over to her as her lower lip trembled as she tried to hold back the tears.

"I asked Santa for something special when I saw him at the store. He said he would do his best to make it happen but I guess he just wasn't able to."

"What did you ask for?" Lacey and I asked at the same time, then laughed. Annie looked down then glanced over at Liam.

"It's okay, you should tell them," he said quietly and I immediately wondered what secret they were sharing and what she could possibly want that meant this much to her.

"I asked Santa for a baby," she whispered.

Lacey's head pulled back in confusion as I leaned forward to try to hear her better.

"Like a baby doll?" Lacey asked.

"No, like a real baby. I asked that Santa would bring me a new baby brother or sister," she sighed. "Well, technically, I asked him to bring one of each." She giggled and looked over at Liam as she brought the stuffed puppy up to her mouth to try to hide the smile.

"Honey, it doesn't really work that way," I started to explain. Lacey and I had talked about expanding our family several times and agreed that when the time was right, we would know it. There had been so much going on these past few months that it didn't seem like now would be the time to add to what we already had on our plate.

"I know, I'm sorry I asked," Annie apologized and looked down again. I looked over at Lacey, wondering what she wanted to do to try to make Annie feel better. We had been trying to work together as a team since we became an instant family but I was feeling completely lost on how to make a little girl feel better about Santa not granting her wish to have a real-life newborn sibling.

There was a calm look of peace on Lacie's face as she smiled sweetly at Annie before she turned to look at me and placed a hand on her stomach.

"Actually…" she said slowly as she caught my eye and looked deep into my eyes. "I have one more gift for you, but it's a little hard to unwrap…"

I nodded as I waited, unsure of what to think.

"I'm pregnant," she said cheerfully, a smile stretching across her face. "With twins."

I felt as if everything around me shifted at once as the kids got up and jumped up and down excitedly as they celebrated the news. I reached forward and grabbed Lacey, pulling her into me as I ran a hand along her stomach.

"I think that might be the best gift you could ever give me," I whispered in her ear as my heart burst with happiness.

A Very Haven Christmas

Samantha Baca

A VERY HAVEN CHRISTMAS

<u>One</u>

"Oh my," I whispered as he planted kisses down my neck and along my collar bone. It had been so long since a man had touched me and I felt like my body was on fire. My heart raced as my fingers itched to reach out and touch his body. For a man approaching sixty, he had the stamina and finesse of a man in his twenties.

I felt his hand slowly move up to caress my breast under the warmth of my knit sweater. I glanced to the side, checking the time on the clock that sat next to the bed on the nightstand. The kids would be here in less than thirty minutes which meant I needed to get him out of the house before they got here.

"We have to stop, the kids will be here soon for Christmas dinner," I breathed as his body pressed down on mine, the bulge in his pants forcing a whimper to escape from my throat.

"Okay," he breathed as he kept kissing, slowly dipping his tongue beneath the top of my sweater that he had been pulled down low enough to almost show my bra. "But I need to give you my Christmas gift before I go."

"We already exchanged gifts, remember that nice watch I gave you and the beautiful necklace you bought me?" I giggled as he nipped at the lace of my bra.

"Yeah, both of those were great. But I'm about to give you the gift you really want, the gift that neither of us can get enough of." His voice was low and husky, filled with arousal.

I planted my hand against his chest and popped up on my elbows as I looked at him. He stopped, confused as he tried to figure out what happened. "Wait— you mean to tell me that you're cooking dinner for me today?" I joked as I struggled to keep my face straight. I watched the smile pull across his gorgeous face, up to his golden-brown eyes.

"You know I would in a heartbeat, sweetheart," he said as he leaned forward and kissed my forehead. "But we're not ready for your kids to find out about us yet."

"I know," I sighed as I laid back down and looked up at him. "I'm sorry."

I felt an enormous amount of guilt that I had been hiding my relationship from my kids for three months but there had been so much going on that it never felt like the right time to tell them that I was seeing someone. He was the first person I had dated since their father passed away eleven years ago, and honestly, I never thought I would ever love another man the way I had loved my husband.

"Don't be sorry, it'll happen when the time is right," he assured me as he lifted himself off of me and climbed over to the empty side of the bed. The mood was totally killed and I felt terrible about it.

"I better get going," he said, smiling as he bent down and picked up his jeans from the floor, sliding them up his muscular legs and zipping them as my eyes focused on the bulge that was still there. His chuckle forced my eyes up to look at him. "Don't worry, I'll come back when the coast is clear and we'll finish our gift exchange," he teased.

I stayed in bed for a few minutes, watching him finish dressing as he pulled the t-shirt down over his head, hiding the perfectly sculpted abs that I had run my tongue down not that long ago. This man was far from anything I had ever pictured, even in my wildest fantasies after reading my romance novels. He was pure masculinity with an erotic twist that made me weak in the knees.

A few minutes later I had climbed out of bed and put on the rest of my clothes, giggling when I remembered making love with nothing on but my Christmas sweater. It was a holly jolly good time, to say the least. I stood in front of the mirror as I carefully ran the wand of mascara through my lashes before adding a light peach colored lipstick to counter the flush that was still lingering on my face. I tucked a strand of gray hair behind my ear, debating whether I should make an appointment to get it colored soon? Maybe a light brown color? Take me back to my younger days...

I walked down the hall holding hands with the man who had started to become such an important part of my life. As we reached the front door, I turned to hug him as he wrapped his arms around my waist. I reached up and locked my hands behind his head as I tilted my head to kiss him. His lips were as soft as they were full, and my absolute favorite things to kiss on him. Okay, maybe my second favorite. Within seconds our G-rated kiss had quickly turned into a groping session as we devoured each other's mouths and ran our hands over every body part we could reach. His hands were firmly dug into the flesh of my ass as he kissed my neck when the doorbell rang.

We quickly pulled apart and stared at the door in horror. There was no way that it was already four o'clock, last I checked we still had at least twenty minutes left. I ran my palms down the front of my jeans, wiping away the sweat as I struggled to figure out what to do next.

"Want me to sneak out the back?" he asked quietly, pulling my attention away from the door. I stood staring at him with panic on my face as I thought about what to do. Suddenly the doorbell rang again, sending my heart into a frenzy.

"Mom, is everything okay?" Chase called from the other side before he knocked loudly on the wooden door.

"It's fine," I whispered and shook my head, my hands trembling as I slowly walked forward and turned the lock, counting each second as it passed by. I opened the door and tried to force my face to smile anything other than the terrified, creepy smile that was plastered to it.

"Hey, are you okay?" Chase asked as his brows pulled together while he balanced the newborn car seat on his forearm. I glanced to the side to find Mia watching me with curiosity as she tried to figure out what was going on as well.

"Yeah, I'm fine, I was just in the middle of cooking and didn't expect anyone so soon," I lied. "Come on in, it's freezing out there and I don't want my grandbabies turned into popsicles," I joked as I stepped to the side, panic filling me as I knew what they were about to say. They walked in, Mia first as she held Rylee on her hip with a diaper bag strapped across her shoulder. As they walked in, both of their eyes went wide when they saw that I had company. Chase pulled his head back in confusion before looking at Mia as if she had the answer.

"Lieutenant Dickson, what are you doing here?" Chase asked before looking over at me while he gently set the car seat down next to the couch on the floor. "Is everything okay? Did something happen?"

I felt my cheeks flush as I looked away from my son and glanced at Mia. Her eyes went wide with amusement, her eyebrows nearly shooting off her head when she quickly caught on to what was happening. Buck looked at me, raising his eyebrows as he waited for me to answer.

"Um, Buck is here to check my furnace," I said quickly, looking back and forth between the three of them. I saw the slightest smile pull at his lips as he looked away and ran a hand down the trimmed gray beard that made him look like a sexy silver fox.

"Your furnace?" Chase questioned as he folded his arms across his chest. "Since when does our local law enforcement come out to check furnaces?"

"I was in the neighborhood and your mom mentioned she was having some trouble so I stopped by," Buck said and shrugged as if it was no big deal. "Not to worry, I've checked everything out and she's definitely getting plenty of heat." He turned his head to wink at me, leaning in to give me a quick, friendly hug before saying goodbye to Chase and Mia. The door closed behind him, leaving us in awkward silence.

"I still don't get why you had the Lieutenant come by to check your furnace? You know I would have helped you with it when I got here," Chase said as he tried to make sense of it. I watched as Mia smiled and chuckled before handing Rylee to Chase.

"Don't worry about it, baby. I have a feeling your mom isn't going to have any cold nights from here on out." She laughed as she wrapped her arm in mine and walked with me to the kitchen, glancing over her shoulder at Chase who was still clueless.

Two

"It's not what you think it is," I blurted out as Mia and I walked into the kitchen, keeping my voice low enough so Chase wouldn't hear me. As the oldest of my rowdy boys, he was also the most protective and the one I worried about the most when I thought about how they would take the news of Buck and I dating.

"Why, Connie, I have no idea what you're talking about," Mia chuckled and smiled at me over her shoulder as she reached into the fridge to put away the bottles of milk she had just taken out of the diaper bag. She closed the door and turned around, smiling at me like two girls in the schoolyard who were sharing secrets about their crush.

There was a knock on the front door, followed by Chase getting up to open it. I glanced at the clock on the stove and saw that it was after four, which meant everyone should be showing up around the same time now. I could hear several different voices floating through from the living room and hoped that this would be my saving grace from having to admit what Mia already knew. I forced a quick smile, as I tried to stop the blush that was creeping up my cheeks again before I turned and walked into the living room to greet everyone as they got settled in.

"Merry Christmas my babies!" I squealed as I leaned forward and opened my arms to Liam and Annie as they came running over. I wrapped them in a big hug and kissed the top of their heads before they rushed off to go finish their rounds of hellos. The door opened again and I saw Noah and Jade walk in with Wyatt right behind them. I quickly hugged and said hello to Grant and Lacey before they made their way into the kitchen to put the pies on the table that Lacey had made.

I watched as my family all shuffled about in front of me, holding a hand to my chest as I wished my husband was here to see this. We always talked about how wonderful it would be to watch our boys grow up and start families of their own and how fun it would be to have our house filled with laughter as the kids played on Christmas day. It broke my heart that he never got to see any of this.

Noah and Jade were the last to come in and I was so happy to see them. Noah had been like having a fourth son all these years. He and Chase were inseparable since the day they first met each other. He had always been a part of our family and I was so proud that he was now sharing his family with me. I rubbed my hands together excitedly as Noah unstrapped Asher from his car seat and picked him up, letting him wake up a little before bringing him over to see me. Jade carefully leaned over and kissed his sweet face, gently rubbing her hand across his cheek. I loved watching her with him, the pure love that radiated out of her for her son.

When they first had him, they were so stressed out with finding the perfect name for him. They wanted something that would honor him as their rainbow baby and showed the strength and determination that he had from the start when Jade was told she would likely never be able to conceive. I had suggested Asher after looking up names for them and told them that it was a biblical name meaning miracle or blessing. When they looked at each other, then down at him, I felt my heart skip a beat when they proudly decided to name him Asher.

Jade reached over and stole the baby out of Noah's arms and cradled him against her chest as she walked over and hugged me. I kissed her cheek then looked down at the sweet baby that was trying to fall back asleep against his mama.

"Do you want to hold him?" she asked softly, starting to lift him off of her. I placed a hand over hers and gently patted it, smiling and shaking my head no.

"You let that sweet boy rest, I'll hold him later when he's awake."

She nodded and walked over to the couch, finding a spot in the corner where she could curl up and rest with Asher. I gave Noah a quick hug and a kiss on the cheek as we wished each other a Merry Christmas before he joined Jade on the couch. The room was quickly warming up with all of the bodies buzzing about, so I went over and slid the kitchen window open, allowing the breeze to help cool things off some.

"Why are you opening the window? I thought you were worried about your heater?" Chase asked from across the room, forcing everyone's attention on me. I looked around and saw Mia still laughing in the corner as she tried to hide her face from the others. Wyatt tilted his head and looked at me while Grant looked over at Chase and pulled his brows together.

"What's wrong with mom's heater?" Grant asked Chase.

"I don't know, she didn't tell me anything was wrong with it until we showed up a few minutes early and I found Lieutenant Dickson here, checking on her furnace," Chase said sharply as he looked from Grant then back to me.

"That's funny, I was just here yesterday to fix it. What happened after I left, mom?" Wyatt chided in as he pushed off the wall and folded his arms over his chest, pinning me with a look that said he knew damn well that no one was here fixing my furnace.

"Oh, it was nothing," I waved dismissively in the air. "Everything is fine. Why don't we get started on presents before dinner?" I smiled as big as I could at Liam and Annie, hoping that they would get as excited as I was so we could focus the conversation elsewhere. I watched as Rylee ran around in circles on the carpet in front of the couch, entertaining the kids so they didn't hear me. I scrunched my nose in disappointment when my plan didn't work.

"Okay—now I know something is wrong because mom NEVER lets anyone open gifts before dinner," Grant said as he studied me. I looked around the room at my three *very* protective sons and struggled with how to tell them. I cast a glance over my shoulder to look at Mia, desperate for someone to save me.

"Yeah, and look at how flushed her face is. I don't think she's cold at all. Maybe we should get her to the doctor and have her checked out?" Chase offered as he started a side conversation between Wyatt and Grant.

"Are you sure that you checked the furnace, Wyatt?" Chase asked, getting an immediate dirty look from Wyatt in return.

"Seriously? You are questioning whether I checked the fucking furnace?" He shook his head and glared at Chase. "I'm the only one who comes by to fix things around here and check on her, I think I of *ALL* people know whether the damn furnace isn't working right."

"Well obviously you missed something or Lieutenant Dickson wouldn't have had to go out of his way to come check on it himself,"

Grant argued and pointed a finger at Wyatt. Lacey walked off to the side and stood next to Mia. She had been in the family long enough to know to get out of the way when the boys started to argue like this.

"Or *maybe* you're all missing something, like the real reason Lieutenant Dickson was at your mom's house on Christmas," Noah said loudly as he raised his eyebrows, everyone's attention shifting to him. He gave me a sly smile that confirmed that he knew what was going on as well.

"Okay, those potatoes are not going to mash themselves," Mia interrupted and walked across the room to stand next to me. "Ladies, let's get in the kitchen and help Connie get dinner going."

I let out the breath I had been holding and gently squeezed Mia's arm as she walked past me, pulling my hand along with her. A few minutes later and I was finally able to breathe as I opened the fridge and stuck my head inside, trying to cool myself off as the blood rushed to my head. Jade and Lacey had joined us and watched me from the table as Mia began working on boiling the water for the potatoes.

"Connie, are you sure you're okay? You look a little overheated," Lacey said as she walked over to the fridge and placed her hand on my shoulder. I could tell that the nurse in her was worried and quickly analyzing whether or not she needed to send me to a doctor.

"I'm fine, dear, thank you."

"She's overheated, alright," Mia giggled from the stove and yelped when I playfully snapped a towel across her butt.

"Mia!" I exclaimed and laughed.

"What?" She pretended to not know what I was talking about. "You know everyone is going to find out sooner than later, and at the rate, the guys are going in there—I would say it's going to be sooner." She lowered her voice as she said it.

"Find out about what?" Jade asked as she sat down at the table and started to breastfeed Asher.

I looked at Mia before looking back at Jade and Lacey, unsure of whether or not to tell them. I knew that everyone was about to find out anyway, and I wanted them to hear it from me, but I had no idea how to tell them that I was seeing someone.

"Umm… well… I… ummm," I stuttered, looking to Mia for help. She nodded and stirred the potatoes once more before setting the spatula on the counter next to the stove and turning to face them.

"Connie had Buck over today to check her furnace because he really knows how to *light her fire* if you know what I mean." She grinned as their mouths dropped in shock as they turned to look at me. I could feel my cheeks blushing again. "Sorry, I can't keep calling him Lieutenant Dickson anymore—not now that I know what's going on," she laughed.

I closed my eyes and covered my face with my hands and I groaned in embarrassment.

"Connie!" Lacey hissed as she giggled from the table. "You naughty, naughty girl," she squealed playfully.

"I can't believe it," Jade said excitedly from the table as Asher continued to nurse. "I'm so excited for you. That might be the best Christmas gift this year."

I lowered my hands and found three beautiful women smiling at me, celebrating the new relationship that I had worked so hard to try to keep hidden because I was scared of what everyone would think.

Three

"Alright, dinner is ready," Lacey called to the guys and kids from the kitchen, getting mumbled responses as they stared at the football game on the television. I rolled my eyes and set the bowl of stuffing on the table next to the turkey and yams. Everything looked beautiful and smelled delicious. I silently stood there, watching my beautiful family as I thought about how wonderful it would be to share all of this with Buck. He had been single longer than I had been widowed and I often wondered why he never wanted to find someone and settle down. I knew he had a bad marriage and that his wife left shortly after his son, Jimmy, started getting into trouble, but Buck was a wonderful man and every woman in town knew that.

"Boys- dinner- now!" Mia yelled from the stove, knowing that none of them had bothered coming when Lacey had called them in a few minutes ago. Two six-foot tables had been set up in the small area between the kitchen and living room to fit everyone in one spot while we ate dinner as a family. For so many years I had given up on wanting to have a formal Christmas dinner and allowed everyone to eat off of paper plates and spread out in the living room, eating on the couch and the floor when there wasn't enough room. But this year—this year was different. I was feeling fresh and renewed, and damn it—I wanted a nice dinner where I could sit down and talk with my family.

Jade adjusted the red table cloth that Asher had grabbed and tried to pull off as Mia set up the highchairs in the corner. It felt weird seeing three highchairs around the table when last year there was only one. Our family was growing quickly and it made my heart a little bit fuller with each addition. I took a deep breath and was about to yell out into the living to call them in when I heard them whining and grumbling about an interference and how 'the ref must be drunk if he didn't see that' as they came into the kitchen and scattered around the table to take their seats.

Once everyone was situated, I did a quick check to make sure we had everything we needed on the table and sat down in the only empty seat, which happened to be the head of the table. I felt my chest tighten as I recalled Christmas dinners when the boys were younger and their father sat at the head of the table. I swallowed hard, busying myself with picking up my napkin and laying it on my lap. The room was quiet overall as everyone focused on passing the dishes around, serving themselves and each other, until everyone's plates were full.

I waited a few seconds, unsure of whether to say grace since we hadn't done that in years. Chase smiled at me as he reached his hands out, taking Mia's on one side, and Lacey's on the other, before bowing his head. Quickly everyone followed his lead and the room was silent as they bowed their heads. I cleared my throat before saying a quick prayer, thanking the Lord for our meal as well as the time we were spending together as a family. As I finished, I sent up a silent prayer that he would help guide me on how to come clean about why Buck was here earlier.

Forks clanked against the plates as they started to eat. I busied myself with cutting my turkey into small pieces, feeling the nervousness bubble up inside of me.

"So, how was everyone's Christmas morning?" I asked, trying to stall as I started a random conversation.

Chase and Mia mumbled *good* as they focused on feeding their girls. Rylee wanted to be a big girl and do everything herself since she was going to be two in a few weeks. Millie was just excited to sit in her highchair and smear mashed potatoes across the top of it, stopping every now and then to lick some off of her hands.

"It was good, I got a baby for Christmas," Annie said proudly as she sat up taller in her chair and took a bite of turkey.

"How exciting, what is your new doll's name?" I asked in between bites. From the corner of my eye, I could see Grant and Lacey exchange nervous looks as they shifted in their seats.

"It doesn't have a name yet, but I'm hoping that one is a boy, and the other is a girl."

"Two babies, wow, that's really exciting! You must have been a good girl to get TWO babies," I said happily.

"I guess." She shrugged her shoulders and pushed her turkey around her plate with her fork as Liam leaned in and whispered something in her ear. Something was going on but I couldn't figure out what. I turned to look at Grant and Lacey who now had a deer caught in the headlights look on her face.

"Something is going on, what is it?" I asked as I narrowed my eyes at my middle child. He was always the first to crack under pressure and I knew he would come clean if I pushed hard enough.

"Actually," he said as he set his fork down on his plate and looked around the table before turning his attention back to me. "Lacey was the good girl. She's pregnant."

I let my fork fall from my hand as I covered my mouth and squealed in excitement. Everyone started talking, offering their congratulations.

"Are you sure she was a good girl?" Wyatt joked, glancing at me from the corner of his eye knowing that I would get on him for being rowdy around the kids. "Seems like maybe she was riding the naughty list when that happened."

I felt the laughter bubble up inside me and tried to hold in before I failed miserably. I burst into laughter at his joke and snorted, causing the room to go into hysterics.

"Mom, what has gotten into you today?" Grant joked playfully as he tapped my arm with his elbow. "You're feeling a little rowdy."

"I think maybe your mom has been riding the naughty list too," Noah teased, ducking as Chase threw a bread roll at his head.

"Shut up, my mom isn't seeing anyone," Chase said defensively before looking over at me. "Tell him, mom."

I tried to keep a straight face as everyone's eyes were on me. Without warning, I burst into another fit of laughter as I tried to think of a more tactful way to say that I had indeed been riding the naughty list.

"Okay, since it's going to come out sooner or later, I might as well just get this over with," I said with a heavy sigh once I was able to stop laughing. I glanced at the kids, making sure they weren't listening before I continued. "Buck—Lieutenant Dickson—and I have been…

working on my furnace for a few months now." I decided to word it carefully when I saw Liam look up and started to listen.

Noah brought his fist to his mouth and tried to hide the laughter as his head rolled back and his chest shook. Jade elbowed him to get him to stop as she laughed and smiled at me. I looked over to Chase, Grant, and Wyatt, trying to gauge their reaction to the news.

Chase stared off into the distance, looking as if I just told him that someone shot down Santa's sleigh and he didn't make it. Grant worked his jaw back and forth as his foot tapped on the floor next to me. And Wyatt looked at me with a huge smile on his face as he shook his head. I raised my eyebrows to silently ask him why he was smiling.

"I fucking knew it," he laughed and slapped the table. "There was no way that anything was wrong with your furnace."

"Language!" I scolded as I looked pointedly next to him at Liam and Annie. He rolled his eyes and smirked as he started laughing again.

"Nope, your mom has definitely had something warming her up this winter," Lacey joked, earning a quick glare from Grant.

Chase stayed silent at the other end of the table, looking upset.

"Are you okay?" I asked, making sure to raise my voice enough to grab his attention so he would know that I was talking to him. He waited a few minutes and just stared at me.

"I just can't believe it…" His voice trailed off as his words lingered in the air. I felt my heart sink, knowing that he would be the one who would have the hardest time with me dating someone.

"Honey, I'm sor—" I started before he looked directly at me and cut me off.

"His name is *Buck?*" He wrinkled his nose and frowned.

"That's what bothers you?" I asked as I tilted my head to the side in concern.

"Yeah, I guess I just never knew him as anything other than Lieutenant Dickson. It feels so weird to hear you call him *Buck.*"

"I'm sure that's not all she calls him," Noah quipped as he ducked to avoid another bread roll, this time from Grant. Everyone laughed and suddenly I felt more relaxed about coming clean and having everyone know my little secret.

"So, are you guys okay with this? I know that I haven't dated anyone since your dad passed," I asked sincerely. I was excited to see where things could go with Buck but at the same time, there was no way that I could continue on with him if one of my kids wasn't fully on board with it. Their happiness has always been the most important thing to me and I wasn't about to change that now.

"We're okay with it, mom, really," Chase said as he looked around the table at his brothers before his eyes locked onto mine. "We just want you to be happy. And if *Buck* makes you happy, then we're happy."

"Are you seriously going to keep saying his name like that?" Wyatt leaned forward to look at Chase.

"What?! I might be happy that mom found someone to make her happy and that she enjoys spending time with—but I will always know him as Lieutenant Dickson- the guy that caught me smoking pot outside of the school and turned me in."

"At least he didn't catch you having sex," Grant said as he nodded across the table at Wyatt who had a faint blush creeping up his cheeks.

"I don't think you want to start sharing dirty secrets, big brother," Wyatt responded and glanced at Lacey's hand. Suddenly everyone turned their attention to her as she desperately tried to pull her hand under the table to hide it.

"Son?" I asked and nodded to Lacey. He pursed his lips and glared at Wyatt before looking around the table.

"Well, I guess since we're all sharing with each other, Lacey and I have more news to share with you guys."

"Besides her being pregnant?" Chase asked, obviously having missed Wyatt's nod at Lacey a few seconds ago.

"Are you ready to tell them?" Grant asked Lacey who was almost as white as a sheet of paper. She nodded her head yes and slowly pulled her hand up from under the table.

"Lacey and I got engaged this morning," Grant announced proudly as she held her hand up for everyone to see the ring that sparkled in the light. "And, not only is she eight weeks pregnant, but we're having twins."

I jumped up out of my seat and waited for him to stand up as I wrapped my arms around him and hugged him. This was turning out to be one of the best Christmases we had had in a long time.

Four

After dinner, I sent everyone into the living room to hang out and watch the rest of the football game while I worked on the dishes. There was so much energy flowing through me that I needed to be up and moving to get rid of it. I scraped the last plate clean, watching as the few bites of food fell into the overly full trash can. I set the plate in the sink on top of the others and turned to open the pantry to get a new trash bag when I bumped into Wyatt. I clutched my chest as my heart began to race.

"Wyatt! What are you doing there? You scared me half to death," I exclaimed, trying to calm myself.

"Sorry, I didn't mean to scare you. I thought you heard me behind you," he laughed as he opened the pantry and pulled out a trash bag. He slid the trashcan over with his foot so it was out of my reach as he took the full one out and put the new one in. He grabbed the heavy bag and carried it outside to the trash for me. I was at the sink, rinsing the dishes when he came back in.

"Here, let me help you," he offered, gently pushing his hip into mine to scoot me out of the way.

"You don't have to help clean up, you should go watch the game with your brothers."

"Eh, my team is losing anyways," he smiled and began filling the sink with hot water to wash the dishes that couldn't go in the dishwasher. "Plus, you did the cooking, you shouldn't have to do all of the cleaning too."

"Well thank you," I said, proud of how he turned out to be such a sweet and caring man, just like his father was. "But don't tell the

others that I let you help me, I forced them out of here and wouldn't let them help me even though they insisted."

"It'll be our little secret," he winked and turned off the water before picking up the sponge to start washing the dishes. I felt myself blush when he said *secret*, wondering if he had known all along that I was seeing someone. He had reacted differently than the others, almost as if he knew.

"It seems there were a lot of secrets revealed today," I said, hoping to lead into the conversation that I really wanted to have with him. One thing about Wyatt was he didn't talk about things if he didn't want to, and I honestly didn't know if this was something he would want to talk about.

"Yeah, there sure were," he answered as he scrubbed the plate and rinsed it. I took a slow, deep breath in and held it for five seconds, releasing it just as slowly.

"How do you feel about everything that came out today?" I knew that he would know where I was going with this conversation and prayed that he wasn't going to force me to just come out and ask him about it.

"I think it's great that Grant and Lacey are getting married and having babies. It's like a big baby factory around here lately," he chuckled and smiled at me.

"Ain't that the truth?" I laughed and finished loading the dishwasher before turning it on. My head was still spinning when I thought about how next Christmas there would be seven grandbabies running around my house. I was so excited, I could hardly stand it.

"But that's not what I'm talking about and I think you know that," I said gently as I stood next to him, my back against the counter so I could look at him while he washed the dishes. He sighed and dropped the sponge, letting it sink into the water as he pulled his hands out and rinsed them before drying them on the towel hanging next to the sink.

"I'm happy for you mom," he said as he turned around and leaned against the counter, facing the same direction as I was. "As long as you're happy, that's all that matters to me."

"Did you know that I was seeing someone?" I asked quietly, not sure that I wanted to know the truth. He nodded but didn't say anything.

"How long have you known?" I looked up at him.

"For a few months," he shrugged and kept staring straight ahead of him.

"How did you find out?" I asked, suddenly worried when he looked nervous and his shoulders tensed.

"It doesn't matter," he said nonchalantly.

"Wyatt…"

He leaned his head back and exhaled heavily before turning to look at me.

"I came by one night to check your actual furnace and didn't know you had company. I thought maybe you were out with your friends when you didn't answer, so I used my key and let myself in. Once I heard you in the bedroom, I left and vowed never to come over unexpectedly again after that." He arched an eyebrow as he watched the color drain from my face.

"So let me get this straight—my boyfriend once caught you having sex, and now you've caught me having sex with the same guy who caught you?" I asked, embarrassed as I processed that new piece of information and added it to the collection of things that I couldn't ever un-know.

"Yup." He made a popping sound with his lips.

"Let's agree to never talk about this again? Ever?" I asked and extended my hand for him to shake. "Not even with your brothers." I raised an eyebrow as I extended my hand further. He laughed and shook my hand as he agreed.

He turned around and went back to the dishes while I grabbed a washcloth and started wiping down the counters.

"So, how are you feeling? Are you still doing your therapy?" I pressed, knowing that he didn't like to talk about it.

"Na, I gave up on that."

"Why? I thought you said they thought it would help?"

He stopped what he was doing and clenched his jaw, the anger evident on his face.

"I know that you don't want to talk about it, but I really think you should."

"I don't need to talk about anything, mom," he snapped, forcing me to flinch at his tone.

"I'm sorry," he apologized softly. "I just hate talking about it."

"I know."

He lowered his head and let out a sigh as the weight of everything that had happened this year sat heavily on his shoulders.

"It's not fair. That's what I hate the most about it. I had a scholarship that I can't do anything with now because the doctors won't clear me to play again because my heart is too fragile," he said sarcastically.

"Wyatt, you were stabbed several times in the chest. You lost a lot of blood. The doctors had to work very hard to keep you alive because your *fragile* heart kept giving up," I said firmly as I reached over and placed an arm around his shoulders. Or at least tried to. He was almost a foot taller than me so it was a hard reach. "I know that it breaks your heart that you can't play baseball anymore, and I know that it sucks. But I thank the Lord every single day for giving you back to me because it's not always that easy. Very few people are given a second chance at life, but you got one."

I gently squeezed his shoulders and felt some of the tension slip away.

"You know, I would do it all again in a heartbeat," he said matter-of-factly.

"What's that dear?"

"Being stabbed and almost dying. I would go through all of that all over again to save Lacey." He gazed over the half-wall that divided the living room and the kitchen. I followed his gaze to where Lacey was sitting on the couch, curled up next to Grant, holding hands as they watched tv by the fire.

"I would never want that, none of us would. But I know that we all appreciate how selfless you were when you sacrificed everything to save her. Especially your brother."

"Well, she's a special girl who deserves to be saved. And my brother needed someone like her in his life, especially after everything he's already been through. He and Liam both."

I blinked to try to clear the tears from my eyes as I thought about sweet Renee and how she was taken too early, forcing Grant to raise their son on his own. I knew the pain of losing a spouse and being left to care for children as a single parent but I never thought my own son would have to experience it at such a young age. When no one else could reach Grant as his life spiraled out of control, Wyatt stepped in and was the one who had saved him from himself. They've had an unbreakable bond ever since.

"Someday you're gonna find a woman just as special, and you'll be adding to the baby factory yourself," I teased, watching as his face scrunched up.

"No way, there's not a girl out there who can settle me down. Not any time soon, anyway," he joked and went back to washing the dishes.

<u>Five</u>

The night slowly went by as we sat around entertaining each other with sharing funny stories while indulging in pie and drinking hot chocolate. My heart felt fuller than it had in a very long time and part of me wondered if it was because my family was growing or if it was because I had finally allowed someone new into it. For the longest time, I swore that I would never love another man, that my heart would forever be closed off to finding new love, because I had made that promise on my wedding day. But the more that I allowed myself to step back and really look at things, I found that I wasn't trying to replace the love that still held a huge piece of my heart. I was simply allowing the love to grow in a place of my heart that I never knew was there.

I glanced down at my watch to check the time, knowing that it was getting late and everyone would be heading home soon so that the grandkids could wind down and rest for the night. I was also starting to feel giddy about calling Buck to let him know that I had finally told my family about our relationship so we no longer had to hide it. This also meant that I didn't have to get creative with ways to hide his vehicle every time he came over. It was seven-thirty when I heard the doorbell ring, puzzled as to who it could be when everyone I knew was already here.

I got up and walked over to the door, looking over my shoulder as I felt Chase's eyes on me. He smiled and looked away, planting a kiss on Millie's head as he bounced her on his knee. I turned the knob and opened the door, surprised to find Buck standing on the other side with a bottle of wine. My reaction must have startled him because he suddenly looked panicked and looked past me to where everyone was hanging out in the living room.

"What are you doing here?" I whispered as I leaned in so no one else could hear me. "I thought we said we would talk later after the kids were gone?"

He opened his mouth to speak but stopped and looked over my shoulder.

"I called him and asked him to come join us," Chase whispered loudly, mimicking me over my shoulder. I tilted my head upward to look at him, surprised that he would do something like this.

"You called him and invited him over?" I asked as I continued to think through this. He nodded his head yes and extended his hand out to Buck.

"I'm really glad you could join us tonight, Buck, please come in if my mom will pick up her jaw and scoot out of the way," Chase teased as Buck shook his hand.

"Thank you for inviting me, it's a pleasure to be here," Buck laughed and handed me the bottle of wine as he wrapped his arm around my waist and leaned in to whisper in my ear, "I'm guessing they know?"

"Mmhmm," I murmured and stepped to the side to let him come in. "It's been a very revealing Christmas with plenty of sharing to go around."

He arched a brow and looked at me, sending a shiver through me as I took in how good looking he was. His short black hair with streaks of gray was freshly trimmed, and it looked like he had shaved since this morning as well. I took a deep breath and inhaled the spicy scent of his aftershave, anxious to rip his navy button-down shirt off of him and strip him of the dark denim jeans that perfectly hugged his ass. I cleared my throat and tried to force the thoughts out of my head as I closed the door and led him into the living room.

"Everyone, I would like you to meet Buck," I said nervously as they all turned their attention to us. "I know you all know him as Lieutenant Dickson, but now that you are aware of our relationship, I would like you to call him Buck and treat him as the special friend that he is to me."

I felt relieved when they all took turns saying hello and coming over to welcome him. I would never have imagined that I would be able to spend Christmas with my kids and my new boyfriend—was he actually my boyfriend??—at the same time. The thought that we were all here together at the same time was blowing my mind.

We found a space on the floor by the fire and sat down to join everyone as they talked about their plans for New Year's Eve. I was sitting next to Buck as he wrapped an arm around my shoulders casually and leaned in close to me.

"Do you have plans for New Year's Eve?" he whispered in my ear. I shook my head no. "Good, because I was hoping that you would join me at my house and I could make dinner for you for a change."

"That sounds wonderful, I would love to." I turned to face him and gently cupped his cheek in my hand, debating on whether it would be inappropriate to kiss him. The kids knew about our relationship, but that didn't mean that they were ready to see us together yet.

"When do you start your new job?" Grant asked Wyatt, pulling my attention away from Buck.

"After New Years'," Wyatt responded, looking nervously at me.

"What new job?" I asked, wondering why he hadn't told me about it. Wyatt and I were probably the closest out of all of my kids, and last I knew he used to tell me everything. He looked down to avoid meeting my eyes as he pulled at a loose thread on the pillow next to him.

"I just accepted a new job as a Recruiting Coordinator for the Haven Brook University baseball program. I'll be scouting new talent across the state, and on occasion, I might have to go out of state. But right now it will be a lot of travel, that's why I was waiting to tell you."

I felt my body tense as he told me, my fears that he would completely abandon his dream of playing baseball again finally being true. I knew that he was having a hard time being patient with his recovery after the stabbing and the numerous surgeries he had to undergo, but I also knew how important it was for him to keep playing. Baseball has always been important to him, ever since he was a little boy and his dad coached his little league team.

"Is this what you really want?"

"It is. I've thought long and hard about it and while I would love to keep playing baseball, I don't think it's going to happen for me. That's why I stopped doing physical therapy. They might hope that someday I'll get to where I can play again, but I know deep down that it's likely over for me. This job allows me to still be a part of it, without having to worry about my own recovery."

I nodded my head and felt Buck gently squeeze my shoulders as he stayed silent. Everyone's attention was focused on our conversation while the kids were off in Liam's room playing.

"If you're happy then I'm happy. That's all I ever want for you. For all of you," I said as I looked around the room and smiled.

"Thanks, mom. I thought you were going to be upset about it," he admitted sheepishly.

"Why would I be upset?" I asked.

"Because I gave up on my childhood dream, I let go of the one thing that I still shared with dad. It's like I let go of him." His voice cut off and I could hear the pain in his words.

"Son, you are more than baseball. You always have been. We've been passionate about it because you loved it so much but we've never wanted you to feel like we would ever love you any less if you didn't keep playing. Your dad would be proud of who you are, regardless of whether you kept playing."

He gave me a tight smile and went back to picking at the loose thread.

"So, do you have any prospects lined up yet?" Buck asked, jumping into the conversation.

"Yeah, I'm actually checking out this kid who is really good in East—" he paused and looked at Lacey with panic on his face.

"Easterville," she finished for him and smiled sadly. "We have a lot of good talent there, I can ask my cousin Kayce if she knows anything about the prospect you're checking out since she still lives there."

"Thanks, but that's okay. I want to slide into town without anyone knowing why I'm there. I think that's how you really learn about someone."

"Don't lie, you just want to sneak around and check out the local girls before you have to do your actual job," Noah teased.

Everyone started laughing and the rest of the night flowed easily from there. Soon, everyone was saying goodnight and heading home. I waved to Grant and Lacey from the door as they packed the kids into his truck and drove off. As I shut the door, I realized that Buck was still there and we finally had the house all to ourselves.

"So, about that Christmas gift you were wanting to give to me this morning…" I teased as I hooked my finger into his belt loop and pulled him down the hall to my bedroom.

A VERY HAVEN CHRISTMAS

<u>Six</u>

I rolled over and snuggled up to Buck, feeling happy and content to be waking up in his arms and not having to worry about him sneaking out before the neighbors saw him there so word didn't get back to the kids. Now that the kids all knew about it, I didn't care about who in town knew and were gossiping. They could say whatever they wanted to at this point, nothing would ruin this new happiness that I had found.

Gently, I ran my fingers along his chest, tracing circles as he slowly started to wake up. I scooted closer and kissed his cheek, whispering good morning in his ear.

"Good morning," he drawled out, still half asleep.

I laid my head on his chest and closed my eyes, still feeling tired from our marathon love making last night. We'll just say that he gives the *best* Christmas gifts and I planned on staying on the naughty list for next year. We stayed snuggled up together for a little while longer and, for once, neither of us worried about the time. I knew that Liam and Annie were coming over later to spend the day with me but we still had hours before they would be here.

"What are your plans today?" he asked sleepily as he rubbed my back.

"I don't have any until later this afternoon, Liam and Annie are coming over for a bit so Lacey and Grant can celebrate their engagement. I'm having the kids sleepover so they have the entire night, though I'm not sure how long Lacey will stay awake," I giggled, hearing Buck chuckle along with me. I had given him the updates on everyone last night after they had all left and excitedly told him that I was going to be a nana again in July and that Lacey was expecting twins.

It felt wonderful to share the news with Buck and feel his excitement along with mine. Things started to feel like they had shifted between us, that we had a stronger connection now that we weren't trying to hide our relationship anymore. Once I saw how genuinely excited he was to hear about all of the things happening in my kids' lives, it made the wall around my heart crack a little bit more, allowing him in.

"Sounds like fun," he said as he looked down and smiled at me. I returned the smile but could swear that I saw a hint of sadness on his face. "I'll be sure to head out before they get here."

When I heard his words, I knew what the problem was. Even though we had made a lot of strides in our relationship in the last twenty-four hours, it was still so fresh that he was having a hard time feeling like he was part of my family.

"What are your plans today?" I asked, leading into my formal invite.

"I don't have any, other than going to visit Jimmy at some point this weekend."

"How is he doing?" I knew that he didn't like to talk much about his son and the trouble he was constantly in because everyone in town judged him for what Jimmy did. If Jimmy was caught with drugs again, it was Buck's fault for not keeping an eye on him as a child when he first started experimenting. If Jimmy robbed a store, it was Buck's fault for not knowing where he was at all times so he could protect the people of the town since he was the Lieutenant. It was really unfair and I hated that he constantly felt the weight of his son's actions.

"He's good, I guess. Staying out of trouble for the most part."

"Well, that's as good as anyone could ask for," I joked, feeling his chest rumble as he laughed.

"If you don't have any plans *today,* maybe you could stay and we could have a pizza and movie night with Liam and Annie?" I felt my voice crack a little as I asked it.

He pulled back and I could feel his eyes on me. I slowly pulled my head back and looked at him. There was a serious look on his face and I immediately started to wonder if it was too soon to be inviting him into all of my family stuff.

"You don't have to if you don't want to, it's not a big deal," I said hurriedly, trying to move past the awkward moment.

"You really want me to be here with you and the kids?" He tilted his head to the side and watched me.

"I do," I nodded. "Buck, I would love nothing more than to have you be part of my family and share everything with me. It's not about spending the holidays together, it's about sharing everything with each other. And I want you to be in my life for a very long time, which means that I would love for you to be here for pizza and a movie night with the kids."

I watched as tears flooded his eyes as he quickly tried to blink them away. Buck and I had talked several times when we first started dating about how hard it was to find someone who would fit so perfectly in the life we had created. For him, it was hard to find someone who understood that no matter how many times his son messes up, he will always love him and be there for him because he is his son. He regretted that he never found another woman to love and that he would likely never have grandchildren that he would know about. For me, it was hard to want to let someone into my life when I finally had things the way that I wanted them and I worried that they would undo everything that I had worked so hard to create.

"I would be honored to be a part of the pizza and a movie night," he whispered as he leaned in and kissed me.

"Okay," I laughed, "But it's going to be at least three movies and none of us can ever agree on one pizza so we end up with at least two different pizzas, the kids split theirs in half with their own toppings. I get the special."

"Well, I just happen to love the special and I would stay through four movies." He winked, making my heart flutter as I leaned forward and wrapped my arms around his neck before giving him the biggest kiss ever.

<u>Seven</u>

It was after two when Grant and Lacey showed up to drop the kids off and I was starting to feel a little anxious about springing it on them that Buck would be hanging out with us tonight. I knew that this was a big change for everyone and prayed that they would be okay with it so that I didn't have to break Buck's heart and cancel on him after all.

I opened the door and smiled as Liam and Annie came running up the driveway with their overnight bags strapped to their backs. They rushed up and wrapped their arms around me. I loved the brother-sister bond they had formed so early on, thankful that Liam finally had the sibling he had always wanted. My heart nearly burst when I found out that they were both going to get to share the experience of having two new siblings in seven months. I let go as the kids ran off and went inside, saying hi to Buck and dropping their bags by the door. Grant and Lacey were a few minutes behind them, smiling as they came up the driveway.

We said a quick hello then went inside to get out of the cold. I waited with bated breath for them to say something about Buck being there but instead I was pleasantly surprised when Grant went over and gave him a quick hug, followed by Lacey. Everyone seemed happy and I started to feel silly for stressing about everything in the first place. Perhaps I had been worried for so long about how it would impact other people if I met someone who made me happy, that it made it hard to accept that I felt this way.

"You look beautiful, Lacey," I said as I went over and sat on the couch next to Buck. The kids were already back in Liam's room, getting their stuff situated and picking which movies they wanted to watch from the list I had made this morning. I tried to make things as fun as I could when they would come over, so today I decided to pretend they were going to dinner and a movie at the theater. I left a menu for them to order their pizza and a list of different movies that would be showing tonight. Buck helped me make tickets for them to use for popcorn and candy that they could 'purchase' at the concession stand.

I don't know who was more excited about it—Buck or the kids. We ran out to the store this morning to grab a few things and ended up coming back with a bag filled with the movie theater-sized boxes of assorted candies, a 12 pack box of popcorn, and a variety of popcorn seasonings. When I gave in and agreed to let Buck get the stuff to make root beer floats, I couldn't stop smiling when I saw how excited he was. It felt wonderful to let him be part of this and to do things with the grandkids he never expected to have on his own but has always wanted.

"Thank you," Lacey said with a quick blush on her cheeks. "Grant and I are going to dinner in Eastern Point tonight and getting a room at the hotel I've been dying to stay in. We figured we might as well enjoy a romantic, kid-free night before I get too pregnant to be able to enjoy it." She laughed and leaned into Grant's shoulder. He wrapped his arm around her and planted a kiss on her forehead.

"We do want to talk to you about something real quick before we go," Grant said, his tone changing the mood in the room. I felt my stomach knot as I dreaded what he was about to say.

"I can leave so you guys can talk," Buck said quietly, patting my knee before standing up.

"You don't have to do that," Grant interrupted. "I think it would be best if you stayed for this."

Buck hesitated for a minute before looking down at me and sitting down. Grant blew out a quick breath and glanced at Lacey before turning his attention back to us.

"Alright, here it goes," he paused and looked at Lacey again, getting an eye roll from her in return. She reached over and playfully swatted at his chest, laughing at how dramatic he was being.

"Just get on with it and tell them, or I will. These babies are getting hungry and you promised me a snack before dinner," she teased. I laughed and was thankful that Lacey's mood was still the light and playful one she had since she came in, hoping that their 'news' wasn't as bad as Grant was making it out to be.

"Okay, Lacey and I have set a date for our wedding," he blurted out as a huge grin spread across his face. "February 14th."

I took a minute to let it sink in, knowing that Lacey and I had talked a while back about how hard it was to date after being widowed, and she had mentioned that she didn't want to rush into getting married again. She wanted a long engagement to make sure that it was the right thing to do before she made that type of commitment again. I felt her eyes lock onto mine and knew that she recognized the puzzled look on my face. She smiled softly as if she knew what I was thinking, remembering our conversation herself.

"When we settled everything with Derek's estate, I found that there were a few boxes that I had left in Montana after we rushed to move in with my dad. I was in such a frenzy as the grief took over me that I had completely forgotten about them. My best friend agreed to ship them to me, and when I opened them, I found my mom's wedding dress." She sighed heavily and took a deep breath before continuing. "I struggled with what to do with it, but in the end, I decided that I wanted to honor my mother by wearing it at my wedding. I didn't have anything that she left to me, nothing that was a part of her. And while the dress felt tainted at first because it was the dress she wore when she married my dad, I decided that I didn't have to look at it that way. When she married him, she thought she was marrying the man of her dreams. She was ready to make those vows to the man that she thought the world of."

She stopped and looked up at Grant as a tear slid down her face.

"And I want to do the same. I love this man so much that I couldn't imagine living a second of my life without him. I don't want to slow down and risk missing out on a minute of happiness."

Grant reached over and gently wiped away the tears that were flowing down her face as he pulled her closer into the side of him and hugged her.

"I think it's a wonderful way to honor your mother, dear." I felt my own tears threatening to spill out of my eyes as Buck reached over and squeezed my hand.

"We know that it's a very quick engagement, but we were hoping that maybe you guys could help us with some of the planning since it's less than two months away and you both have some connections in town." Grant looked between Buck and me as we sat in stunned silence.

"You want me to help?" Buck asked quietly.

"We would be honored if you would," Lacey chimed in with a smile.

"After all, you are a very important part of the wedding party now that you're family."

"Thank you, Lacey, but I think you have the wrong idea," Buck started and I could feel his body tense against mine. Lacey's face fell and her shoulders slumped as she waited for him to speak. "I'm the one who would be honored."

I felt the tension in the room evaporate as quickly as it had mounted.

"Well, it looks like we have a lot to do in a short period of time," I joked, confirming that I was fully on board to help them with whatever they needed. "Not that I'm not excited about the wedding coming so quickly, but what made you guys decide to get married on Valentine's Day?"

"My mother was four months pregnant with me when she got married, and I'll be right around four months with the twins at that time. I just pray that I can still fit in her dress with *TWO* babies instead of one."

The room was filled with laughter as we joked and teased each other for a few minutes before they left for their date. Liam and Annie were still in their rooms, arguing over which movie to watch first. I curled up on the couch next to Buck and tucked my feet under me as he wrapped a blanket around me and let me snuggle against him.

"Well, this Christmas has been a whirlwind of changes with everything happening so fast," I said as I listened to his heart beat beneath my head. "I still can't believe that they're getting married in less than two months," I chuckled.

"I'm really honored to be a part of everything," he said quietly. "I know we've talked plenty of times about how we wanted to take things slow and how hard it is to allow someone into your life after so long. If things are starting to move too fast, or if I'm getting too much into your space—please tell me and I'll gladly back off some."

I shifted my position so I could look up and see him better.

"Buck, there's nowhere else I would ever want you to be. I thought that this would be a hard thing to do, but it turns out that it's really easy to open up and share your life with someone when you've found the right person."

His face lit up as he smiled. I wasn't sure when he was happier- now that I'd confessed my feelings for him, or earlier when he was loading our shopping cart to the top with junk food for the kids tonight. Either way, I was glad that not only did I get to be a part of it but that I was the reason for it. It turned out that once you started letting the walls down on your heart, it was easy to want to take them away completely when you found someone that fit so easily into the empty space you never thought you could fill.

<u>Eight</u>

The days seemed to fly by after Christmas and before I knew it, it was already New Year's Eve. I had spent time with each of the kids throughout the week, each of them having their own plans for New Year's. Buck had stayed with me almost every night, only going home for short periods to change his clothes and take care of a few things. It felt so weird that we went from sneaking around and hiding our relationship a week ago to having him practically live with me. I enjoyed his company so I didn't complain other than when he had to leave.

Tonight, Buck had invited me over to his house for dinner and I was feeling anxious like a teenage girl who was expecting her first kiss. I had no idea why I was so nervous, it wasn't like we hadn't slept together already. The thought of him cooking me dinner and having me go to his house felt like we were taking our relationship to a whole different level when it forced me out of the comfort and safety of my house. When we were together at my place, I felt like I was in control of almost everything. Now he was in control and I was feeling completely out of sorts.

I glanced in the mirror one last time before deciding to put on my pearl necklace that would go great with the black lace dress I was wearing. It was sleeveless which made me feel self-conscious, but Mia and Jade had assured me that I looked sexy when they stopped by earlier to help me get ready. They were both so sweet and caring to come over and walk me through a handful of wardrobe options as they told me how stunning I looked in almost everything that I tried on. It felt like I was young again, getting ready for a date with my best girlfriends by my side to help me.

Mia loaned me a pair of black strappy shoes that had a four-inch heel that I was terrified would trip me and I would break my neck before we even had dinner. She assured me that I would get used to them in no time and Jade confirmed that they made my legs look even longer and sexier with the dress that hit my legs mid-thigh. My fingers trembled as I clasped the necklace in place and rubbed my lips together, watching as the red lipstick vanished then reappeared. I took one final deep breath before picking up my cell phone from the nightstand and stuffing it into my purse before heading out the door to Buck's.

Ten minutes later I was walking up to his door, legs shaking as I started to doubt my ability to walk in these heels without making a complete ass out of myself. I knocked on the door and waited. Finally, I heard whistling as he got closer and opened the door. He had a towel slung over his shoulder, the smell from inside floating out around me and making my stomach growl. He stepped back to let me inside as his eyes traveled up and down my body.

"The food smells delicious," I said as I leaned in and kissed him. His hand slid down my waist and cupped my ass as he leaned in and kissed me back.

"You *look* delicious," he replied with a sexy smile. I looked down at myself nervously, pulling my lip in between my teeth.

"Thank you."

"Dinner is almost ready, why don't you come in and I'll pour you a glass of wine?"

He closed the door behind me and turned to walk back to the kitchen, extending his hand out for me to take it as I followed him inside. I had only been inside his house a few times but it reminded me so much of my parent's house from when I was a little girl. Suddenly, I felt the calmness take over as I walked with him through the living room to the kitchen that was attached. I loved that his house was wide open and wished that mine was bigger and had the space he had. I would love to be able to cook in the kitchen while my family hung out in the living room, laughing and talking, and I could still be a part of it.

I sat on the barstool he pulled out for me at the island that separated the two rooms. The island was huge and had four cushioned stools that slid under it so they weren't in the way. I loved that there was hardly any clutter in his kitchen, everything having its own place. He opened the wine and poured two glasses, extending one to me before taking a sip out of his glass. He set it down and walked to the stove behind him to check on the food that was cooking.

I slowly sipped my wine as I watched him move about the kitchen, admiring his abilities to move so easily without spilling anything or burning himself. He looked at ease with every movement and I wondered if he had been an actual chef at some point. My eyes gazed on his nicely sculpted body as the button-down shirt he was wearing pulled tight across his shoulders when he bent down to pull a pan out of the oven. He was wearing the same jeans he had worn over to my house on Christmas—the ones that really showed off what a great ass he had.

Ten minutes later, he led me to the table in the dining room that had a beautiful bouquet of red roses in the middle with a cream-colored tablecloth underneath. He had taken the time to set the table, including a bottle of champagne that was chilling in a bucket of ice beside the roses. I brought a hand to my chest and gasped at how beautiful everything was as he smiled proudly. I took my seat and allowed him to serve me, feeling like a pampered princess as he waited on me.

Dinner was delicious and I made a mental note to wear baggy clothes the next time I let him cook for me. After we finished, I offered to help with the dishes but he shook his head no and led me to the living room where he started a fire and laid out a blanket on the floor in front of the fireplace. He ran off to the kitchen as I got situated on the floor and brought back the bottle of champagne and our glasses. I grabbed a few pillows from the couch behind us as he sat down to join me.

I kicked off the heels that I had been wearing and tossed them to the side while he situated the pillows behind us. When I turned around I found him on one knee in front of the fire, holding out a black box with a red ribbon on top.

"I know it's not Christmas, but I have one more gift I would like to give you," he said nervously. I watched anxiously as he slowly opened the box, showing me a beautiful diamond ring.

"Connie, I know that we haven't been dating long and we both agreed to take things slow, but I thought long and hard about what Lacey said the other day about not wanting to miss a single second of happiness. You make me happier than anyone I've ever known and I don't want to miss a single second of happiness with you either." He stopped and pulled the ring out of the box, his fingers trembling as he held it out to me. "Would you do me the honor of being my wife and making me the happiest man in the world?"

I felt my heart skip a beat as I looked back and forth between the ring and the man who had stolen my heart.

"Yes," I said breathlessly as I extended my hand and watched as he slid the ring onto my finger. What I expected to be a moment of doubt and sadness ended up being a moment of absolute certainty as I kissed the man that I was excited to spend the rest of my life with.

Nine

Buck and I rang in the new year cuddled up by the fireplace, drinking champagne, and making love. I was blissfully satisfied with how my year ended and even more excited about how the new one was starting. There had been so much that had changed in my family over the past few years that it felt weird for the change to finally be with me. We agreed to sleep in and start the first day of the new year on the right foot—fully rested and in each other's arms. I rolled over and cuddled into him, feeling the roughness of his beard as it tickled my face when he leaned in to kiss my neck. I wrapped my arms around him and giggled.

"Good morning," he mumbled against my shoulder.

"Good morning, *fiancé,*" I whispered back to him, feeling on top of the world.

"I love the sound of that." He leaned forward and kissed me softly.

"Me too," I said, meaning every word. I ran my fingers up along his shoulder then down his back, making lazy circles.

"When did you want to start telling the kids?"

I froze for a second, the first time I had thought about having to tell them. I wasn't worried that they would be upset about it given how quickly they had warmed up to him already, but I did wonder if they would feel like it was too soon. For me and Buck it didn't feel rushed at all given that we had already been dating for a few months but for the kids, it might feel like it happened in the blink of an eye since they barely found out a week ago.

"I don't know," I said nervously. "I want to tell them right away but…"

"But you're scared that they'll think we're moving too fast," Buck finished my sentence for me. I nodded and slowly pulled in a deep breath, hoping it would help relax me.

"I understand your apprehension and if you want to wait a little while before we tell anyone, that's fine with me."

His words soothed me better than any calming breaths could. That was one of the things that I loved the most about him was that he knew me so well, he could tell when I was stressed or upset about something, and he was able to easily defuse the situation before it overwhelmed me.

"I'll tell them soon, I promise," I assured him with a smile. "There's just a lot going on right now with Wyatt starting a new job on Monday, Grant and Lacey rushing to plan a wedding, and Chase and Mia getting ready for Rylee's birthday next week—it's so much at once and I don't want to add to anyone's stress right now."

"It's okay, Connie, really." He reached over and gently ran the pad of his thumb across my cheek.

"Thank you, I appreciate your support."

"Well, you better get used to it because you're going to marry me and from what I've heard—that's what married folk are supposed to do," he joked, lightening the mood between us.

We spent the rest of the day together, putzing around the house while talking about random things in between the meals he cooked. I was definitely going to take him up on any future offers to cook from here on out. I found that he could make even the most basic things—like grilled cheese and tomato soup from a can—taste like it was made in some gourmet restaurant. After lunch, we cuddled up together on the couch to watch a movie but I couldn't help but notice how tense and nervous Buck was suddenly acting. Every few minutes he would check his watch or his phone, keeping an eye on the time instead of paying attention to the movie.

"Is everything okay?" I pulled away and looked up at him so I could read his expression. I was a mom of three rowdy boys so I knew how to easily read when someone was lying to me.

"Yeah, I'm fine," he said nervously, avoiding my eyes and focusing on the tv. Liar. I folded my arms across my chest and continued to glare at him until he turned to look at me. I waited as he squirmed in his seat, adjusting his position anxiously.

"Buck…" I warned with the same tone that usually worked with the boys.

He slightly turned his head to look at me, a forced smile on his face that looked almost painful.

"What is going on?" I demanded, my irritation growing the longer he avoided me.

"Nothing, let's watch the movie." He patted my thigh a few times and looked back at the tv as if he had any idea what the movie was about. Then, when he thought I wasn't looking, he looked down at his watch again.

"Okay, that's it," I said as I stood up and threw my hands in the air. I knew that all of this was a big change for him as much as it was for me, but if we were going to make this relationship work, he needed to be honest with me and tell me that he wanted some time to himself. Maybe it was a little too soon to get engaged?

I reached down and picked up my cell phone from the coffee table and shoved it into the pocket of the sweatpants he had loaned me so I didn't have to wear my dress all day. I debated changing back into it so I could give him back the clothes he let me wear but I was too angry and frustrated to care about it right now. I would go home, fix something for dinner, and toss them in with the load of laundry that was still waiting for me from a few days ago.

"Where are you going?" he asked as if he had no idea why I was so upset. This infuriated me even more.

"I'm leaving, Buck. I'm going home and giving you your own space so you don't have to check your watch and phone every few minutes. If you wanted me to leave, you should have just said so," I bit out angrily.

"I don't want my own space, Connie. You know that. I wouldn't have asked you to marry me if I did," he explained with a stern tone.

"Then why have you been sitting here watching the time for the last hour? Something else has clearly had your attention and I don't want to be the thing that is keeping you from whatever it is that you'd rather be doing." I put my hands on my hips and waited for him to respond.

"Why don't we get out of the house for a few, get some fresh air? Maybe we can head back to your place and spend some time there?" he suggested with the grin I couldn't resist. I eyed him suspiciously, wondering what he was up to. "I'll even cook you dinner…"

I laughed and rolled my eyes. Had I been reading the whole thing wrong? Maybe he wasn't wanting me to leave so he could do something else—maybe he was feeling restless from being at home for so long and he really did need to get out and get some fresh air. We did spend a lot of time at my house so it would make sense that he would want to go there and hang out for the rest of the night. I let out a sigh and felt calmer as he guided me out the door and to his truck.

A few minutes later, we pulled into my driveway and I felt the comfort of being home again. He reached over the console and gave my hand a quick squeeze before we got out and walked up to the door. I unlocked the door and walked inside, holding the door open for Buck to follow. When I turned the corner to go into the living room I felt my heart jump out of my chest as everyone screamed 'surprise' and threw confetti in the air toward us. My eyes quickly scanned the room, finding that all of my kids and their families were there, smiling while they waited for me to process what was going on.

I felt Buck's hand on my lower back before he leaned down and chuckled in my ear.

"Surprise," he said playfully.

"What in the world… what is all of this?" I asked, watching as Chase and Grant came over to shake Buck's hand while the girls came over to hug me.

"Congratulations! We're so excited for you!" Lacey squealed and held my hands.

I looked up at Buck who was grinning from ear to ear, soaking up the excited energy that was flowing through the room.

"Did you plan this?" I asked him as everyone started to quiet down some to listen.

"I didn't plan this, no. But, I did tell the boys that I was going to propose before I did it. I wanted to get their permission beforehand and they were all very supportive of it. They were excited for us and asked if they could tell the ladies and before I knew it, a surprise engagement party was being planned," he laughed, spreading his arms out.

"This is amazing, thank you guys so much!" I brought my hands up to my cheeks and looked around the room at the beautiful family that was the symbol of what love is.

I made my way around the room getting hugs from everyone and showing off the ring. The kids had put everything together for us, including order pizza for dinner so no one had to cook or clean up. We laughed and talked for hours, my heart feeling fuller than it's ever felt. Soon everyone was packing up and heading home to get ready for the new week. I was standing at the door, waving goodbye to Chase and Mia when I saw Wyatt lingering in the hallway.

"Are you heading out too?" I asked, noticing the look of concern on his face.

"Yeah, here in a few."

"Is everything okay?" I reached over and gently squeezed his hand.

"I'm not sure about taking that new job tomorrow," he said nervously.

"Do you want to come sit down and we can talk about it?" I asked, nodding to the couch. Grant and Lacey were still packing up their things while Liam and Annie went through the stuff in their room that they needed to take home. He looked over at them then shrugged his shoulders as he made his way over to the couch. I followed his lead and sat down beside him.

I waited a few minutes to let him start the conversation but when he sat there in silence, gently rocking back and forth, I decided to take charge.

"What happened with the job? Why are you reconsidering?" I asked gently, grabbing Grant's attention as he turned toward us.

Wyatt looked up at Grant then over to Lacey before blowing out a heavy sigh.

"I don't know, something just doesn't feel right. I can't explain it but it feels like if I take this job, something bad is going to happen."

"Do you think maybe you're just nervous because it's a different type of job than you've had before?" I kept my tone soft to make sure he knew that I wasn't judging him or trying to tell him how he should feel. Honestly, I was worried about him taking this job as well but for different reasons. I hated the idea of him having to travel so much for work because it meant that I wouldn't know where he was most of the time or if he was okay. Buck had already laughed and thought I was borderline crazy when I asked if we could sneak a GPS tracking device onto his car so I could know where he was at all times. Then Buck reminded me that I probably didn't want to know where he was at *all* times.

"I guess it could be nerves," he sighed. "But it feels like if I take this job then I'm admitting that this is what I am. This is all that I'll ever be. I will have officially given up on trying to pursue a baseball career of my own. What if I'm giving up on myself too soon?" His voice rose slightly, the desperation and fear creeping up with it.

I reached over and held his hand again, finally understanding what was bothering him. I was struggling to find the words to say when Grant came over and kneeled in front of him. He arched an eyebrow and waited until Wyatt looked at him.

"What have I always told you?" Grant asked as he stayed at eye level with Wyatt.

"You've told me a lot of shit—some of it helpful, some of it not," Wyatt joked until Grant gave him a pointed look. "Fine," he sighed dramatically. "You have always told me that I'm whatever I want to be."

"Exactly," Grant replied. "And taking this job does not mean that you're giving up on yourself. It means that you value and respect yourself enough to go after new challenges. Your body is healing and trying to recover. You can't force it to do what you want it to do, Wyatt. That's not the way it works. If and when you heal the way you need to, baseball will still be waiting for you. If not, then you remember it as a wonderful part of your past and your work your ass off to create the future you want."

I leaned back against the couch and watched my two sons, the bond between them stronger than I could have ever prayed for. It made me happy to know that they loved and would always be there for each other. Wyatt sat in silence for a few minutes, processing Grant's words.

"Is there anything we can do to help you with the stress you're feeling with taking the new job?" I asked.

"Na, I think that helped," he said with a smile. "I just need to get out there, try something new, and see what the future holds for me. Who knows, maybe it will be good to get out of Haven Brook and see what else is out there."

"Yeah right, you just want to get out there and see what *girls* are out there," Grant joked, clapping him on his back as he stood up and walked over to Lacey.

"Well, you found Lacey and she's a catch… just saying, there might be more to Easterville than this kid I'm supposed to scout." He winked at Grant who had wrapped an arm around Lacey's shoulders and scowled at him.

"Trust me, you don't want to mess with the girls in Easterville," Lacey laughed. "They're all a little bit crazy. Except for me, I was one of the good ones."

"What about Kayce?" Grant asked, looking down at her. "Is she one of the good ones or one of the crazy ones? Just so I know how deep the crazy runs in that side of the family before these babies get here," he joked as he rubbed a hand along her stomach.

"Oooh, Kayce is a good one but she is also crazy. She's equal parts." She giggled and wrapped her hand over Grant's.

"Maybe I'll have to find her and say hi while I'm out there," Wyatt teased with a wink, back to his usual self.

"Oh sweetie, that girl is a man-eater. She will eat you alive," Lacey warned playfully.

Buck walked over and sat next to me on the couch, joining in on the conversation as we laughed and teased Wyatt about his rowdy ways. He wrapped an arm around me and snuggled me close as he whispered, "I really love this family."

"So do I, and that includes you," I said before I tilted my head up and kissed him.

THREE STRIKES, YOU'RE GONE

Three Strikes, You're Gone

Samantha Baca

THREE STRIKES, YOU'RE GONE

One

Kayce

"I'll be right there," I called from under the car I was working on. I waited for a response from whoever it was that had come in but was met with silence. I slid out and pushed the creeper to the side so it was out of the way before wiping my hands on the worn-out towel that hung from my pocket.

As I was walking out of the garage, I spotted someone dart out of my office and run out the front door. The icy chill from outside sent a shiver through me as I raced down the hall to my office, wondering who had been there and what they were doing.

Everything looked normal, nothing was out of place. It was a small office to begin with, so there wasn't much in the way of valuables for someone to take. I pulled the chair out and sat down, feeling shaken up by the random visitor.

Just as I had convinced myself that it was nothing, I looked down on my desk and found a large white envelope with my name on it. My gut instinct said to leave it alone and call the police, but I quickly pushed that irrational fear to the side. What was I going to say? Someone came into my office and left an envelope for me? That wasn't exactly a crime and I would probably be the laughing stock of our tiny police department. It would likely be the highlight of their day on this dreary Monday morning.

I shook my hands in the air, trying to force my nerves to calm down before picking it up. It was silly to be this nervous about a damn envelope. I pulled the top out, noticing that it hadn't been sealed, just tucked inside. My fingers started shaking as I slid the contents out onto my desk.

There were a handful of pictures that were laying facedown. I picked the first one up and flipped it over, gasping when I saw what it was. Quickly, I turned the others over, my stomach souring over the sight in front of me. At the bottom of the pile of pictures was a note written on an old concert ticket in black marker.

Just in case you forgot...
Because I didn't.

Two

Wyatt

The dark sky was a quick reminder that I only had a short window left to make it to Easterville and get checked into my hotel before I lost my reservation. Between stopping for gas more often than I had expected to and dealing with the check engine light, it was taking me a lot longer to get there than it should have. Needless to say, I hadn't gone into all of those details with my mom when she called and asked about the truck, and reminded me that my brother Chase had said that it needed to be looked at before I ended up stranded somewhere on the side of the road.

I looked down at the gauges on the truck and blew out another frustrated breath. There was no way that I was going to be able to make it the rest of the way without filling up. This thing was guzzling gas faster than a college kid in a beer-chugging contest. I saw a sign up ahead for a gas station and pulled off at the exit. I went inside the small convenience store to grab some snacks for the road since I was probably going to miss dinner at this point. I didn't know much about Easterville, but I assumed that since it was a smaller town than Haven Brook, most of the decent places to grab a bite to eat would be closing by the time I had a break to go eat.

I tossed the bag full of snacks and a few bottles of water into the passenger seat of the truck and shut the door. Gas was more expensive here than it had been at any of the other stops, but thankfully, I was getting reimbursed for it. I would go through the receipts and cut them in half, turning in the fair amount of gas that a normal person would use. It wasn't their fault that I had a truck that sucked down gas quicker than any other vehicle I'd ever seen.

The truck was having more issues than I was willing to admit right now, mainly because I hadn't had the time or energy to work on it. My fingers trembled from the frigid cold as they struggled to turn the key in the ignition. I groaned as the truck failed to start after several attempts. I gave it a little more gas as I tried again, feeling the frustration build as I saw the white smoke floating out of the exhaust once it started. *Fuck...*

The highway was empty when I got back on, most likely due to the heavy snow that had been falling the majority of the day. I was thankful that the exit I needed for Easterville was only an hour away. I was going to be pushing it, barely making it on time for my check-in, but I was trying to keep my faith that somehow luck would intervene and things would go my way. Just one little break to get me started on the right foot. That was all that I needed.

I felt like I was on pins and needles the entire way, not knowing when the truck was going to decide to give out and leave me stranded on the side of the road in this terrible weather. I let out a long, heavy breath when I saw the first exit sign for Easterville, knowing that my hotel would be at the next exit. Only a short way to go.

I gripped the steering wheel tighter, praying that I would make it to the next exit. In the rearview mirror, white smoke was billowing out from the exhaust. There was a loud pop as the truck backfired and the engine started to die. I swerved to the right at the last minute, barely making it onto the offramp. I continued to pull to the right and felt as if luck was mocking me as I slid right into the parking lot of an auto shop as the truck died.

Three

Kayce

I was just about to turn the lights off and leave for the night, when I saw a truck come sliding into the parking lot, a trail of white smoke clouding behind it. At first, I panicked when I thought about the stranger who had been in my office earlier, but then I remembered that Lacey's soon-to-be brother in law was supposed to be heading to town soon, and if I remembered right, this looked like the kind of truck he would be driving.

My cousin Lacey had been checking in with me nonstop for the last hour to see if I had heard anything about whether or not Wyatt had made it to town. She was worried about his old truck being on its last life. She was right about that. Just by looking at the amount of smoke that was still coming out, I had a list of things in my head on what was likely wrong with it. And unfortunately, none of them were quick or easy fixes.

I watched as he climbed out with a scowl on his face, and what I assumed were a string of curse words filling the crisp air around him. I had briefly caught a glimpse of him last year when I went to see Lacey after she was released from the hospital. Things had happened so quickly while I was there that I didn't remember much about him, other than he was recovering from being stabbed while trying to save Lacey's life.

Of course, there were the constant pokes and prods from her about how good-looking he was, and oh, did she mention that he was single too? *Wouldn't it be the cutest if we got together? Then her little cousin could fall in love and marry her fiancé's little brother…* She had been fantasizing about a relationship between us for as long as I could remember. I simply humored her, letting her believe that I was open to the idea of her setting me up with him the next time I went to Haven Brook, which might also be the same reason I hadn't gone back…

As he ran a hand down his face in frustration, I caught a glimpse of how muscular his body was. She wasn't lying when she said that he was in good shape, however, she forgot to mention that he had the body of the guys that women drooled over on the cover of dirty romance novels. He reached up and adjusted his baseball cap, the tight-fitted hoodie stretching across his broad shoulders and pulling up slightly at his waist. I felt my cheeks flush as I saw a sliver of skin before he lowered his arms and looked at me.

I had been staring for so long that I completely forgot that he might turn around and notice me. I offered an awkward smile and a little wave, feeling like a complete idiot as he headed my way. I stepped back and opened the door, inviting him inside. A blast of cold air came in with him, sending a shiver through me as I took in the dark chestnut eyes that were watching me with amusement.

"Sorry to barge in here," he said, rubbing his hands together. "My truck decided to die on me so it looks like I'm stranded for the time being. Is it okay if I leave it here for now? I can call a tow truck to come get it in the morning."

"A tow truck? Where do you plan to have them take it?" I asked, my brows pulled together as I tried to keep the smile off my face. It seemed as if I knew more about him than he did about me. From the looks of it, he had no idea who I was, which I was suddenly thankful for.

"A mechanic?"

"Like the one you're currently standing in?"

I watched a faint blush creep across his face as he looked down in embarrassment.

"I didn't want you to think that I just assumed that you would work on it. I know usually most shops have a waitlist and I really need to get my truck up and running."

"Well, I hate to break it to you," I sighed. "But I'm the only auto shop in Easterville. And, not to brag—but I'm the best." I winked.

"You're Kayce," he said with a smile and nod of his head.

"And you're Wyatt," I replied with a cheesy grin.

"I didn't see the sign outside, Lacey just told me that you worked at Wrenched, but she didn't mention that you were the only mechanic in Easterville. I guess I could have assumed that this was your place when you opened the door, but I just thought…" His thought trailed off, leaving the words unspoken.

"That I was the receptionist?" I offered.

A sheepish grin crossed his face as he nodded.

"Sorry," he said sincerely.

"Don't be." I waved him off. "Honestly, I get it all the time. Even though I've lived here all my life, there are still a handful of folks here who refuse to believe that the only mechanic in town is… wait for it… a *woman!*"

"Eh, it's their loss," he said as he leaned back against the wall and shoved his hands in his pockets.

"Why's that?"

"Because it's fucking hot to see a woman working on cars." He licked his lips and locked eyes with me, forcing a blush to creep up my neck. I remembered that Lacey had warned me that he was the town playboy back home, but honestly, I didn't expect to be on the receiving end of his charm within the first ten minutes of talking to him.

"No offense," he added, noticing my embarrassment.

"None taken, I appreciate the comment." I narrowed my eyes. "I think…"

He laughed, the corners of his lips curling up into the sexy dimples in his cheeks. No wonder he could get any woman he wanted. That smile alone had me wanting to strip my panties off and throw them at him.

"So, is it okay if I leave my truck here for the night?" He pointed his thumb over his shoulder to the parking lot. "I have to get to the hotel and see if they'll still let me check-in." He glanced down at his watch. "And I'm already almost an hour past the cutoff time they gave me."

"Which hotel are you staying at?" I asked, knowing he was out of luck.

"There's more than one hotel in this town?" He pulled his brows together in suspicion.

"Two, actually," I laughed.

"I'm staying at the Honey Lodge," he said, squinting his face as he looked upward, trying to pull the information out of his head. "Which, if I run over there, I might be able to get there in time."

"You're going to run two miles to the hotel?" I pulled my head back and looked at him like he was some sort of alien.

"I run five miles every morning," he assured me with a cocky smirk.

"For fun?" I scrunched my face and earned a burst of laughter from him. I should have known that he was a runner by how lean and sculpted his body was. He was also probably one of those health-nut freaks that only ate organic foods and avoided the greasy, good stuff. My stomach growled in response as I thought about the barbeque food that I was planning to stop for on my way home.

"Well, more for training. But I don't mind it." He shrugged his shoulders nonchalantly, the hoodie moving fluidly with his body as it gave me more assurance as to what I would find if I were to take it off of him right now. I knew that Lacey was head-over-heels in love with Grant, but now I understood why she was constantly going on and on about his little brother and how attractive he was. As he stayed leaning against the wall in his dark denim jeans and black work boots, I could easily see what her obsession was all about. Apparently, good genes just run in that family.

"I hate to tell you, but you're not staying there tonight." I shook my head and shifted my weight, trying to balance my bag on my hip as it started to get heavier. "And you'll have to get there first thing in the morning, with a candy bar, if you want to grab a room for tomorrow. I wouldn't run there though." I laughed, envisioning it in my head.

"Why won't I get a room tonight?"

"Because Mr. Ashby is a stickler for the rules. He's a cranky old man that hates late check-ins as much as he hates when people want to extend their stay. However, Mrs. Ashby will be working in the morning and she's a sucker for candy bars—Paydays, to be specific. A couple of those, combined with that sexy smile—and you'll have a room for tomorrow."

I felt his eyes widen at my words and realized my mistake as soon as I said it. I swallowed hard, hoping to force the embarrassment away before the blush stained my cheeks again.

"You think I have a sexy smile?" he asked, pushing off the wall and taking a step toward me. He was tall—way taller than me, forcing me to lift my head to look at him. His scent was intoxicating, cedarwood with hints of vanilla that made me want to lean in closer for a better whiff.

"It's nice, but I wouldn't go too far with thinking that it's overly sexy," I stammered nervously. "I mean, it will probably get you the hotel room tomorrow if that's what you're looking for…"

"Good to know." He pulled his bottom lip in between his teeth and let it pop free as he took a step back, allowing me some space to breathe. What the heck was that? It was like I couldn't think within such close proximity to him. My brain was foggy while his magical voodoo smile worked its wonders on me. I tried to force a smile, but it came out as some awkward movement of my face which made him turn and fake cough to keep from laughing.

"Well, I'm closing up here for the night," I blurted out, desperate to change the conversation. "You can leave your truck here, and I'll look at it in the morning."

"Sounds good, thanks," he said, turning to walk outside. I followed him out and pulled the door closed behind me after turning off the light switch. The cold air whipped past me, sending a chill through my body while my fingers trembled against the cold metal of the lock. A few minutes later, the door was locked and I shifted the bag up higher on my shoulder, knowing that I was going to pay for this in the morning. It was too much weight to try to carry for this long, but I hadn't been smart enough to set it down while I was talking to Wyatt.

He walked to his truck and yanked on the handle to get the rusty, old door to open. I thought he was just grabbing what he needed from the truck but was surprised when he pulled the door closed and sat there.

I walked over and knocked on the window, feeling silly as he rolled it down to talk to me.

"What are you doing?" I asked, lifting my hand in the air beside me.

"I'm staying in my truck because it's freaking cold outside," he explained as if it should make sense. "I don't have a candy bar to offer the cougar at the hotel, so I'm waiting it out inside of my truck."

I rolled my eyes and brought my palm to my face.

"Boys are so stupid," I sighed playfully, rolling my eyes. "Get out of the truck, you're gonna come stay with me tonight."

I stepped back, allowing him room to open the door to get out.

"Kayce, thank you for the offer, but I can't put you out. I'll be fine in the truck, thank you though." I watched as a shiver ran through him, the cold air biting at his skin. The sucky thing about older trucks, like the one he was driving, was that they were all metal and that meant that nothing was going to keep the cold out of it tonight. The snow had finally stopped falling, but the temperature was supposed to plummet in a few hours with more snow on the way.

"Your brother is marrying my cousin which makes us practically family. Get out of the truck you big oaf, before we both freeze our asses off." I raised an eyebrow at him and folded my arms while I waited. He sat there for a moment, thinking about it before I added, "I'm not afraid to call Lacey and have her tell Grant what a stubborn ass you're being."

Now it was his turn to roll his eyes as he rolled up with the window and climbed out of the truck. He grabbed a duffle bag from the passenger seat and slung it across his shoulder before walking with me to my car. I watched as his eyebrows raised when he saw the 1998 Dodge Ram 2500 that was parked at the opposite end of the parking lot.

"That's your ride?" he asked, a hint of amusement in his tone.

"Yeah, why?" I replied, my eyes narrowed.

"Don't get me wrong—it's a dope ride," he said, putting his hands up in front of him. "I just didn't expect it to be your truck, that's all."

I couldn't blame him for his reaction. It was the same one that I had gotten from almost everyone who saw me driving it. With a 6 inch lift on it, I had mastered getting in and out without killing myself or causing a scene for people to gossip about. She was a beast, there was no doubt about that. I had put in hours of love, sweat, and tears to make the modifications that I wanted. It was the best damn truck in all of Colorado, and you could bet your ass that no one was talking shit about it when I was the only one in town that could pull vehicles out of the thick, muddy areas after a heavy snowstorm.

"I may be short, but trust me, I have no problem getting where I want to go," I replied sarcastically, knowing that it was an open-ended meaning.

"Her name is Oakley," I added when we got closer. I ran a hand down the side of the truck, touching the black pinstripes that were added to the crimson red color I had recently painted it.

"Oakley? As in…"

"Yup, Annie Oakley. Because she was a badass that made her own way in a male-dominated world. We're doing the same thing," I said proudly, patting the vehicle as if it was a dog that had just earned some praise.

"Very fitting, I like it."

I pressed the button to unlock the doors, praying that they weren't frozen shut. Relief washed over me when I heard the click and opened the door. Wyatt walked around to the other side and climbed in, shivering again as the cold followed us inside the cab. He set his stuff on the floorboard in front of him and buckled up.

I pushed the key inside of the ignition and turned it, hearing the beautiful purr she made every time I started her up. There was something about the sound of a 5.9 diesel engine coming to life that made my skin tingle with excitement. Once we were both situated, I put the truck in reverse and pulled out of the parking lot.

"Do you like barbeque?" I asked, glancing over at him before turning my attention back to the road.

"Is that a trick question?" he joked. "I think it's a sin not to like barbeque."

"So am I taking you to grab some, or do you need me to drop you off at a church for confession first?"

"Lacey was right about you," he laughed, turning to look out the window.

"What do you mean?" I asked, feeling partly amused and slightly worried.

"She told me you were a wild one, warned me about your sarcastic humor and wit." He winked as he turned slightly in his seat to look at me.

"If you only knew," I muttered with a low laugh before turning into the parking lot of the Tasty Pig.

Four

Wyatt

"This is good," I mumbled before sinking my teeth into the last bite of meat left on the rib. Kayce wasn't lying when she said the Tasty Pig had the best barbeque she's ever had.

"I told you." She winked and popped a piece of fried okra into her mouth.

We got back to her apartment less than thirty minutes ago and she promised she would give me the official tour of it after we ate because she was starving. It was a nice place but small enough that I could see the majority of it without needing a tour. The living room and kitchen were combined in one area that was barely big enough to fit her couch and coffee table, which I found out served as her dining table as well. It was a simple piece of black, beat-up wood, but it lifted to make a table in front of the couch.

The TV was mounted on the wall, a small bookshelf underneath it that was overflowing with books that don't fit in the tiny space. She didn't strike me as a reader, but shit, she also didn't strike me as a mechanic either. Guess it was true what they said about not judging a book by its cover. Or in this case, don't assume the beautiful girl with dark purple hair isn't a successful businesswoman who is handling her own shit and isn't afraid to get her hands dirty.

"Do you guys not have a good barbeque place back home?" she

asked, nibbling the side of the corn she held between her fingers. Her question pulled me back to reality and I stopped for a second to think about who had the best barbeque back home.

I shook my head and frowned.

"We don't really have a real barbeque place back home," I said with a shrug. "We have Slow-Mo's. They have some killer ribs and barbeque chicken, but other than that, I've always just grilled at home."

She tilted her head to the side and thought about what I had said, as if it seemed strange to her.

"What's that look for?" I laughed, wiping the barbeque sauce from my mouth with the napkin.

"Nothing," she snickered. "I guess I just can't imagine a world where there's no Tasty Pig."

"Well that's because you haven't tried my food yet—it would make you forget the Tasty Pig ever existed," I assured her with a smirk.

"How can you be so cocky about that?" She lowered the empty cob to her plate alongside her napkin and demolished ribs. "You don't even have a real barbeque place to compare yourself to."

"Trust me, I don't need anything other than a grill and some meat and I'll have your mouth watering."

My eyes followed the trail of crimson that flushed across her skin as she tucked her chin and looked away. Without giving it much thought, I licked my lips and wondered what she tasted like. The thought of Kayce reacting to me this way sent a direct message straight to my dick, making my jeans suddenly tighter than a few seconds ago. The problem was that I knew there was nothing that could happen between us. She was Lacey's cousin, and Grant had already threatened to break my neck if I even *looked* at her the wrong way.

"Well, I guess we'll just have to agree to disagree." She got up to throw her plate away and looked down at my empty plate, asking permission to take it as well.

I nodded and stood up, picking up my mess before reaching over to take hers.

"What are you doing?" she asked guardedly.

"Cleaning up." I walked around the table and wandered into the kitchen, looking for the trash can.

"It's under the sink, but you can just set it on the counter and I'll run it downstairs later with the other trash."

"I can run it down now, I don't mind."

I added the plates to the bag that contained the empty take-out containers and pushed them down, making sure they didn't leak.

"We can take it later." She scooted past me, her grin spread from ear to ear as she opened the freezer and pulled out a tub of vanilla ice cream. She wiggled her eyebrows before opening another take-out box that was pushed off to the side of the counter, away from the empty boxes. The scent of peach cobbler filled the air and I found myself leaning closer to inhale the delicious aroma.

"Their barbeque is amazing, but this peach cobbler is downright divine. It's better than an orgasm," she whispered, her eyes barely meeting mine before she ducked her head and looked away.

"Sounds too good to be true," I teased. "Or maybe you just haven't found the right guy to give you better orgasms."

I watched the way her body reacted, the sharp intake of air that filled her lungs. In all fairness, I had tried to turn it off and not pursue her, but her orgasm comment screamed game on. I was pretty damn good at reading women, and she was giving me all of the signals that she was just as interested in whatever this was as I was.

"Maybe you just haven't had the best cobbler in the world?" she countered, pulling a spoon out of the drawer beside her before closing it. She dipped it into the container, scooping out a small piece of cobbler before turning to me and lifting it to my mouth.

I parted my lips, opening my mouth to allow her to put the spoon in so I could take a bite. As her golden-brown eyes watched me, I reached up and gently held her wrist, pulling her hand away as slowly as possible while my lips wrapped tightly around the spoon. Once it was out of my mouth, I allowed the cobbler to sit on my tongue for a second as I locked eyes with her. I moved it around, swallowing before licking my lips.

My hand was still holding her wrist, the tension between us getting thicker by the minute. Her chest rose and fell heavily, a look of desire flooding her face. She pulled her bottom lip in, releasing it when I moved my hand and took the spoon from her.

"My turn," I said softly, my voice deeper and hoarser than normal. I scooped out a piece of cobbler, making sure it wasn't too much for her to take. I scolded myself for the inappropriate thought before realizing that there was nothing appropriate about what we were doing. We had already started to cross a line, and there was no going back at this point. Hell, I wasn't sure that either of us would if we could.

"Open." I nodded subtly, lifting the spoon to her lips as she opened her mouth to accept the bite. Her breathing was heavy, her full breasts spilling over the top of the t-shirt that pulled tight against her body. The temperature was definitely rising in here, there was no doubt about that.

I watched her eyes close, a soft moan escaping her mouth as she pulled the cobbler from the spoon. I felt my erection get harder as I imagined what she would look like with something other than that spoon in her mouth. The way she slid her tongue along the bottom of it before it went in wasn't lost on me. She was teasing me as much as I was her.

"If your reaction to the cobbler right now is comparable to the best orgasm you've ever had, you might need to find a new boyfriend," I said dryly.

"I don't have a boyfriend," she replied matter-of-factly, opening her eyes and meeting the challenge in my stare.

"Good."

"Good?" she repeated, turning it into a question.

"Mmm-hmm," I murmured, scooping another bite of cobbler from the container. I held it in the air between us before adding, "because I'm about to show you what a real orgasm feels like." I popped the spoon into my mouth and smiled, watching the curiosity in her eyes as she watched me chew.

"Who said I was willing to have sex with you?" she asked, her hands moving to her hips.

"I never said anything about sex," I countered, scooping out more cobbler onto the spoon. "I simply said that I'm going to show you what a real orgasm feels like. You know, for comparison." I shrugged my shoulders and laughed when she reached over and pulled the spoon to her mouth, taking the bite before I could.

"You're full of shit," she scoffed, wiping the corners of her mouth with her finger before pulling it into her mouth and sucking it clean.

"Why's that?"

"Because there's not a guy alive that would just give a woman an orgasm without wanting something in return."

"Sure there is." I pulled my head back in disbelief that she would think that. Who the fuck had she been with that was so selfish and self-centered that they didn't take care of her without having their own agenda?

"Bullshit." She folded her arms over her chest and pursed her lips. Maybe it was the way she had her hair pulled up on top of her head, exposing her slender neck, or maybe it was the way her ass looked in the leggings she had put on when we got home—either way, she had my body reacting to every inch of her.

I stepped closer, setting the spoon down beside us. She was pinned in the corner where the counter joined the short island that jutted off into the living room, leaving her no way to escape as I took another small step toward her. I gently reached forward and put my hands on her hips, guiding her further back until there was nowhere left to go. She watched me closely, unsure of what I was doing as she braced herself against the counters with her hands.

I bit the inside of my cheek, trying to distract myself from leaning down to kiss her. Now wasn't the time for that, and I sure as hell couldn't let feelings get in the mix. I promised her the best orgasm of her life, and damn it, I was going to deliver. My eyes never left hers as my fingers slid across her waist and dipped below the waistband of her leggings before pushing them down her hips.

Her eyes widened as she felt them move down her legs and land in a pile on the floor at her feet. I chuckled softly, bringing my hands back up to her waist as I sat her on the counter. She looked surprised, but thankfully she didn't reach down to try to cover herself. Instead, she leaned back slightly on the palms of her hands and smiled. I licked my lips as I got down on my knees and reached forward, pulling her to the edge of the counter as my hands wrapped around her ass.

My tall frame aligned perfectly with the height of the counter, allowing me plenty of room to move around. She was wearing a pair of cotton boy short panties that looked fucking sexy on her. I debated on whether to push them to the side and get started or if it would be easier to just take them off. Being a selfish man, I decided to get rid of them so I could have a perfect, unobstructed view of her pussy.

"Lift your ass," I commanded, sliding her panties off her when she did. "Good girl," I murmured, trying not to sound condescending.

I looked over and found the container with the rest of the cobbler and handed it to her, along with the spoon.

"For comparison," I teased with a wink. She laughed as she took it, sliding the spoon into her mouth at the same moment I leaned forward and licked her slit. She gasped loudly, earning another chuckle from me.

I pushed her legs open, pinning them against the counter with my shoulders as I slowly licked her again, tracing a path across her lips. I heard the spoon scrape across the Styrofoam container as she got another bite of cobbler. Pushing myself closer to her, I parted her folds with my fingers and slid my tongue inside, feeling her body react to my touch. Her legs started to push back against me as she squirmed on the counter while my tongue slid in and out of her. I held them in place with my shoulders while I slid two fingers inside, bringing my mouth to her clit and sucking. I could hear her labored breathing as I sucked harder, my fingers pumping inside of her easily with how wet she was.

"That's right, come for me baby," I groaned against her pussy. "Come on my face." I sucked harder, knowing that it would send her over the edge by the way her body was responding. The sound of metal clinking to the floor confirmed that I had won this battle against the cobbler as her hands dug into my hair, pulling it as she arched her back and moaned.

I fingered her faster, rotating my hand so I could rub her g-spot as I sucked her clit harder. She panted as her legs trembled against my shoulders.

"Fuck!" she screamed as her pussy spasmed around my fingers, her orgasm ripping through her. I kept going, waiting until I knew she couldn't take anymore before I pulled them out and stood up. I stayed close to make sure she didn't fall given how close she was sitting on the edge. Her eyes fluttered open, the rush of blood flushing her cheeks.

I glanced down and laughed when I saw the rest of the cobbler on the floor in a mess.

"I'm gonna venture to guess that I won that round," I said with a smirk, nodding to the floor.

"I can't even answer that until the blood makes its way back to my brain," she laughed and shook her head.

"Do you need help down?" I offered, extending my hand to her.

"I'm not that short," she balked, taking my hand anyway. "But thank you." She hopped down and grabbed her leggings and panties from the floor.

I turned to give her some privacy so she could get dressed but felt her hand reach out and grab my arm. As soon as I was facing her, her hands snaked up around my neck as she pulled me close to her and planted her lips on mine.

I leaned down and kissed her deeper, her mouth parting as my tongue slid inside. I could feel the energy between us and knew that I needed to stop, if I wanted to keep things from going further between us. But the way she kissed me—I knew there was no going back now. I slid my hands down and lifted her, her legs wrapped around my waist while her bare pussy hovered above my throbbing dick. I wanted to be inside of her, to fuck her senseless, but I needed to make sure this was what she wanted.

"Are you sure you want to—"

"Fuck you?" she interrupted. "Yeah, I'm sure," she panted, moving her lips down the side of my neck as I moaned. I walked her into the living room, not sure where she wanted to do this. It wasn't my apartment so it wasn't like I had any idea about where she was okay with having sex. Fuck, if it was my apartment, I would fuck her on every surface until we claimed the entire fucking space.

"Where?" I asked in between kisses, her fingers clawing my back.

"I don't care. Pick a spot and get naked," she moaned as she slid down me and planted her feet on the floor. We stood in front of the couch, staring at each other for a half of a second before she lunged forward and starting pulling my hoodie off. Within seconds, I was down to my boxer briefs. I reached over and lifted the shirt over her head, desperate to bury my head in her cleavage. Things had slowed down slightly for us, a quick moment to breathe—or stop and think. I worried that she might come to her senses and reconsider, but instead she reached over and pulled my underwear off before leading me to the couch.

I bent down and grabbed a condom out of my wallet before sitting down beside her. My dick was hard, desperate for relief when she reached over and stroked me a few times. Her hand was soft, but her grip firm as she pumped up and down, watching as precum dotted the tip. She licked her lips and leaned back against the couch, spreading her legs. As quickly as I could, I ripped open the package and covered myself before I climbed over and slid inside of her. Her legs were wide open as she took me in, scratching my back as I pushed myself in deeper.

We fucked in this awkward position for a few minutes before I grabbed her and rolled her on top of me, pulling her down on my dick as she started grinding her hips against me. I leaned back and ran my hands up her thighs, over her hips, and along her sides before I reached up and caressed her breasts. The fabric of her bra was thin, her nipples pebbled from my touch. I wanted more. Needed more.

I reached back and unclasped her bra, freeing her tits before tossing the fabric across the room. She rode me harder, grinding down on me as I leaned forward and pulled a nipple into my mouth. I sucked hard, feeling her pussy clench around me in response. The harder she fucked me, the more her perfect breasts bounced in my face. I shifted to the other, pulling that nipple into my mouth and sucking as she arched her back and came hard on my dick. I pulled back and dug my fingers into her hips as I felt my orgasm rip through me moments later.

When I opened my eyes, she was looking at me with a devious smile on her face as she bit the tip of her finger.

"You're right," she said playfully. "That was better than cobbler."

Five

Kayce

Awkward. That's how I would describe the feeling between Wyatt and me after our little—whatever the hell that was. Fun? It was definitely fun. And good. But now that it had happened, I had no idea what I was supposed to do next. It's not like we were together, so it felt weird to act like we were. But, he also just ate me out on my kitchen counter like I was better than the barbeque he had just devoured a few minutes before. And then, we fucked. On my couch. Where I've sat to have tea with my grandma when she came over to visit.

When I offered him to stay with me tonight, it was because it was the right thing to do. I knew that he had already blown his chance at getting a late check-in with Mr. Ashby so I did what anyone would do to help family. Keyword—FAMILY. Because that's what we would be once his brother married my cousin. We're not blood-related, but it still felt a little like maybe it was a line we shouldn't be crossing. So yeah, things were awkward.

I had no idea what I was supposed to do next. Do I allow him to give me the best orgasms of my life, and then ask him to sleep on the couch because it would be too intimate to share my bed with him? I leaned against the wall in the bathroom and closed my eyes. I had come in here to freshen up ten minutes ago, and if I didn't go back out there, he might think something was wrong with me. I mean, technically he wouldn't be wrong. Something had to be wrong with me with what I just did.

My phone vibrated on the counter, startling me. I picked it up and groaned when I saw Lacey's name on the caller ID. There was no way to avoid talking to her so I sighed and slid my finger across the screen to answer the call.

"Hey," I said as cheerfully as I could muster.

"Hey, what's wrong?" she asked immediately. I could picture the frown she was wearing and knew that she had already sensed that something was off from the tone I used with the one measly word I had said.

"Nothing's wrong, I'm just tired." I leaned forward and looked in the mirror, making sure there were no random hickeys that he had given me that I hadn't seen yet. I kept my voice low, struggling to find the right level to keep Wyatt from hearing me in the other room and to avoid having Lacey guess why I was muffled. The bad thing about living in an apartment this tiny was that you could hear *everything* easily through the thin walls.

"Bullshit," Lacey snorted. "Something is off, I can hear it in your voice…"

"Really, I'm just feeling a little worn out."

"Alright," she said suspiciously. "If that's what you're sticking with then I guess I'll just have to wait for you to give in and spill the beans when you're ready."

I ran a hand through my hair to fix it, even though I wasn't going anywhere other than to bed. The thought of Wyatt seeing me like this made me feel self-conscious.

"What do you mean Wyatt didn't answer his phone?" Lacey asked away from the phone. I could hear Grant talking in the background and my stomach started swarming with butterflies.

"Maybe Kayce can go look for him? See if maybe he got stuck somewhere and needs her help?" Lacey continued her conversation with him as if I wasn't there on the other line. I wanted to tell her that Wyatt did get stuck somewhere and that's why he missed his brother's call. He was stuck in between my legs, and I enjoyed every second of it.

"Wyatt's here with me," I blurted out. I closed my eyes and waited for it. Three. Two. One.

"He's there with you?" Lacey asked, bringing her attention back to me. "How long has he been there? Grant's been trying to call him for over—"

"Kayce!" she hissed out loudly. "You didn't!"

I closed my eyes and lowered my face to my hand, immediately feeling ashamed of what I had done. Not that she was trying to shame me. It was more likely that she would start planning our wedding by the end of the phone call. I was the one who was getting ready to slap a scarlet letter across my chest.

"What did she do?" Grant asked in the background, loud enough that I could hear him clear as day. I groaned again, sitting down on the closed lid of the toilet.

"Nothing, I'll tell you about it later," Lacey whispered, either not noticing that she said it loud enough for me to hear, or not caring.

"Really Lace? You're going to talk to your fiancé about what I just did with his little brother?"

"I knew it," she giggled. "I knew you two would get together. I just didn't think it would happen so fast."

I shook my head in frustration. *You're telling me.*

I heard a phone ring through the door and wondered if Grant was calling Wyatt. It would be weird and uncomfortable, but I wouldn't doubt it. Lacey was going on with how she just knew this would happen, but I wasn't listening to a word that she said as I got up and moved closer to the door to listen.

"What's up, man?" Wyatt said, answering his phone. In the background of my call, I could hear Grant asking how Wyatt's drive was and if he had any problems with the truck. The conversation seemed to be steering clear of our little fuck fest, so I moved away from the door and sat down on the toilet, trying to catch up with whatever Lacey was rambling on about.

"And I think white lilies would be the perfect accent," she cooed.

"What are you talking about?" I asked confused.

"I knew you weren't listening," she laughed. "I guess you've got it bad. Can't say that I blame you."

"I don't have *anything* other than some feelings of guilt and embarrassment," I assured her, lifting my butt off of the seat to pull out a brush that I had been sitting on. "And maybe a little pain in my butt," I muttered, reaching back to rub the sore spot.

"Really? I didn't know you were into that, but okay," she giggled and I knew she was enjoying every second of this.

"No, not really. I sat on a brush, you pervert."

"I wasn't going to judge if you were into it."

"We're not having this conversation about your future brother-in-law," I assured her. "It's just gross."

The line went quiet for a minute so I pulled the phone away to make sure I hadn't lost the call. Nope, she was still there.

"Lace?"

"I'm still here. But you're right—that is gross. Thanks for ruining the fun I was having."

"Sorry, but at least you still have an attractive fiancé to have fun with when we hang up."

"Ugh, probably not," she grumbled.

"Why not?" I stood up and listened at the door again to see if Wyatt was still on the phone. I couldn't stay in the bathroom forever, and it felt weird hiding in here to talk to Lacey about him.

"Because Grant doesn't want to have sex or do anything until I'm at least twelve weeks. He thinks it's bad luck and doesn't want to risk hurting the babies."

"Well, you are having twins, so I'm sure that makes things a little more difficult than just one. You can't blame him for wanting to be careful, he just loves you and the babies."

"I know," she breathed out heavily. "Thankfully, I'll be ten weeks on Wednesday so he won't be able to use that as an excuse for much longer. I'm literally counting down the *days*."

"I think you might have a problem," I laughed.

"How do you think I got in this position to begin with? Even with Liam and Annie running around the house, I find myself trying to find reasons to send them over to his mom's house so I can jump on him. My doctor assured me that it's just the hormones, but I swear, he's never looked so good as he does right now."

"Right now, right now?" I quirked an eyebrow, wondering if she had finally lost her damn mind. It was a Monday night and he worked as a PE coach at the kids' school. I couldn't picture anything about that being sexy.

"Yes!" she hissed, pulling the phone closer to her mouth. "He's wearing a snug white t-shirt with gray sweatpants!"

"NO!" I gasped dramatically, playing along. "Not GRAY sweatpants!"

"Laugh now, but when you see a sexy man wearing them, you'll know what I'm talking about."

"I don't know, I don't tend to see many men parading around in sweats. I guess married life is just too much for me. Maybe it's a good thing I've vowed to stay single?"

"Just wait and see," she laughed harder. "Well, Grant is talking to Wyatt now so my reason for calling is taken care of. I'll let you go so you can get back to *whatever* it was you were doing."

"I'm getting ready for bed and calling it a day. And was your reason for calling was to find out whether I had sex with Wyatt?"

"No, I called to make sure he had gotten there okay. I just happened to be pleasantly surprised to hear that things had happened between you guys after all."

I rolled my eyes and shook my head. Ever since we were little girls, Lacey and I have always shared everything with each other so it was no surprise that she would find out about me and Wyatt right away. I felt bad for not telling her about the incident at work today with the random envelope and pictures, but until I knew who had left them and what they wanted, I didn't want to scare her. Hell, I didn't want to scare myself either, but I found that I had been cautiously looking over my shoulder all day after that.

"Alright, get those cute kids of yours to bed, and I'll talk to you soon," I said, suddenly missing Liam and Annie. Maybe it wouldn't be bad to make a trip down there soon to visit them. Both of their birthdays were coming up soon, which would be a good excuse to get down there. Not like I was hoping to see Wyatt again while I was there… even if he was Liam's uncle and would likely be there for his birthday as well. All purely innocent motives, if you asked me.

"Keep me posted on how things are going?"

"Lacey, I'm not going to keep you updated on my sex life with Wyatt," I snapped with a little more frustration than was necessary.

"So there's a sex life? You made it sound like it was a one-time thing when I first called," she said smugly.

"It was a one-time thing. A stupid, not thought through, one-time thing. That's it."

"Why are you fighting this so hard? You don't have to put a label on what happened, but Kayce, you're a single woman, and he's a single man. There's nothing to be embarrassed about if you both wanted it."

"I know, but Lace, he wasn't even around me TWENTY-FOUR hours before we had sex. That has to be some sort of new record for me," I admitted with embarrassment.

"Maybe because you guys—"

"Don't you dare say *are meant to be*," I groaned.

"No. Maybe because you guys have an insane amount of chemistry. Sometimes it's impossible to pull away from someone that you feel such a strong pull with. I know that things were hard for Grant and me given our pasts. Neither of us wanted to jump right in, but we also couldn't walk away if we tried. Sometimes, it's just better to give in to the attraction."

I knew what she was saying, and it made sense, but it didn't make me feel any better about what had happened. That wasn't the impression that I wanted to make on Wyatt. I also didn't want him to think that I was some tramp that just threw herself at any man that walked in her path.

"Alright, I gotta go," Lacey said, interrupting my thoughts. "But try not to overthink this. You're both grown-ups who had a good time. Leave it at that if you have to."

"Talk to you later," I replied, ignoring the rest of what she said.

I hung up the phone and gave myself a quick glance in the mirror before I opened the door and walked into the living room. Wyatt was sitting on the couch wearing the same hoodie he had on earlier and a pair of sweatpants. Not just any sweatpants. GRAY fucking sweatpants.

"Sorry, Lacey called while I was getting cleaned up," I said nervously, pointing over my shoulder to the bathroom.

"No worries, I just got off the phone with Grant."

"Everything okay?" I asked, my voice rising an octave as I worried about whether Grant knew what had happened between us.

"Yeah," he breathed, rubbing his hands together. "He promised to come down here and break my neck if I put my hands on you again."

I felt my heart skip a beat as I walked closer to him and sat on the opposite arm of the couch.

"What did you say?" I felt nervous asking him but it seemed like one way or another, we were going to address the elephant in the room.

"I told him that it wasn't my hands he needed to worry about… it was my tongue."

I felt the heat prickle my skin as the blush crept up my neck and across my cheeks.

"You didn't?!" I gasped, bringing my hands up to cover my face.

I felt him scoot over on the couch before he reached up and pulled my hands down.

"No, Kayce, I didn't. I don't talk about my sex life with my brother. You don't have to worry about that. But if you want to talk about where my tongue might be going, I'm always open for that conversation." He winked, the sexy dimple in his cheek making another appearance.

His words stunned me for a moment, turning me on as I thought about what had happened less than thirty minutes ago.

"Still thinking about that peach cobbler?" he asked as if reading my mind.

"Shit!" I exclaimed, jumping up and running into the kitchen. I looked at the carton of ice cream that was still sitting out on the counter that we had never gotten around to eating, along with the cobbler that was now in a puddle on the floor. I felt Wyatt walk up behind me and chuckle when he saw the mess that we had made. The ice cream had already melted and left a puddle in the middle of the black countertop.

"Sorry about the cobbler," he said quietly, with a hint of humor in his voice.

"Don't be," I sighed. "I was willing to part with it in exchange for that orgasm." I kept my back to him, afraid to turn around and look him in the eye.

"Here, let me help clean this up, then I'll run the trash out for you." He gently ran his fingers up the side of my arm, leaving goosebumps in its trail.

He stepped past me and grabbed the pile of napkins that came with the barbeque. With ease, he bent down and scooped up the cobbler, tossing it into the already full take-out bag that was now serving as a trash bag. I grabbed the mop from the closet by the front door and waited until he had picked up the last few pieces before we swapped places. He grabbed the carton of ice cream from the counter and added it to the stuff he was taking to the trash.

"I'll wipe the counter down," I said when he looked around for something he could use to clean up the melted ice cream.

"Okay, I can help when I get back. Where is the dumpster?"

"Downstairs, on the left, just past the giant, overgrown tree."

He nodded and carried everything gracefully out the door, careful not to spill anything on his way out. I quickly wiped down the counter and tossed the rag back in the sink to rinse it later before squirting some of the cleaning solution into the bin of my Swiffer mop. I loved this thing more than I loved any of my other cleaning appliances. Just a couple of sprays and my floor would be spotless and smell like pine.

I had just finished mopping the floor when I heard the door open and Wyatt walked in. I took off the cleaning pad and tossed it in the sink next to the dishrag while I drained the rest of the cleaning solution and rinsed it out. Everything else could wait until tomorrow, the essential stuff was done for now. I heard the door to the bathroom close and took the opportunity to get situated on the couch. I had turned on the tv and was flipping through the channels to find something to watch when he came out.

Wyatt joined me on the couch, given there was nowhere else to sit. We sat in awkward silence for a few minutes, both pretending to be interested in the infomercial. I knew it was still early, but I couldn't handle any more of the tension between us. I pretended to yawn while bringing my arms up over my head, trying to sell it that I was tired.

"Well, I think I'm going to call it a night," I said as groggily as I could. "Do you need anything?"

"I'm good," he said as he shook his head. "Thanks again for letting me stay here, I appreciate it."

"No problem." I smiled and got up. I was walking away, feeling confident that I had dodged a bullet when he spoke.

"Hey, Kayce?"

I stopped in my tracks, frozen and afraid to turn around to look at him.

"About tonight—I don't think any less of you and I hope you don't think any less of me. I'm sure you've heard that I have a reputation back home, but I wasn't going for a quick score with you. As much as I wanted to back off and *not* touch you, I couldn't. There's this electricity between us, and I couldn't walk away if I tried. For what it's worth, I'm sorry if I've overstepped or made you uncomfortable. I don't mind if you'd rather that I leave."

I slowly turned to look at him and tried to swallow past the lump in my throat as I listened to his words. He was being honest, I could see it in his eyes.

"Want to sleep next to me?" I asked nervously. As weird as everything had felt earlier, it now felt even stranger to not let him sleep with me in my bed. We did have sex after all, so nothing should be awkward or uncomfortable at this point—even though it was for me. Plus, I knew that my couch sucked to sleep on. I had done it a handful of times after having a few too many drinks and regretted it more than the hangover that usually came the next day.

"Is that what you want?" His face was stoic, his body tense as he waited.

I nodded and turned on my heel, walking to my bedroom before I could overthink it and change my mind. I heard his footsteps behind me and forced out the breath that I had been holding.

I stood next to the queen-sized bed and pulled back the comforter and sheet. I reached down to take my leggings off when it suddenly hit me. My face froze in panic as my cheeks reddened.

"What's wrong?" he asked from the other side of the bed, setting his phone down on the nightstand.

"Nothing," I lied in a whisper.

"Kayce…" He dropped his head slightly and pinned me with a look.

"Fine—I sleep naked. Okay?" I muttered in frustration.

"Okay… so why is that a problem?"

"It's not, I just—I can't just strip down and climb into bed knowing that you'll be lying next to me."

"Why not? Are you worried that you won't be able to keep your hands to yourself?" He arched a brow.

The temperature in the room increased tenfold as my palms started to sweat. As discreetly as possible, I ran them down the front of my pants.

"No, that's not it at all. It's just weird and awkward…"

"Because I would see you naked?" He paused for a minute, processing the information. "Again."

"It was different earlier," I whined. "That was for sex. There was an end goal. This is for sleep."

He turned to the side and pretended to cough to stifle his laugh. His dark brown hair caught in the light by the bed, casting a warm glow through it. He coughed again, clearing his throat before he turned back to look at me with a straight face.

"Okay, I have a solution to the problem," he assured me with a nod. It was my turn to arch a brow at him as I waited.

He reached down and pulled his hoodie up and over his head, revealing a ridiculously perfect body underneath. His abs were on point and his chest was more solid than an engine block. I let my eyes travel leisurely down his body, taking in every beautiful inch as his fingers hooked into the waistband of his sweats and he pulled them down.

While part of me was relieved that he had underwear on underneath, the dirty girl inside of me was hoping for another view of his rock-hard dick. My eyes lingered there for a second too long when I felt his eyes watching me, noticing what I was staring at.

"Problem solved," he said, stretching his arms out at his sides. "Now it's your turn."

I laughed and bit the inside of my cheek to keep from saying something stupid. Instead, I pulled my shirt over my head and tossed it to the floor before slipping out of my pants. I was still wearing my bra and panties but this was easier than trying to sleep in full clothes.

"I thought you slept naked?" he teased with a smirk, not bothering to hide that he was blatantly checking me out. "Did you need help with the rest?" He wiggled his brows.

"I'm not going to strip down naked in front of you," I said sarcastically. "This will be fine."

"Alright, suit yourself." He shrugged and reached down, pulling his underwear down and kicking them to the side with the pile of his other clothes. He looked overly confident standing there naked, not an ounce of fat anywhere on his perfectly fuckable body. I fought the urge to look at the one-eyed monster as it started to rise in greeting.

I turned my back to him and reached behind me, unclasping my bra and sliding it down my arms before I let it fall to the floor. I tucked my fingers into the top of my panties and slid them off, tossing them in with the other pile of clothes before I lifted the covers and slipped into bed. I felt childish and immature, but something about the way he was looking at me made me so nervous and aroused that I didn't care. Maybe it wouldn't be that bad to share my bed with him tonight after all…

THREE STRIKES, YOU'RE GONE

<u>Six</u>

Wyatt

His eyes looked like they were bulging out of his head as he held a hand to his chest and looked around, panicked.

"Dad!" I screamed, trying to force him to snap out of it.

I watched as he leaned against the truck, his body slowly slumping to the cold cement floor of the garage, the wrench falling out of his other hand. I kneeled down beside him, trying to help, but not knowing what to do.

"Dad, what's wrong? What can I do?" I begged, watching as different emotions flashed through his eyes. The most obvious one—fear. I jumped up and looked around, hoping that one of our neighbors would hear me. No one else was home so it was pointless to call Grant or Chase.

"HELP!!! PLEASE, SOMEONE!! HELP MY DAD!!" I screamed into the silent air around us.

I turned back around and found my dad lying beside the truck. Our eyes locked onto each other's one last time before he let out his final breath.

I leaped forward in the bed, gasping for air the way I always did when I had this dream. Only this wasn't a dream. It was a fucking nightmare that I couldn't stop no matter how hard I tried. I felt the bed shift beside me, glancing over to make sure I hadn't woken Kayce. Her purple hair was fanned out across her back as she laid on her stomach, face buried deep in the pillow. The contrast of the blue sheets to her bright colored hair made her look like some sort of beautiful mermaid.

I forced a deep breath out, then slowly pulled one in. My heart was racing, and I knew that there was no way that I was going to be able to go back to sleep after that. The week had already started out rough but I had prayed that today would be a better day. It was still early enough to try to turn it around.

As quietly as possible, I climbed out of bed and slipped my sweatpants on. There was a chill in the air so I threw my hoodie on as well. Glancing down at my phone, I found it was barely four-thirty in the morning which meant that I had a lot of time to kill before I could head over to the hotel to get things situated. I also needed to find a rental car for the time being while I had Kayce look at the truck. There was plenty on my plate, and nothing that I had planned to have to deal with when I first came out here.

My first meeting with the possible recruit wasn't until Wednesday morning, but I came down early to see what the town was all about. This was my first recruiting job, and I knew from personal experience that if I was going to try to convince this kid to leave his hometown, I'd better have a good argument on what he would be gaining by moving to Haven Brook. If I could lay low for the first few days without him knowing I was here, I would get a good idea of who he really was and that meant that I would have an advantage with getting him to commit.

I grabbed my duffel bag and went to the living room to work for a bit. I considered making coffee, but given that I didn't know where she kept anything, I didn't want to risk waking her up by looking for stuff. I decided to just wait until she was up and see if there was a coffee shop close by. I had already had sex with her but had no idea if she drank coffee. Yeah, I was off to a good start.

I rolled my eyes and shook my head, trying to force the sarcastic thoughts away. Grant had been quick to lecture me about what happened, reminding me that she wasn't just some girl in a new town that I would never see again. Nope, she was the cousin of his fiancé and at this point, I believed him when he said he would cut my dick off and beat me with it if I did anything to hurt her.

Thankfully, I was able to divert the conversation to the truck which held Grant's attention long enough to forget about everything else. It was a hot topic in our family whenever it came up, but I appreciated that Grant held a little more sentimental attachment to the truck like I did. Chase didn't understand why we were still messing around with it, but Grant knew why I couldn't just walk away from it. I would go to my grave with that truck by my side because it was the last memory I had with my dad. I owed it to him to take care of it and keep it in our family for as long as I could.

I opened my bag and pulled out my laptop, hoping that I had enough battery to get through a couple of hours' worth of work. I had made sure it was fully charged before I left, but given how everything else was going so far, I wouldn't be surprised if it died in five minutes. It would be just my luck.

I leaned back against the cushion on the couch, propping my feet up in front of me as I set the computer on my lap. I was so focused on waiting for it to start up that I hadn't heard Kayce come out of the room. The screen lit up as the icons started popping up and a picture of me and my mom displayed as the wallpaper.

"Oh my gosh, that is the cutest picture," Kayce said over my shoulder. I felt myself jump as she startled me, turning to look at her while making sure I didn't drop the laptop.

"Sorry, I didn't mean to scare you," she laughed, resting her hand on my shoulder.

"You're fine," I laughed with her, enjoying her touch. "I just didn't hear you come out. You're like some early morning sly ninja."

"Hmmm." She pursed her lips and tapped her finger to her chin. "You're right. I think I'll add that to my resume." She shot me a playful smile over her shoulder as she turned and walked into the kitchen. "Do you want some coffee?" she asked, bending over to get something out of the cabinet.

"Sure, if you're making some for yourself, I'd love a cup. If not, please don't go through the trouble for me."

"It's not a problem at all," she said breathlessly as she pulled a blender out from under the sink and set it on the counter.

I raised an eyebrow, wondering what she was doing.

"Where exactly do you put that filter thingy?" She raised on her tiptoes and lifted the lid, looking inside before looking over at me. Her face was utterly adorable, but I worried that she might be serious.

"You're going to make coffee in *that*?" I asked, setting my laptop down on the coffee table.

"Uhhh… yeah." She tilted her head to the side and looked at me like I was the crazy one. "Why, are you too good for my coffee? Do you need some sort of hipster coffee drink with organic beans and cream whipped by a leprechaun?"

I walked over to the counter, resting my hands as I lowered my head to look her in the eyes.

"You do know that this isn't a coffee maker. Right?"

Her face fell as she lifted her hand to her mouth. The golden brown color of her eyes had flecks of green in them as the corners of her lips turned up and she burst into laughter.

"Yes, Wyatt, I know that this isn't a coffee maker," she laughed hysterically. "But man, you should have seen your face." She pointed a finger and kept laughing before she bent down and pulled the coffee pot out from under the same cabinet.

"You're rotten." I shook my head playfully, walking around to the other side of the counter. She was wearing a pair of black leggings with a loose t-shirt that was probably two sizes too big for her. While it would probably make other women look frumpy, she looked incredibly cute in it with her hair pulled up into a messy knot on the top of her head.

"Do you need help?" I offered, noticing the hoarseness in my voice again.

"Nah, I got it. Thank you."

"I take it you don't make coffee much?" I nodded to the blender that she had to pull out to get to the coffee maker, which also made me wonder if she even had coffee if she didn't make it often.

"Coffee runs through my veins," she said as she plugged it in. "But, Saturday was girl's night which meant frozen margaritas. Priorities." She gave me a quick wink before she scooted over and opened the cabinet, pulling out a bag of coffee grounds and a filter.

"How do you like your coffee?" Her hand froze in the air while she waited for my answer before filling the filter with coffee.

"Strong, but I'll drink it however you want yours."

"Good. I like it strong too."

I watched as she packed the filter with as much coffee as it could take before she plopped it into the maker and added the water. A few minutes later the room was filled with the delicious aroma of coffee brewing.

"Why are you up so early?" She asked as she busied herself around the kitchen, pulling down coffee mugs and grabbing the creamer from the fridge. She set everything between us, then stopped and gave me her full attention while she waited for me to speak.

I didn't want to talk about the dream or how the nightmares of the day my dad died still haunted me, so I just blew it off with a shrug.

"I had work to get done. Nothing major. I couldn't sleep so I figured I would start looking into the fabulous town of Easterville."

"What did you find?" She turned her back to me to grab a spoon out of the drawer. Flashbacks of eating her out on the counter last night came flashing through my mind, making my dick twitch at the thought.

"Not much, someone scared the shit out of me before I could look," I laughed. "Why are you up so early?"

"I'm naturally an early bird. Always have been, which is odd because I'm also a night owl. I like to stay up late and get up early which has never made sense. I guess I'm just one of those people who doesn't need a lot of sleep." She held her hands out to the side. The coffee trickled to a stop before she pulled the carafe out and poured each of us a cup.

She held hers with two hands and lifted it to her lips. Before taking a sip, she closed her eyes and took a deep breath, inhaling the aroma of the steaming mug of coffee first. Her lips parted while her eyes stayed closed, the hot liquid forcing its way inside. Everything about what she was doing was so fucking arousing that I was worried I was going to break the mug I was holding in my hand just to keep from coming from the image in front of me.

Slowly, her eyes opened after taking a drink, embarrassment washing over her when she saw the way I was looking at her. There was no hiding what I was thinking, but I was thankful that I had moved back to the other side of the counter so she couldn't see the erection that was trying to force its way out of my sweatpants.

"Well, if you're up for it, I'll take you to breakfast this morning," she offered, setting her mug down in front of her. "That way you can get the best breakfast burrito in all of Easterville since you're looking at what we have to offer." She raised her eyebrows with faux excitement.

"Are you telling me that the best thing Easterville has to offer is a breakfast burrito?" I asked wearily, lifting my mug to take a drink.

"No, not the best *thing*. Just the best breakfast option. Trust me, it's delicious and you'll never want another breakfast burrito again after you try this one."

"Alright, fine," I sighed dramatically. "If you insist that it's the best, then I guess we'll have to go try it. But there is one condition…"

"What's that?"

"I'm paying," I said flatly, making sure she heard the tone to know that I wasn't playing.

"Don't be such a caveman," she replied, rolling her eyes as she grabbed her mug off the counter. "I can and I *will* buy you breakfast. I just need fifteen minutes to shower real quick, then you can jump in while I get ready," she called over her shoulder as she walked away and closed the bathroom door behind her.

I took my coffee to the couch and sat down, still shaking my head at the thought of her paying for my food. It was bad enough that I had crashed at her place last night, but my only other choice was to freeze my ass off in the truck since I didn't get in early enough to secure my hotel room. I set the mug down and opened my laptop, trying to think about what could possibly be the most interesting thing in Easterville.

While most people would google things like *places to eat, things to do,* I found myself googling 'Wrenched'. A few seconds passed by before the screen changed and a general search of the auto shop popped up. There were a handful of pictures linked to it with comments about how hot the mechanic was, but there wasn't an actual website for Wrenched. I looked through a few of the photos before I clicked on one of her and some guy.

I leaned forward and read the caption underneath.

Jolted lead singer Brent Fallows with girlfriend Kayce Fields

Girlfriend? I clenched my fist, wondering if she was still with this douchebag-looking prick who was caught on camera checking out another woman's ass as she stood next to him. In a way, I hoped she was, only so I could make her scream my name while he listened, knowing he would never be able to please her the way I had.

I scrolled through more pictures of them together. Aside from her hair changing colors, they all looked the same. He was constantly focused on every other woman around them, while she stood there, looking unimpressed and bored.

A squeak from the bathroom drifted under the door as the shower turned off. I closed out the browser window I had opened and shut down the computer. The door opened a few minutes later as I was sliding the laptop back into my duffle bag. As I looked up, I found Kayce walking out with her hair wrapped up in a towel on her head, her cup of coffee in one hand, and her other hand holding the corner of the towel against her body.

My eyes took their time, slowly scanning her body as the blush crept across her skin. I licked my lips, fighting the urge to walk over and strip her of the fluffy material that was covering her sexy fucking body.

"I saved you some hot water," she whispered as she stood in the living room. She didn't look like she wanted to walk away from this either, but one of us had to force ourselves to think straight. I grabbed my bag from the floor and stood up, pulling it over my shoulder.

"Thanks, I think a cold one is in store for me at this point," I muttered as I walked past her and closed the door.

She was gorgeous, there was no doubt about that. But it was like there was some secret language that our bodies were speaking to each other and neither of us knew what it was. Our heads were able to rationalize that we were doing something stupid, but our bodies were the ones who weren't getting the message.

I turned the handle and didn't bother waiting for the water to warm up before I stripped down and climbed inside. Maybe the burst of cold water would convince my dick to stand down before we got ourselves in over our head.

I hadn't thought to pull my toiletries out of my bag beforehand so I was stuck using whatever she had in the shower. I was thankful to find that she wasn't one of those girls who used expensive products or things that were heavily scented. I reached for the bottle of shampoo and squirted some in my hand, wondering if it would be helpful to deal with the other situation while I was here.

The subtle vanilla scent filled the shower, making me think of her naked body under the hot water a few minutes ago. I groaned as I added more shampoo to my hand before reaching down and gliding it over my cock. I pictured Kayce's mouth as it wrapped tightly around my dick, sucking hard as she worked me over with her tongue. I stroked faster, the smooth glide from the liquid coating me as I imagined being inside of her slick, wet pussy. I held my hand against the wall to brace myself while I jerked hard and fast, my dick growing harder as my balls started to ache. My breathing grew more rapid as I imagined her riding me, her thighs clenching around my body as she threw her head back and came on my dick. The way her mouth parted and her nipples perked when she was about to come had me jerking harder until I shot ropes of cum across the shower.

I cleaned up and finished washing my body before I got out and felt the cold chill of the tile floor beneath me. Suddenly, I was regretting not taking a hot shower after all. I pulled the towel around my waist and dug through my bag, grabbing a fresh pair of jeans and a clean t-shirt. I had left my suitcase in the truck but knew better than to not pack at least one clean outfit in my duffle bag, which had worked in my favor this morning.

By the time I had brushed my teeth and got dressed, Kayce was already in the kitchen when I came out.

"I hung my towel on the hook behind the door, I hope that's okay," I said as I walked out and pulled the door closed behind me.

"That's perfect, thank you."

She looked sexy with her hair pulled up into a high, messy bun that sat on top of her head. The front was puffed up like the retro girls I used to see in the calendars my dad would buy me every year. He would tell my mom that he got them for me because of my love for classic cars but then would wink when she wasn't looking to let me know that he only bought them for me because of the girls. I could totally picture Kayce as a pin-up model next to an old muscle car.

"You ready to get going?" she asked, breaking me free from my thoughts of her climbing up the hood of a hotrod, her ass in booty shorts on full display with her lips parted open.

"Yeah, sorry." I shook my head and smiled.

She reached down and picked up the same bag I had seen her with last night. It looked heavier than it did last night and I wasn't sure how she was even able to carry it. I rushed over and grabbed it before she could slide it up onto her shoulder.

"Here, let me help you with that," I said softly, our fingers brushing against each other as I took it from her.

"It's okay, I got it. It's heavy," she countered, not bothering to move her hand from mine.

"Which is all the more reason why I should help you with it."

She paused and narrowed her eyes at me.

"Are you insinuating that because I'm a woman, I'm not strong enough to carry it myself?"

I met the glare she was giving me and smiled. A genuine smile. Not some dickish smile that she was probably expecting.

"Not at all. I think it's fucking amazing that you carry this to begin with, and I have no doubt that you are strong. However, I was raised to be a gentleman, which means that if a woman is carrying something— I'm going to offer to carry it for her. Not because you can't do it yourself, but because my momma raised me better than that."

Her features softened a bit but her grip on the strap of the bag remained firm.

"Can I please be a gentleman and carry your bag?"

She paused for a moment to think, making it obvious that she was messing with me.

"Fine," she sighed. "But I get to buy breakfast."

I rolled my eyes as I took the bag from her and lifted it onto my shoulder. I shifted the duffle bag around my shoulders to balance the weight, then followed her downstairs to her truck. I handed her the bag before she got in, then walked around and climbed in. I wasn't going to be nosey and ask what she had in that damn thing, but part of me wondered if it was the body of the fucking loser wanna-be rock star she was dating. If it was, I would gladly help her bury that shit in some abandoned field where no one would ever find it.

The roads were empty, and I didn't know if it was because it was barely six in the morning or if this was just the normal for Easterville. We passed by Wrenched, and I was relieved to see the truck still sitting where I had left it, all in one piece. It had been hard to walk away last night, not knowing if it would still be there this morning. A wave of calm hit me and reminded me why that truck meant so much to me.

Ten minutes later, we were parked in an empty parking lot and walking into a building that looked like it belonged in the 1970s. A bell chimed as we opened the door, with a nauseating wave of orange shag carpet greeting us as we walked inside. There was wood paneling along the walls and off in the corner were a few animal heads that had been mounted. I pulled my lips together, forcing myself to stay quiet so I didn't say anything rude while we waited for someone to come seat us.

Kayce peered up at me, a smug smile on her face as she studied me. I knew she could tell how uncomfortable I was and that I was definitely judging the town by this so-called treasure. Haven Brook wasn't known for much in the way of food, but at least our breakfast burritos had surpassed the time capsule that we were currently trapped in.

I looked around for a sign so I could text Grant and let him know where to send the coroner to come to collect my body. Time of death: six-fifteen. Location: Jumping Joe's.

Just as I was taking stock of the things around me, a woman in her twenties came flying around the corner, screeching to a stop right in front of us.

"Howdy! Dine-in or to-go?" she asked, tucking a strand of curly blond hair back behind her ear.

"Dine-in," Kayce confirmed.

"Right this way," the woman said cheerfully before grabbing a few menus and making her way over to the table. She stopped and waited for us to sit down before she walked off.

"So, this is the best of Easterville," I said carefully, picking up the menu to look it over. It was a long piece of laminated paper that looked promising until I saw that there were only two options listed on the menu. Kayce's eyes danced wildly as she watched me examine the menu, flipping it over to see if there was more on the back. I raised an eyebrow and looked past the menu at her.

"The only options are burrito or," I paused and looked back at the menu for dramatic effect. "Or burrito."

"Well, things here are simple." She shrugged, smiling as the waitress came back with two glasses of water.

"Alright, what can I get you?"

"You mean there's more than burritos?" I asked dryly, setting the menu down in front of me. I placed my hands on the table and looked up at her.

"Well, duh," she snorted, laughing with Kayce as if I just said the funniest thing.

"Humor me," I prodded. "What else is there to get here?"

"Trust me, sugar, you don't want anything else. This is *the place* to go for breakfast burritos in all of Colorado. Don't you go messing that up by trying to order something different."

I clicked my tongue against the roof of my mouth and looked at Kayce. Her smile was still stretched across her face as if she was enjoying every second of this.

"I'll have the bacon burrito," she said, turning her attention away from me and back to the waitress.

"I'll do the same," I replied, pushing my menu to the edge of the table. She nodded and scooped the menus up before walking off to the back, yelling *two bacon!* on her way into the kitchen.

"So… what do you think?" Kayce asked, trying to stifle her laugh.

"I think you might be someone to keep an eye on. Lacey insisted that I could trust you, but I'm starting to wonder if her pregnancy brain is impacting her judgment," I teased, squinting my eyes at her.

"Trust me, it looks totally like something you'd find in an outdated horror movie, but their burritos are the best."

"I guess we shall see."

I looked around the small room, noticing a few of the other tables starting to fill up with customers. The clock on my phone said it was almost six-thirty, so maybe this was the time the town started their days. It would be good to get a feel for how things worked here so I could compare them to how things would be in Haven Brook.

"So, Lacey mentioned that you were here for work. What do you do?" Kayce asked, pushing the paper off of her straw and crumbling it into a small ball in her hands.

"I'm a Recruiting Coordinator for Haven Brook University."

"What does that mean? Sorry, don't hate me, I've never been much into sports." She squinted her eyes and scrunched up her face.

"Basically, it means that I find talented players and essentially stalk them until they commit to our university," I laughed, knowing there were many levels of truth in that statement.

"High school kids?"

"Yeah, mostly juniors. Some seniors. It just depends. Right now, I'm here to meet with a senior at Easterville High. He has a lot of talent and the potential to do two years with Haven Brook before moving up."

"What's his name?" she asked, leaning back as the waitress returned and set our plates down in front of us. The burritos were massive and took up the entire plate. The smell of bacon made my stomach growl as my fingers itched to pick it up and dig in, though I wasn't sure that I could even pick the beast up.

"You might want to give it a few minutes," she warned, watching my fingers as they started to reach for the burrito. "They crisp the burrito which is what makes it so delicious, but it takes a few minutes before it's edible without scalding your mouth."

I nodded and pushed the plate away to keep the temptation at bay.

"Junior Soto," I said, ignoring the loud growl from my stomach. Maybe there was some truth to these being the best breakfast burritos after all?

"He's definitely one of the best that we have," she agreed, cutting into her burrito with a knife to let some of the steam out.

"Well, that makes my job harder," I joked.

"Why is that?"

"Because I have to convince him that Haven Brook is *the place* to be so he'll commit to our school." I paused to cut into my burrito like Kayce had. I took a bite and closed my eyes as I chewed. This was beyond delicious. "And unfortunately, we don't have breakfast burritos like this in Haven Brook."

Kayce covered her mouth as she laughed, the sound almost as wonderful as the food in front of me.

THREE STRIKES, YOU'RE GONE

Seven

Kayce

I was pleasantly surprised by how much Wyatt had enjoyed breakfast, even though I knew he would be crazy not to. We finished breakfast and when he wasn't looking, I slipped some cash to Naomi, the waitress, for our meals. We climbed back into the truck and made a pit stop at the gas station before heading to the hotel. I advised him to grab at least three Paydays and couldn't help but laugh when I saw him come out with a bag filled with them. I'm not sure how much bribing he thought he was going to have to do, but this should cover him.

A few minutes later, we were parked in front of the Honey Lodge, patiently waiting inside at the front desk for someone to come greet us. I had assumed that Trudy would be working but almost burst into another fit of laughter when I saw Fred round the corner, his eyes narrowed at us behind the thick lenses of his bifocals.

"Can I help you?" he grumbled, sitting down on the padded chair behind the desk. He glanced over at the bag of candy bars that Wyatt was trying to discreetly pull to the side, out of his view.

"Um, hi, I'm Wyatt Walker. I had a reservation yesterday but wasn't able to make it in time due to some car trouble," he said, forcing a smile as Fred glowered at him. "I apologize for the late notice, sir—"

"Mr. Ashby," he corrected.

"Mr. Ashby," Wyatt repeated. "However, I wanted to see if I might be able to get a room for the rest of this week. I'm here on business."

Fred looked between us, studying me then Wyatt. I had known him long enough to know that he was as harmless as a butterfly, even though he liked to act like he was tough.

"Where's Trudy?" I asked, interrupting his thoughts as he glared at Wyatt again.

"She's home, sick, probably from all of the candy that the good-looking out-of-town kids bring her to bribe her to give them a room," he said sarcastically, looking back at Wyatt who was now pushing the bag further away. "She has diabetes, you know?"

I turned my head to the side and coughed, trying to hide the laughter that was threatening to come out.

"We hope she feels better soon," I said sincerely. "What do you say, do you have a room that this good-looking out of towner can have?" I tilted my head to the side and gave him my best smile.

"No."

He picked up the newspaper that was lying on the desk, shaking it open. I gently reached over and pushed it down, making sure he could see me.

"I'll give you a free oil change…" I offered.

He lowered the newspaper to his lap and thought about it.

"Two. Trudy needs one too, even though Lord knows she never goes anywhere other than to Bingo to blab about Tracy Miller." He shook his head as if this was a heated topic for him.

"Deal," I said, interrupting him before he could go on. I stuck my hand out, smiling when he reached over and shook it.

Ten daunting long minutes later, Fred was handing Wyatt two key cards to his hotel room and confirmed that he would need to call down daily for the Wi-Fi password if he wanted to use it. He grumbled about how the kids around town try to use it for free, and he had to put a stop to that. I laughed, knowing how true and funny it was, even though his scowl confirmed that he didn't see any humor in it.

"Thank you again for the room, sir, I appreciate it," Wyatt said, grabbing the bag of candy from the desk.

"Leave the candy," Mr. Ashby said with a sheepish grin. "Trudy's not the only one around here who likes a sweet bribe." He wiggled his eyebrows and smiled for the first time.

"Fred!" I gasped and brought my hand to my chest. "You just got two free oil changes from me, AND a bag full of candy out of him." I shook my head and tsked at him. "If Trudy knew…"

"Who do you think she learned it from?" He shrugged and laughed hysterically as we walked out and left him to his stash of sugary treats.

The air was bitterly cold as we walked outside, the wind sending a chill right through us. We jumped in the truck, and I turned the heater on to help warm us up.

"So, did you want me to drive you around back to your room?" I asked, not sure what his plans were for the day. I needed to get to the shop before long, but since I didn't have any clients waiting on me, I wasn't in a rush.

"Sure, that would be great. Thank you," he said, looking down at his phone. "Do you remember him giving me the Wi-Fi password?" he asked, his brows pulled together as his fingers swiped across the screen.

"He did, I think it was NOCANDY, all capital letters," I laughed.

"I put that in, but it's showing spotty service. Maybe it will be better in my room."

I looked around at the mountain that the hotel was butted up against and knew that he wasn't going to have any better luck in his room. The internet service here was crap because of the lack of towers nearby and the thick forest that surrounded the hotel on three out of four sides.

"It's not going to be any better in your room," I said, shaking my head as I pulled around to the row of rooms by the back parking lot. "Why don't you go get yourself settled inside and then bring whatever you need for work, and I'll take you to my shop. I have great service there and you can work out of my office."

"I don't want to be in the way," he insisted with his hands up.

"You won't. Besides, I might have questions about your truck, and it'll be helpful if you're right there to answer them." I smiled but didn't miss the look that flashed across his face. The sadness mixed with pain when I mentioned working on the truck. "Unless you don't want me to look at it?"

"No, it's not that. Sorry, I'm just out of it today. I'll go drop off my stuff real quick," he said before climbing out and shutting the door.

I leaned back against the seat, taking in the warmth of the heater as I tried to relax. There was negative energy in the air, and I couldn't put my finger on what it was. I closed my eyes and focused on my breathing. In. Out. In. Out. It was weird, when Wyatt was around, I felt fine, safe even. But once he got out of the truck and went into his room, I had this terrible anxiety that crept up on me. I hadn't quite shaken this feeling since yesterday in my office, but for whatever reason, I felt better when he was around.

Eight

Wyatt

It was almost one o'clock, and Kayce had spent most of the morning helping one of the locals with their work truck that had broken down over the weekend. She promised to look at my truck when she was done, but I reminded her that I wasn't in a hurry. Now that I knew how small the town was, I was confident that I could easily get around where I needed to without my truck. As long as it was up and running by the end of the week so I could head back home, that was all that I needed.

I had been working on my laptop, going over the paperwork that had been sent over for Junior. There were plenty of other students that we could have been recruiting, but he was listed as the top priority and based on his stats, I could see why. This kid was the wet dream of baseball. My phone vibrated across Kayce's desk, showing the head coach's name on the caller ID.

"Hey, Chuck," I answered.

"How's the great town of Easterville treating you?" he snickered sarcastically.

"Well, I finally got a room at the luxury Honey Lodge after bribing the owner with a bag full of candy bars, and I had the best breakfast burrito in all of my life," I said with a laugh.

"So, you've been to Jumping Joe's. It's definitely a must while you're there."

"Yeah, I think that's all that's really a *must*," I countered. "Other than The Tasty Pig. That was pretty good too." I thought back to the cobbler incident last night and felt my dick twitch in response.

"Are you ready for your meeting with Junior Soto tomorrow?" he asked, interrupting my dirty thoughts.

"Yeah, I have all of the paperwork printed and I've gone over his stats sheet. This should be quick and easy unless there's another school that he decides to commit to instead."

"Don't go putting that karma out in the universe, kid," he warned playfully, even though we both knew that it was a possibility. The only good thing about him being from such a small town was that it was more likely for him to be under the radar of the larger D1 division schools that would try to snatch him up as well.

"Don't worry, I'll make sure I don't leave here without his commitment," I assured him. This was my first recruit, and I was determined not to screw it up. I remembered how excited I was when I committed to Haven Brook University and how huge it felt when I was picked up by a pro team before my injury. I tried to push the thoughts away of what could have been as I hung up with Chuck. My life had done a complete 180, and even though I wouldn't change anything about saving Lacey's life, I hated that it cost me everything I had worked hard for since I was a kid.

I still went to my follow-up doctor appointments as part of my agreement with the Colorado Cougars and humored them by continuing the physical therapy even though I knew it wasn't helping. Numerous doctors had told me that the likelihood of pitching again was slim. Being a left-handed pitcher who had to have three separate heart surgeries to repair the damage from being stabbed was pretty much a death sentence to my career as a professional ballplayer.

I heard the door open up front as Kayce came back inside from dealing with another customer. She had made it seem like she wasn't usually that busy, but today seemed to be slammed for her. I felt bad about taking up her office and keeping her from getting work done. I logged out of my email and shut down my computer before unplugging it and stuffing it back into the backpack that I had brought with me.

"Hey, how's it going?" she asked as she came in and picked up the bottle of water that was sitting on the edge of her desk. She twisted the top off and took a drink.

"It's good," I said, standing up to move out of her way. "I'm all done with what I needed to do, so you can have your office back."

"Oh, no worries," she said and waved it off. "I'll do all of my paperwork tomorrow. But I'm done with the other cars, did you want to go show me what's been going on with your truck?"

I felt the lump in my throat as I tried to push my words out.

"Sure," was all that I was able to get out. I set my backpack down on the couch against the wall and followed her out to the parking lot where it was still sitting. The snow was beginning to fall again which didn't feel promising that I would make it back to Haven Brook this weekend after all. Thankfully, it wasn't as cold as it had been which was keeping the snow from sticking.

"Lacey mentioned that you were having some problems with it backfiring recently," she stated as she walked to the back of the truck and squatted to look at the tailpipe.

"Yeah, it's been guzzling gas and I've seen clouds of white smoke as well. My guess is that it's the carburetor."

"When was the last time that you had any work done on it?" she asked as she walked around to the front and waited for me to pop the hood. I closed the door and went to help her lift it when she gave me a glance that told me she didn't need my help.

"It's been a while," I shrugged, not wanting to get into the details. "I've done basic maintenance on it, but it hasn't needed much other than that until now."

"It's a 1969?"

I was impressed. She definitely knew vehicles, and I could tell by the way she was treating mine that she also respected them.

"Yeah." I felt my hands starting to sweat, the memories of my dad trying to push their way to the surface.

"Do you know if there was ever any major work done to it before you bought it?" she asked as she turned away from the truck and looked at me.

I shook my head, partly trying to answer her questions but also trying to force the thoughts of that day out of my head. My dad and I were getting ready to start a big project on the truck before he died, but we never got around to it. I had always hated that I didn't know much about what work it still needed because I always spent my time with him rambling on about baseball.

"It's okay if you don't know," she assured me, stepping closer. "I can get in there and find out what's going on. I agree, I think it's the carburetor as well, but I'm worried you might have a bad head gasket. I'll poke around some more and see what I can find."

His eyes looked like they were bulging out of his head as he held a hand to his chest and looked around, panicked.

"Dad!" I screamed, trying to force him to snap out of it.

I watched as he leaned against the truck, his body slowly slumping to the cold cement floor of the garage, the wrench falling out of his other hand. I kneeled down beside him, trying to help, but not knowing what to do.

"Dad, what's wrong? What can I do?" I begged, watching as different emotions flashed through his eyes. The most obvious one—fear. I jumped up and looked around, hoping that one of our neighbors would hear me. No one else was home so it was pointless to call Grant or Chase.

"HELP!!! PLEASE, SOMEONE!! HELP MY DAD!!" I screamed into the silent air around us.

I turned back around and found my dad lying beside the truck. Our eyes locked onto each other's one last time before he let out his final breath.

I gasped as I felt her hands on my arm, pulling me out of the nightmare that had been trying to consume for almost eleven years now.

"Hey," she said softly. "It's okay, we'll figure it out."

While her words were meant to be a comfort, there was one big problem with them. No matter how hard I tried, I would never be able to figure it out. My dad's death was the one thing that continued to haunt me, no matter what I did to try to stop it.

<u>Nine</u>

Kayce

After a slew of curse words, Wyatt was able to get the truck to start and pulled into the garage bay. It wasn't a big garage, especially with my project car off in the back of it that I hadn't had a chance to work on in a while.

I took note of several things that helped solidify my suspicions about what was wrong with it. He put it in park and turned off the engine, while I went back to my office to grab the bag I needed. I carried it into the garage and set it down on the work table, hearing the loud sound it made from the weight of it. There was something strangely satisfying about that sound.

I opened it up and started pulling some tools out, deciding what I needed first.

"Oh, thank God," Wyatt said. "It's just tools…" A cheeky smile spread across his face.

"What did you think it was?" I asked, laughing as I stopped what I was doing to wait for his answer.

"A dead body."

My eyes bugged out as I stared at him, the grin on my face pulling tighter as I tried to cover it behind my hand.

"Why on earth would you think that I have a dead body in here?"

"I don't know… it's super heavy and I guess I just thought it might be Brent Fallows—boyfriend and the lead singer of Jolted." He shrugged his shoulders but the grin didn't fade.

"You Googled me?" I asked. I tilted my head to the side and rested my hand on my hip.

"Maybe."

My eyebrows slowly inched higher up my face as I waited for him to come clean.

"Alright. Fine. I Googled you this morning."

I shook my head and pretended to be offended by this blatant invasion of privacy, but secretly I felt excited and giddy that he had been interested enough to do it in the first place.

"So, did you find what you were looking for?" I kept my head down, while I rifled through the bag, looking for my favorite wrench. Once I had the tools I needed lined up, I straightened and looked at him, wondering why he hadn't answered me.

" I found lots of articles about your boyfriend, Brent," he said cautiously.

"He's not my boyfriend. We broke up," I clarified a little too sharply.

He nodded as if that was the answer he was hoping for.

"Now that we've settled that, is there a girl back in Haven Brook that's going to threaten to come kick my ass for sleeping with you?"

"Probably more than I can count," he mumbled and turned his head away.

I grabbed the tools from the table and debated whether or not to bother responding. Lacey had told me plenty of times how Wyatt had a different girl every day of the week, so why did this bother me so much all of a sudden?

"Let's take a look at the truck, shall we?" I said through gritted teeth, hating the jealousy that was running through me at the thought of

Wyatt with another woman.

He gave me a devilish smile as if he was enjoying the fact that I was flustered by what he said. From that point on, we didn't talk. He stood off to the side, while I did my thing. I pulled out the creeper and slid under the truck, making sure that I checked everything before reporting back to him on what I thought was wrong with the truck. Plus, I just wanted to be able to hide for a few moments and not feel the pull of his body so close to mine.

When I couldn't delay any longer, I scooted out from under the truck and got up. I set the tools down next to the bag and brushed my hands on the front of my pants.

"It's your carburetor," I said as I stood at the table and looked at him. "Usually you'll find that the vehicle is acting more sluggish, so you give it more gas. Well, that extra fuel that you're going through is forcing it to stall out and is also creating the backfire. I also noticed that the head gasket is bad, which is what's creating all of the smoke that's coming out of the exhaust. I can fix both, but I'll have to order some parts."

"How long do you think before it's up and running?"

"Honestly, I don't know." I shook my head. "It'll be at least a few days for the order and with the storm that's supposed to hit this week, I don't know if that will delay things further. Also, I won't know if there's anything else going on until I get in there to fix those items. If I find additional problems, then that will add on to the time it takes me to get it running again."

He closed his eyes and let his head fall backward, rotating it along his neck.

"I'm sorry it's not better news," I added gently.

"It's not your fault, I just have terrible luck this week," he replied with frustration. "I should have been more focused on taking care of it to keep it from getting to this point, to begin with."

"Why haven't you?" I asked politely. One thing that I'd learned in this business was that those who had older vehicles tend to take good care of them. If you're not interested in the maintenance and upkeep of an older vehicle, you get a new one with a warranty and let the dealership handle things that come up. But when you have a 1969 Chevy C10, you'd better be taking care of that beautiful piece of art.

"My dad and I were working on the truck when he died," he said quietly.

He looked at the floor and avoided me as my soul crumbled at the heartbreak in the words he'd just spoken.

"I'm so sorry, Wyatt, I didn't know," I apologized.

"Not many people do. It's not something that I like to talk about."

"I get that," I said quietly, stepping closer, reaching out to touch his arm.

"No, you don't," he bit out, pulling away from me. "I don't avoid talking about it, because I'm sad that he died. I avoid talking about it because I'm the one who killed him."

He gave me an icy cold glare before turning and walking away. I saw him grab his backpack out of my office before he walked out the door and let it slam shut behind him. I stood there in the quiet, wondering what in the world had just happened.

Ten

Wyatt

I felt like a dick. A big, hairy, unattractive dick that no one in their right mind would ever want. Not even the crackhead that was offering to blow me for a pack of cigarettes outside of The Tasty Pig when I stopped to grab dinner before heading back to my hotel room.

While I hadn't run like I had told Kayce I would yesterday, I did walk all the way from her shop to my hotel room as I burned off the anger and frustration that was still pulsing through me. It had been a long time since I had talked to anyone about my dad and the words burned as I said them out loud. The worst part was the pity on her face that I didn't deserve.

I knew that it was wrong to storm out of there the way that I did, but I couldn't risk staying any longer and saying something that I would regret. Besides, what was she going to think of me now, anyway? I wasn't Grant's cute little brother to her anymore. No, now I was the monster who was responsible for killing my dad, and then letting his truck waste away because I refused to take care of it the way that my dad would have.

The TV blared in the small room as the local news channel started reporting new road closures due to the storm that was barreling in. *Fucking lovely.* As if I needed any more delays to keep me here any longer.

I flipped through the channels until I found something with sports and finished the last few bites in my to-go box. I had debated grabbing a side of the peach cobbler because it was indeed *delicious*, but decided against it when I thought about how eating Kayce on her counter was much more fulfilling.

After my last bite, I tossed the plastic fork in the box with my used napkin and closed the lid. I was too lazy to run outside to find a dumpster to put the trash in so instead I piled it neatly on the counter by the bathroom and sat down on the bed. It was still early, barely almost seven o'clock, but my body felt tired and drained from the past few days.

I was just about to pull off my hoodie and get ready to lay down when I heard my phone vibrate. Hoping it was Kayce, I picked it up and slid my finger across the screen to unlock it. The disappointment of not hearing from her since I stormed out of her shop was beginning to irritate me and put me in an even worse mood. Not recognizing the phone number, I ignored the call and set the phone down.

It was already dark outside and the snow was still falling which ruled out any physical options for relieving some of the tension. Instead, I settled for a quick workout in my room that consisted of the basics—jumping jacks, sit-ups, and some squats to keep my ass nice and firm. Thankfully, I was on the ground floor and at the end of the building so it wasn't likely that my work out would bother anyone. Hell, I wasn't sure if there were any other guests at this damn hotel in the first place. For all I knew, I was the only guest.

When I was done, I debated on calling Kayce to apologize for my behavior earlier but decided that my mood was still too sour to risk ruining her night. I settled on taking a hot shower instead. Hopefully, the water would pull some of the tension out of my body and let me relax enough to get a good night's sleep. Tomorrow morning was my meeting with Junior at his school, and I needed to make sure that I was at my absolute best so I didn't fuck anything else up this week.

Eleven

Kayce

Today had gone a lot differently than I would've thought. I had no idea what to do after Wyatt stormed out of the shop. It was apparent that he was still harboring some heavy guilt over what happened to his dad, but it wasn't like I could chase after him and convince him that it wasn't his fault. In all honesty, I had no clue. He didn't seem like the kind of guy who would kill someone, but then again, that's been said about plenty of murderers. *He seemed like such a nice guy… everyone just loved him… surely he didn't mean to kill all of those people.*

I rolled my eyes at the thought, knowing how completely ridiculous and absurd it was. I didn't have to know Wyatt to know that he wasn't capable of anything violent. For heaven's sake, he saved Lacey from her father when he showed up at Grant's house to kill her. He sacrificed his life to save hers—without even knowing her, so yeah, I was pretty confident he wasn't some sort of monster in disguise.

I held the phone between my ear and my shoulder while I leaned back in the chair at my desk, tossing the small Nerf ball between my hands. The sound of elevator music played while I waited for someone to come back on the line. After Wyatt left, I was able to clear my head and focus on the truck without being distracted by his presence. It wasn't even just his cologne that triggered me. It was his voice when he spoke and the way he ran his hand through his short hair that made me want to volunteer to have his babies. There was something about him that made me crazy, and I felt like I was walking around in a fog every time he was in my presence.

After some poking around, I was able to find a few other things that needed to be fixed as well. The head gasket was pretty much blown, so I went ahead and called to order a new one from the shop in Glenview. They were the closest automotive repair shop that had a full inventory of parts, and I had been going to them for years.

Leroy let out a low whistle when I rattled off the things that I needed and asked if maybe I should just toss in the towel on this one and buy a new car. All joking aside, he meant well. I had known him since I was a little girl and my grandpa would take me there to pick up the parts he had ordered. Leroy knew my abilities as a mechanic, and while he didn't doubt my ability, he knew how big this job was going to be. Especially when I added a few things to the list that weren't needed right now. It wasn't my fault that I had such a strong, emotional pull to that truck. Someone needed to take care of it, even if it was me.

As I was getting ready to close up the shop, I heard a noise outside in the parking lot. My stomach dropped, panic rushing through me as I worried that it was the same person who had been in my office yesterday. I had my bag hung on my shoulder, the weight of my tools comforting on my hip. I reached down and patted the bag, making sure that I could easily get into it quickly if needed.

I walked slowly down the hallway, keeping my steps as light as possible as I approached the window in the front lobby. The lights in the garage bay were off which sent a chill through me since I knew that I had purposely left them on. I always waited to turn them off until I was locking the front door because I hated the idea of someone hiding in the shadows when I wasn't looking.

My chest heaved as I struggled to control my breathing, the fear mounting with each passing second. I slowly walked forward, keeping my eyes focused for any sort of movement around me as I crept along the wall. The front door was still closed but the door to the garage was open. I didn't want to deal with any of this, I just wanted to get the hell out of there and hide under my bed until it was safe.

A few more steps and then I would be at the end of the hallway, forced to choose a door. The one outside that led to darkness and the unknown. Or the one to the garage bay that also led to darkness and the unknown.

I took a deep breath and tried to steady my hand as I reached into my purse and pulled out the first tool that I could find. I gripped the wrench tightly and kept my back against the solid wall as I took the few steps I needed toward the garage. With shaky fingers, I reached in and flipped on the light switch, allowing my eyes a few minutes to adjust to the bright lights as they flickered over Wyatt's truck.

I quickly scanned the room, looking for an intruder. My heart was racing, the blood rushing in my ears. I stepped inside, glancing over my shoulder to make sure no one had snuck up behind me, turning my attention to the envelope that was placed on the windshield of Wyatt's truck.

Slowly, I walked toward it, still unsure of whether it was safe. A quick look around the room confirmed that no one else was in it with me. It was a small area with a bay big enough for two cars but wide open with plenty of space to work. While it was ideal for working on vehicles, it was lacking as a place to hide given everything was out in the open.

I pulled the envelope out from under the wiper blade and read the words written on it in red marker this time.

Ready or not—Here I come.

I looked around, hoping to find something that would give me a clue as to what these secret messages meant and who was leaving them. Deciding that I had enough, I tucked the envelope into my bag and adjusted it on my hip before making my way to the front door. With one hand gripping the wrench, I used my free hand to lock the door which was freaking difficult to do when your fingers won't stop shaking. I walked quickly through the parking lot, constantly checking my surroundings while making sure I didn't slip and fall on the patches of ice that were starting to form from the snow that had fallen earlier.

My phone rang, vibrating against my thigh as I hopped up into my truck and locked the doors. I set my bag down on the passenger seat, making sure it was within reach if I needed it while putting the wrench in the cup holder next to me. My grandpa always joked that they were tools, not weapons. Little did he know that they came in handy a time or two when I needed them. I lifted my butt and slid my phone out of my pocket, seeing a missed call from Lacey.

Looking around one last time, I made sure everything was safe before unlocking my phone and calling her back. I put it on speakerphone and set it in the other cup holder as I put the truck in reverse and started backing up.

"Hey," Lacey said sweetly, and for a second, I wondered if she was talking to me.

"Hey—son of a bitch!" I screamed, slamming on the brakes. My heart pounded against my chest as I looked in the rearview mirror and found a deer standing behind me. Where in the hell did that asshole come from?!

"What's wrong?" Lacey asked, her voice laced with concern.

"Nothing," I said shakily, my heart feeling like it was beating in my throat. "A damn deer jumped out behind my truck and scared the shit out of me."

I watched it in the rearview mirror, waiting to see if it was going to move on its own or if I was going to have to go around it. After a quick stare down, it gave me one last look before turning and walking back to the empty field across the street. *Stupid deer.*

"Are you okay?"

"Yeah." I felt my shoulders fall as I exhaled heavily, checking my surroundings one more time before pulling out of the parking lot. I was desperate to get the hell out of there and get home where I felt safe. Suddenly, I missed the calm that I had been feeling every time Wyatt was around.

It was already late. I was exhausted, and my stomach was growling. I listened to Lacey tell a quick story about the deer that had decided to live at Grant's mom's house last summer and laughed when she rattled off the string of curse words Connie had used when it started eating her petunias. I still wasn't ready to tell her about the mysterious envelopes, so I tried to force myself to relax as I focused on the false sense of security I found with the number of other people who were out on Main Street tonight.

"I think Connie and I would be great friends," I joked, hoping she didn't pick up that it was fake or that I hadn't been listening as much as I should have.

"Well, if you come down here for the wedding next month, you can spend some time with her," Lacey suggested.

"You know I wouldn't miss it," I assured her as I pulled into the parking lot and circled around to the drive-thru, ignoring the loud growls that were coming from my stomach. I inched forward and stopped at the speaker to place my order. It wasn't a fancy dinner but it was what I could afford right now, and let's be honest—it was delicious.

"Are you at Taco Bell?" Lacey asked with a laugh.

"What? It's Taco Tuesday!"

"Every day is Taco Tuesday with you." She laughed harder, and I joined in, knowing she was right.

"Hey, don't judge. Their food is delicious and cheap. You can't get that anywhere other than Taco Bell. Besides, plenty of people do Taco Tuesday, it's a real thing," I added as I pulled forward and handed the cashier my debit card.

"Yeah, but does it still count as Taco Tuesday if you don't eat tacos?"

"Well, I guess I can challenge them to have a chalupa day. But I really feel like every day should be chalupa day."

I smiled at the woman who handed me my bag of food at the next window and set it down on the seat beside me, behind the bag of tools. Not only were they also weapons when needed, but they also made a handy seat belt for my precious food. I pulled out onto Main Street and went to my apartment. I could hear Annie and Liam in the background talking about starting a chalupa movement at their school in my honor. I smiled and remembered how silly Lacey and I had been when we were their age and the fun we used to have before we hit those teen years and had to worry about stupid stuff—like boys.

"How's she doing?" I asked as I hopped out of my truck and walked around to the passenger side to grab my things. I stayed alert, making sure I watched for any sudden movement around me before rushing up to my apartment.

"She's good. They go back to school next week. They were supposed to start back this week, but we keep getting hit with these snowstorms that have been shutting everything down. I swear, I haven't seen a winter like this in Colorado in all of the years I've lived here."

"Yeah, we're supposed to have a bad one move in by this weekend, but I heard it might come earlier. We're just barely starting to thaw out from the last one." I said as I stood at my door, making sure not to drop my food as I fumbled with the key.

Finally, the door opened and the warmth of the room helped push away some of the icy chill that had clung to my skin. There was no doubt that the next storm was going to be a bad one. I locked the door and slid the deadbolt into place before I set the keys down on the counter next to my bag. I set the food down as well and did a quick sweep of my apartment, making sure everything was okay before I got comfortable. After the weird and creepy things that had been happening at work, I didn't want to assume that my apartment was safe, even though I knew it was a lot harder to get into it than my office was.

Feeling content, I grabbed the bag of food and made my way over to the couch.

"How's Wyatt's truck? Grant said that you're going to help him fix something on it?" Lacey asked as I opened the bag and dug out a chalupa. The heavenly aroma of chicken floated through the air around me as I pulled it out of the wrapper. I closed my eyes and took a bite, savoring it while forgetting that I was still on the phone. A soft moan escaped my lips before I took another bite.

"Is that noise what I think it is?" I heard Grant ask in the background. I started coughing as I almost choked on a piece of chicken, realizing that she must have had me on speakerphone, and he heard me.

"Yeah, it's exactly what you think it is," Lacey confirmed.

"I knew it was a mistake for them to meet…" Grant mumbled in the background.

"Lacey!" I exclaimed, feeling the heat pinch my cheeks. "Stop it! Grant, it's not what you think—"

"Yes, it is," Lacey interrupted. "And stop judging her for her love of chalupas. Let the girl enjoy whatever she wants to. It's not like I don't have stories to tell about you and brownies."

"I don't even want to know," I muttered, taking another bite while reminding myself not to make any embarrassing noises. It was bad enough that he knew that I had sex with his brother. I didn't need him to have any inklings of what I might sound like during climax.

"I thought Bunny was there." Grant's voice was louder as he got closer to the phone.

"Bunny?" I asked around a mouthful of chicken.

"He's talking about Wyatt," Lacey giggled.

"Okay, why do you call him Bunny?" I hoped that maybe it was some sort of cute nickname from when he was little.

"Let's just say his reputation around town earned him that nickname from all of the women who claim he can go as long as the Energizer—"

"Okay, I get it!" I blurted out, desperate for him to stop so I didn't have to hear about Wyatt with other women.

"Is he there? I mean, I get that you're just molesting the damn chalupa, but is he there with you?" Grant asked seriously.

"No," I responded, wiping my mouth with the back of my hand as I pushed the food to the side with my tongue so I could talk. "He had been with me at the shop for a while but then he got upset and left. I haven't talked to him since."

I wished he would have stayed. Maybe if he had, whoever it was that had been in my garage wouldn't have had a chance to get in there to begin with. I knew that they had to have gone in there while I was in my office on the phone, but I hated the thought of someone creeping around in the building without me knowing. I shivered as I thought about it.

"Why did he get upset? What happened?" Lacey asked, pulling me back to the conversation.

I crumpled up the empty wrapper and tossed it in the bag after pulling another chalupa out. I took a smaller, more manageable bite before answering.

"We were talking about the truck and the lack of maintenance on it over the years. I asked him why he hadn't had any work done and when his dad came up, he got upset and stormed out."

"Shit," Grant whispered loudly.

"I'm sorry, I didn't know," I explained, setting my food down in my lap. "I was just trying to figure out why he hadn't done any maintenance on it."

I bit my tongue after I said, realizing how rude it sounded.

"You know, we've told him for years that he should look into selling it and get something else. Something newer that doesn't need the upkeep. But Wyatt," he sighed. "He won't listen. He's been driving that truck since the day he got his license. I think it's just too hard for him to let go of it because he thinks that by doing so, he's also letting go of our dad."

"Did they work on it a lot when he was growing up?" I asked, eager to know more about him.

"Nope," he laughed. "Wyatt was always into baseball. That's where his heart has always been. My dad was the one who was into cars and I think part of him always hoped that at least one of his sons would share that same passion with him. By the time Wyatt was old enough to learn, my dad really gave it his all, hoping that maybe he could get him to fall in love with that old truck."

"So, did it work? Did Wyatt finally fall in love with the truck?" It seemed like a possibility given the way he reacted to it and how protective he was over it.

"Wyatt fell in love with the time he got to spend with my dad. They had an agreement that every night after dinner, they would work on the truck for an hour. During that time, my dad would show him things as they went, and Wyatt would talk to my dad about baseball. It was this perfect mix of combining the two things they both loved while spending time together. My dad loved that Wyatt was into baseball. He even coached his little league team. But there was this special bond between the two of them when they were working on the truck that none of us ever had with him."

My heart fluttered at the thought of Wyatt as a kid, excitedly telling his dad about baseball. I could imagine the twinkle in his eyes as his whole face lit up.

"When my dad died, Wyatt was the only one home with him at the time. They were outside, working on the truck when he had a heart attack. Wyatt called for help, but it was too late. Ever since, no one has been able to touch that truck. Wyatt's heart shattered that day. My dad was his best friend, and he lost him in the blink of an eye. That's why he'll never give it up, and more importantly, why he hasn't been able to work on it. The truck is the last piece of my dad that he has."

I felt the tears fall down my face, my heart breaking for him. Everything made so much sense now, and I felt like an ass for pushing him earlier. If I had known, I never would have said the things that I did.

"I feel terrible," I admitted sadly.

"Don't, you didn't know. I wasn't trying to make you feel bad, I just wanted to let you know why he is the way he is with the truck. I'll call and check on him in a few."

I didn't bother telling them that I had ordered the parts to fix the other stuff that he would need sooner than later. It was bad enough that I had already overstepped by insinuating that he hadn't bothered to take care of the truck. I wasn't ready to admit that I had also been out of line with taking it upon myself to fix stuff that he may not want fixed. Maybe he was planning to do some of the maintenance himself later? Who knew, but it wasn't my place to decide for him. If anything, I could always give him the parts I ordered, and he could decide if and when to do it.

I talked to Lacey for another hour after Grant went upstairs to help the kids get ready for bed. They were probably one of the cutest couples I had ever seen, and they seemed to mesh so well together that being a blended family had been an easy transition for everyone. I had to laugh at the irritation in her voice when she told me that he was limiting how many times she was able to go up and down the stairs during the first trimester of her pregnancy. Luckily for her, she only had a few more weeks.

"Alright, I better get going," she said with a yawn. "Grant said the kids are in bed and waiting for me to come say goodnight. I'm going straight to bed after that."

"Sounds good. I'll talk to you later this week," I confirmed and hung up.

My mind was busy as I thought about what Grant had told me about Wyatt and his dad. I still felt terrible and reached for my phone, deciding whether or not to give him a quick call to apologize. It was after eight-thirty so I assumed he was still awake, but I didn't know him well enough to know for sure.

As I swiped my phone to unlock it, I found a text message from an unknown number.

Unknown: Did you remember to lock your door?

Twelve

Wyatt

"I'm not a big fan of *no news is good news*," my mom scolded on the other end of the phone. I had forgotten to call her yesterday with the update from the doctor that I had seen last week.

"It's the same news that it always is. *You're making progress, slowly but surely. Your body has been through a lot. You're lucky to be alive, focus on what else will make you happy other than baseball,*" I said each word in a whiney, high-pitched tone to make sure she understood my level of irritation.

"Well, I'm sorry that it wasn't better news. I know how frustrated you are, and I'm not trying to dismiss that. I just wanted to know what they said because I care," she explained softly.

"I know, Ma. I know."

"So, how is the new job going?" she asked cheerfully, changing the subject.

I laid back against the padded headboard and closed my eyes. My head was killing me this morning from sleeping like shit last night. Between the guilt that was still eating away at me for how I treated Kayce and the bed being hard as a rock, I couldn't fall asleep.

"The job is fine," I said lazily, rubbing my temple with my fingers.

"There have been a few delays, but I'm hoping to be home this weekend."

"What about the storm that's supposed to hit? Please tell me that you're not considering driving through that…"

"I don't think it really matters right now, ma. My truck is stuck in Lacey's cousin's garage while she tries to fix it. At this point, I'm not going anywhere."

"Do you need some money to extend your stay at the hotel?" she asked.

I hadn't even thought about that until now. Not that I needed her money—that wasn't the problem. I was more worried about Mr. Ashby being a stickler and not letting me extend my stay. Who knew how booked they were? I couldn't imagine that they were so busy that he couldn't tack on another week, if needed. I made a quick note to go down and see him before I went looking for breakfast.

"Thanks, Ma, but I've got it covered."

"Okay, if you're sure…"

"I promise," I laughed, knowing that I could be forty and she would still mother me like I was her baby boy who needed her help.

"Alright. Well, I better let you go. Buck and I are going shopping to get some stuff for Lacey and Grant's wedding. I can't believe that it's right around the corner, there's so much to do," she said light-heartedly.

"We'll get it done, don't worry. I can help you when I'm back in town, but just make sure you leave all of the manly stuff for me. I don't want to come back to pressing flowers and folding napkins into swans," I teased, remembering the last time I got roped into helping her with setting up for a party.

"That was one time, and if memory serves me correctly, you were very proud of those swans and showed all of the girls at the Country Club." She paused for a minute. "Maybe that's where I went wrong with you. I gave you the greatest weapon that those poor girls never saw coming—a sensitive guy who helped his mama."

"Hey, none of them have complained since then, have they?" I clicked my tongue against the roof of my mouth.

"Oooh, honey, you don't want to hear half of the things I've heard," she laughed.

I was just about to ask her what exactly she had been hearing when I heard Buck in the background.

"Gotta go, sweetie, I'll talk to you later. Love you!"

"Love you too. Tell Buck hi for me."

I heard him holler hello in the background before she hung up. It still felt a little odd to see my mom's relationship out in the open now given that I had known about it for so long when she thought she was still being sneaky. I was glad that she had finally found someone to spend her life with who truly made her happy. She spent the last eleven years by herself, raising us boys after my dad died. She deserved to have fun and live life for herself for once.

It was still early in the morning, not even eight o'clock yet. I took a quick shower to help wake me up before wandering down to the front desk to ask about extending my stay. If only some miracle would appear out of thin air; Junior would commit to Haven Brook University, and Kayce would have my truck fixed before the weekend. Then I wouldn't need the room longer than my original reservation. But I doubted that luck was going to find me any time soon. Well, *good* luck anyway.

I stood at the front desk, waiting patiently as I heard the toilet flush down the hallway. A few minutes later, an older woman came walking toward me. Her salt and pepper hair frizzed out around the ponytail she had it in. I smiled as she got closer, watching the way her pale blue eyes lit up when she saw me.

"You must be Wyatt Walker," she said, her voice a tad bit gruff.

"And you must be Mrs. Ashby," I replied warmly, turning my body to face her as she walked behind the desk and sat down.

"Please," she waved her hand. "Call me Trudy."

I nodded in agreement and offered her another smile, hoping it would work in my favor since I had forgotten to bring a candy bar.

"What can I do for you?" she asked, pushing her reading glasses up her nose before moving the mouse around to wake the computer screen up.

"I was hoping that I might be able to extend my stay." I rocked back on my heels. "I know it's last minute, and I apologize, but with my truck breaking down and the storm that's coming…"

"Oh dear," she chuckled and winked at me. "Let me see what I can do."

She took a few minutes looking at the computer and part of me wondered if she was really checking for availability, or if she was just messing with me.

"NO!" A man's voice boomed down the hallway. I looked up to see Fred heading our way, a scowl plastered on his face.

"Oh Fred, stop being so cranky," she scolded as he walked around the counter to stand behind her, giving me a cold glare on his way.

"The answer is no, Trudy."

"But, Fred, he's stuck—"

"No."

She turned in her seat to look at him and folded her arms over her chest. He mimicked her as he looked down at her. Neither of them budged for a solid three minutes, and I started to feel awkward and uncomfortable just standing there.

"Fred, we're giving this boy a room and extending his stay, and that's the last of that." Her tone was curt, but I could swear I heard a tad bit of playfulness behind it.

"He brought candy to bribe you with… A LOT of candy," Fred said disgustedly, looking up at me before returning his attention to his wife.

"Yeah, and WE ate the candy… remember? That night, in bed, while we were watching that movie with the really steamy love scene." She lowered her voice but not enough to shield me from the details she was giving him.

I groaned and looked away, not caring if they heard me. She burst into laughter as he whispered something in her ear, the scowl he was wearing a few minutes ago replaced by a grin that split his cheeks.

"Okay, fine," he sighed, looking up at me. "He can extend his stay."

I forced a smile even though I was still struggling to keep any images of them messing around with the bag of candy bars I brought out of my head.

"But—" Fred said sharply, pointing a finger at me as the scowl returned. "It will cost you more candy bars."

"You got it," I said quickly, slapping my hand on the top of the desk. "An extra week stay for me and twice as many candy bars coming your way!"

I heard Trudy squeal with delight as I waved and walked out, ready to be away from their weird little love fest. The snow that had fallen last night had turned into ice this morning, making it a difficult walk to find food. I hated not having my truck and being stuck in this tiny little town. If I was back home, I could call one of my brothers or Noah, and they'd come get me then we'd all be on our way again. But no. I was stuck here, pretending to be some sort of ice skater just to find decent food to silence the grumbling in my stomach.

What felt like hours later, I had finally made my way onto Main Street. I was walking toward Jumping Joe's when I saw Kayce's truck drive past me. I lowered my head, hoping that she hadn't seen me while also praying that she was going somewhere *other than* where I was going. When she turned into the parking lot and waited at the back of her truck, I knew I hadn't been lucky on either wish.

I quickened my pace, making sure not to slip on a patch of ice on my way. She was smiling as she waited for me, shivering every few minutes as the wind blew a gust of cold air in her face.

"Good morning," she said, her teeth chattering.

"Morning," I forced out. The cold had settled into my bones, and I wasn't sure that I was thawed out enough to get more words out if I wanted to.

"Let's go inside where it's warm," she suggested, turning to walk to the front door.

I followed behind her, shivering as another gust of wind whipped past us. The bell chimed as we went inside, the heater blowing full force through the small space.

"What in the world are you doing walking in this weather?" she asked, looking around to find the hostess.

"I was hungry." I half shrugged, unsure of what else to say without sounding like a dick again.

"Why didn't you call me? I would have come and picked you up."

"I didn't want to bother you," I answered, as the same girl that waited on us yesterday walked up to the front and smiled.

"Back for another one?" she asked happily, clutching the menus to her chest. "Do you need a menu, or have you had enough to know what's good?"

"I'll have the same as yesterday," I laughed. "And coffee. Lots of coffee."

She smiled and pointed to the selection of tables that we could choose from while she went to the back to put our order in. Kayce and I slid into a booth toward the back and waited as she brought a pot of coffee and two cups with her. She set them down, then rushed off to help another customer who had come in for a to-go order.

We sat quietly, drinking our coffee as we waited for the other to talk. I knew I owed her an apology, I was just struggling with how to start it since I also owed her an explanation for what had happened. Talking about my dad had never been an easy thing to do, and I didn't want Kayce to pity me the way everyone else had.

"About yesterday," I said quietly, setting my cup on the table. "I'm sorry for the way I acted. I was being a jerk, and I didn't mean to take it out on you."

"It's okay," she held her hands up. "Really, don't worry about it. You don't owe me an apology. If anything, I owe you one. I was completely out of line with asking you the way I did."

I could see the empathy on her face, the sadness in her eyes as she looked at me. I lowered my head and gently spun my coffee cup around on the table, avoiding looking at her.

"Who told you? Grant or Lacey?" I asked softly.

"Grant." She waited for the waitress to set our food on the table before she spoke again.

The smell was intoxicating, and I now knew why she was obsessed with coming here. Hell, I would probably be here every morning too if I lived here.

"He didn't tell me on his own," she said quietly, as she cut into her burrito to let some of the steam out. It was too massive to hold it to eat. "I mentioned that you weren't with me when they called and that you had been upset earlier. I told them what happened, and Grant filled me in on everything else. I'm sorry if you didn't want me to know."

I looked up at her, our eyes locking.

"It's okay that you know," I assured her. "It's not that I try to hide it, I just don't like talking about it. But, I owed you an explanation for my behavior yesterday, and I'm glad that you got it."

Things felt weird and awkward between us, and I hated it. It wasn't like we had spent that much time together since I had only been in town for a few days. However, the time we had spent together before this was easier and there was less tension than right now. It was like the opposite of what you would expect to happen—we had sex without really knowing each other, and it was fine, not much had changed, but then we have a personal conversation about real life, and it was as awkward as having your first kiss as a horny teenager.

"I went ahead and ordered the parts for your truck," she said, interrupting my thoughts as she took a bite of her burrito.

"Thank you, I appreciate you getting that done. How much do I owe you for them?"

She took another bite and shook her head.

"Don't worry about it, I've got it covered. I order from a store in the next town over, and they put everything on my account and I pay when I pick it up."

"Well just let me know how much it is. I'll give you cash, or I can go with you and pay for it."

I had no idea if she wanted the company, but I hated the idea of her paying for my stuff on her own. It was beyond me if that was something that mechanics typically did, but she wasn't *just a mechanic.* I didn't like the thought of her spending her money on me, even if I was going to pay her for it later.

"About that…" she said wearily. "I'm hoping the order will be ready before the storm hits, but if not…"

"Then I'm stuck for a while longer," I finished for her before taking a bite of my burrito.

"Sorry, I know it's not the news you were hoping for," she apologized.

"Don't worry about it, it's fine," I said, meaning it for once.

It was weird but sitting across from Kayce made everything feel right again. The tension and stress that I had been feeling all night last night and this morning seemed to evaporate the moment I saw her. Suddenly, I didn't feel as concerned about whether I was going to get back home anytime soon and that should have scared me more than it did.

Thirteen

Kayce

I rubbed my hands together to stay warm while I waited for Wyatt in my truck. He insisted that I didn't need to wait for him while he was in his meeting with Junior, but I assured him that I would be here when he got out. It seemed like waiting for him was just the polite thing to do since he didn't have a ride, and it was almost a blizzard outside, but deep down, it was really because I didn't want to go to the shop by myself.

The text from the unknown number last night had left me feeling rattled and uneasy as I read it over and over while obsessively checking all of the locks in my apartment. It was a small space, so I didn't have to worry about anyone hiding where I couldn't see them, but it didn't take away from the unnerving feeling of someone watching me. I tried to convince myself that it was all in my head and that I needed to shake it off and move on. The only problem was that I couldn't ignore the pictures that were still sitting in the envelope, tucked into the bag behind me.

I smiled when I saw Wyatt rushing back to my truck, jogging carefully so that he didn't slip on the snow or ice beneath him. He opened the door and jumped in, letting a gush of cold air in with him in the process.

"How did it go?" I asked, feeling the excitement that was reflected on his face. He buckled up and turned to look at me, the dimples in his cheeks prominent as his grin stretched tightly across his face.

"I got his commitment!" he said happily.

"That's awesome!"

"Thank you, I was a little worried at first," he admitted sheepishly.

I put the truck in reverse and pulled out of the parking spot.

"Why's that?" I asked, glancing over my shoulder to check for other cars before pulling onto Main Street.

"Just nerves, I guess. He's my first recruit, and I know how talented he is. I wouldn't be surprised if other schools weren't swooping in to grab him first."

"Benefits of living in a small town," I joked. "People barely know that Easterville exists, let alone that we have an amazing ballplayer at our high school."

"Ain't that the truth," he agreed, pulling his cell phone out of his pocket as it rang. "Sorry, I gotta take this," he apologized with a smile as he pushed the button to answer it.

I turned my attention to the road, trying to give him as much privacy as I could even though we both knew that I would be able to hear everything in the small space we were stuck in. The drive back to my shop was quick, and then he would have the opportunity to take his call wherever he wanted.

"Hey, Chuck," he answered. "I got his commitment, and he's very excited to join our program."

I loved hearing how proud he was when he talked about it. The way he lit up every time he talked about baseball reminded me of what Grant said about Wyatt as a child and how much he loved it. It warmed my heart to know how passionate he was and wondered if I would ever find something that I was *that* obsessive over. Yeah, I loved being a mechanic, but it didn't feel like I had the same spark with it that he had with baseball.

"I'm not sure when I'll be back to town, but I can keep you posted. My truck is currently out of commission, and we're waiting for the parts to come in. On top of that, there's a blizzard rolling through that is going to make travel difficult," he explained as we pulled up to the shop.

I put the truck in park and climbed out, grabbing my bag of tools from the backseat. I heard Wyatt's door close but was distracted by the giant hole in the window of the shop. My heart started racing as I hoisted the bag up onto my shoulder and rushed over, staring at the shattered glass that covered the freshly fallen snow.

"Chuck, I gotta go. I'll let you know when I'll be back as soon as I have an update," he said distractedly before he hung up. He was standing next to me, looking at the mess.

"What in the hell happened?" he asked, his voice barely a whisper.

"I have no idea," I murmured as I unlocked the door and walked inside.

Laying on the floor was the rock that had been thrown through the window. I bent down to pick it up, finding another concert ticket with a note written in black marker wrapped around it. My fingers trembled as I pulled it out from under the rubber band that was holding it in place.

The note was simple, just like the others.

Payback is a bitch.

My stomach dropped, and I felt the tension sitting heavy on my shoulders again. The pictures from the envelope on Monday were enough to shake me given that very few people had ever known about what had happened that night. I couldn't remember anyone that would have taken pictures. It would've been a sick and demented thing to do. But then again, whoever was breaking into my shop to leave me threats didn't seem like they were really sane either.

"Hey, are you okay?" Wyatt asked, gently touching my arm. I looked up at him as he looked down and read the note in my hand. He jerked his head toward it, his brows knitted together. "What's that?"

"I wish I knew," I exhaled, feeling defeated by the constant mystery.

"We should call the police."

He turned to walk away, pulling his phone out of his pocket.

"No!" I cried out, rushing over to stop him. I placed my hand over his. "We can't call them yet," I tried to explain, though I couldn't tell him why. The last thing that I needed was for the police to show up and start asking questions, especially since I couldn't tell them about the photos. There was no way that I could tell anyone about them. They needed to be burned in a fire so that they would never be seen again, but the problem was that I had no idea who had taken them to begin with. Most likely, they would just keep making copies until they got whatever they wanted.

"Kayce, someone threw a *rock* through your window and shattered it. And on top of that, they left you a threatening note that said—*payback is a bitch*. I don't see why you wouldn't want to notify the police..."

I held my breath for a second and puffed up my cheeks, trying to figure out what to say. Slowly, I released it and tried to get my courage up to talk to him.

"I can't go to the police because this isn't the first note they've left me. If I tell them about the others, then I have to show them what they've left, and I can't do that."

I kept my voice as steady and even as possible even though I was shaking from the inside out.

"What do you mean this isn't the first? How many have you received?"

"A few?" I wanted to be vague enough to keep from having to tell him everything without being too vague that he still pressed to call the police.

"Since when? When did they start, Kayce?"

I avoided him for a moment, trying to stall, when I felt him step closer to me. He lifted my chin with his finger, forcing my head up as his eyes locked onto mine.

"When?"

"Monday," I said wearily. "Right before you got here."

He ran a hand through his hair, shaking his head in frustration.

"Why didn't you tell me?" he asked.

"I barely knew you," I scoffed. "You came flying into my parking lot, like a bat out of hell, so I was a little bit distracted."

It wasn't a lie, I had been distracted from the moment that I saw him. Partly because of the way he showed up but more so by his devilish good looks and the way my knees felt slightly wobbly every time that he was around.

"How many notes have you gotten? Where? I want all of the details," he pushed assertively as he stood next to me, legs slightly parted with his arms folded over the Haven Brook University logo that wrapped across his chest.

"I can't give you all of the details, so please don't push me on this."

"Why not? Someone is obviously threatening you…"

"So?" I snorted. It wasn't the most mature response, but I had nothing to say to that. Someone was threatening me, and it scared the living shit out of me, but I wasn't about to admit that to him. I had been taking care of myself long enough to not need some knight in shining armor to come rescue me from a weirdo who had a grudge against me.

"So? That's your response—so?" He arched a brow as he pinned me with a look. I could feel the intensity as I squirmed beneath it.

"Yeah, that's my answer. Whatever this is—I'll handle it." I shifted the bag on my shoulder and walked down the hallway to my office, holding the rock and concert ticket in one hand. I could hear his footsteps right behind me, which didn't surprise me given how he had yet to give up.

His phone rang again. I silently prayed that he would answer it and forget about all of this. He looked down, rolled his eyes, and slid his finger across the screen.

"Hey, Grant," he answered sharply. "No, I'm fine, just dealing with something."

He gave me a look and continued to stare at me as he talked.

"Yeah, I got his commitment, which is great news, but I'm not sure when I'll be home."

I swallowed hard, listening to his conversation, hoping that he didn't say anything about this. The last thing that I needed was for Lacey to get wind of it and freak out. Her pregnant ass would be here in a heartbeat, blizzard or not.

"We're waiting for parts to come in for the truck, and then there's another storm that's supposed to hit soon so I'm sure I'll be here for another week or so." He paused and held my gaze so I couldn't look away. "Maybe longer."

They talked for a few more minutes, the conversation fading as I heard someone up front and went to see who it was.

"Leroy!" I exclaimed as I walked down the hallway and saw him standing by the front door, looking down at the mess of glass and snow that was blowing through.

"My goodness, what happened here? Did the storm do this?" he asked, handing me the box that he was holding as he looked back at the floor.

"I don't know, I just got in a few minutes ago, but it looks like maybe that old window was no match for this blizzard," I joked, trying to force a smile as I situated the box against my side.

"You didn't have to come drop these off," I said softly. "I would have gladly come to pick them up from you, Leroy. That storm is bad. You shouldn't be driving in it."

"Nah, don't worry about it," he replied, still focused on the broken window. "My son was coming into town anyway, so I just hitched a ride with him. You know, safety in numbers or something like that… that's what my Judy used to say."

I smiled warmly, remembering his sweet wife from the handful of times she had been at the shop when I went to pick things up. She had recently passed and the sadness in my eyes when he talked about her never seemed to fade.

"Did you come with Greg?" I asked, turning to set the box down on the empty chairs by the front desk.

"Yeah, he has that big truck that can handle anything," he laughed, nodding to the vehicle outside. "Kind of like your beast out there."

I waved to Greg, not sure if he could see me or not. Wyatt walked down the hallway, not noticing that someone was there. He stopped short and looked between us, before turning to go back to the office.

"Wyatt," I called, getting his attention. "This is Leroy, and he was kind enough to brave this blizzard to drop off the parts for your truck."

He beamed as he walked our way and extended his hand to Leroy.

"Thank you, sir, that was very nice of you," he said as they shook. "But you didn't need to come out in this storm to get them to us."

"Like I was telling Kayce, I caught a ride with my son, so it was no skin off my back."

We stood there in silence for a few seconds before he turned back to the window.

"Do you want me to help you fix this?" he asked with a shudder. The building was freezing cold, despite the heater blowing at full force. The hole in the window was definitely a problem, just one that I wasn't in the mood to deal with right now. But then again, neither was the massive gas bill that I was going to get from running it all day at the level I needed to keep us somewhat comfortable.

"That's okay but thank you. I'll get it taken care of soon," I assured him, feeling Wyatt's eyes on me. "Do you want to send me a bill for the parts since I didn't go down there to pick them up?" I asked, hoping to change the subject.

"Nah, we'll settle it the next time you come in."

"I'm happy to offer you some cash while you're here, at least for your time bringing it down here," Wyatt offered, glancing at me for guidance.

"I'm good, really," he laughed. "But unless you need help with that window, I should get going. Greg gets grumpy when he has to wait too long." He rolled his eyes and pointed over his shoulder to where the truck was parked.

"We've got the window, thank you." I walked over and hugged him before he made his way outside in the frigid cold.

I felt the wind whip past me, blowing a cloud of snow in my face as I pulled the door closed and looked at the window.

"Do you have any wood that I could use, and I'll get the window taken care of?" Wyatt asked, reading my mind.

"I think I have some scraps in the garage," I said, leading the way.

I flicked on the light, getting a flashback of the fear that I had last night as I made my way through the dark, not knowing what would be waiting for me. I pushed the thoughts aside and walked to the back of the shop where I kept the random crates and pieces of wood that I used when I needed to create a makeshift workstation.

There were a few decent-sized pieces that would likely cover the majority of the window but not the whole thing. We would have to bust out the rest of the glass that was left in the frame because it was too splintered to try to work around. That meant that I would have to get creative to fill the spots that the wood didn't cover.

I handed Wyatt the pieces that I had and kept looking for anything else that I could use while he took them up front and started cleaning the floor. I never knew that watching a man sweep the floor could be so sexy until I found myself practically drooling as I stared.

"Did you find more wood or were you too busy watching me?" he called over his shoulder with a chuckle.

Shit! I had been caught and there was no way to deny it.

"I'm still looking," I called back stupidly.

"I hate to break it to you, but I don't think the *wood* that I have will help your window at all."

His voice was louder this time as he made sure there was no way that I had missed what he said. I felt my body warm up at the thought of what he was saying, getting distracted all over again.

"It would be a lucky window if so…" I muttered under my breath as I pushed stuff to the side and found a few more scrap pieces of wood.

I carried them over to where Wyatt was finishing up sweeping and added them to the pile.

"Hopefully that will be enough," I said with my hands on my hips.

"Yeah, but I don't know that it will be enough to withstand the storm. Is there a place in town that you can call for a replacement?"

"No one that will come out today," I sighed.

"Well then, we'll have to make do with what we have and pray that my erection isn't needed," he laughed, gently bumping my shoulder as he walked around me to get a piece of wood.

I bit down on my tongue to keep from telling him that it wasn't the window that was suddenly in need… It was me.

Fourteen

Wyatt

I took a step back and looked at my work. It wasn't half bad given that all that I had to work with were scraps of wood that weren't the right size to cover the full window. I did the best that I could with what I had, but I still hated the idea that she wasn't going to be able to get anyone out here to replace it for her before the worst part of the storm hit.

I grabbed the tools that I had used and took them back to Kayce's desk, smiling when I passed by the garage and saw her bouncing her head to the sound of Pantera floating out of the room. Her mood seemed to have shifted some from earlier, and it was nice to see her enjoying herself. I was still frustrated that she wouldn't tell me what was going on or who the note was from, but I didn't know her well enough to push her. I could be a jerk and tell Grant, knowing that he would tell Lacey and she would find out for me, however, that was a one-way ticket to her hating me and shutting down even further.

I leaned against the doorframe and watched her for a few minutes before she looked up and noticed me.

"You scared the shit out of me," she gasped, laughing embarrassedly.

"Sorry, I didn't mean to. I just finished up with the window and thought I'd come check to see how you were doing."

"So far, so good," she said, looking at the truck. "But then again, I haven't gotten to the hard part yet."

"I see," I laughed, walking over to where she was standing. "Anything that I can help with?"

"Not that I can think of, but you can keep me company while I work if you want to."

I pulled out the rolling stool that was pushed under the table and sat on it, trying to stay out of her way as she climbed onto the creeper and slid under the truck. As much as I should have looked away, I couldn't. The sight of her on her back, legs slightly parted as she moved around was sending every inappropriate thought through my head quicker than a four-seam fastball.

"Can you hand me the wrench on the table?" she asked, reaching her hand out toward me.

I looked around, not seeing a wrench anywhere on the table. I moved a few other things around and still couldn't find one.

"I don't see one," I replied. "Is there somewhere else it could be?"

"It's probably in my bag," she sighed as she started to push herself out.

"I can look if you want me to," I offered.

"Thanks, it should be right next to the table, on the floor."

I looked down beside me and saw the bag that she was talking about, the same one that I was convinced held the dead body of that musician she had been dating. I pulled it over to me, knocking it over in the process. On the top of the bag was an envelope with Kayce's name on it. I set it down on the table, then went back to looking for the wrench. Finally finding one, I turned to ask her if it was the right one and bumped the envelope, knocking it to the floor.

A handful of pictures fell out of it and scattered across the floor. I bent down and picked them up so I could put them back in the envelope for her when one caught my eye. It was a picture of Kayce in the back of a limousine with her arm wrapped around the shoulders of another girl who looked like she was so strung out that she had passed out. Kayce's hair was bright pink and matched the tube top that she was wearing with the mini skirt that barely covered her. Her tongue was out as she posed for the camera.

No one else was in the picture other than her and some drunk chick.

I gathered the rest of the pictures and fought the urge to look through them when I heard Kayce's feet shuffle as she moved around.

"Did you find it?" she asked.

"Yeah, sorry," I mumbled as I set the pictures back in the envelope and handed her the wrench.

She worked in silence for a few minutes while I sat at the table, staring at the photo of her with that girl. Something about the photo just didn't sit right with me and gave me the creeps. Maybe it was the visible track marks on that girl's arm or the way her mouth slightly hung open, just like my dad's looked after he was… dead.

I glanced over my shoulder, making sure Kayce was still busy under the truck before I turned around and picked up the pile of pictures. It was a total invasion of her privacy, but I couldn't stop myself. I moved the picture to the back of the others and stared at the next one. My stomach clenched when my fear was confirmed—she was dead and Kayce was the one holding the baseball bat that was covered in blood as the girl's body slumped down the wall beside her.

Fifteen

Kayce

After calling his name from under the truck twice, I figured he had left since he didn't answer me. It wasn't until I scooted out from under the truck and found him sitting at the table, staring at something with such an intensity that he was oblivious to the world around him. I wiped my hands on the rag and tucked it back into my pocket before walking over to see what he was so focused on.

I walked up behind him, gasping when I saw the photos spread out on the table in front of him. His forehead wrinkled as the harsh expressions set in. I knew what he must be thinking when he saw them. It was the reason why I couldn't go to the police. All they needed was one look at the pictures, and they wouldn't believe a word I said after that.

"What the hell are you doing?" I snapped, stepping around him and snatching the photos from him. I clutched them to my chest as if that would somehow protect me from the harsh judgment in his eyes when he looked up at me.

"I'm sorry," he started, running a hand down his face as if that would erase what he had just seen. "I wasn't trying to invade your privacy."

"But you did anyway," I scoffed.

"You're right, I did. And again, I'm sorry for that. But, Kayce…"

"Don't." I held up my hand to stop him. It was a mistake to cross the line with him the other night when we had sex. I knew better. I should have left things as casual as possible. Now things were complicated with him sharing my deep, dark secret. The one that no one was ever supposed to find out about. Including Lacey.

"You know that I can't just look the other way and pretend like I didn't see those," he said softly, pushing the stool away from the table as he stood up. "And I'm not going to forget about what happened with the window either."

I swallowed hard, clutching the pictures tighter against my body as I wished this would all just go away.

"Please, Kayce, just tell me what's going on and let me help you."

His face was soft, the hardened features from a few minutes ago vanished.

"I can't," I stuttered, my voice cracking under the pressure. I wanted to tell him, to confide in someone and admit what I had done, to allow myself a moment of weakness to succumb to the grief that I had been trying to swallow down since last summer. Just one quick break, then I could lock it all up again and live with the consequences of the stupid decision that I had made one night after one too many shots of tequila.

"Kayce," he whispered my name as he stood in front of me and put his hands out for me to take. "You can trust me. Whatever this is—I will help you. Just please, let me in. Talk to me…"

A tear slid down my cheek, escaping the prison it had been confined to for the last six months. He reached out and grabbed me, pulling me into him. The warmth of his body as his arms wrapped around me felt heavenly.

"It's not what it looks like," I said against his chest.

"Okay," he said reassuringly, rubbing my back softly. "Do you want to go talk about it in your office? That way you have some privacy in case someone comes in?"

"Trust me, no one comes in unless they're sneaking around to leave me these stupid notes," I mumbled as I pulled away and looked up at him. Surprise flashed across his face before it was replaced with anger.

"I want the details, Kayce. All of them."

He pulled me by the hand and led me out of the garage and down the hall to my office. Once we were inside, he closed the door and stood against it, as if making sure that I wasn't going to try to make a run for it.

"I don't know where to start," I admitted as I sat down at my desk.

"Let's start with the pictures," he offered, nodding to where I had set them down beside my computer.

"Like I said, it's not what it looks like. I didn't kill her."

I pulled my shoulders back and tried to take a slow, deep breath to calm my nerves.

"Brent and I had been broken up for a while and I hadn't talked to him for months. Last summer he reached out to me because they were going to be passing through Colorado, and he wanted to get together. I agreed to meet him in Denver and ended up going to their concert. He always gives me a backstage pass, so I was hanging out, waiting for them to finish their set when I met this girl—the one in the pictures— who said she was dating Dray, their drummer. We talked for a bit, and she seemed like a nice girl."

I wiped a stray tear away from my face as I thought back to that night. The light that had been in her eyes when she talked, how full of life she was.

"We went to an after-party with the band and everyone was only drinking, except Dray and Stella. They were going a little harder than everyone else, and by the time we got to the party, they were both pretty high. The picture of her and me in the limo was taken before we got to the party. After that, everything just got out of hand. The night was a blur, but long story short—Dray has a short temper, and it's even worse when he's on drugs. They got into a fight, and he started hitting her. Brent didn't want the bad publicity, so he packed the band up, and we all left.

"We were driving on some deserted back road, in the middle of nowhere, when Dray just lost his shit and started hitting her again. Brent had enough. He told the driver to pull over, and he kicked Dray out of the limo. Well, Stella being high and in *love,* decided to go with him. The second they were out of the car, he started attacking her again. So, Brent got out, and the other guys tried to help him pull Dray off of her, but nothing worked."

A shiver ran through me as the memories came back. No matter how hard I had tried to forget, nothing would ever erase this night or the scars it left behind. I swallowed hard and forced the emotions back down to where they belonged.

"I saw a baseball bat on the floor when I had gotten in earlier, so I grabbed it and tried to help. I swung it a few times, aiming for Dray's head. That's whose blood was on the bat in the picture. It was enough to knock him out but not kill him," I paused and forced out the breath that I had been holding. "But it wasn't enough to save Stella. He had beaten her to death."

"Fucking asshole," Wyatt grunted from his position in front of the door. His arms were still folded across his chest.

"We were in the middle of nowhere with a dead girl and a passed-out drummer who was high on cocaine. It wasn't like we could just call the police. Brent had just booked their first international tour and if this went public, they would be done. His career would be over. So, they drug her body into the woods, out behind an abandoned barn. They dug a hole as deep as they could without any shovels, and made me bury her."

I remembered the anxiety I had felt that night, the hole in my stomach that filled with acid as I gently rolled her body into the shallow grave and used my hands to push the dirt around to make sure it covered her.

"They made you?" he asked, anger laced in his tone as his eyebrows nearly shot off his head.

"Brent said that the only way to guarantee that none of us ever talked about what happened, was if we all had something at stake. If one of us talked, it would take everyone down. I would be just as guilty for hiding a dead body and not reporting it."

"So, how did someone get these pictures? And why are they sending them to you?"

"I wish I knew," I sighed heavily. "I really do. I have no idea. The only people that were there that night were the band members, myself, and their manager—"

The words stopped abruptly when I finally put it together.

"Oh my God," I whispered, bringing my hand to my mouth. "He didn't get out of the car that night, he stayed inside. None of us had even thought about it because he had just as much to lose if anyone got wind of what happened. Without the band and their international tour, he wouldn't have a paycheck. So, if anything, he had even more to risk than the rest of them. Jolted was his only client and that meant a lot was at stake for him."

"Which would mean that he took pictures of what happened—in case he needed them later."

"I guess so, but that meant that he would have had to have gotten out of the car and found us because we were far from where the car was pulled over and it was pitch black out. And why now? Why would he be sending them to me with these vague notes? I had nothing to do with him—we barely knew each other. What could he gain from harassing me? " I asked, knowing that Wyatt wouldn't know any better than I would.

"Maybe I should call Brent and see if he's had anything strange happen to him?" I pondered out loud.

"I wouldn't," Wyatt said, pushing away from the door. "Until you know for sure that it was their manager, I wouldn't talk about it. You never know who you can trust in these types of situations. Best to keep this one quiet for now." Something in his tone changed that sent a shiver through me.

"That's a good point," I said cautiously, as I watched Wyatt pull out his phone and press it to his ear. He was the one convincing me that I could trust him, yet now he was saying that I should be careful of who I trusted. There was this nagging feeling in my gut that told me that maybe I should be worried about what he said.

"Hey, I need a favor," he said into the phone as he reached down and locked the office door behind him, keeping his eyes on me.

THREE STRIKES, YOU'RE GONE

Sixteen

Wyatt

I watched the reflections in the mirror above Kayce's head while I waited for Buck to grab a pen and piece of paper. She looked guarded as she watched me, her eyes following my every move as I reached down and locked the door.

"Get under your desk," I whispered, covering the phone with my hand. "Now."

I could hear footsteps approaching and knew whoever it was, they were headed our way. I pushed myself against the wall, trying to make sure I could see them without risking them seeing me through the blinds of her small window. Unless they were smart enough to look for someone in the reflection of the mirror, like I had, I should be safe.

She looked at me like I was crazy, then did as she was told and crawled under her desk a few seconds before there was a loud thud on the door. I whispered to Buck, telling him to hold on, while I waited to see what they were going to do.

I could hear muffled voices from the other side but couldn't make out what they were saying. My fist clenched at my side, ready for them to kick in the door and come for Kayce. Instead, a piece of paper was slipped under the door, and the voices faded as they walked down the hallway and left. Or at least I hoped they had left, there was no way to make sure without walking out there to check.

I waited a few minutes to make sure the coast was clear before I bent down and picked up the piece of paper.

"It's okay, you can come out now," I said to Kayce, rolling my eyes as I stared at the piece of paper in my hands.

She climbed out from under the desk and looked around, panic evident on her face as she tried to locate the threat. I extended the paper to her and pulled my lips into a thin line as she took it, her brows furrowing when she read what it was.

"You made me hide from Johnnie? The loyal customer who came in to pay on his account?" She held the paper out in front of her with her other hand planted firmly on her hip.

"I'm sorry, I didn't know. I just assumed because you said that no one ever *just shows up*, that maybe it might be the person leaving you notes," I explained quietly as I heard Buck come back on the line.

"Alright, what do you need?" he asked kindly.

"I hate to ask for this kind of a favor, but can you look into someone for me?"

Kayce raised a brow and glared at me. It seemed that I had some sort of knack for pissing her off, and I was getting better at it by the minute.

"What's the manager's name?" I asked her, praying that she would tell me.

"Mike Sullivan," she replied through gritted teeth.

I turned away from her, mainly to escape the look she was giving me, and finished my call with Buck. He promised to get back to me within a few hours with whatever information he was able to get. I knew that I should have talked to her about it before I asked him, but I was worried that she would refuse to let me help her. I trusted Buck and knew that he would help however he could without pushing me for details on why I needed it.

I slid my phone back into my pocket and unlocked the door. It seemed silly to be so paranoid but after what she had told me, I was feeling on edge, and I could see that she was too. I turned the knob and opened the door, blindsided by the baseball bat that came flying at my head before I hit the ground and everything faded to black.

<u>Seventeen</u>

Kayce

"You don't have to do this," I begged as Mike grabbed hold of my hair and dragged me down the hallway. I looked down at Wyatt's body that was slump on the floor, a small puddle of blood forming under his head.

"Shut up!" he yelled, his voice bellowing through the narrow corridor as his grip on me tightened. I glanced outside, thankful that it was still light outside, and prayed that someone—anyone, might be around to see what was happening. A gust of wind pushed a blanket of snow up against the door, the sound whooshing in through the small gaps between the wood, confirming that no one in their right mind would be out in this.

We had plenty of snowstorms living in Colorado, but I couldn't remember ever seeing one this bad in all of my life. The locals had been busy prepping after the news anchors asked everyone to find shelter and to avoid going out if they didn't have to. I started to panic, knowing that unless Wyatt regained consciousness soon, I was on my own against Mike.

I hadn't seen him since that night last summer, but a lot had changed. He wasn't the tall, skinny guy that I had remembered. Now, he was in shape and muscular, someone who had taken control of his fitness and appeared to be going to the gym regularly. Being in his early thirties without a wife or children probably meant that he had the spare time to go when the band wasn't on tour—which if memory served me right, they had just finished one.

I looked around for anything that I could use as a weapon as he dragged me to the front door. The wind was howling and the wood on the windows rattled. If I had enough time, I could pry off a piece of wood and use that, but I wasn't that quick, and apparently, Wyatt had done a damn good job of making sure each piece was well secured.

He fidgeted with the lock on the door for a few minutes, grumbling when it wouldn't turn to open. I was thankful that the damn thing was acting up again when he let go of my hair for a second to use both hands to get it to open. Knowing that this was the only chance that I would have, I carefully planned my next step. The lock clicked as he finally got it to turn and the door flew open with the wind. I ducked down and grabbed the brick that I use to hold the door open in the summer. I pulled my arm back and slammed it against the side of his face, cringing at the sound it made before dropping it and running outside. I didn't have a second to spare to watch his reaction as his head whipped to the side.

I darted out the door and into the thick snow that made it impossible to see more than a few inches in front of you. I heard him yell out a cuss word followed by another one as I ran as fast as I could, slipping on the ice as I went in the direction of the forest that sat behind the shop. My heart was about to beat out of my chest as I kept running, thankful that I knew the area better than he did. I felt terrible for leaving Wyatt behind, but there was no other choice. I was what he was there for, and I knew that he would stop at nothing until he got what he wanted.

Eighteen

Wyatt

My head was pounding as I sat up and leaned against the wall, trying to remember what had happened. I was desperate to get up and find Kayce, but every time I tried to pull myself up off of the floor, I felt lightheaded and had to sit back down. I looked around the office for any sign of her and felt my stomach knot when I knew that she wasn't there. Whoever had been there had found her the second they knocked me out with the bat. There was no way that they didn't.

I patted my pocket, trying to find my phone. My fingers felt around, desperate to locate it so I could call for help.

"Looking for something?" A man asked, walking down the hall, holding my cell phone in his hand.

I had no idea what Mike looked like, but my guess was that this was him. I had pictured the typical older guy with a beer belly and balding head, not a tall guy with muscles for days and a tattoo of a skull on his hand.

He squatted down in front of me and held it out. When I refused to take it, he shook his head and chuckled as if it somehow amused him.

"You know, when I came here to find Kayce, I didn't expect to find you," he admitted, standing up.

I wanted desperately to stand up and show him that I wasn't

intimidated by him, but my body refused.

"Not that I need to know who you are—it doesn't matter at this point," he gave a half shrug. "But, I am curious to know who Lieutenant Dickson is and what information he has on me."

His brown eyes darkened as his hand gripped my phone tighter. I bit the inside of my cheek in frustration, hating that I had reached out to Buck in the first place. And honestly, I was surprised that he had tried to get back to me so quickly. It had barely been a few minutes since I had called him. Hadn't it? I didn't know how much time had passed from when I had called him to when I woke up from getting clobbered in the head with a baseball bat. My mind was still focused on Kayce and whether she was okay. If Mike was here, talking to me, where was she?

"I don't know who that is," I lied, raising my eyebrow to match the look he was giving me. He scoffed and shook his head.

"I was able to see the text message even though your phone was locked," he continued to explain. "You might want to change that setting in your phone. You never know who might read your messages without you knowing."

"Where's Kayce?" I asked, forcing the words out as my body fought the urge to sleep. I had been hit by a bat more times in my life than I cared to admit, but I had never felt this out of it afterward. After having several surgeries from the stabbing incident, doctors had warned me that I needed to be careful if I was still considering a career in baseball. One hit to my head of any kind and it could have a devastating outcome.

"Well, that's where you come in," he replied through clenched teeth. "It seems she's decided to play a game of hide and seek, and I'm going to use you as bait for her to come find us."

"She won't do it," I laughed, deliriously hoping that she would go find help and not try to be some sort of hero. "She barely knows me— there's nothing for her to come back for. If she left, then it's for good."

"See, that's where you're wrong." He tsked his tongue on the roof of his mouth. "I've known Kayce long enough to know that there are certain things that she's willing to fight for. And the way that she looked at you when I dragged her out of the room—that told me everything that I needed to know. Women in love do stupid shit all the time."

My head lifted as I looked him over, waiting for him to tell me that he was just bluffing to see if it would get a rise out of me. When his features locked in, I knew that he was telling the truth and that could only mean one thing—Kayce was in even more danger than she knew. We both were.

Nineteen

Kayce

I shivered in the cold, listening for any signs of footsteps approaching as I tried to make sure that I didn't get too far from the area that I knew. The forest was thick behind me, and it would be easy to get lost in if I made one wrong move. The blinding snow that was decreasing my visibility by the second. Soon, I would be in over my head, succumbing to the elements around me.

It was stupid to run off into the woods during the middle of a fucking blizzard without a jacket or a cell phone, but it wasn't like I had much of a choice. If I didn't run, then I would likely be dead by now anyway. I had no idea what Mike wanted, but I could tell from the look in his eyes that I wasn't going to live to find out either.

In an act of desperation, I patted my pockets one more time, praying that somehow the keys to my truck would magically appear. If I could get to my truck, I could go find help. Not that anyone in town would be able to do much, or even believe me, but now Wyatt's life was at risk. I needed to do something to save him.

I grumbled in frustration when my pockets came up empty. I was stuck in the woods, during the worst snowstorm that we have had in over fifty years, and someone was trying to kill me. Things couldn't possibly get any worse unless some wild animal suddenly decided to come hunt me for dinner. At this point, it would have been a welcoming invite.

I found a spot in front of a tree that sat off to the side of my shop and leaned against it. It was far enough away from the building that no one would easily spot me but close enough that I would be able to hear if someone left—if the wind wasn't whipping past me. I had thought about running out to Main Street and trying to find someone to come help, but I knew that would be a waste of time and energy. Most of the shops had already closed and everyone was hunkered down at home, waiting out the storm.

That is, everyone except Mike who was still in the shop doing God knows what to Wyatt. I pinched my eyes closed and said a quick prayer that he would be alright. He was strong—there was no doubt about that, but the impact to his head from the bat was enough to knock anyone out, including him. I tried to shake away the image of his body lying limp on the floor as Mike dragged me past it, completely helpless.

My body temperature was dropping as the cold dug its sharp claws into me, and I knew that I wouldn't be able to stay out here much longer without risking severe hypothermia or worse—death. If I could somehow sneak back into my shop, I could get out of the cold and save Wyatt. I pushed away from the tree and took a few steps, balancing myself with each one to keep from falling. The frigid cold had already turned everything to ice beneath me, making each move more treacherous.

I slowly took a few more steps, inching my way closer to the shop. The snow had started to slow down, allowing a small amount of visibility around me. I felt relieved that I hadn't gotten turned around in the woods. Just a few more feet, I would be on the side of the building and could sneak around to the back where the garage was. There was a spare key that I kept back there, just in case I needed it.

As I was about to take another step, I heard a man's voice and stopped. I froze in my tracks, straining to hear it through the wind that was muffling it.

"What the fuck do you mean *you lost her?*"

"I mean she fucking clocked me in the face with a brick and took off running," Mike said, his voice closer and clearer than the other one.

"And you didn't think to run after her?"

"In this weather? Are you fucking kidding me?" Mike scoffed. "Besides, there was another situation that I had to deal with."

I leaned closer, desperate to hear the other person without risking that they would see me. I needed to know who he was talking to, who was with him.

"This just gets better by the second," the other voice said sarcastically. "What's the other problem?"

"She wasn't alone. And whoever this guy is—he's been talking to a cop."

"Well then, I guess we better go shut him up before he says anything more than he already has."

"What about Kayce?" Mike asked.

"She'll either die in the woods or she'll pop up when she's ready to try to save the day. Either way, she'll be dead soon enough."

I peeked my head slightly around the tree that I was hiding behind and focused on the parking lot as I watched Mike walk back to the shop with the other guy. He looked familiar, but I couldn't figure out why. As they got to the door, Mike walked in first while the other guy held it open. When he turned his head to scan the area, I noticed the scar on his face and felt my stomach drop when I realized who it was.

Twenty

Wyatt

I sat tied to Kayce's office chair, pulling at the knots in the rope that held me in place. Mike had gone outside to talk to someone. I knew that I didn't have long to try to get out of this mess, but I still had to try. The rope somehow felt looser than it had a few minutes ago. Either that or my hands were getting too numb to actually feel any movement around them. I heard voices coming down the hallway and stopped moving.

Mike walked into the office first and sat down on the chair across from me, resting his ankle on his other knee. When the other person walked in, I felt a hysterical laugh bubble out of me, unable to believe the irony of the situation. The amusement on Mateo's face matched mine as if neither of us could believe this was happening.

"Wyatt fucking Walker," he snorted and stood in the doorway, arms folded over his chest. "I didn't think I would get the opportunity to beat your ass again so soon."

Mike looked between us in confusion.

"You two know each other?" he asked.

"Oh yeah, Wyatt and I go *way* back."

I felt his icy stare on mine and knew that he was remembering the bar fight from last year.

"How's Mandy?" I asked with a cocky grin. I might have been tied to the chair with no way to defend myself, but that didn't stop me. "Is she still wearing those tight little miniskirts?"

His jaw clenched as he pushed off from the doorway.

"Looks like you don't know when the fuck to shut up and walk away," Mateo said.

"Just here getting my truck fixed so I can get back on the road," I said nonchalantly. It wasn't a total lie, but they both saw right through it.

"Is that so?" Mateo asked, stepping closer to me. "And you just happened to get stuck in *my* town?"

"I was here for work."

"And what work is that?" Mike asked from the chair he was still sitting in.

"None of your damn business," I said, keeping my eyes locked onto Mateo's. I discreetly tried to loosen the ropes behind me as Mateo took another step forward.

"Everything that happens in this town is *my* business," Mateo snarled as he stood in front of me. "Maybe next time you'll think twice before you come to Easterville. We're not too fond of *outsiders*."

I watched as Mateo's eyes landed on the duffle bag on the floor behind Kayce's desk. The Colorado Cougars logo was displayed front and center with my name underneath it. I hated that I wasn't an active player anymore, yet I still carried the bag with me proudly as if I was part of the team.

"Three strikes, you're gone, motherfucker," he taunted as he looked at me.

I held my breath as I watched his fist fly toward my face, clocking me straight in the temple.

Twenty One

Kayce

I waited a few minutes to see if I could hear anything inside before I turned the key and unlocked the back door that went to the garage. It was risky to be in the open with nowhere to hide, but my only other option was to die in the cold. My feet were already numb and my socks were soaked from the snow that I had to walk through to get back here. The back of the shop was nothing but forest and had a good four feet of snow that had been piled up from the wind.

I slowly closed the door, keeping it from slamming shut as I heard the latch click. Quickly, I scanned the room to make sure no one else was around, before I rushed over to the table and squatted down behind it. Thankfully, it gave me enough space to hide. My bag full of tools on the floor allowed me easy access to a weapon if I needed it. Granted, I had no idea what kind of weapons Mike and Mateo had on them, but I was sure they were packing something stronger than a wrench.

The muffled sound of voices floated in under the door, which meant they were either in my office or in the hallway since I couldn't see them. I worked quickly to pull a couple of things out of the bag and tucked them into my pockets. If I could get to my office, I could grab my gun and get Wyatt away from them. He wasn't the one that they were after and I knew that they would get rid of him the same way that they did Stella—as if he didn't matter. But, he did, and I would go to my grave making sure that everyone knew that.

I heard a vibrating noise and looked up. Carefully, I reached up from under the table and felt around until I found my cell phone. I felt a sudden rush of relief wash over me as I grabbed it and pulled it under the table. I could call for help, but honestly, who would I call? Our local police department was as tiny as my pinky and didn't have the manpower to stop Mike or Mateo. I could call Lacey and have her get help, but that would mean that she would send Grant in this deadly snowstorm, and I couldn't risk having something bad happen to him, not with a family of his own and twin babies on the way.

I swiped my finger across the screen to find a text message from an unknown number again.

Unknown: So, you like to play games? How about we'll hide your boyfriend, and you can see if you can find him. We'll even leave clues along the way to help you.

My fingers trembled as I held the phone, watching the dots bounce as another message was being typed.

Unknown: Just look for the random body parts and trail of blood.

I heard footsteps heading down the hallway and held my breath, as I froze beneath the table. A few seconds later, the front door opened and then slammed shut. I couldn't tell if someone had really left or if they were just doing it to try to freak me out. It was unlikely that they knew that I was in the garage, but not impossible. The door wasn't open long enough for all three of them to leave, which made me wonder where they were and if they had split up.

I knew that I had to make a decision quickly. I couldn't hide under the table forever—sooner or later they were going to find me. For once, being tiny and petite would come in handy, as I brainstormed a plan to hide in the shadows and make my way back to my office. I had to be fast, which meant that there was no time to second guess myself or be afraid. It was now or never.

I quickly moved out from under the table and was about to run when I looked in front of me and stopped in my tracks.

"Found you," he growled.

Twenty Two

Wyatt

I was pretty sure that the doctors would be banging their heads against the wall if they knew that I'd had two severe hits to my head in one day. My eyes fluttered open, and I looked around, unsure of where I was. It wasn't Kayce's office—that was for sure. Everything was dark and somewhat blurry as I blinked my eyes and tried to get them to focus.

My hands were still bound together with rope, but this time, instead of being tied to a chair, I was sitting in the back of a van. I felt my body jerk to the side as it went over a bump and wondered where they were going and why the hell they were driving so reckless in this weather. Not that they gave a rat's ass about whether I lived or died, but I figured that they at least wanted something from Kayce or all of this would be for nothing.

There were no windows and the only light that came in was from under the cracks of the doors at the back of the van. My back was leaning against something solid, but I couldn't tell what. Whatever it was, they had apparently braced me against it, while I was unconscious. I looked around, desperately trying to find anything that I could use as a weapon.

Suddenly, the van came to an abrupt stop, and I felt myself slide forward. I tried to pull my hands free from the rope, knowing it was my last chance. The doors opened and a gust of snow blew in, whipping me in the face. I held my breath for a second until the next gust passed before catching my breath. Mike was standing at the door, looking off to the side as he nodded and turned to look behind him. It seemed like he was looking for someone which meant that I needed to act fast.

I scooted forward as quickly as I could without him noticing. When he turned to face me, I leaned back and brought my legs up, kicking him square in the chest with everything I had. His body immediately tumbled backward as he fell into the snow, struggling to catch his breath.

I slid the rest of the way out of the van and jumped down, thankful that my hands were tied in front of me, instead of behind my back. It was stupid on their part, but they didn't seem like the smartest kidnappers in the world. My guess was that this wasn't something that they did often. I looked around, hoping to find somewhere to go for help and felt my stomach sink when I realized where he had taken me.

We were in the middle of nowhere and off to the side of the road was the abandoned shed from the pictures. I could hear Mike groaning and cussing as he fought to get up and out of the snow. The force of the kick to his chest seemed to have done the amount of damage that I had hoped it would.

I could run, but there was nowhere to go and no one to ask for help. That left only one option, and it was the one thing that I really didn't want to do…

Twenty Three

Kayce

His fingers wrapped tightly around my throat, cutting off my air supply as my feet dangled in the air like some limp rag doll. I watched his eyes darken as he enjoyed seeing me squirm, my fingers digging into his skin as I struggled to breathe.

"You've always been such a feisty little thing, haven't you?" he teased, tilting his head to the side to look at me.

I could feel myself getting lightheaded. It wouldn't be too much longer before I passed out. Maybe that would be best? At least I wouldn't feel anything and wouldn't have to know what had happened.

He finally let me go to fall onto the concrete floor of the garage, as if somehow, I bored him and he had lost interest in the game.

I gasped loudly, pulling in as much air as I could, my lungs burning with each breath. I scooted away from him quickly, trying to put distance between us.

"You know, things didn't have to be like this," he said lazily as he slowly started stalking over to me. "We could have done this the easy way—but no, you wanted to make it harder than it needed to be."

I looked around, still trying to catch my breath. I could read the look on his face and knew that he was enjoying this. He turned to the side when something upfront caught his attention for a split second, most likely the wind rattling against the boards in the window. The fluorescent lights overhead caught the scar on the side of his face, reminding me of who I was and what I was capable of. I had protected myself from him before, and I would do it again.

When he turned back to face me, I locked eyes with him and pulled my shoulders back. I didn't make an effort to get up from the floor which seemed to amuse him as he chuckled and took another step closer. I crawled backward, slowly and deliberately, to where I needed him to follow me.

Off in the corner of the garage, in the other bay was the project car that I had been working on for over a year now. It was completely stripped and lifted onto a jack while I fussed around with it when I had time. When I took it off the hands of its owner, it was the same as it was now: tireless and needing more work than money could buy. Right now, it was the biggest weapon that I had.

I relied on my memory to guide me as I kept crawling backward like a crab trying to escape a starving seagull. One quick glance over my shoulder confirmed that I was right where I wanted to be. I turned back and smiled at him, before I flipped over and dashed under the car. I knew that it was easy enough for me to maneuver underneath it since I was already familiar with being down here—and my petite size was an added bonus compared to his husky build.

He laughed maniacally, the sound vibrating off of the walls of the garage, coating the room in its evil.

"That's your grand plan?" he snorted as he bent down to look at me. "You're going to hide under this piece of shit?"

I pulled my lips into a thin line and waited. I could tell that I was already getting under his skin, and if I pushed him enough, he would come after me.

"What? I thought you liked a challenge?" I replied snarkily, making sure that I was moving far enough to the back of the car while also keeping an eye on where he was at all times. Timing and position were everything right now- one small miscalculation and this could end badly for me.

"Since when has anything with *you* been a challenge? Your legs are open more often than the twenty-four-hour convenience store on Main Street."

I bit the inside of my cheek, trying to remember that the goal was to lure him in, not hit him with my best comebacks. I let the anger that was boiling inside of me fuel me for what I was about to do. There was no time to rethink this or second guess myself. If I wanted to live, I *had* to do this.

"Well then, what are you so afraid of? A teeny, tiny, little girl?" I mocked, tilting my head to the side as I challenged him.

"You asked for it," he growled as he climbed down onto the floor and started crawling toward me.

I rushed to the back as quickly as I could and got out from under the car in time to kick the jack out. I stepped back and gasped when I saw the car crash to the ground. The sound of metal hitting the concrete boomed through the garage, echoing off the walls. Bright red blood started spilling out in every direction as I took a step back and covered my mouth with my hand.

I fought the urge to scream and freak out; there wasn't time for that. I needed to find out where Mike and Wyatt were before it was too late.

It looked like a scene from some terrible, low-budget horror film. His legs were sprawled out in front of the car with his torso pinned beneath it. It looked as though he tried to turn at the last minute to escape, which resulted in his head getting caught as well. I looked away from his face, unable to handle the image as his brains pushed through the holes of his cracked skull.

There was no doubt that he was dead, yet I still approached his body with caution. I forced the bile down as it started to rise up at the metallic smell of blood permeating the air. I tried to breathe through my mouth to avoid throwing up, but it wasn't helping. The image alone was enough to trigger a vomit reaction. My breaths were more labored and intense as I struggled to keep it together. My sanity was hanging by a string, and that string was the lifeline that Wyatt was holding onto. One wrong move and it would break, costing him his life.

I slowly kneeled down, my fingers shaking as I fumbled around in his front pocket, trying to find his cell phone. I had to block out the thought of touching his *dead* body from my mind to get through it. If I stopped to think about what I was doing, I wouldn't be able to do it. I had to keep reminding myself that there was still work to do. Wyatt was counting on me right now and I couldn't let him down. If Mateo really had been working with Mike, then I assumed he would be calling to check in with Mateo soon, which meant that I needed to find his phone.

I groaned when I came up empty and knew that I was going to have to go around and check the other pocket. I sucked in a deep breath through my mouth, trying again, to avoid the smell of the blood around me. I stepped carefully as I walked around to the other side, making sure to avoid walking in the mess if I could.

My fingers were still shaking as I reached into his pocket and pulled out his cell phone. I held it in the air in front of me, praying for some sort of miracle that it wouldn't be locked. I was almost relieved when it vibrated with a new text message. I tried to open it, but his phone was locked. I let out a string of curse words until I looked down and found that he hadn't set it up to unlock with a password. It required his thumbprint. There was no turning back now, so I bent down and picked up his limp hand, pressing his thumb against the screen.

The phone vibrated and the screen bounced as it confirmed that it wasn't the right fingerprint. I tried again, reangling the finger to see if maybe it just hadn't read it right the first time. It did the same thing, confirming that it was still wrong. I only had a few more tries before I would be locked out. I stopped for a moment and studied my hand, thinking about which finger would be my go-to finger if I used a fingerprint sensor to unlock my phone. I was right-handed and it just felt natural that I would use my right thumb. I looked down at his body, remembering that his left was my right and vice versa. I rolled my eyes and tried again, this time with the other thumb. The screen lit up as it unlocked and I felt relief spread through me quicker than a wildfire.

I quickly went to the settings and changed the password, using his thumb one more time to gain access. After changing it from fingerprint to the code that I had created, I didn't have to worry about getting locked out again—not that I would need it for long once I found what I was looking for.

The text message was from Mike, confirming that he was there. It was vague, and I knew why. They weren't going to give those kinds of details in a text message that could be traced or used as evidence against them for what they were planning to do. I needed to know where *there* was, but I knew that I couldn't text him and ask because that wasn't something that Mateo would do. I had to be smarter and think like a criminal.

I decided to call him instead. I pressed the button and muted the phone on my side so he couldn't hear anything. I didn't want to give anything away and hoped that he was stupid enough to start talking before waiting for Mateo to say why he was calling. Mike had a habit of doing that and I was praying that he would be as predictable as I remembered.

"Hey, are you on your way, or did you already get lost?" he asked.

I stayed quiet, waiting him out.

"Shit, I can't hear a thing. Must be the shitty reception out here. We're at the abandoned shed that we talked about. Text me if you need directions."

The phone disconnected, and I smiled at how easy that was.

I opened Mateo's text messages and rolled my eyes at the ones at the top of the thread that he had recently received. You know, the ones that were from other girls that *weren't* his wife. I found Mike's name and opened the thread. My stomach sank as I read the last text message from Mateo to Mike. It was quick and to the point: *dealing with the problem now.* I shook my head to clear it. I had to stay focused on what really mattered right now.

I needed to confirm that *Mateo* had heard him on the phone and acknowledge that he was heading to the shed. I tried to think of what Mateo would say but had no idea how they talked to each other. I decided to just keep it short and simple.

Mateo: On my way.

I waited until I saw that the message was read before I exited out of the message. I pulled my hands inside of the sleeves of my shirt and tried to quickly wipe down the phone to get rid of my fingerprints. I didn't have time to deal with his body right now, but I also didn't want my DNA all over it if someone randomly found him, before I got back to take care of this. Not that I had any idea *how* to take care of it. After I wiped it down several times, I bent down and tossed it under the car. I had the information that I was looking for, so I no longer needed it.

Now that I knew that Mike was with Wyatt and Mateo was dead, I didn't have to sneak through the building anymore. I made a quick pitstop in the bathroom before going to my office to grab the things that I needed. I pulled my gun out from the safe and checked to make sure that it was fully loaded before tucking it in the back of my jeans. Once I had everything that I needed, I grabbed my keys and jumped in my truck. Now I just had to pray that Wyatt would still be alive by the time I got to him.

Twenty Four

Wyatt

Not much had changed for me other than where I was sitting. I was still tied up and had the marks on my wrists from where I had been pulling at the rope, trying to break free. I chewed at the inside of my cheek in frustration when my master plan of trying to escape was quickly thwarted by a patch of black ice. Everything was going perfectly—Mike was still on the ground, trying to recover from the kick to his chest. Mateo was nowhere to be seen. All that I had to do was run from the back of the van to the front, and hope that Mike was stupid enough to leave the keys in the ignition.

Unfortunately for me, the long patch of ice that ran along the side of the van was my undoing as I slid Bambi style and hit my head. By the time that I was able to try to get back on my feet, Mike was already back on his and standing over me. There was nowhere to run at that point, and he knew it.

He had grabbed me by the rope and yanked me up, shoving me against the van until I caught my balance. I was surprised that we both didn't take another tumble on the ice. Luckily, the van was pulled over off the side of the road far enough that it was a quick walk to the shed, not that the abandoned shed in the middle of nowhere was an ideal place to want to be.

The door was barely hanging on the hinge, swaying with the wind as it whipped past us. Mike pushed it open and shoved me inside, not caring as I stumbled in and tripped on a piece of wood that was splintered up on the floor. He cast a quick glance at me before turning his attention to the small window by the door, keeping an eye out for someone. Or maybe some*thing*? At this point, everything that had already happened was so fucking wild and unbelievable that I wouldn't be surprised if a yeti came down from the mountains and ate us all alive.

The inside of the shed was dark and damp from the recent snowstorm, making everything smell mildewy. It was a small space with nothing inside and a few broken windows. I decided to get out of his way and sat down on the floor against the wall, shivering as the cold air blew around me. Thankfully, there was a small amount of light that had trickled in through the missing glass—enough to see what was around me. Aside from the resident rat that was dead in the corner a few feet away, there was nothing but cobwebs and dust.

I was starting to feel helpless, wondering where Kayce was and whether she was okay. I always thought of myself as a strong man, but here I was, sitting in the corner of an empty room, hiding like a damn pussy. Maybe it was the likely concussion that was keeping me down, but my body just didn't have the energy that I needed right now to try to fight back. I closed my eyes for a brief second, ready to just give up.

This was never how I had expected to die. Hell, I had imagined a whole different path for my life altogether. I had hopes and dreams, just like any kid, but I never thought that they would all come crashing down and end when I was twenty-five. A lot had happened in a year and I still couldn't wrap my head around the failure that was knocking on every door. It seemed like no matter what I did, I couldn't find success. I could feel the tears sting my eyes as I swallowed the harsh truth in the thoughts that were running through my head. As the guilt of disappointing my father started to build up, I saw an image of him that sent a chill right through me.

I had to fight, I couldn't give up. Out of all of the things that he had taught me growing up, it was that we always fight for the things that we want. And right now—I wanted Kayce. I needed her more than I needed the air around me to breathe.

More determined and focused, I started looking around again. As I looked closer, I found a sliver of glass laying on the floor, over in the corner. It wasn't that far from where I was sitting, I just needed to get to it without drawing attention to myself.

As quietly as I could, I started slowly scooting over toward it. I had to play my hand right this time and couldn't afford any more mishaps. I was only a few inches away when I heard the sound of a loud vehicle outside. I waited to see if Mike had heard it too but was relieved when I saw him with his head down, focused on his phone. The noise got louder as whoever it was got closer. Mike lifted his head, turning his ear in its direction at the same time that it stopped.

I slowly released the breath that I had been holding and scooted closer to the glass. Without drawing attention to myself, I carefully pushed it underneath my leg before resting my hands in my lap on top of it.

The wind picked up and whipped past the shed, howling through the room as we heard a car door slam outside. Mike's face lit up in excitement as he rushed over to the front door and opened it. Another gust of snow blew in, taking him by surprise as he turned his head to catch his breath. He held his arm up to cover his mouth before looking outside again, but another gust came through and he pulled back to avoid it.

I listened closely, trying to hear what was going on and praying that Kayce was okay. For all I knew, it could have been Mateo showing up with her dead body. I had to force those thoughts out of my head and try to focus on getting out of this mess.

Once the wind stopped for a moment, Mike stuck his head out of the door again. He pulled back in surprise, then leaned further outside to get a better look. When I heard the car, it sounded like it was at the back of the shed—not the front, where the van was parked. I felt a spark of hope, wondering if it was Kayce. She knew the area from that dreadful night, and she was smart as fuck. It would make sense for her to park in the back to stay hidden and give her the advantage.

"Son of a bitch," Mike muttered, pulling his jacket tighter against him as he stepped outside and pulled the door shut behind him.

That was it—the moment I had been waiting for. I picked up the piece of glass, ignoring the burn as it cut into the palm of my hand the harder I gripped it. It wasn't as sharp as I needed it to be, but I could feel it cut through the rope. In less than a minute, I had my hands free and tucked the rope into my pocket. I laid the glass down beside me and made sure it was hidden in case I needed it again.

I waited for Mike to come back in, but after several minutes had passed, I started to wonder what was going on. My nerves were already shot, but I could feel the anxiety clawing its way up my back, making my body tense as I waited out the unknown. I wanted to get up and make a run for it, but I had no idea whose car I had heard outside. It could have been Mateo showing up with Kayce, or it could be a group of mobsters that Mike is doing some shady business with. Who the fuck knew what I was in the middle of at this point.

Just as I was about to get up to go sneak a peek out the window to see what was going on, I heard voices outside and sat back down. The door flung open and Kayce stumbled in as Mike pushed her from behind. Our eyes immediately locked on each other, making sure we were both okay. I wanted to run over and hold her, to pull her as far away from Mike as I could, but I couldn't let him know that I had gotten out of the rope that I was supposed to be tied up with. There was still too much unknown, and I couldn't risk either of our lives by trying to be the hero just yet.

Mike wiped his nose on his jacket sleeve, leaving a smear of blood behind. I raised an eyebrow at Kayce, and she just shrugged while trying to keep the smirk off of her face.

"Sit your ass down next to your boyfriend," he demanded, nodding to where I was. I lowered my hands even further between my legs, keeping my knees up as a shield so he couldn't see them. Kayce walked over and sat down beside me. Her eyes quickly scanned my body before returning to the spot on my head where I had been hit earlier. Her brow furrowed as she stared at it before she looked at me and mouthed *I'm sorry.*

"Where's Mateo?" he asked her, as he continued to wipe at the blood that was dripping down his face. She shifted her attention from me back to where he was pacing back and forth by the door. A loud vibrating noise filled the room around us, and I wondered if it was Kayce's cell phone. I prayed that Lacey wasn't trying to call her right now because I knew that she would call over and over until she got her on the phone, and that could be deadly for us.

"He got pinned down," she said lightly. "He was crushed he couldn't be here."

Mike glared at her before pulling his cell phone out of his pocket and answering it. I felt my shoulders relax some when I saw that it was his phone that had been vibrating, and not hers.

"Yeah?" he huffed into the phone, walking back over to the door. "It's the same place as before."

"Are you okay?" I whispered quietly in her ear, making sure Mike didn't hear us.

"I am," she sighed. "You?" Her eyes went back up to the bump on my head.

"Yeah, I'm fine." I smiled and desperately wanted to reach over and grab her hand but didn't. I was just thankful that she was alive and from the looks of it, she didn't seem to be hurt. I prayed that she wasn't because if either of them did anything to her, I would go to my grave making sure that they paid for it.

"If you passed the windmill then you're almost here," Mike snapped at whoever he was talking to. I took the opportunity to focus on Kayce while he was distracted.

"Your head looks pretty bad," she whispered, concern laced in her tone. She lifted her hand to touch it but pulled away as I jerked back. I had no idea how bad it looked, but it fucking hurt like hell, not that I was willing to admit that to her.

"It's okay, really," I assured her as I kept an eye on Mike. He finished his call and slid his phone back into his pocket.

"Did you pass out?" she asked, not worried about Mike being done with his phone call. Maybe she hadn't noticed, or maybe she just didn't care?

I nodded, unable to say anything more as Mike turned back to look at us before opening the door. As another gust of wind whipped past as I heard car doors slamming. Not just one door, but two or more. Whoever it was had parked out front, and there was definitely more than one person.

The cold air forced its way inside the room as he held the door open. Two men walked in, neither of them acknowledging Mike, other than a shoulder check from the taller, skinnier guy.

When they turned to face us, I immediately recognized the shorter one as Brent, Kayce's ex-boyfriend. He looked at her, a tight smile on his face, before glancing at me. For a moment, it looked like he was worried about her as he worked his jaw back and forth and took in the situation before him.

"So, why are we here?" Brent asked Mike assertively, his eyes shifting from him back to Kayce.

"Because I have something that you want," Mike said dryly, walking over to where Kayce was sitting. He reached down and pulled her up off of the floor by her jacket. I clenched my fists, ready to pop up and clock him for putting his hands on her, when I remembered that no one could know that I wasn't tied up anymore.

Kayce stumbled from the force and caught herself before Mike grabbed her by the back of her hair. He reached into his coat pocket and pulled out a knife, holding it to her throat.

"Kayce?" Brent laughed hysterically. "You did all of this because you thought you could use Kayce to get what you wanted?"

Apparently, I had been sorely mistaken when I thought that he had been concerned for her when he first came in. Her eyes narrowed at him as she gave him a look that I never wanted to be on the receiving end of.

Mike's features hardened as Brent laughed at him.

"No offense, Kayce," he paused and held his hands up. "But she isn't of any value to me. I don't know what you thought you were going to get by kidnapping her."

"I just figured that maybe her *life* was worth something to you," Mike replied angrily. I could see his hand shaking as he tried to control himself. "But if not, then maybe I need to show you that I'm not fucking around anymore!"

He forced her to walk across the room, towards Brent, as we he kept the knife pressed to her throat. They were standing in front of Brent and the other guy when Mike reached into his jacket and pulled out an envelope, still keeping his grip on Kayce.

"Take it," he instructed, extending it to Brent.

With a dramatic eye-roll, Brent grabbed the envelope and opened it. His jaw tightened as he pulled the contents out and flipped through the pictures that were inside. He didn't say anything as he handed them to the other guy and kept his eyes on Mike. The room was eerily quiet as his friend looked through them before he chuckled and wiped at his nose.

"What do you want?" Brent asked sternly.

"Five million, in my account, by tomorrow." Mike pulled harder on Kayce's hair, making her gasp in pain.

"We fire you for embezzlement, and you think the best way to get revenge is to blackmail us for five million dollars? You're out of your fucking mind," the other guy laughed, handing the pictures back to Brent.

"I'm not playing!" Mike shouted, his voice booming through the small room. "I will release those photos to all of the magazines and tabloids—your career will be over. I will ruin you!"

The tension was mounting as the two guys looked between each other, not saying a word. This seemed to piss Mike off even more as the vein in his forehead throbbed while they ignored his outburst.

I tried to make eye contact with Kayce, but her head was forced up as Mike kept his grip on her. The knife was pressed so hard against her throat that I could see the red mark from where it had already nicked her. My anger was ready to boil over with every second that she stood there with him. I needed to get to her, but I was outnumbered and couldn't trust that Brent was on her side. He had already made it clear where she stood, why would I think that he would let her walk away from this if I saved her from Mike?

"You know, Mike, we don't take well to being blackmailed and threatened," Brent warned, stepping to the side.

In an instant, the guy beside him reached behind him and pulled out a gun. Without any warning, he aimed it straight at Mike and pulled the trigger. The bullet whipped past Kayce's head—barely missing her, and went straight through his forehead. I jumped up and rushed over to Kayce, pulling her away from him as his body hit the floor with a loud thud and the knife landed at my feet. She turned and curled into my chest, looking away from the gruesome scene in front of us. I watched Brent carefully as I waited for him to make his move.

394

Twenty Five

Kayce

I felt like I was living in a nightmare that I couldn't wake up from. I wished that I could hide forever as Wyatt held me, but I also knew that neither of us could trust Brent or Dray. I forced myself to pull away from him and turn around. I looked down at Mike's dead body beside us, the puddle of blood getting closer to where we were standing.

There was a stare-down between the men as nobody moved or spoke. I took a moment to catch my breath, as I tried to figure out what was going on at this point. If Mike was working with Mateo to blackmail Brent and Dray, and now both of them were dead, then maybe this whole thing could just be over? It was wishful thinking but worth a shot.

I watched as Dray wiped at his nose again. Obviously, some habits never die for others either. He looked high as a kite, just as I remembered from the last time that I had seen him. It was hard to believe that the night we all swore to forget was the very thing that brought us here again.

The knife that Mike had been using was still lying on the floor between all of us. Without strinking twice, I bent down and grabbed it. I saw Dray move the gun in my direction before Brent's hand reached over and pushed it away. My heart was racing as I stood next to Wyatt and handed it to him with shaky fingers while keeping my eyes on Brent and Dray. I felt confused by Brent's behavior, and it made me even more uneasy than I was before. He hadn't seemed to care that

Mike had kidnapped me and was trying to use me against him, yet he quickly pushed the gun away so I wouldn't get hit if Dray pulled the trigger.

An awkward silence lingered between all of us for a few more minutes before Brent finally spoke.

"Does anyone else have copies of these?" he asked, holding the envelope up in front of me.

"I have no idea," I admitted. "I didn't know about them until he started leaving them at my office a few days ago."

Brent nodded but said nothing.

"I wasn't a part of this and I didn't tell anyone about the photos or the notes he had left me," I added. I felt Dray's eyes on me and squirmed the way that I always did when he was around. He was one of those people that could naturally make you uncomfortable without trying. It was the pure evil that ran through him and tried to creep into your soul every chance it got.

"Then why is *he* here?" Dray asked, jerking his head toward Wyatt.

"He got caught up in it by accident. I'm working on his truck and he got stranded while here for work. He was at my shop when Mike came by. Mike had the wrong idea and brought Wyatt here. He doesn't know anything about what happened, and it will stay that way," I lied. I felt Wyatt's hand drop from my waist and knew what he was doing. If we were going to act like nothing was going on between us, other than me fixing his truck, then he couldn't touch me the way that he was.

"Look, there's nothing to worry about anymore," I pleaded, my voice rising when I realized what they were thinking. " Mike was the one who wanted to release these photos—not me. Can't we all just walk away and go our own way like we did last time? I think I've already proven that I won't say anything…"

"It's not that easy," Brent muttered, running a hand over the scruff of his jawline.

"Sure it is," I laughed nervously.

"No, it's not," he snapped. "Even if he doesn't know what happened before, he saw what just happened with Mike. How do we know that he's not gonna go snitch on us and tell someone?"

"I have a lot to lose if anyone got word of this," Wyatt said, speaking up beside me. All eyes, including mine, turned toward him.

"I'm the relief pitcher for the Colorado Cougars. If word got out that I was involved in something like this, I would be removed from the team, and my career would be over. Trust me, no one wants this to go away and never be spoken of again more than I do."

Brent and Dray exchanged a look between the two of them that I couldn't read. I hated that Wyatt was even pulled into this mess, to begin with, and I couldn't wait for it to be over.

"Well then, you'll know how important it is to tie up loose ends," Brent said, reaching into his pocket and pulling out a needle.

My eyes went wide and I stared in disbelief as I watched him turn around and plunge the syringe into Dray's arm before taking the gun from him. Now that Brent had Dray's gun, I felt even more anxious that I didn't have mine. I had reached for it when Mike attacked me outside, and during our struggle, it fell to the ground, lost in the thick snow on the way to the shed. *You don't take a knife to a gun fight...*

"Dude! What the fuck?!" Dray yelled as he jerked away and shoved Brent off.

"Problems have to be taken care of, and that includes you," Brent replied nonchalantly, stepping back and folding his arms over his chest. "Soon, things will be cleaned up, and I won't have to worry about all of these little *issues*."

"Why did you do that?" I shrieked as I watched Dray stumble toward the door.

"He was already high from a couple of hits he took on the way over here." He shrugged one shoulder and looked over at him. "I just helped top him off."

"With what?" I gasped. I knew that it was stupid to ask but there wasn't any point in trying to pretend that we didn't see what he did. He was roping us in and dragging us down with him. If he was willing to get rid of Mike and Dray, I knew what our fate was.

"Heroine. It'll be the quickest, and honestly, aside from the trouble breathing, he'll be too high to even know what's happening. I'm doing him a favor if you ask me."

I stepped back, unable to believe what I was seeing and hearing. Even though Brent and I weren't serious when we dated, I thought I knew him better than this. I never would have thought that he was this evil.

"Dray's had this coming for a long time," Brent explained, even though no one had asked. "He's been in a downward spiral ever since Stella died. Which is funny," he snorted, "because he killed her. And then I had to clean up the mess. But, I did it because we were going places, and I was finally getting where I needed to go in my career. We were selling out at international venues and we had a stellar tour lined up for next year—the sky was the fucking limit!"

He pumped his fist in the air excitedly as Dray leaned against the wall and started to slide down it. I tried to keep from looking at him as he gasped for breath, knowing that he was overdosing on the lethal combination of drugs in his system.

"That's the funny thing though—it was all just temporary. I needed everyone to keep their shit together for a little while longer while I got things set up, then they could ruin their lives however they wanted to. Mike had some great connections and made some killer deals for us, but now, I don't need him anymore. He started to get in the way and was too nosey for his own good, worrying about what business I was getting into and whether or not it was good for *everyone.* And Dray— well Dray has been a drag for far too long now. But the thing about him is that drummers are a dime a dozen. I just needed to get Jolted on the map, and then, I could easily find another drummer to replace him."

"You're a monster," I muttered under my breath, even though it was loud enough for him to hear me.

"Why? Because I look out for myself? I know what I'm worth and I'm willing to make whatever sacrifices that I need to get what I want. I'm the lead singer of the hottest fucking band in America right now and *nothing* is going to stop me."

I turned my head away from him in disgust and caught a glimpse of Dray hunched over, his head down as foam poured out of his mouth. His skin was turning blue as his eyes settled in the back of his head.

"Two problems down, two to go," Brent said bitterly, as he looked at

Dray and laughed. He raised the gun and aimed it at us.

"Which one of you want to go first?" he asked, moving the gun back and forth between us.

"Ladies first," Wyatt said coldly, gently pushing me to the side. I turned to look at him, unable to believe what he had just said. Was *everyone* going to betray me today?

Brent tossed his head back, laughing hysterically. I looked over and saw Wyatt grip the knife at his side. His face was hard and his attention focused on Brent. Out of nowhere, he lunged at him with such force and speed that I almost missed it. I couldn't see much of what was happening as Wyatt's body blocked my view. There was a scuffle as Brent tried to fight back and push Wyatt off of him, but at that moment, Wyatt was stronger and used his full force to shove Brent up against the wall. His body leaned slightly to the right as his arm turned, and I saw the horror on Brent's face as Wyatt plunged the knife deeper into his stomach. Wyatt stepped away slowly, walking backward to where I was standing as we watched Brent slide down the wall, leaving a streak of blood along the way. I covered my mouth with my hand as I tried to keep the scream from escaping my lips and filling the silence as his body crumpled to the floor with a heavy thud.

THREE STRIKES, YOU'RE GONE

Twenty Six

Wyatt

I watched as Brent fell to the floor, not bothering to check him to see if he was still alive. While I had never killed anyone before, I was confident that the stab wound to his internal organs was enough to do the job. Besides, we didn't have time to waste with that right now. There were things we needed to do before we got the hell out of there before any more villains decided to show up.

I reached down and dug my cell phone out of Mike's pocket. A quick glance at the screen showed that there were seventeen missed calls and thirteen unread text messages. There was probably an equal number of voicemails too, but I would have to deal with those later. There wasn't time right now. We needed to get moving and were wasting seconds that mattered.

"We need to get out of here, Kayce," I said gently, placing my hand on her elbow as she stood there, covering her mouth with her hands. "Can you help me find the keys? We need a vehicle…"

My mind was scattered, trying to think through everything at once. All it took was for me to forget one tiny detail and this whole thing could blow up in our faces.

"Kayce!" I snapped, starting to lose my patience.

Her head jerked up, eyes filled with tears as her body trembled. I scolded myself for being so hasty with her. It wasn't like she was in an abandoned shed filled with dead bodies every day. Hell—neither was I. I forgot to account for the fact that she was likely in shock—anyone would be and that I needed to be gentle with her. It was hard to keep that in mind when I was scrambling, trying to figure out how to get us out of here and to somewhere that was safe.

"My truck is outside," she stammered, her hands slowly reaching down to pat her pockets. She reached in and pulled out her keys, handing them over to me.

"Thank you," I said as I took them from her. "We've got to get out of here, okay?"

"Okay," she whispered, looking around the room as if she was missing something.

"What are you looking for?"

She bent down and started picking up the pictures that were scattered on the floor.

"Don't worry about them," I said softly as I placed my hand on her shoulder.

"But if someone finds them…" Her voice trailed off, the thought forgotten for a brief moment.

"They won't," I assured her while helping her back up. "Where did you park?"

"Behind the shed."

"Okay, go get in the truck and I'll be right behind you."

Her eyes widened with a mixture of fear and curiosity.

"You're not coming with me?"

"I need to take care of something first. Please go wait for me in the truck," I urged. "I promise, I'll be right behind you."

I waited until I heard her close the door behind her before I turned and looked at the gruesome scene in front of me. While we could just run and leave here as if nothing happened, I couldn't guarantee that someone wouldn't stumble upon the decomposing bodies at some point. On top of that, I had to assume that there would be evidence of Kayce and I being here—whether it be fingerprints or a strand of hair, it wasn't worth risking it.

I rushed over to Dray and felt around in his pockets, making sure to avoid the mess that had cascaded down his hoodie. I didn't know much about drugs given that I was never into them, but I was willing to bet that he had a lighter on him given he reeked of pot on top of whatever he had done on the way over.

My fingers pushed through the tight fabric of his jeans, forcing their way into his pocket. After a few seconds, I felt something hard, cold, and metal. I pulled it out and grinned when I saw that it was a Zippo lighter. I jumped up and ran over to the photos that were laying on the floor by Brent. I flipped the top back and pushed my thumb down until the flame appeared. Holding the lighter steady, I carefully held the photos over it until the fire spread to them. I let them fall to the floor, watching as the flames licked the old, rotted wood. Next, I burned anything else that I could find, hoping that it would spread quickly. Unfortunately, it was an old shed with nothing in it and the inside had already been exposed to the snow which would make it more difficult.

It wasn't a brilliant plan, but it was the best that I could come up with while rushing to get the hell out of there. I watched as the flames danced around the floor and climbed the walls, sticking to the parts that were still dry. I pulled my hands through the sleeves of my hoodie and quickly wiped the zippo before tossing it on the floor next to Dray.

By the time I got outside and trekked through the thick snow to the truck, Kayce was already inside, warming up in the driver's seat. I climbed into the passenger side and buckled up. We didn't say anything, just a silent look, asking if each other was okay before she put the truck in drive and got out of there.

I would have offered to drive, but Kayce looked like she needed it more than I did. Instead, I unlocked my phone and scrolled through the list of text messages and missed calls from my mom, Buck, Grant, Lacey, and a number that I didn't have saved in my phone. There was too much to try to deal with all at once so I tackled the biggest item first: my mom.

I pressed the button to call her and held the phone to my ear while I shifted in my seat. I hated talking on the phone in front of other people, but it wasn't like I had much of a choice at the moment. If I didn't get back to my mom right away and let her know that I was okay, she was guaranteed to be in her car and on her way to look for me within the next ten minutes. Her last three texts had confirmed it.

"Wyatt Eugene Walker—where the hell have you been, and why aren't you answering your phone?!" she yelled through the phone. I pulled it away from my ear for a second, the shrill tone of her voice, when she was pissed, was too much for me to take with the pounding headache I had from getting hit so many times in one day.

"I'm sorry that I missed your calls, mom," I started slowly. "But I'm okay. You don't have to come down here."

"Too late," she snapped. "Buck and I are already on the road."

I looked around us at the blanket of snow that was falling around us. Kayce was used to driving in this kind of weather, but even she was going under the speed limit and had to use her high beams to see more than two feet in front of her.

"Mom, please turn around and go home. This storm is intense and you guys should not be driving in it."

"I'm not stopping until I make sure that you're okay."

I grounded my teeth in frustration, knowing that she wouldn't stop until she had some sort of proof that I was fine.

"Are you driving, or is Buck?" I gritted my teeth. I hated this idea but if it meant that she would turn around and go home, then I would do whatever it took to keep them safe.

"Buck is driving. For whatever reason, he wouldn't let me. He insisted that he drive us there," she scoffed as if it was the most ridiculous thing she had ever heard.

"Okay, I'm going to FaceTime you so you can see that I'm fine. But you need to promise me that you'll turn around and go home once you have seen for yourself that there's nothing wrong."

I glanced at Kayce, noticing the way she flinched at my words. I knew that there was dried blood on my head from the first time I had been hit, but I had no idea how bad the rest of it was. She tried to give me a reassuring smile before returning her focus to the road.

"Fine, but I will make no promises until *I've* decided that you're okay."

"Deal," I muttered and pulled the phone away from my ear so I could press the button to change the call to a FaceTime call instead. I held the phone in front of me, waiting for her to show up on the screen.

Even though she tried to force a smile, I could see the wrinkle lines in her forehead as she leaned closer to her phone. I expected her to gasp or let out a shriek, but instead, she stayed calm and her features became harder to read.

"Buck, can you please pull over?" she asked politely. I swallowed hard and looked out of the window. It was rare that my mom was this calm and collected when she knew that I had gotten myself into some sort of trouble. I almost always preferred the angry, screaming side of her because then I knew that she was just mad in the moment and that she would forget about it sooner than later. When she was calm that usually meant that she wasn't going to forget anytime soon.

I could hear Buck in the background as he agreed. My mom waited patiently for the car to come to a stop before turning her phone to Buck.

"Which one of you is going to go first and tell me what the hell kind of trouble you got into this time?"

Buck and I stared at each other for a second, neither of us bothering to answer her.

"Well?" she prodded impatiently.

I felt bad that Buck was even getting brought into this, yet I had no idea what he had told her. Did he mention to her that I had asked him to look into Mike? That couldn't have been that big of a deal, could it? There was no way that he knew anything about what had happened. No one did.

"Buck wasn't involved in any of this," I said, noticing the way that his features hardened before he looked over at her.

"Then why was he getting information on someone for you?" my mom asked, turning the phone back to look at her. "And what on earth happened to you?!"

"There was a fight, that's all," I lied. I couldn't tell them the truth, especially with Buck being a cop. There was no way that I could ever burden him to carry this secret for me of what I'd done. No, that would be something that I would take to my grave and never speak of ever again.

"Why did you get into a fight? With who?"

I could feel the irritation start to build again, each question forcing me slightly closer to the edge.

"Look ma, I really don't want to get into it right now. Okay? I'm fine, I just have a knot on my head and a terrible headache."

"You're just as stubborn as your father was," she sighed. "Fine. We'll turn around and go home. But promise me that you'll get to a doctor and have that bump on your head looked at…"

"I'll deal with it later, mom."

My attitude was getting more sour by the second. I knew where she was going with it and she knew how much I hated to talk about it.

"The doctors said, one more hit and you could—"

"I know, mom!" I snapped angrily into the phone. I looked away to avoid seeing the look of hurt that flashed across her face.

"Okay," she whispered, holding her hands up in front of her. "I won't push you. But keep an eye on it and don't be a dummy. If the pain starts to get worse, you better get your butt to a hospital and this time—call me."

"I will, mom, I promise," I assured her before wrapping up the call and hanging up.

I didn't feel like discussing it, so I was relieved when Kayce kept her attention on the road and didn't bother asking me about it. I turned my focus to the voicemails so that I could clear the notifications. I deleted the messages from my family and almost deleted the last message from an unknown number before deciding against it.

I held the phone up to my ear and waited for the message to start.

"Hey, Wyatt, this is Rudy Villanueva from the Colorado Cougars. I wanted to chat with you about the recent progress update that came in from your doctor. Give me a call when you have a chance."

I felt my blood pressure start to rise, the weight of the day starting to take its toll on me. I deleted the message and let my phone drop into my lap as I bit my fist and looked out the window.

"Everything okay?" Kayce asked, glancing at me for a quick second.

"Yeah, it's fine."

I didn't want to take my bad mood out on her. It wasn't fair and she had been through plenty of heavy shit today as well. It was already late, the sky eerily bright from the snow that had gotten thicker the closer that we got to town.

"How's your head feeling?" she asked cautiously as she slowed down for a red light.

"Not you too," I moaned, pinching the bridge of my nose between my fingers to push the headache away.

"I'm not trying to nag you," she laughed. "I'm genuinely concerned."

"I'm fine. Thanks," I said, forcing a smile that was reluctant to appear.

"I'm not a doctor, but I don't think you should be alone tonight—just in case." She rushed the words out, and I couldn't help but notice that she seemed nervous.

"What are you suggesting?" I asked, turning slightly in my seat to face her.

"I'll buy us dinner, and maybe you can come stay with me tonight… You know, so I can keep an eye on you with your lumpy head."

I laughed and felt some of the tension start to lift from my shoulders. She was afraid to be alone, and it felt oddly satisfying that she wanted me to stay with her for comfort.

"Deal," I said happily. "But—I have two conditions."

"Oh great," she replied sarcastically, easing on the gas pedal as the light turned green. "Let's hear what the diva wants this time…"

"Diva?!" I shrieked, pulling my hand up to my chest in mock exasperation. She laughed and looked over, her eyes immediately finding the cuts along my wrists from the rope. I lowered them and tried to pretend she hadn't seen them. "I'm not the diva, however, I'm also not budging on my requests."

"Okay, let's get this over with," she teased, driving slowly as she turned onto Main Street.

"First—I need to have some Tasty Pig tonight. Barbeque is the equivalent of nature's first aid. It'll make everything better."

"That's doable. What's the second item on your request list?"

"I'll tell you when we get there."

Ten minutes later, we were in line at The Tasty Pig, thankful that they were still open when everything else had already shut down from the storm. It would have been nice to go home and have it delivered but unfortunately, they never jumped on the modern train of food convenience.

"I guess it's a good thing that I wanted barbeque," I said, looking around at the empty parking lots around us. "There weren't any other options, even if we wanted them."

"Yeah, The Tasty Pig is one of the few businesses that will stay open for pretty much anything and everything. The owner has a house close by, so they never worry about the weather since they can just walk home if they need to. It's actually that little house, right over there," she said as she leaned closer to the steering wheel and pointed to the house sitting on the corner of the side street that was behind us.

The car ahead of us pulled forward and Kayce placed our order. As she was talking, I dug out my wallet and got my debit card ready. When she pulled forward, I handed it to her, watching her narrow her eyes as she looked at it.

"What's that for?" she asked with a quirked brow.

"My second requirement. I'm buying dinner."

She opened her mouth to speak, but I held my finger up to stop her.

"Look—I get to buy dinner because if not, then it'll feel like this weird prostitution thing where you buy me dinner and lure me back to your place. I don't know what you've heard, but I'm not that kind of guy."

Her face flushed red as I winked and pushed the card toward her. She reluctantly took it and handed it to the cashier at the window, after they gave her the total. A few seconds later, they handed it back to her, with a receipt. I tucked both of them into my wallet and reached over to grab the bags of food from Kayce.

"It'll be just a second," the cashier said. "We're just waiting on the peach cobbler."

I laughed hysterically at the look on Kayce's face as she turned beet red and sank back against her seat.

"I stand corrected," I laughed. "Apparently, you are trying to buy your way with me tonight, aren't you?"

She rubbed her lips together in an effort to not say anything. I could see the comeback sitting on her lips and wished that she would say it. Instead, the cashier slid the window open and handed her the last bag that had the cobbler in it. Kayce handed it over to me without looking and drove off.

Twenty Seven

Kayce

By the time we got back to my apartment, the snow was blowing so hard in every direction that you couldn't see more than an inch in front of you. We sat down on the couch to eat but the tension was thick in the air between us as the events of the day sat heavily on our shoulders. There was a lot that we needed to talk about, but I had no idea where to start.

I set the boxes of food in a line on the coffee table and opened the lids, allowing the heavenly smell to float out around us. It felt almost dream-like, sitting on the couch next to Wyatt, eating dinner while the snow fell peacefully outside. Never mind the dried blood on his head from getting hit earlier or the cuts on his wrists from where they had tied him up. If you looked past the physical evidence that we were wearing, you could pretend that we hadn't spent the day in a blood bath with a handful of people who wanted us dead.

"You okay?" Wyatt asked gently, handing me a paper plate.

I took it and set it in my lap, pulling a deep breath in before I trusted myself to speak and not have a meltdown.

"Yeah, I think so," I replied, turning my head to look at him. "Are you?"

He shrugged dismissively so I didn't push it any further. I didn't blame him for not wanting to talk about it. I wasn't chomping at the bit myself.

"Do you want some ribs?" I asked, changing the subject as I picked up the container from the far end of the table and held it in front of him. He smiled and scooped a few onto his plate with his fork.

I served myself before setting it back on the table and then went about filling my plate with the rest of the food. We didn't bother to talk after that. It was just two people who were quietly enjoying a much-needed meal. My stomach rumbled, a gentle reminder that I hadn't eaten anything since this morning with Wyatt before everything crashed down around us. I glanced over, pleased that he was devouring his food as quickly as I was, so he couldn't judge me for being such a piggy.

Once we were finished, we leaned back against the couch, too tired to move. Part of me wanted to get up and take a shower to wash the day off of me, but the other part of me was too tired and sore to get up to make the effort.

I still hadn't told Wyatt what had happened, and honestly, I had no idea where to start. It sat there with the other topics that we were strategically avoiding with our silence.

He lifted his hand and rubbed the side of his head, wincing as he pulled his hand away.

"We really should take a look at your head," I said, turning to face him. "Lean over so I can see it better."

He scooted closer and leaned toward me, angling his body so his chest was lined up against mine and his arm pinned me on the other side. I could smell the subtle scent of his cologne as it teased the edges of my mind, bringing the memories of the other night back to the surface.

It seemed so strange that it was just a few nights ago when everything now felt like it was longer. Today was so long and exhausting that I was sure it had been at least a week and not just a few hours.

I gently reached up and pushed his hair back away from the cut on the side of his head. There was a large knot sticking up beside it that faded into his hairline and disappeared. My fingers tenderly traced along it as I tried to see how bad it really was. As I got closer to his temple, I felt him flinch and jerk away.

"Sorry," I apologized softly.

"It's okay," he said as he looked into my eyes. "It's just a little tender."

"I can see why. It looks like he got you pretty good."

I pulled my hand away, afraid that I would start running my fingers through his hair if I didn't.

"Yeah, they both did," he chuckled, even though there was nothing humorous about it.

"Both?" I asked, pulling my brows together.

"Mike got me the first time, then while you were gone, Mateo got me the second time."

Hearing his name on Wyatt's lips sent shivers down my spine.

"You know Mateo?" The words almost stuck in my throat as I tried to force them out.

"Not really. I knew his wife, Mandy."

A faint blush crept up his cheeks as he tucked his chin and looked away.

"You slept with his wife?!" I gasped, putting two and two together.

He grinned sheepishly as his eyes slowly made their way back up to mine.

"I didn't know she was married."

I raised an eyebrow and waited for him to come clean. I had known Mandy long enough to know that there really was a good chance that she hadn't told him that she was married, but there was a very small one that someone in town wouldn't have said something and ratted her out.

"I was in Eastern Point on business, so was she," he explained with a shrug.

"Man, Lacey was right about you, wasn't she?" I laughed, feeling more relaxed now that we were talking and not avoiding the heavy elephant in the room.

"Hey, that one wasn't my fault!" he said, putting his hands up in front of him defensively.

We laughed together for a few minutes. It felt so good that I didn't want it to end, even if it was from talking about Wyatt having an affair with another woman.

"How did Mateo end up finding out anyway?" I asked, genuinely curious.

"Turned out that he was supposedly there for business, but his *colleague* looked like she was paid by the hour, if you know what I mean."

I rolled my eyes and grinned, knowing exactly what he meant.

"There's something—" I started saying at the same time he said, "Do you—"

We both stopped and waited for the other to finish their sentence.

"Go ahead," I offered, suddenly feeling too nervous to tell him about Mateo.

"It was nothing," he replied with a half-smile that pulled at the dimple in his cheek. "I was just going to ask if you wanted me to clean this up?" He looked down at the empty boxes on the table.

"Nah, I'll take care of them in a little bit. I'm too tired to care about that right now."

"Why don't you relax, and I'll clean this up?" he offered, reaching forward to grab the boxes at my end of the coffee table. The light caught the cuts on his wrist, making my stomach clench in response. I hated that he had these injuries because of me.

I reached forward and gently pulled his arm away, making sure not to touch his wrist.

"Leave them," I said quietly. "Really. They'll still be there tomorrow."

I could see the tension in his neck as he rolled his head back to relieve it. What had started out as a good day for him with getting Junior's commitment quickly turned sour because of me.

"Why don't we go take a hot shower, then get ready for bed?"

His eyebrows lifted in surprise, a cheeky smirk splitting his cheeks.

"We?"

"What?" I pulled my head back in surprise. "I said *you*. Not *we*." My mind was racing, trying to remember if I had just said that or if he was messing with me.

"You totally said *we*," he assured me, the stupid grin still plastered across his face. "First you try to bribe me to come over with dinner, then you add in the peach cobbler—which we've yet to eat by the way. Then you ask me to take a shower with you… I gotta say, maybe Lacey should have been warning *me*."

I sat there with my arms folded over my chest, refusing to give in and admit that I had said it. There was no proof either way, but he was having way too much fun believing that I did.

"I did not lure you over here with food and the promise of showering together," I said matter-of-factly.

"Well, then, I guess it was just your natural charm and hospitality that pulled me away from my cozy room at the Honey Lodge hotel tonight."

I fought the smile that was tugging at the corner of my lips, threatening to spread across my face when I pictured him trying to get comfortable on those hard-ass beds. I had never stayed there myself, but it was a running joke around town about how old and hard the mattresses were, yet there was never any talk of them getting new ones.

Out of nowhere, a huge yawn took over, making me realize how exhausted I was.

"Come on," Wyatt said, standing up and holding his hand out to me.

I tilted my head to the side, confused.

"Let's go take a quick shower, then we'll get to bed. It's been a long day."

THREE STRIKES, YOU'RE GONE

Twenty Eight

Wyatt

Kayce tilted her head back, letting the water run down her face and chest. I stood next to her, my fingers itching to follow the droplets of water as they rushed down her stomach. The water was relaxing, while the heat of it burned the cuts on my wrists. I didn't complain and tried not to act like a pussy about it.

I had told Kayce to go first so that way there was enough hot water. If it ran out by the time she was done, then I would be the one to take a cold shower—which I obviously needed with the erection that I had no way of hiding. Thankfully, her eyes were closed as she scrubbed the shampoo bubbles out of her hair so she hadn't seen it yet.

Not that it should be surprising that a man had a hard-on while showering with a beautiful woman. I didn't know a man in his right mind who could be around a naked, wet, woman and not have a bulging boner. Unless he was gay—then I guess he wouldn't care much about the naked woman. But I was neither gay nor crazy, and my dick was making sure that I knew it.

Her eyes fluttered open after she leaned her head forward and wiped the water off of her face. She looked breathtakingly beautiful. Completely natural—no make-up or silly filters that most girls had started to rely on for their constant selfies on social media. That didn't show you what someone really looked like. This did.

I studied her face, even though she gave me an odd look while I stared intently at her. She had high cheekbones that complimented her beautiful smile. It was perfect—like the kind you would see in a magazine ad. Straight, white teeth, and full, pouty lips. As I looked closer, I saw a small cluster of freckles on her cheeks that I must've missed this entire time. Or maybe I just hadn't gotten close enough to notice them before.

"You're being creepy," she stated before squirting a blob of conditioner in her hand, then ran it through her hair. It smelled sweet with a heavy vanilla scent that lingered in the air.

"I'm not creepy," I laughed, leaning my shoulder against the shower as I crossed my arms over my chest to keep from touching her. "I'm just admiring the beauty before me."

She stopped mid-rinse and looked at me as if I just said that two plus two equaled eighteen.

"What?" I laughed, suddenly feeling self-conscious.

"Nothing," she giggled. "But, if you have a thing for my shower, then I'll move and get out of your way." She wiggled her eyebrows as she squeezed around me and gently pushed me toward the water. I loved the feeling of her hands on my back as I stepped forward and let the hot water hit my face and chest. I closed my eyes and took a moment to enjoy it.

"The showerhead has different pressures," she laughed, "You know, in case you're into that sort of thing."

I turned around, running a hand down my face to wipe the water away before I looked at her.

"Trust me, I don't need a damn showerhead."

Her face flushed red as our eyes locked onto each other.

"All I heard was head," she muttered, taking a step closer.

I could feel the heat and electricity pulsing between us as the small gap between our bodies closed. Her chest rose and fell heavily against mine as her fingers reached down and trailed along the length of my shaft.

My dick twitched in response, ready for a release but not yet. I wanted to take my time with her, to enjoy every second. To watch her face as she came undone from my touch as I fucked her senseless.

I ran my hand down her side and over her hip before reaching back and cupping her ass. She gasped in response, her eyes darting up to look at me. Her lips parted as I leaned down and kissed her, my tongue greedily pushing its way into her mouth. I wanted to taste her—no, *needed* to devour her like I was on my death bed, and she was my last fucking meal.

She deepened the kiss, reaching up to wrap her arms around my neck as my dick pressed against her hip, desperate to be inside of her. Her breasts pushed firmly against my chest, our bodies perfectly lined up and ready for each other.

As quickly as it started, it ended when she pulled away and stepped back.

"I'm sorry," she whispered. "I don't think we should be doing this."

Without another word, she turned and got out of the shower. She quickly wrapped a towel around her body before she walked out and closed the door behind her.

THREE STRIKES, YOU'RE GONE

Twenty Nine

Kayce

I sat on the couch with my knees pulled to my chest as I waited for him to come out of the bathroom. I felt terrible about what had just happened, but something about the way that he looked at me forced me to pull back. It was more of a natural reaction—step back and put my guard up before anyone had the chance to get close enough to hurt me. But I had seen the way his face fell when I got out of the shower and walked away.

It wasn't his fault and I couldn't expect him to know what was going on in my head. After everything that we had been through today, it felt nice to forget long enough to distract ourselves from the reality of it all. The problem was that both of us were used to using the same coping mechanism—sex, which used to work when we were single and carefree. Not that we were dating, but it felt different with Wyatt. I was already feeling myself fall for him, and that was even more terrifying than the things I had been through today.

A few minutes later, the pipes squeaked as he turned the shower off. It was warm in the apartment after I cranked up the heater, but I still couldn't shake the chill that had settled in my bones. I rubbed my hands together to try to warm up as my nerves frayed, when he opened the door and walked out.

He gave me a sheepish grin, almost as if he was unsure of how to act around me now. I hated that in a split second, I had completely ruined the light-hearted, fun vibe that we had found with each other.

"Hey," I smiled and waited for him to come sit beside me on the couch.

He was wearing a pair of sweats and a t-shirt that fit so perfectly around his body that I wanted to curl up next to him and sink into his comforting arms. I pulled at the string on my hoodie by my neck, wondering if it would be easier to just cover my head and pull it shut so I didn't have to look at him and deal with any of this.

"Hey," he replied warmly as the cushion next to me dipped with his weight as he sat down.

"I'm really sorry about what happened—"

"Don't be," he interrupted, holding his hand up to stop me from continuing my sentence.

I looked down, too uncomfortable to look up at him as I made my confession.

"I got scared," I blurted out, keeping my eyes on the piece of lint across the room on the edge of the rug by the wall. "I didn't know what to do, so I walked away."

He nodded his head and ran a hand down the scruff on his jaw from missing a few days of shaving.

We sat there for a few moments, neither of us speaking.

"Why were you scared?" he asked suddenly, turning to face me. His eyes were soft and sympathetic as they studied me.

"I don't know," I exhaled loudly with frustration. "It just felt— different. I don't know how to explain it. I wanted someone to comfort me and make everything go away for just a little while, but then when you looked at me, I realized that it felt…"

"Different," he repeated with a smile.

"Exactly. And I don't know why or what it means, but I knew that it was better to stop it before things went any further."

"I get it," he sighed. "I really do. Because things felt different for me too."

He reached over and lifted my chin with his finger. Our eyes locked and that same feeling from the shower started tingling in my stomach again.

"I like you Kayce," he continued, still holding my chin between his fingers. "And I think that you like me too."

I bobbed my head in agreement, too afraid to say the words out loud.

"But it's new for both of us. Or at least for me," he laughed, pulling his hand away so I could move from my frozen position. It was like his touch had some magic spell on me. "I've been with my share of women—hell, I've been with more than my fair share, but I've never met anyone like you before, and that scares the shit out of me."

I ran my tongue along the backside of my teeth as I tried to process what he was saying. It was something I had done since I was a little girl. Usually, it would help me to clear my head and find the right answer, but sitting here next to him as he stared at me with those eyes—I had never felt more foggy-brained in my life.

"What if this is just some sort of coping mechanism?" I asked, jumping ahead and speaking my thoughts before thinking them through. I saw the confusion on his face as he raised a brow in response to my random question. "I mean, what if what almost happened between us in the shower was just our way of escaping reality for a little while. Maybe that's why it felt different?"

Deep down, I knew better. I knew that this wasn't just some random thing that we were doing to pass time and forget the unthinkable. It was the very thought-out and deliberate thing that we both wanted to do because there was this insane chemistry that sizzled between us whenever we were next to each other.

"Is that what you think this is?" he asked calmly, not sounding offended or upset by it.

I paused for a moment and tried to force the words out of my mouth. I needed him to believe that I did. Then, he would walk away, and I could deal with my feelings for him on my own, after he went back to Haven Brook. It wasn't like this was something we could continue, even if we wanted to, because we didn't even live in the same town. Sure, it was only a few hours between Easterville and Haven Brook, but I couldn't imagine that either of us was going to be good at long-distance relationships when we avoided commitment at all costs to begin with.

"No," I admitted, betraying myself. "I don't think that is what *this* is." I moved my finger between us before he reached up and grabbed it, pulling my hand onto his lap.

"We don't have to label anything right now, Kayce. It's enough just to say that we like each other, and that maybe, this is more than just a fling."

His words were exactly what I needed to hear to calm the storm that had been brewing inside of me.

"Okay," I agreed, rubbing my thumb across the top of his hand.

His grin spread across his face, showing off the sexy dimples that I couldn't get enough of.

"Okay," he repeated with a laugh before reaching over and pulling me across the couch so I was leaning against his chest. He wrapped his arms around my waist and rested his head on mine. The warmth from our bodies was enough to send my body into complete shutdown as a yawn tore through me and made my eyes water.

"It's been a long day, we should get to bed," he offered when he noticed.

I didn't bother saying a word since my mouth was busy with another yawn. He chuckled behind me as we made our way to my bedroom and climbed into bed. I set my phone down on the nightstand beside me, looking for the cord to the charger when it started ringing. I groaned when I thought that it might be Lacey wanting to check in and see how the day had gone. Then I realized that it was late and there was no way that she would be up and calling me at this hour unless something was wrong.

I checked the caller ID and froze when I saw the name displayed on the screen. My fingers trembled as I picked it up and stared at it.

"What's wrong?" Wyatt asked, leaning over to touch my shoulder.

"It's the police," I whispered. I swallowed hard and slid my finger across the screen to answer it. The last thing that I needed was for them to show up at my apartment if I didn't take the call. While it was late and I could say that I slept through it, it would be terrible to have to talk to them about anything in person. I was a terrible liar and had always been told that my flushed cheeks gave me away.

"Hello," I croaked out, my voice getting stuck in my throat.

"Hey, Kayce, sorry to wake you. It's Dan," he said, assuming that I had been asleep and that was why I had sounded weird. That's the nice thing about small-towns though—everyone knows each other on a first-name basis and no one ever assumes that you were part of a mass murder earlier that day.

"No biggie," I lied, nervously biting my finger while Wyatt listened from the other side of the bed. "What's up?"

"Well, I was driving by your shop earlier, doing my nightly rounds, and I noticed that it had been broken into. The window up front was busted."

"Oh, yeah," I said lightly, finally releasing the breath that I had been holding. "Sorry that you had to bother with that, unfortunately, that was from the weather and I had tried to deal with it this morning. I boarded it up the best that I could but wasn't able to get anyone out to replace it because of the storm. Hopefully, it will hold up for another day or two."

"Yeah, um, I think there's a bigger problem than that," he said awkwardly. "The boards weren't up on the window anymore so I went ahead and checked it out."

Shit. This was it. I held my breath and waited for him to say it as Wyatt's eyes frantically searched my face for a clue as to what was going on.

"Okay?"

"The problem," he continued, "is what I found in the garage."

My mind was racing as I desperately tried to remember where Wyatt and I had left the photos from Mike. Were they on my desk? Did we leave them on the table in the garage? Were they the photos that Mike had with him at the shed? Why the fuck hadn't I gone back there to deal with Mateo before someone found out about it? I was so stupid!

I could hear him clear his throat on the other end and knew that he was waiting for me to respond.

"What did you find?" I asked stupidly, closing my eyes as I waited.

"A body."

THREE STRIKES, YOU'RE GONE

Thirty

Wyatt

There were flashing lights bouncing off the walls and onto the trees outside of Kayce's shop, when we pulled up. There wasn't much time for her to explain in detail what had happened or why Mateo's body was in her garage, but she insisted that the less that I knew—the better.

"Thanks for coming, Kayce, I'm sorry to have to drag you out this late and in this weather," an older man in a police uniform said, hugging her before glancing over at me.

"I'm sorry that this happened to begin with," she muttered before realizing what she said. "Dan, this is Wyatt Walker. He's Lacey's future brother-in-law and is in town to recruit Junior Soto for the Haven Brook University baseball program."

She looked up at me with a smile that begged me not to correct her if any part of that statement was incorrect. I extended my hand and shook his as he gave me a warm smile.

"Let's get inside where we can talk without losing a limb to frostbite," he said, leading the way.

We walked carefully through a handful of officers and the crime scene unit that was busy taking pictures of the broken glass that was still scattered on the outside of the building. I was disappointed that the wood I had used to fix it earlier wasn't strong enough to withstand the storm after all. The opening in the window was completely exposed, with a pile of snow that had started to accumulate inside.

We made our way into the garage where there were even more people scattered about and crime scene tape wrapped around the project car in the back of the room. I saw Kayce's eyes immediately go over to the area, but it wasn't curiosity that shone in them. It was fear.

"You don't have to go over to where the body is," Dan said, breaking the silence between us. "I can confirm that it is Mateo Villareal."

"Do you know what happened?" I asked, knowing that I had a better chance of getting information than Kayce did right now. She was a nervous wreck and I prayed that Dan didn't start getting suspicious as to why. Since I still had no fucking idea what happened, I could easily play along with whatever he could tell me.

"They're still conducting their investigation, however, it looks like a break-in that went terribly wrong. I have no idea what he was trying to steal, but we found a cell phone under the car that we believe he was trying to get to before the car fell on him."

Kayce turned and looked away, tucking her chin to her chest. It wasn't a look of admission, but it still made me wonder if she was responsible for this. I looked over to where they were working and waited for the heavy-set cop to move out of the way so that I could see what had everyone's attention. Finally, he stood up and walked over to talk to another cop. For a brief moment, I had a completely unobstructed view of Mateo's body that was crushed under the car that had been knocked off of the jack that it had been on earlier today.

I stole a glance from Kayce and slightly raised my eyebrow to ask all of the questions that I knew she couldn't answer. Subtly, she nodded her head yes while pretending to cough, before she turned and looked in the opposite direction.

"So what happens now?" I asked Dan who was looking down at a report that someone had just handed him.

"Well, for now, we continue with the investigation and make sure that it's thorough and complete. But honestly, I don't think we're going to find much other than what we already have. It doesn't appear that anyone else was here when it happened, so there are no witnesses. The window up front was already broken, and according to Kayce— temporarily fixed. Now the wood might have been ripped off by the wind with that terrible storm, or it might have been an easy target for someone who counted on everyone being at home because of the weather. I'm sticking with an attempted robbery that went bad."

"Do you need anything else from Kayce right now?" I prodded. I knew that we were both tired and likely to slip up and say something that could get us in hot water the longer that we stuck around.

"No, I don't imagine so. Just keep your phone on you and I'll be in touch. I would also recommend taking the day off tomorrow, since I don't know when we'll be able to clear everything out and give you your shop back."

I saw her eyes quickly dart over to the table where I had been sitting when I found the pictures earlier. I knew that she had to be thinking the same thing that I was—where had we left them?

"I left my duffle bag in your office earlier, I'm gonna go grab it," I said to Kayce, gently grabbing her elbow to get her attention.

"Okay," she said quietly, not drawing any attention to it.

I rushed off, stepping past the officers that were still moving around in the lobby as I jogged down the hallway and opened her office door. I walked around behind her desk and picked my duffle bag up off of the floor. It was obvious that no one had been in here since they found Mateo's body because the pictures and envelope were still sitting on her desk. I quickly grabbed them and unzipped my bag, pushing them into Junior's folder that was sitting on top of my stuff. I zipped the bag shut and slung it over my shoulder, looking around to make sure there was no other evidence that we were leaving behind.

"Can I help you?" a man's voice asked.

I looked up, my heart feeling like it had jumped out of my chest and into my throat. A plainclothes officer stood in the doorway, arms folded over his chest as he studied me. I tried to regain my composure as I shifted the bag behind me in some subconscious, desperate attempt to conceal what I was hiding. My eyes quickly took him in, noticing the gun on one hip and the badge on the other.

"I just came to get my bag," I said, patting it for good measure. "I'm here with Kayce," I added, when he didn't blink or budge from his spot.

"No one is allowed back here," he replied in his official police tone.

"This is a crime scene."

"I apologize, I wasn't trying to interfere," I stammered, suddenly feeling my nerves shoot through the roof as he pinned me with his look. "I had mentioned to Dan that I had left my bag in here and that I was coming to get it."

He nodded his head, the muscles in his neck pulling tight with the movement. This guy looked like he ate steroids for breakfast, lunch, and dinner.

"Alright, then you won't mind if I check it before you go," he said, staying put as he continued to block the door.

"Of course not," I said through somewhat clenched teeth. I was screaming internally, begging for some sort of miracle intervention to get me out of this one.

I walked out from behind the desk, feeling the weight of the bag heavy on my shoulder. Every step that I took felt like I was one inch closer to having everything blow up in my face. This was it—this was how everything was going to end for me. I would end up going to prison for crimes that I didn't necessarily commit, and then, my career would forever be down the drain. Unless, there was some sort of professional baseball team in prison.

I was almost to Robocop when I saw Kayce and Dan come down the hallway and stop just outside of her office.

"Hey, did you get what you needed?" Kayce asked, looking up at the beast of a man beside her. "What's up, Logan?"

I closed my eyes to keep from rolling them. Why did it not surprise me that Kayce would know this meathead?

"Just caught this guy rummaging around in your office," he stated, with a nod in my direction. "I was just about to go through his stuff. Make sure he wasn't taking anything that didn't belong to him."

"Seriously?" she said sarcastically, before she nudged him out of the way. "He's Lacey's soon-to-be brother-in-law. He's practically family."

She stood beside me with her hands on her hips and glared at him. I had to give it to her. For someone as small as she was, she sure packed a lot of sass into that little, tiny body.

"The boy is fine, let him go," Dan said from the hallway. "They need you to go help outside."

Logan gave me one last glare before he turned and followed Dan out of the office and down the hallway.

"Are you good?" Kayce asked, glancing at her desk.

"We're good," I confirmed, patting my bag to let her know that I had what she was looking for.

We kept our heads down and quickly made our way outside and into her truck. The drive back to her apartment was quick now that the worst of the storm had passed through already. Even if I wanted to ask her about what had happened with Mateo, I was too exhausted to stay up and listen.

We made our way back to the bedroom, where I tucked my duffle bag under the bed, then crawled in and fell asleep listening to the loud snores of the incredible woman next to me.

432

Thirty One

Kayce

I rolled over and felt a hard body next to me, forgetting for a second that Wyatt had stayed the night. My fingers felt cold against his warm back, and I wondered when he had stripped down last night without me noticing. Knowing me, I was already passed out and snoring before he even reached the bed.

Feeling a little silly, I gently lifted the sheet to see if he had fully stripped down like he had done last time or if he was still wearing his pants.

I looked over, holding it slightly in the air, waiting to see if he had felt the cold air on his skin. I didn't want to wake him, and I definitely didn't want to get caught red-handed. He didn't move, so I lifted it the rest of the way, disappointed to find that he was wearing his sweatpants. He was rolled onto his side, facing away from me, so I almost missed it when he mumbled into the pillow.

"Are you checking to see if I'm naked?" he asked sleepily, slowly rolling over onto his back and turning his head to look at me. I let the sheet fall from my hand and tried to pretend that I hadn't just been caught doing exactly that.

"You know, you can just ask if you wanted to see me naked," he teased playfully, opening his eyes to look at me. I could feel the blush covering my skin and tinting it pink in the mid-morning sun that was filtering in through my curtains. I couldn't remember the last time that

I had slept in this late, but I also couldn't remember the last time that I had been this exhausted.

"I wasn't trying to see if you were naked," I scoffed, picking up my cell phone from the nightstand to distract myself, so I didn't have to make eye contact. It was bad enough that he knew that I was lying because he had just caught me in the middle of it. I didn't want him to have the satisfaction of seeing the guilt branded across my face.

I had a few unread text messages from Lacey that had come in this morning, but other than that, nothing was needing my attention. I don't know what I expected. Somewhere deep down, I had this nagging feeling that someone would find out what I had done to Mateo, and I would get a call from Dan, letting me know that they knew what really happened.

"Then why were you lifting the sheet and looking at my crotch?" he asked as he rolled onto his side and propped himself up on his elbow.

"I thought I felt something tickle my leg." I set my phone on the nightstand and laid down on the pillow, pulling the blankets back up to my chin as an added layer of protection to keep him from reading more into what he already knew was the truth.

"So, you checked to see if it was my dick tickling your leg?" he laughed hard and let his head fall back as he enjoyed himself at my expense.

"You're impossible," I muttered, frustrated that he wasn't letting up on my blunder this morning. I could have come clean and just admitted what I had been doing, but that would have been too easy, and apparently, I didn't do anything easy these days.

"Alright, I'll stop giving you a hard time," he conceded.

I pushed the blankets off of me and swung my legs over the edge of the bed. It seemed like a better idea to put some distance between us before I got tempted to reach over and see just how good he could tickle me.

"But, I will promise you one thing," he added, rolling over and climbing out of bed. I turned to look at him, waiting for him to continue. "It wouldn't be your leg that you would have to worry about it tickling."

He tossed me a playful wink before grabbing his hoodie from the floor and slipping it on as he walked out of the room and into the living room.

I grumbled and ran a hand through my hair. I totally walked into that one, and after last night, I deserved the mounting sexual tension that was frustrating me.

I grabbed a hair tie from the nightstand and pulled my hair into a messy knot on top of my head. There were plenty of things for me to worry about—my hair wasn't one of them.

Wyatt was sitting on the couch, looking at something on his phone, when I walked out of the bedroom. He didn't look up from his phone, so I went about my business and started a pot of coffee. At this point, I was sure that even *my coffee* needed coffee this morning.

My body was sore and achy, but I was thankful that I didn't have the physical marks to show what had happened like Wyatt did. The knot on his head turned a nasty purple-black color and looked a little more swollen today than yesterday. I wondered if maybe I should convince him to go to the hospital to have it checked out when my phone rang with a call from Lacey.

I looked over at Wyatt, who was still busy on his phone, so I slid my finger across the screen to answer it. I didn't pay attention until the last minute that it was a FaceTime call and not a regular phone call until I saw Lacey's face on my screen. She went from smiling and happy to see me to major mom mode with squinted eyes as she tried to look closer at me to see what was wrong.

"Good morning to you too," I muttered when she didn't say anything, just kept staring at me.

"Why aren't you at work?" she asked, tilting her head to the side.

"I took the day off," I said with a shoulder shrug. I waited anxiously by the coffee maker, hoping that it would work its magic, and put something stronger in my coffee for me today. Lord knew that I needed it.

"*You* took the day off?" She tilted her head to the other side, a look of concern still stretched across her face. "Are you sick?"

I pulled my head back in surprise and shook my head.

"Why would you assume that I'm sick? Just because I haven't showered or gotten ready on my day off?" My tone was a little more hostile and aggressive than I had wanted it to be, but my mood was quickly growing sour.

"No, I just know that you don't ever take days off. It's ten o'clock on a Thursday, and you look like you just rolled out of bed," she replied softly. "I just wanted to make sure that you're okay."

"I'm fine," I assured her. I set my phone down for a second while I poured myself a cup of coffee, wondering if I should pour one for Wyatt as well. I didn't want to tell Lacey that he was here with me—again. How was I going to explain that?

"Okay, well, I wanted to call and talk to you about next month. Are you going to be able to make it down?"

I picked up my phone and took a drink of coffee, trying to figure out what she was talking about. My brain was too tired to try to think through the endless possibilities of why she would want me to go to Haven Brook next month.

I was about to answer when I heard Wyatt's cell phone ring loudly from the couch. I froze in place, my mouth slightly hanging open as I wondered if she had heard it.

"Whose phone is ring—" She pressed her lips together as she stopped talking once she realized what she was about to say. My face turned red in embarrassment as I glanced over at him, completely oblivious to my conversation with Lacey as he answered his phone.

"He stayed over?" she asked quietly.

"Let me call you back," I said quickly, not giving her a chance to respond before I hung up. Wyatt had stood up and was standing by the window, looking outside as he raked a hand through his hair. I couldn't imagine that it was one of his brothers calling, given how stressed he looked by whoever he was talking to.

I pressed the button to call Lacey back, this time making sure to avoid FaceTime. I wanted to have privacy for my conversation, yet I found that I wasn't able to walk away from his. What if it had something to do with what happened yesterday? I needed to know if there was trouble heading our way because I couldn't get past the idea that somehow we had managed to escape everything without anything more than some minor injuries. Things like that never happened for me, so I was sitting idly, waiting for the other shoe to fall.

"Okay, do you want to tell me why Wyatt is at your apartment, and you're not at work today?" Lacey asked when she answered the phone.

"It's a long story," I murmured as I stirred the creamer around in my cup with a spoon. I was too distracted to focus on what she had said while I tried to hear what Wyatt was talking about.

I tuned Lacey out as she mentioned something about a double wedding and how she could have Connie get busy on ours. Wyatt was still at the window with his back turned to me, but his shoulders were tight with tension.

"Yeah, I know what the reports say," he replied heavily, the agitation in his tone strong.

His head dipped down to his chest, a look of defeat washing over him.

"I know what it means," he bit out angrily. "What are my options?"

I lifted my mug to my lips and carefully took a sip, my curiosity peaked as to what he was talking about. There was no doubt that it had nothing to do with yesterday, but whatever it was seemed to be upsetting him.

"So, basically, you're saying that it's your professional medical opinion that I will never play professional baseball again."

I felt my heart sink when I heard the words, fully understanding what was going on and how devasting this news was for him.

"Did you hear a word that I said?" Lacey asked, a hint of irritation in her voice.

"I'm so sorry, Lace. I was distracted for a moment," I apologized. I turned my back to Wyatt to give him the privacy that I should have given him all along. "Can you tell me again?"

She sighed dramatically on the other end, the sound of her breath heavy in my ear. I knew that she did it on purpose because she knew how much I hated it. I couldn't blame her. I was being a terrible cousin to her by not listening or making the time for her the past few days that I should have.

"I said that Mia and Jade are trying to convince me to have a bachelorette party. I told them that I don't need one since I've been married before and I'm knocked up with twins, but they're insisting that we do *something*. I was hoping that maybe you could help me come up with an idea of something fun that we could do?"

I felt myself smiling as I listened to her talk, the familiarity of our close relationship a comfort that I didn't realize that I needed. Part of me wanted to confide in her and tell her what had happened, but I knew that I couldn't. This would be another secret that I would have to take with me to the grave. I just hoped that Wyatt would do the same.

"I think it would be great for you to do something fun to celebrate before the wedding. Since the weather will still be bad for a few more months, it will be hard to do anything outdoors. But you could always have a fun slumber party—a girl's only night. We could rent movies and make popcorn, and stay up super late—"

"You do remember that it's me that we're talking about, right?" she joked. "I'm asleep by seven-thirty every night. Eight o'clock if I'm feeling a little wild that night."

"Well, then, I guess we're going to have to do a tea party and Parcheesi. I'll make sure to get you back to the senior center before supper at four o'clock."

I took a sip of coffee and waited for her to snap.

"I happen to think tea is a fabulous idea," she said sarcastically. "But I'd rather play Monopoly."

I snorted and felt the burn of the coffee as it shot out of my nose and all over the counter in front of me. I set my cup down and reached over to grab a handful of napkins.

"Are you okay?" Wyatt asked from across the room, walking over to where I was standing.

Great. I rolled my eyes at how embarrassing this was as I looked down at the splattered coffee on my white hoodie.

"Yeah, I'm fine. Sorry to startle you," I mumbled as I held the phone between my ear and shoulder and continued to wipe at the stain on my shirt with the napkin.

He nodded his head slowly as if he didn't believe that I was okay. A few seconds later, he walked away and went back to his phone call.

"What in the world was that all about?" Lacey asked.

"I was taking a drink of coffee when you mentioned Monopoly, and it came shooting out of my nose when I remembered the stupid strip-Monopoly you told me that you and Grant played," I explained, tossing the dirty napkin onto the counter.

"Oh, yeah," she giggled. "I forgot about that… Well, okay, I didn't forget about it. I think that's actually when I got pregnant. His boat and my shoe made one hell of a—"

"Stop!" I shrieked, not wanting to hear the rest.

"Maybe you should play a game with Wyatt today since you're both there and you have the day off," she suggested casually.

"Yeah, I don't think so," I said dismissively, not wanting to get into the details about him and me.

"Why not? If he's sleeping over at your apartment, I'm guessing you guys are getting along pretty well and pretty much doing it nonstop at this point, right?"

"Not technically."

I watched as Wyatt got off of one call, only to take another. He seemed to be rather popular this morning, and I wondered if this was what a regular workday looked like for him. I knew that he was supposed to get back to Haven Brook as soon as he had Junior's commitment, but that had been delayed due to the crazy blizzard that had just passed through. Maybe they were letting him work remotely while he was stuck here?

"What's going on, Kayce? You seem off."

"It's nothing, really." I rushed the words out too quickly to make them sound believable. Lacey knew me better than my own mom and would instantly pick up on the lie.

"Go somewhere where you can talk," she instructed while waiting silently for me on the other line.

I grabbed my cup of coffee and went to my bedroom, glancing at Wyatt on my way. He was still preoccupied, so I didn't bother him as I went inside and closed the door behind me. I climbed up on my bed and set the coffee down beside me on the nightstand while I got comfortable.

"Okay, spill it," Lacey said.

"It's a long story and one that I can't get into," I said wearily.

"Does it have something to do with the knot on Wyatt's head?" Lacey asked, catching me off guard.

"How did you hear about that?"

"Grant just got off of the phone with Connie. Apparently, she saw it when they were Face Timing after he went missing for a while, and no one could get ahold of him. He convinced her to stay put and not drive in the storm, but she called Grant to ask if he and Chase could go down to Easterville this weekend to pick him up and bring him back home."

I felt my stomach sink as I thought about him leaving.

"There was an incident and a small altercation," I said vaguely, not getting into the details. It was up to him what he wanted to share with his family, but we definitely needed to talk about things this morning to make sure we both had our stories straight.

"Is that why he stayed the night?"

I loved how she assumed that he had stayed the night, but also, how else was I going to explain why he was at my apartment at ten in the morning on a day when I should have been at work?

"Yes."

"But you can't talk about what happened?"

"No."

"Okay," she said with a breath. "I won't push you about what happened as far as why he has a knot on his head, but I am going to ask what's going on with you guys. You seem so standoffish about him when I ask, but yet you guys have spent a ton of time together in the few days that he's been there."

"I don't know, Lacey, it's complicated," I groaned, not wanting to think about it.

"Why? Do you like him?"

"Yes. A lot."

"More than Brent?"

His name sent a chill through me, along with a brutal reminder of the big secret that I couldn't talk to her about.

"More than anyone," I whispered. I pulled the pillow that Wyatt had slept on up to my chest and cuddled it, smelling his cologne.

"Oh, Kayce," she cooed, giddy with happiness. "That's wonderful! You're finally in lov—"

"Don't you dare say it," I warned.

It felt like saying Beetlejuice. Once you said it out loud, nothing but bad things were going to come.

"Alright, alright," she laughed. "I won't push you to say it, but I am so excited to hear that it's happening. And so soon, too!"

She hit the nail on the head without even trying.

"It is too soon, isn't it?" I asked, chewing on my nail. "I've only known him for three days, Lacey. THREE. DAYS."

"Yeah, and you guys have obviously gone through something together—that you can't talk about, but something that pushed you guys even closer. Life works in mysterious ways, but I believe that everything happens for a reason. Like Wyatt taking this job and getting his first recruit in Easterville. Or how you came to his rescue with his truck and letting him stay the night at your apartment when he couldn't get his hotel room situated. Whatever it is that you guys went through, it might just be the one thing that solidifies the bond you've already created."

"I don't know," I sighed heavily. There was so much that had happened in such a short time that my head felt like it was spinning.

"He doesn't even live here, Lacey. I can barely commit to having this tiny apartment, how would I ever be able to do a long-distance relationship?"

"You *could* just move to Haven Brook… I mean, Annie and I would love to have you here with us, and I know I would love for you to be here when the new babies are born."

I thought about what she was saying. It wasn't like I had anything significant to keep me in Easterville, other than my parents still lived here, and I had my own shop. But then again, my parents were starting to travel more now that my dad was retired, which meant that I hardly saw them anymore. On top of that, my shop only did well because it was the only automotive repair shop in town. If a man decided to open up a shop of his own, I would easily be out of business the first week.

But it was ridiculous to think that I would pack up everything I have and move to another town for a man that I've barely known for three days. Who did that sort of thing?

People in love. I rolled my eyes at the thought and dismissed it just as quickly as it had popped into my head.

"I can't just up and leave, Lacey. You know that."

She waited a few minutes before responding, knowing that this was a sensitive subject for me every time she had asked.

"I know. But sometimes things change, and we find ourselves doing crazy stuff we never imagined we would."

I heard footsteps on the other side of the door and wondered if Wyatt was looking for me.

"Well, I hate to run, kiddo, but I have to get going for my doctor's appointment. Call me if you need anything."

"Okay, I will. Let me know how my future nieces or nephews or both are doing."

She laughed and agreed to text me with an update when she was done. I hung up and climbed out of bed, grabbing my cup of cold coffee from the nightstand. When I opened the door, Wyatt was sitting on the couch, his head in his hands.

I didn't want to let on that I had been eavesdropping on his conversation earlier, so I had to pretend that I didn't know what was wrong. I set my phone and coffee cup down on the counter and then walked over to where he was sitting.

Gently, I rested my hand on his shoulder and waited for him to look up at me.

"Are you okay?" I asked softly.

He looked around the room as if he was searching for the answer.

"I don't know," he muttered, still seeming lost.

"Did you get bad news?" I walked around and sat down next to him on the couch.

He rocked back and forth for a few seconds, his jaw clenched as he thought about it.

"No, not bad news. Life-changing news."

I held my breath and waited for him to drop the bomb that had been silently ticking inside of him.

"I just got offered a professional scouting position with the Arizona Rattlers. It's my dream job to work for a professional baseball team since my career as a player is officially over, but I would have to…." His voice trailed off, fading into the silence as I processed what he was saying.

"Move to Arizona," I finished for him. The knot in my stomach grew tighter as it moved up higher to wrap around my heart.

Thirty Two

Wyatt

My heart had felt like it was beating out of my chest with the excitement of getting the job offer. I had applied for the position shortly after several doctors confirmed that it would be unlikely for me to continue to play baseball, but when I didn't hear anything for a few months, I gave up and applied for the job at Haven Brook University.

Never in a million years did I think that I would be given the opportunity to work alongside some of the best athletes in the world, and yet now that I had it, I wasn't sure what to do with it. I saw the look on Kayce's face when I told her that the job would require me to move to Arizona. The way her eyes watered and how she blinked the tears away before they could fall. None of that was lost on me. In fact, it was the reason that I was coming down from my high and thinking of reasons that I should say no and stay in Colorado. It felt strange to be so worried about what she thought, but secretly, I had hoped that she would be as excited about it as I was.

I was about to talk to her about it when her phone rang, and she excused herself to take the call in her bedroom. I could tell that she was upset, but I couldn't put my finger on the reason why. I was starting to feel restless and needed to clear my head.

My phone vibrated against my thigh as it rang. I pulled it out and answered it, seeing Noah's name on the caller ID.

"What's up?" I asked with a little more irritation than needed.

"Woah, I should ask you the same," he joked.

"Nothing, it's just been a long day," I replied, running a hand down my face. I needed to shave. It had only been a few days since I had taken the time to clean up before I met with Junior, but the scruff on my jawline was already irritating me. I liked to take pride in my looks, and this gruff-messy look wasn't for me.

"It's not even eleven in the morning. How is it already a long day?"

"It just is," I sighed heavily, not wanting to get into any of the details on the phone.

"Alright, well, Chase and I are heading to Easterville in an hour or so to pick you up. Should be there around five or six, depending on what the roads are like on our way over there."

I could hear Kayce's voice from under the door. Something about it made me want to stay and talk to her, but I knew that I had to do the right thing. And given how upset she looked a few minutes ago, the right thing was to walk away before I hurt her even more. Maybe some distance between us would be what I needed to clear my head and get back to normal.

Fuck if I even knew what normal was anymore. In four days, everything that could go wrong had gone wrong. Not to mention the crazy shit that went down yesterday. Maybe Lacey was right about Easterville being a place you needed to escape from. The real problem was that I wanted Kayce to run away with me.

"Are you still there?" Noah asked when I hadn't answered him.

"Yeah," I coughed to clear that throat that suddenly felt constricted. "You guys don't have to come for me. I can find a way back."

"We were given orders," he said with a hint of humor.

"Orders?"

It took a second before it hit me—my mom.

"When did she call?" I asked. I stood up and walked over to the window, looking at how peaceful it looked outside with the snow covering the roads.

"About twenty minutes ago," he laughed. "She insisted that we bring you home so she can keep an eye on the knot on your head. Which, by the way, what the fuck happened to you anyway?"

"It's a long story," I mumbled.

"Alright, but if it has to do with you knocking up one of your former one-night stands, please leave that shit in Easterville. We don't need any more of that here."

I laughed and shook my head, remembering the ordeal Noah had gotten himself into with Cindy, a one-night stand that went crazy and kidnapped his girlfriend.

"Nothing like that," I assured him. There was no way that I could tell anyone what really happened. Kayce and I still needed to talk about it to make sure we kept our stories straight.

"Thank God," he chuckled. "Send me the address to your hotel, and I'll text you when we're almost there."

I heard the bedroom door open and looked over to see Kayce walk out.

"I'm not at a hotel," I said with my eyes locked onto hers. "I'm at Kayce's apartment. Ask Grant for the address, he can get it from Lacey."

The line was quiet for a second. Kayce was standing still by the couch, her phone clutched to her chest as she watched me.

"Wyatt, you son of a bitch," Noah laughed. "You slept with—"

I pressed the end button and hung up, afraid that Kayce would hear what he was about to say.

"Is everything alright?" I asked as I slid my phone back into my pocket and walked over toward her.

She slowly nodded her head.

"That was Dan, the officer from last night," she explained. "They found drugs in his system with the toxicology report. Apparently, he was pretty high when he *broke in*. They believe that he accidentally knocked the jack out while trying to get something from underneath the car. The case is closed, and I should be able to go back to the shop later today or tomorrow morning at the latest."

"Closed?" I repeated, unable to believe it myself.

She bobbed her head in agreement.

"Wow. That's a relief," I said, still processing the news. "But I have to ask, Kayce, what really happened yesterday with Mateo?"

I sat on one end of the couch and patted the other, offering her to sit with me. She curled up into a ball on the other side and wrapped her arms around her knees.

"Right after you got hit—the first time, Mike dragged me down the hall by my hair. He was trying to get the door open, but it was stuck. He had to let go to mess with the lock, and when he turned around to grab me again, I punched him in the face and took off running. I thought I was in the clear and snuck around to the back entrance of the garage, where I keep a spare key. I could hear voices, so I hid under the table until the front door closed. I thought they had left. I was coming to find you, but when I got up, Mateo was right there, waiting for me.

"I didn't have a chance to run before he held me by my throat. By the time he let go, I was gasping for air and didn't have the strength to run. I was still freezing from being outside for so long, my body was just too weak. So, I led him to the back of the garage where my project car is, and I slid underneath it. I knew that he wouldn't easily be able to catch me unless he climbed under after me. I purposely antagonized him to get him mad, so he wouldn't have time to think about it. Once he was under the car, I got out as quickly as possible and pushed the jack out from under the car. He was dead in an instant."

Her bottom lip slightly trembled as she told me what happened. I sat there in awe of this incredible woman who was so strong and independent that she did what she had to do to survive. Knowing that she had done all of that by herself made my heart full.

"How did you know where I was?" I asked, trying to put together the rest of the puzzle.

A blush spread across her cheeks as she guiltily looked away. This immediately piqued my interest.

"Kayce?"

"I um… I might have stolen Mateo's phone to get the information from Mike."

"How did you get into his phone? Wasn't it locked?" I asked, remembering Mike's comment about how I should have better privacy settings enabled on mine.

"It was," she admitted. "But I got lucky because it was set with fingerprint access."

My eyes went wide with shock as I listened.

"Don't worry," she laughed nervously. "It's not like I cut off his finger and put it in my pocket for future use. I just unlocked the phone and then changed it to a four-digit password that I made up myself."

I nodded in approval. She was definitely smart and quick thinking—there was no doubt about that.

"I'm impressed," I said proudly. "You did really well with thinking on your feet and getting creative to find answers to your problems."

"Thank you." She smiled the first genuine smile that I had seen in days, and I found how much I had missed it.

"It still seems crazy that everything just happened yesterday. It feels like it was weeks or months ago." I looked down at the cuts on my wrist, making note that I would need to hide those from my family until they healed. Thankfully, it was still bitter cold outside which was the perfect excuse for wearing long sleeves and hoodies.

"I know," she sighed heavily as she leaned back and let her knees rest against the pillow beside her. "I would never have imagined something like this would happen, but I'm thankful that it's over."

I didn't say anything because it felt like I would jinx it if I did. While things felt like they were over because no one was actively trying to kill us, I had no idea if we were that lucky. Two members of a well-known rock band were soon going to be reported missing, along with their former manager. People were bound to start talking about that, and what if it led back to Kayce and me? Did anyone know that they were coming to Easterville? Was anyone looking for them?

"About earlier," I started, my voice feeling a little shaky as I worked up the courage to talk to her about it. "You seemed a little upset when

I told you that I got offered the job in Arizona."

She looked up at me, her golden-brown eyes darkening as the sunlight shifted position in the room.

"I'm sorry that I wasn't more excited for you earlier. I've been feeling a little tired and run down today," she lied. "But I'm very happy for you, and I think you'll love it in Phoenix. There's plenty of hot women out there. Literally and figuratively," she joked.

I felt the sting in my heart as her words stabbed right through it. Did she really think that I was that shallow that I would want to go there to find another woman? How could she not know how hard this felt to think that I would have to leave—whatever this was between us— behind if I took this job? It soured my stomach to think that by going after my dream, it was going to also create a new nightmare. One where I had to live in a world without Kayce in it because there was no way she would go with me.

Thirty-Three

Kayce

It had been twenty minutes since Wyatt left with Noah and Chase. I had offered to take him by his hotel to grab his stuff and check out before they got here, but he insisted that they would do it before they headed back to Haven Brook.

The afternoon was more painful than I had imagined after he told me that he was leaving. I had selfishly hoped that he would be here until his truck was fixed, but it was silly of me to think that he didn't have a life back home that he needed to get back to.

Maybe it was for the best that he left when he did. I could feel myself getting closer to him, and that scared the shit out of me. While he had tried to assure me that what we felt for each other was real and not just a reaction to the trauma we had endured yesterday, it didn't really feel that way after he easily packed up and left with his family.

Everything felt chaotic around me, so I grabbed my jacket and left to get some fresh air and dinner since I was in no mood to cook. I passed by the shop and felt a pain in my stomach when I saw the crime scene tape still wrapped around the building. Dan had said that they were trying to move as quickly as possible but that it might not be ready for me to go back until tomorrow. I couldn't honestly say that I was looking forward to going back.

My shop had been a part of me for so long that I thought that it defined who I was. I needed people to see me as a strong, independent woman who enjoyed working on cars, but I don't know that anyone ever saw me as anything other than the daughter of Mel and Betty—the son they always wanted but never had.

The gossip had never bothered me growing up, and I was happy spending time with my dad and grandpa as they taught me everything they knew. So what if I didn't want to sit around and play Barbies and have tea parties? I could take an engine apart and put it back together wearing my fanciest princess dress without missing a step.

I pulled into the parking lot of Taco Bell and waited for my turn to order. My phone rang, and I ignored it, not having the desire or motivation to answer it. The car in front of me moved forward, so I scooted along with it. I had just finished placing my order when my phone rang again. I knew that if I didn't answer it, Lacey would just keep calling until I did. I waited until after the cashier had given me back my credit card and handed me my bag of food before I answered the phone.

"Kayce! Did you see the news?" Lacey shrieked. It wasn't the excited tone she had when Chris Hemsworth was on tv. It was the one she used to use when we were little, and she would share secrets with me about her dad.

I felt a chill run down my spine as I pulled forward and turned onto Main Street.

"No, what news?"

"That singer you were dating- the one from Jolted—he's dead!"

I slammed on the brakes, sending the bag of food flying across the seat and onto the floormat of the passenger side of the car as I stopped at the red light. I hadn't been paying attention and didn't realize it had already turned yellow long before I came barreling up to it.

"What?!" I gasped. Surely, she had to be mistaken. There was no way that the news already knew about his death. How could anyone know? Unless someone was around and saw us? Or unless he told someone where he was going.

"Hold on, I'm listening to the story now," she said. I waited impatiently for her to tell me what was being reported as the light turned green. I carefully headed back to my apartment.

"It said that Brent Fallows and Dray Long were found in an abandoned shed, along with their former account manager. According to the other band members, Mike, their manager, had recently been fired for embezzling money from their fan club. Brent and Dray had planned to meet up with Mike to recover the stolen funds when something went wrong. They haven't released the details of what happened, but police were sent out after someone called in to report an abandoned structure on fire."

"Oh my God," I whispered, covering my mouth with a hand as I turned into the parking lot and found a spot close to the stairs by my apartment.

"I'm so sorry," she said sympathetically. "I know that you guys haven't been together for a while, but I thought you should know."

"Yeah, thanks for calling to tell me."

I rushed up the stairs and went inside, desperate to get out of the cold. My stomach growled, reminding me that I had once again neglected to feed it consistently for the past few days. I tossed my keys and purse on the counter and took my food to the couch.

"Are you okay?" Lacey asked softly as I unwrapped a chalupa and set it in my lap.

"I'm fine, really," I assured her and took a bite.

"Are you eating?"

"Yeah," I said as I moved the food around with my tongue. "I was starving, and you caught me while I was out grabbing dinner."

"Are you eating chalupas?"

I swallowed my bite and laughed.

"Is there ever a time when I'm *not*?"

"That's true," she laughed. "Maybe I'll have chalupas at my bachelorette party, so you'll be sure to make it."

I rolled my eyes and took another bite. It wasn't the worst idea and probably would be an easy way to lure me there.

"Have you decided when you're going to have it?"

"Grant and I talked about it last night, and since we're not doing the traditional bachelor and bachelorette parties, we're just going to do them that Friday before the wedding. That way, everyone that comes in from out of town can be there for all of it in the same weekend."

"You mean me. So *Kayce* can be there for all of it," I laughed and took another bite.

"It's important to me, and I don't want you to miss any of it," she said light-heartedly.

"I know, and you know that I would never miss anything if I could avoid it."

"I just don't want you to have to miss so much work and fall behind," she added with her mom tone.

"You don't have to worry about me, Lacey. I promise, I'm an adult and can manage my bills and taking a few days off from work. I will be there."

I could hear the sound of my chewing as I waited for her to say something.

"I didn't mean to upset you."

"You didn't," I fibbed and took another bite. I hated that this was something that we talked about often. She constantly worried about me and whether or not I should keep the shop open. It wasn't that I was wild and carefree with my money. No one in town valued what I did, and lately, I had more lulls than busy days.

"Okay, well, I won't keep you so you can enjoy your food. But call me soon so we can chat and catch up?"

I thought about everything that I desperately wanted to talk to her about and felt frustrated when I realized that I couldn't. Not only did I have to keep the stuff about Brent a secret, but I also didn't want to unload my problems with Wyatt on her either. I had no clue whether he had told any of his family about his new job offer, and I sure as hell didn't want to be the one to slip and tell Lacey. She would tell Grant and his entire family would know before he even made it back to town tonight.

I promised her that we would sit down and talk this weekend, knowing that it would be enough to keep her from pressing me about what was going on between Wyatt and me. By that time, he would already be home and likely would have already told his family about his new job in Arizona. Then I wouldn't have to tell Lacey what was wrong. She would already know why my heart was broken.

Thirty Four

Wyatt

I hadn't spoken to Kayce after I left her apartment on Thursday. Part of me tried to convince myself that it was for the best, while the other part of me wanted to ram my head into the wall for a brief escape from the pain that I was feeling from leaving her. But wasn't that what I was planning to do anyway if I decided to take the job in Arizona?

The weekend was a blur, filled with plenty of beer as I tried to drink away the nagging voice that told me to call her. I had heard from the grapevine—aka Lacey told Grant—that one of Kayce's ex-boyfriends had been killed in a fire. Grant didn't know many of the details, and I didn't bother to ask because I didn't want him to think that it had anything to do with my obsession with Kayce. Instead, I got on my laptop and found the article without having to do much digging. There was suspicion that Brent had been stabbed before he shot and killed Mike; however, they were having a hard time collecting evidence due to the fire. The good news was that they didn't believe anyone else was involved as two of the band members went to recover embezzled funds from the recently fired band manager.

The entire thing looked like a big, steaming pile of shit, and I was glad that they weren't bothering to dig any deeper. Between a random car that passed by and called in the fire and the other band member that reported them missing, no one seemed too concerned by the incident.

I sat in my recliner with the paperwork for the new job sitting on the table beside me. I had picked it up several times to fill it out, and each time I would think about Kayce and set it back down. I tried to force myself to focus on the football game playing on the tv but couldn't seem to muster the enthusiasm to pay attention to who was playing. My depression was starting to sink to a new low.

My mom had sent me a text message earlier, asking me to come over for family dinner. She tried to get all of us together every Sunday, but it didn't always work out with everyone's busy schedules. For whatever reason—maybe all of the stars were perfectly lined in the fucking sky—everyone was free for this one, and I was the last person she was waiting on.

It wasn't like I could decline because I was grumpy and didn't want to go. That would never fly with my mom, nor should it. But I also couldn't show up, mopey and depressed, and talk about how I broke Kayce's heart, and therefore broke my own. I hadn't told them about the new job yet either, which felt odd as I was now the one with all of the secrets in the family.

My phone dinged with a new message. I groaned as I reached into my pocket to get it.

Kayce: Did you see the news about that tragic accident with Jolted?

Just seeing her name on my phone had me pushing the foot rest down so I could sit up straight. My fingers quickly moved across my phone as I typed.

Me: I did. It's so unfortunate.

I didn't know what else to say. We both knew that we had to keep our messages about this vague, and I knew what she was asking when she sent her message. Did I see that we were in the clear? Yes, I had seen that.

It felt good to talk to her, even if it was just a quick text message. I didn't want to stop, but I also didn't know what to say.

Me: How are you?

It was such a lame message when I really wanted to ask her a thousand different things. I needed confirmation that she was okay and that I hadn't really broken her heart the way that I feared I did. She didn't deserve it, and I couldn't shake the feeling that she was just as torn up as I had been the last few days.

Kayce: I'm good. How are you?

I rolled my neck back on my shoulders, feeling the tension across them.

Me: Honestly?

I waited for a few seconds as the dots bounced at the bottom of the screen as she typed.

Kayce: Yes.

Me: I feel terrible about how we left things between us.

Kayce: Me too.

Me: Can we talk? There has to be a way for us to work this out?

I stared intently at my phone for a few minutes, waiting for her to text me back. Just as I had given up hope that she would respond, I got her message.

Kayce: I don't think that there's anything for us to work out. Our lives are too different, and neither of us should give up the things we want to try to make this work.

Kayce: Your truck will be ready next week. I'll call and let you know when you can come pick it up.

I tossed my phone onto my lap and closed my eyes as I leaned back in the chair. A few seconds later, I felt it vibrate with another text message and quickly grabbed it, hoping that she had already changed her mind about what she had said.

Grant: Dinner is in 30 minutes. Get your ass over here.

I blew out a heavy breath along with some choice curse words as I got up and got ready.

Forty minutes later, I was sitting at the table at my mom's house, listening to everyone talk as they got situated. Jade and Noah were at one end of the table, getting their son, Asher, situated in his high chair. My older brother Chase was at the head of the table, where my dad used to sit, helping Mia get their girls situated. Riley was giving them sass about how she was a big girl and didn't want to sit in her high chair. I laughed when my mom reminded him that he was worse at two years old and that he better be prepared for when Millie caught up to her big sister's attitude.

It felt good to be around my family and see my brothers settling down as they started their own families. For a while, Noah and I had joked about how we would be the ones to stay single and have all of the fun while Chase was settling down with Mia. But then Noah met Jade, and everything changed after that. Even Grant fell quickly for Lacey. I was fine being the only single one out of the bunch, but now as I looked around at how happy everyone was, it made me want that same happiness too. Hell, even my mom had secretly been dating someone without anyone knowing. It seemed like it was only time before I would find someone to settle down with, but my career seemed to have another idea.

"How did your doctor's appointment go?" my mom asked Lacey as she scooped some green beans on her plate before passing the bowl to Buck.

We hadn't spoken about the information that I had asked him for on Mike, and I prayed that he hadn't heard about what happened on the news. Buck was a quiet man, and I trusted that he wouldn't say anything unless it was when we were in private. And even then, I still hoped that he would avoid it.

"It went well," Lacey said as she leaned over to put a piece of fried chicken on Annie's plate for her. It was incredible how much Annie looked like her mom. I was curious to see what the twins would look like and if either of them would look more like their mom or dad.

I always felt like Chase and Grant looked like my dad, but I never thought I looked like my mom or dad. For years I had worried that maybe I had been adopted, but my mom assured me that I wasn't. My curiosity always got the better of me, and I wondered what my dad would look like as he got older.

"They'll do her twelve-week ultrasound in two weeks," Grant added as Lacey got distracted with Annie. "I'm hoping we'll be able to find out the gender soon after that. They're doing the genetic testing at that appointment and said that they could tell the gender with the bloodwork they'll be collecting anyway."

"We are not finding out," Lacey chuckled and gently elbowed him in the ribs when she was done helping Annie. "I want it to be a surprise."

"Finding out you are pregnant was a surprise. Finding out it is twins is a surprise. I think we've had plenty of surprises already," he teased, planting a kiss on her cheek.

"Well, then you won't mind waiting for one more." She pursed her lips and narrowed her eyes at him, and it immediately reminded me of Kayce. I looked down and pushed my mashed potatoes around with my fork.

"How's the new job?" Buck asked me, changing the subject as everyone began eating. I felt my cheeks turn red as I panicked, wondering how he found out. My mom turned to look at me, her brows pulled together in confusion.

"How did you find out?" I asked, wondering if Kayce had told Lacey about it.

Buck slowly lowered his fork to his plate and looked at me with the same confusion my mom had.

"Umm, you told us about it, son," he said cautiously. "We all knew that you were taking the position with the university. Your mom even checked on you a time or two while you were in Easterville."

I wanted to smack myself in the head for being so dense. Of course, that was what he meant.

"Oh, yeah, um, it's going well. I got the kid's commitment," I said quickly before anyone could question why I was acting so strange.

I shoved a bite of chicken into my mouth and chewed, hoping that it would be the end of the conversation and someone else would start talking.

"What's going on, Wyatt?" my mom asked, turning to look at me after setting her fork down next to her plate.

All eyes were on me as my heart thudded in my ears. I could feel the sweat dot along my forehead and wondered if this was what it felt like to be in a police interrogation room.

"Nothing," I blurted out, my voice cracking in the process.

She tilted her head slightly to the side and said nothing. Her eyes searched my face, confirming that I was lying as I blushed the harder she stared at me.

"Okay, fine!" I exclaimed, slamming my hands down on the table. "I got offered a new job, and that's what I thought Buck was asking about. I haven't told anyone about it, so it caught me off guard when I thought he knew."

"What new job?" Grant asked, leaning forward to listen.

"Why didn't you want to tell us?" Chase asked right after him.

I pulled in a deep breath, trying to calm myself so I could speak without looking like an idiot again.

"I had applied a while back and never heard anything, so I figured they weren't interested. I got a call on Thursday from the Arizona Rattlers, offering me the scouting position that I had interviewed for last year."

I swallowed hard as I turned and looked at my mom. Her eyes were wide with surprise, her hand fiddling with her necklace as she processed my words.

"When did you interview?" she asked quietly.

"Last year. When I said that I was meeting with the rehab specialist in Phoenix, I was actually there to interview for the position."

"And you never bothered to tell me?"

"I'm sorry, I didn't mean to upset you. I knew that you would have told me not to rush things, to wait and see if my shoulder got better."

She pressed her lips into a thin line and turned forward in her seat. She picked up her fork but held it in the air before taking a bite. I could see the wheels turning in her head as she tried to figure out what she wanted to say.

"You're right. I would have told you to wait. But only because I knew how much playing baseball meant to you. Not because I wouldn't want this other opportunity for you."

She took a bite and kept her attention focused on her plate instead of me.

"I know you want the best for me. You all do. But this job means that I would have to move to Arizona."

I saw the look on everyone's face as I said it. The realization of why I had kept this a secret finally hitting them.

"Is this what you want to do?" Noah asked gently.

"It would be my dream job," I admitted, feeling guilty for it.

"Then you should take the job," Grant said from the other end of the table.

"You have to do what's best for you," Chase added. "Besides, Mia and I will need a vacation to someplace warm soon. We can come to visit and show the girls what warm really means."

"We all support you, Wyatt. You know that," Buck said as he squeezed my mom's hand.

"I know," I sighed heavily. It felt better having them know about the job, but that still didn't solve my biggest dilemma. "But it's not that easy. I can't make up my mind on whether or not I should take it."

"Why not?" Grant asked.

"Because maybe it's better if I stay in Colorado," I blurted out. I wasn't ready to talk about this. Not yet, and definitely not with my family.

"What's in Colorado that is worth giving up on your dream?" my mom asked, turning to look at me again.

My face fell, and I closed my eyes. I could see the look on her face when she realized what it was. She had seen it with my brothers and Noah.

"Oh," she whispered. "I see."

I looked up and found Lacey watching me, a look on her face that I couldn't quite figure out.

"I knew it," she said quietly, her eyes never leaving mine.

Thirty Five

Kayce

It had been over three weeks since I had talked to Wyatt. The last message I had gotten was a quick text, letting me know that he had taken the job in Arizona and that he wouldn't have time to come get his truck for a few more weeks. He offered to pay me to have it stored somewhere until he could come for it and apologized that things were so busy and chaotic for him right now.

Whenever I talked to Lacey on the phone, we both avoided any conversations about Wyatt. She didn't give me any updates on him moving to Arizona, and I didn't bother asking for one. He had made up his mind, and as of February 1st, he would be starting the next chapter of his life. He was moving forward—which was something that I needed to do as well.

I, on the other hand, was sitting at my desk, drinking a cold cup of coffee and staring at the stack of bills that I couldn't afford to pay. I almost laughed when I saw his offer to pay me to keep his truck in my garage a little bit longer because he didn't want to cost me any new business by having it sitting there, in the way. If I thought business was slow before, it was even slower after word got out that someone had been killed here. Small towns were just funny like that. It didn't matter whether people thought I had killed Mateo or not; they had already made up their mind that they wouldn't give me their business from there on out.

My parents had offered me to move back home with them, and while

I hated the idea, I didn't have much of a choice. My rent was due in a week, and my bank account was sitting at a measly four dollars—not even enough to buy a few chalupas as one last "pity me meal."

It was almost one o'clock, and my stomach growled loudly, thanks to my daydream about chalupas. I opened my desk drawer and rummaged around, looking to see if I had any hidden snacks that I had forgotten were in there. My phone vibrated across my desk, distracting me from my food search.

"Hey," I said, sitting upright as I answered Lacey's call.

"What are your plans this weekend?" she blurted out with a hint of panic in her voice.

I almost laughed, thinking about how I had no plans because I had no money to do anything.

"I have no plans," I said lightly, trying to force the stress to roll off my back.

"Well, you do now," she informed me with a little more cheer.

"I do?"

"Yes. I'm getting married *this* weekend."

I felt the excitement that I had started to feel deflate.

"The wedding is supposed to be three weeks away. On Valentine's Day. Remember?" I asked, wondering if pregnancy brain was making her crazy.

"I know, I know," she groaned. "But my dress barely fits, and I *really* want to wear my mom's wedding dress. It's important to me, Kayce. So if I don't get married this weekend, then I won't be able to wear it. These babies are making me *huge,* and they're supposed to go through another growth spurt again soon."

"Okay," I said quietly, frantically trying to figure out how to get out there with a quarter tank of gas and no money. It would be nearly impossible unless I found some way to come up with cash—and quick. "You know I wouldn't miss it. I'll be there."

"Oh, thank goodness." She let out a breath, and I could hear the relief in her voice. I was glad that at least one of us was feeling less stressed because I, on the other hand, was way more stressed than before, if that was even possible.

I was chewing on my nail, lost in my own thoughts, struggling to figure out how I was going to pull this off and make it happen.

"Kayce?" she asked, and I wondered if she had asked me something and I had missed it. I had a terrible habit of doing that, but usually only when Wyatt was around.

"Yeah?"

"I've already transferred some money into your account for this weekend," she said sternly. "I don't want to hear about how you don't need it or how you can handle things on your own. This was a last-minute decision on our end, so I wanted to make sure that it didn't put any stress on you. There's enough for food, gas, and for you to have a girl's day with us for the bachelorette party on Friday."

"Friday? As in two days?" I gulped, not even realizing that today was already Wednesday and that she really was throwing a total curveball at me.

"Bachelorette party on Friday—we're going to go get manis and pedis, then go for massages, and then we'll have a nice lunch and relax. The boys will be doing their own thing while we do ours. After that is the rehearsal dinner, and Saturday is the wedding."

"Wow," I said, completely impressed with how organized she sounded. "It looks like you have everything figured out. I'm really happy for you, Lace."

"Thanks." I could hear the smile in her voice. "Wyatt's mom, Connie, has been a total life-saver, as well as Mia and Jade. I can't wait for you to meet them!" she squealed. "They're so amazing, and I know that you will just love them as much as I do."

"I can't wait either. It'll be a fun weekend."

I thought about how I felt about seeing Wyatt again. My stomach was flipping back and forth, which matched what my brain was doing at the moment as well.

"Do you think you can take off tomorrow and drive down early? You can stay with us, so you don't have to get a room. We have the guest room already set up," she offered.

I looked down at the blank calendar on my desk and almost laughed.

"Yeah, I can leave tomorrow. I'll let you know when I'm in town."

We hung up, and I leaned back against my chair as I thought about what all I needed to do before I left. Finally, I grabbed my purse and keys and headed out to the store.

Thirty Six

Wyatt

"Did you get the contract signed for your new lease?" my mom asked as she moved about the kitchen, putting the food from lunch away. I had come over to help her with the last-minute wedding details for Grant and Lacey after she called me in a panic that they had moved up the date.

While I knew that it was more stressful for my mom to put everything together and make it perfect, I was secretly relieved that it had been moved up to right before I had to leave for my new job in Arizona. I couldn't imagine that they would be as lenient with giving me time off after only being there for two weeks, and it broke my heart to think that I would miss my brother's wedding. Or maybe, it was more that I was worried that I would miss seeing Kayce.

I had no idea if she was going to show up or not. It wasn't like I could ask Lacey without having another heart-to-heart conversation about why I was being such an idiot and not calling her. I knew that she deserved better than what I could give her, which was why I was walking away from her. It didn't do any of us any favors to pretend that whatever this had been between us—could work out.

"Yeah, I signed the paperwork, and they'll have my keys at the front desk when I get out there."

"I still can't believe you're leaving in a week."

She smiled, but I could see the sadness underneath it.

"Me neither." I leaned back in the wooden chair at the table and crossed my ankles.

"Are you having second thoughts about going?" she asked cautiously, while washing a plate.

That was a hard question to answer with no right answer. Did I want to go after my dream and work for a professional team? Yes. Did I want to pack up and leave everything I had come to know as my home for the past twenty-five years? No. Was I ready to explore and broaden my horizons? Yes. Did I want to walk away from Kayce and never see her again? No. And that was the part that kept me up at night, reconsidering whether I was making the right decision.

"No," I lied, staring down at my shoes to avoid meeting her eyes. She would know I was lying—hell, she probably already did. But at least I could say that I didn't look her in the eye and lie to her. That was better, right?

"Grab a towel and wipe down that table," she said, changing the subject for me. I loved that she knew when not to push, and this was one of those times. "If you're gonna sit there, you may as well make yourself useful."

I chuckled and got up, grabbing a clean towel from the drawer. I sprayed some cleaner on it and began wiping the table down when I heard the front door open. I assumed that it was Buck coming home but was surprised when Grant and Lacey walked in.

"Hey, what are you guys doing here?" I asked as I walked over to hug Lacey.

"We were out doing some last-minute wedding shopping," Lacey explained as she shrugged out of her jacket as Grant helped her. "And I started to feel funny, so we came here so I could take a break and maybe help Connie?"

"What's wrong? Are you okay?" my mom asked, wiping her wet hands on a towel before rushing over to see Lacey.

"I'm okay, just feeling a little tired, and I think walking around so much was aggravating the babies. I had a couple of Braxton-Hick contractions, and Grant freaked out," she laughed, looking over her shoulder at him with a playful smile.

"You don't *know* that they weren't real ones," he replied, looking past her to my mom.

"Why don't you sit down, and I'll get you a glass of water. We'll see if that'll help those pesky guys go away," my mom teased, leading Lacey to the table with her hand on her lower back. I stepped to the side and pulled a chair out for her.

"I'm sure that it's nothing, really." She sat down and winced as she leaned forward and cradled her stomach.

"See—that's not nothing," Grant said with panic in his voice.

My mom looked between them, unsure of what to say. I could see the doubt on her face and could tell that she was worried that these might not be fake contractions either.

"Why don't I run Lacey over to the hospital and have them take a look?" I offered, clapping a hand on Grant's shoulder. "Mom's going to need your help with some of the wedding stuff anyways," I added when he gave me a strange look.

My mom tried to hide her grin when she realized what I was doing.

"I can take her to the hospital," Grant objected, looking between all of us as if we were crazy for thinking that he couldn't.

"I know, big brother, we don't doubt that you can." I squeezed his shoulder gently. "But Lacey needs someone who will stay calm and *not* send her into labor right now. So, how about I take her to get checked out, and you help mom with the doilies or whatever girly project she has on her agenda today?'

I felt the sting of the towel after my mom whipped it at my arm, giving me a fake evil glare for making fun of her. I laughed and ducked when Lacey tried to swat at me with the towel I had left behind on the table.

"See, there's plenty of violence, so it's like a *manly* girl project. It's right up your alley!"

I laughed and moved out of the way as he turned to put me in a headlock.

"Gotta be faster," I teased, reaching up to wrap him in one first. "How are you ever going to survive in a house with four kids if you can't even catch me?"

That one got him riled up as he tried to get out of the hold that I had him in. I heard another groan and looked over to see Lacey bending forward again as my mom gently rubbed her back. Grant and I immediately let go of each other and stopped horsing around.

"You better get going," my mom said calmly, keeping her eyes on Lacey. "My keys are hanging by the front door. Take my car."

I nodded and turned to Grant. I could see the look of helplessness that was on his face.

"It's okay, I'll take care of her," I assured him. "Keep your phone on you so I can call with an update, okay?"

He shook his head and helped Lacey stand up before walking her out to the car. I was thankful that everything happened at my mom's house because it didn't look like Lacey was in any position to be climbing up and out of Grant's truck. Thankfully, my mom had a comfortable little Sentra that was easy for Lacey to get in.

I gave a quick wave to my mom and Grant as I made my way to the hospital.

"You didn't have to take me to the hospital," Lacey said as I reached over and turned down the radio. "But thank you. I don't think I have the energy to keep Grant calm today," she laughed. "He's already so stressed out with getting everything done for the wedding, I can't imagine what he'd be like at the hospital if he thought something was wrong with the babies."

"No worries. I'm glad that I could help."

I drove slowly, making sure to stay right around the speed limit and to drive as carefully as possible to the hospital. Luckily, it wasn't that far of a drive, and the roads were already clear after the snowstorm that barreled through a few nights ago.

"I'm going to miss you when you leave," she said softly, turning slightly in her seat to look at me. "I know that Grant is going to miss you too."

I could feel the burn in my throat from her words. It was hard to think about moving and leaving everything behind. More importantly, it was *who* I would be leaving.

"I'll miss you guys too," I replied as I focused on the road. "But hopefully, you guys will come to visit when the babies are a little older?"

"You know we will."

We didn't say anything else until we got to the hospital. I offered to run inside and get a wheelchair, but she swatted the idea away as she pushed past me and made her way to the front desk. She explained what was going on, and then we were asked to have a seat.

A few minutes later, a nurse came to take Lacey back. I offered to go with her, unsure whether she wanted her privacy or wanted the support. I was surprised when she asked me to go back with her. We followed the nurse down a long hallway, then into a room with a bed that raised up too high for Lacey to sit on. There was another woman in the room, standing next to the bed, entering information on the computer. I was about to help her up when I saw the tech push the keyboard away before she reached over and pushed the button to lower it.

Lacey sat down and lifted her shirt as she was asked. I turned away to give her some privacy and kept my head turned when I heard the sound of gel being squirted. I prayed that this wasn't one of those vaginal ultrasounds where they stick the probe up inside of the girl because if it was, this was about to get *real awkward, real fast.*

"You can look now," Lacey laughed, followed by a giggle from the nurse.

I turned and looked at the screen that they were both staring at, feeling my heart swell when I saw two very distinct babies on the monitor. It wasn't like when people showed you pictures of their babies, and you had to guess which end was head or tails. The image was crystal clear, and these cute little tadpole-looking creatures were my nieces or nephews or some combination of both.

My cheeks split as the grin spread across my face. I turned to look at Lacey, wondering if she was seeing the same thing that I was. She burst into another fit of laughter when she saw the excitement on my face.

"It's pretty amazing, isn't it?" she asked quietly.

I nodded and turned back to look at the screen, not wanting to miss a single second of it.

"So, I saw that you've been having some discomfort today?" the tech asked, glancing over her shoulder at Lacey as she kept moving the wand around on her stomach.

"Yeah, I think I was having Braxton-Hicks contractions. My soon-to-be husband was worried, so I agreed to come and get checked."

The woman smiled back at me, likely assuming that I was Grant.

"When are you getting married?" she asked as she turned her attention back to the monitor.

"This weekend," Lacey said excitedly, resting her arms over her head. "We were planning to get married in three weeks, on Valentine's Day, but my dress is getting a little too snug, so we moved it up."

"How exciting! Congratulations, you two!"

"I'm not the husband," I blurted out randomly, feeling my cheeks flush immediately.

I looked over at Lacey to see her arching a brow at me. I could see the humor on her face and knew that she was trying, yet again, not to laugh at me. Apparently, I was the comedy relief for everyone today.

The ultrasound tech stayed quiet. Either she hadn't heard me or was polite enough to pretend that she hadn't. She finished up and set the wand back in its holder before reaching over and wiping the gel off of Lacey's stomach.

"Everything looks fine. Both babies are very active and have plenty of fluid around them, which is a good sign. I'm going to hook you up to a monitor that will monitor any contractions, as well as the babies' heartbeats. The midwife will be in to check on you shortly, and we'll have a better idea of what's going on then."

I stepped to the side to allow her room to get everything set up. When she was done, Lacey had so many bands wrapped around her stomach with cords everywhere that I couldn't imagine that she was comfortable. A few minutes later, a nurse came in with a Styrofoam cup filled with ice water that she asked Lacey to drink.

Once we were alone, I stood off to the side, too afraid to go near her, so I didn't accidentally bump any of the monitors that were hooked up. She looked tired as she leaned her head back and closed her eyes after taking another drink of water.

"What a way to spend the last few days before the wedding, right?"

"It'll all work out, don't worry," I said gently, trying to reassure her.

"As long as the babies are okay, that's all that matters," she said, opening her eyes.

"They'll be just fine. And then we'll get back to putting together the wedding of your dreams."

I smiled when I saw her face light up with excitement.

"I'm so excited about the wedding, I just can't wait! It'll be so nice to have the family all together as we get married. Liam and Annie are just thrilled that they get to be in it, and they're over the moon that Kayce will be spending the night with us when she gets here tomorrow!"

I felt the weight of her words as they smacked me straight into my heart. She continued, not realizing what she had said or that she was rambling on about how happy she was that Kayce was coming to Haven Brook. She wasn't the only one.

Thirty Seven

Kayce

The drive to Haven Brook wasn't bad. I had gotten up surprisingly early, given how late I had been sleeping lately. Ever since Wyatt left, I no longer had the desire to get up and out of bed in the mornings, and I hated that part of my life. I needed a change—something to make me feel like *me* again. Not the sad, lonely, depressed me that signed the paperwork to sell her business this morning before getting on the road.

My hand had trembled as I scribbled my name on the papers, knowing that I didn't have any other options. Aside from taking out a loan to pay my bills for a few months and flashing people on the street corner to try to draw up new business, I was out of ideas. Now I was twenty-five years old, single, unemployed, and getting ready to move back in with her parents. Life was just freakin' peachy.

The only good part about my day so far was the breakfast burrito that I had grabbed from Jumping Joe's and the latte that I had treated myself to from the new coffee shop that had just opened in the next town over. I'd spent the first three hours listening to every sad, break-up song that I had on my phone, then shifted gears to a party playlist to try to get myself hyped up for the weekend. It was a wedding, and I was the maid of honor, so I needed to get my shit together.

I saw the sign for Haven Brook coming up and reached over to grab my phone. Without getting too distracted, I found her name and pressed the button to call her so I could let her know that I was almost there.

"Hey, are you getting on the road?" she asked happily.

"I'm actually getting ready to get *off* the road," I said with a smile as I slowed down and pulled off onto the off-ramp. "I just got off the freeway and should be at your house in fifteen minutes."

"You're here? Now?!"

The way her voice went shrill had me worried that maybe I shouldn't have come so early. I had hoped to come in and help her with any last-minute stuff for the wedding. Instead, it seemed like I was possibly adding to the stress that she was already dealing with.

"I'm so sorry," I rushed out. "I should have called before I left to make sure that this was okay with you. Don't worry about me—I will keep myself busy until tonight—or whenever you're free."

"Kayce—" she snapped, pulling me out of my panic. "Don't be ridiculous. I'm happy that you're here early. I just didn't believe it, you surprised me," she laughed.

"Are you sure?"

"Yes," she groaned. "Now, get your butt over here so I can give you a hug!"

"Okay, I'll see you in a few."

I was smiling for the first time in weeks as I headed to the only person who could ever calm me with just a hug.

Ten minutes later, I was parking in front of their house. I paused for a moment to look at it, completely blown away by how beautiful it was. Lacey had sent me plenty of pictures of it when they were having it built and after it was done, but I hadn't been back to Haven Brook since then. When I was here last, most of my time was spent at the hospital with Lacey after her dad tried to kill her.

I opened the door and climbed out, grinning when I saw Lacey come running out of the door, her baby bump on full display as Grant followed after her.

"You shouldn't be running," I called over to her, walking around to the passenger side of the truck to get my stuff.

"That's the same damn thing that I just told her," Grant grumbled, trying to catch up with her.

"Oh shush," she snapped over her shoulder at him. She waited for me to grab my duffle bag out of the truck before she wrapped her arms around me in a great, big hug.

I let my bag drop to the sidewalk and wrapped my arms around her. It was at that moment that I realized just how *okay* I was not. I hugged her tighter, desperate for the comfort that she was giving me as the tears spilled down my cheeks. My shoulders shook as I crumbled in her arms, unable to hold it together any longer.

"Oh honey," she whispered. "What's wrong?"

She pulled back and looked at me as she held my face in her hands. We were standing so close that her warm belly pressed against me. I reached down and rubbed a hand over it, amazed by the life she had growing inside of her.

"Look at this perfect belly," I said in awe. I looked up at her as she wiped my tears away. "You look stunning, Lace. Such a beautiful bride-to-be and a glowing mama."

Now it was her turn to cry. The tears ran down her cheeks as she swiped them away with the back of her hand. Grant smiled and gave me a quick nod before reaching down to grab my bag. He carried it inside and closed the door to give us some privacy.

"Look at you," Lacey commented as she ran a hand through my hair. "This color looks amazing on you. I really love this cut. It's so cute and frames your face perfectly!"

I felt my cheeks flush from the compliment. I was worried about making such a drastic change—well, drastic for me anyways. The purple in my hair had faded, and I felt I needed something *normal* for once. I decided to go with a dark ash brown, but that didn't feel like enough of a change, so I called my friend and had her help me cut six inches off. My hair felt lighter and touched the top of my shoulders, which I found was a better length for me.

"Thank you," I replied nervously, tucking my chin to my chest. "I wanted to make sure that you had good pictures from your wedding without having some crazy girl with bright hair."

I laughed and tugged at a piece of hair.

"You know that I don't care what color your hair is. All that I needed was *you*."

We linked our arms and went inside to get out of the cold. Lacey gave me the official tour of the house and showed me to the guest room, where Grant had already left my bag on the bed for me. The room was packed full of boxes with stuff for the wedding, so it was a little hard to see anything but the bed. It was a beautiful house with plenty of room. But, in an odd way, it made me feel sad as I thought about them starting their new life together as a family.

"The bathroom is down the hall, but feel free to use the one downstairs if this one is tied up. Liam and Annie fight over who gets to use this one, so it might be easier just to use the other one," she laughed as we walked out of the bedroom.

We were walking down the stairs when I heard voices. I knew that Grant was home but didn't know that anyone else was there. I was about to take a step when I looked up and saw Wyatt walking out of the kitchen with Grant. My heart skipped a beat as I missed a step and landed hard on my ass.

Thirty Eight

Wyatt

"Kayce!" I ran over and reached a hand out to help her up. "Are you okay?"

I could see the embarrassment on her face as it turned bright red, but I didn't care. I continued to hover around her, looking her up and down to make sure she was alright.

"I'm fine. Thank you." She pulled her hand away as soon as she could and leaned against the side of the wall, furthest away from me.

For a moment, I had barely recognized her. She looked completely different—not that she wasn't hot as hell with her long, dark purple hair that she had a few weeks ago. But the way that the dark brown color made the gold in her eyes sparkle, I found myself hypnotized.

"Hey, Wyatt," Lacey said from behind Kayce. I stepped back to let them finish walking down the stairs and scooted off to the side. My hands felt sweaty, and my stomach was starting to knot up from seeing Kayce. I felt like a teenage boy who had just said hi to his crush for the first time. While I had thought that time apart would be good for us, I was finding that it hadn't been. If anything, it had made the longing that I had for her even worse.

"Hey," was all that I was able to get out as my eyes wandered back over to Kayce. She tucked a strand of hair behind her ear and wrapped her arms around her stomach while she avoided looking at me. I knew that she was feeling as awkward and uncomfortable being around me as I was around her. I just didn't know if it was because she was trying to fight the pull between us that I was feeling, or if maybe it was because she no longer felt anything.

"What are you doing here? I thought you were packing today?" Lacey asked as she walked past me and led Grant to the living room by the hand. Kayce lowered her eyes and sucked in a deep breath when she heard it, which led me to believe that I was right after all. She did still feel something for me, or she wouldn't care if I was leaving.

"I came by to check on you," I replied, glancing over at Kayce before I walked into the living room and sat in the recliner off in the corner.

"That's so sweet of you, thank you," she gushed, leaning back against Grant on the couch. "I'm doing much better. Thank you again for taking me yesterday.

Kayce narrowed her eyes and tilted her head to the side.

"What happened yesterday?" she asked Lacey, completely ignoring me as she sat down in the recliner next to me—which happened to be the only empty seat in the room unless she wanted to sit on Lacey's lap.

"I wasn't feeling well, so Wyatt took me to the hospital to get checked out. The babies are fine, and it turned out that I was just a little dehydrated, which was causing some contractions. Some rest and a couple of gallons of water, and I was feeling ten times better."

"You need to rest and take it easy," Kayce scolded, earning a scowl from Lacey.

"You sound just like Grant," she teased, playfully elbowing him in the side.

"At least someone does," he snorted. "Maybe you'll listen to her since you don't listen to me."

"I listen to you!"

The room got quiet for a few minutes before Lacey burst into laughter, and we all joined in, knowing that it wasn't true.

I found myself staring at Kayce, watching the way her eyes wrinkled in the corners as she laughed. It was killing me being this close to her and not being able to touch her. I had only had a small taste of her, and

I needed more. I wanted to devour her in every way possible.

"What are your plans for the day?" Grant asked me when the laughter finally died down.

I looked at Kayce, wondering what her plans were, before blurting out, "I don't have any."

"Good, then you can help us set up for the wedding."

I could feel his eyes on me, and I knew what he was thinking. He had already made it clear when I was in Easterville that he wanted me to keep my hands off of Kayce. And now, it appeared he was going to do everything in his power to make sure that I didn't go anywhere near her while she was here.

"You know that I'm always happy to help," I replied smugly, matching his look from across the room. I wrapped my hands around the end of the armrests and stared him down.

"Okay, okay, enough of the chest match, you two," Lacey scolded and pushed off from Grant as she stood up. "We do have a lot to do before the wedding, and Wyatt, if you're able to stick around and help us, we would greatly appreciate it. However, I know that you need to get your stuff packed, so we won't have any hurt feelings if you can't."

I nodded and smiled, loving how Lacey always took control and put Grant in his place.

"I'm going to take Kayce to grab a bite to eat, and then we're going to head over to The Vine. Chase said that we can store stuff in the back and start decorating tomorrow afternoon when they close. First, I need to go see what we have and what we still need to get. Grant, you and Wyatt can work on taking the rest of the stuff from upstairs over. Otherwise, Kayce won't have a place to sleep tonight."

"What about us? Don't we get lunch?" Grant asked with a grumpy face. Lacey smiled as she reached up and patted his cheek a few times.

"There is stuff in the fridge to make sandwiches," she teased. "Or if you're lucky, maybe your brother will fix you something when you go drop stuff off."

"You know that I would rather *eat sandwiches* with you," he whispered in her ear, too loud, so I was able to hear as well.

"Ugh, get a room," I groaned and walked past them.

Kayce laughed and watched them for a few seconds before she looked away. I desperately wanted to talk to her, but not in front of them. I needed to find a way to get her alone and tell her how I felt about her. Not that it would change anything, but deep down, I hoped that it would.

"Come on, let's get going. Noah promised me a few meals before I leave, so lunch is on me today," I joked, clapping him on the back before heading upstairs to start packing up the boxes.

Thirty Nine

Kayce

"That was so good, but now I'm stuffed," I said as I leaned back in my chair and pushed my plate away.

"Slow-Mo's will do that to you," Lacey laughed and raised her hand to get the waitress's attention.

I had heard her talk about the food here plenty of times, and even Wyatt had mentioned it when I asked if they had any good barbeque places. But no one told me that their southern comfort food could put you in a food-induced coma. My stomach was as hard as a rock, and I was uncomfortably full after devouring a plate of fried chicken and mashed potatoes.

"I might be too tired to work now," I joked, relieved to see the smile on Lacey's face. Thankfully, even though there was still a lot left to do, she didn't seem that stressed out about it. Which was helpful given that she had been in the hospital the day before and hadn't told me.

"It's okay, we have the easy job. The guys have the hard part."

The waitress came over and slid our ticket onto the table before clearing the empty plates. I reached over to grab it. Lacey frowned as she swatted my hand away and swiped it across the table to her. She was digging in her purse for her wallet when her phone rang.

I leaned back against the booth and closed my eyes for a minute while she answered her phone. I felt strangely calm now that I was in Haven Brook, and I tried to justify that it was because I was with Lacey and that it had absolutely nothing to do with Wyatt.

"No!" she gasped, clasping her hand over her mouth as she closed her eyes. "You've got to be kidding me...."

I stared at her, waiting for her to finish.

"Okay," she sighed heavily, tapping her fingers on the table as she shook her head. "There's nothing else that we can do. Can you guys get everything packed up and take it back to the house?"

I could feel the stress radiating from her and worried that she was going to work herself up too much and end up back in the hospital.

"Keep me posted, and I'll try to see what I can come up with as a plan B."

She hung up the phone and set it on the table. Her brow furrowed in disappointment as she stared out of the window.

"What's wrong?" I asked, reaching over to touch her hand.

"That was Grant. A pipe burst in the kitchen at The Vine, and we can't store anything in the back breakroom because the floor is flooded. Chase and Noah are working on getting it fixed, but they don't think the room will be dried out anytime soon.

"You said that they're closing early tomorrow so you guys can start setting up, right?"

"Yeah, but there won't be enough time for us to pack everything up from the house, take it over there, and get it set up. Plus, we have the bachelor and bachelorette parties, the rehearsal dinner—there's just too much. It's not going to work," she sniffled.

"It will work, Lacey, I promise. We just have to break it down into smaller pieces and go from there. Okay?"

She nodded her head and wiped at the tear that had slid down her face.

"Okay."

"So, the guys are taking everything back to your house now, right?"

"Yeah, they'll put it in the—" Her face fell as she realized what she was going to say.

"Lace, it's okay. They can put it in the guestroom. Just have them move my bag to the living room, and I'll sleep on the couch tonight. My dress is still hanging in the truck, so I'll move it into the guest bathroom. Everything will work out."

"You can't sleep on the couch, it'll be so uncomfortable, and it's loud in the morning when the kids get up."

"It'll be fine."

"Okay. It'll be fine," she repeated.

"Tomorrow after they close, we can have everyone help move everything back from your house to The Vine. Since they'll be closed, we can put stuff up front and just unpack and decorate at the same time. I'll go back after the rehearsal dinner and finish whatever we don't get done before then."

"Crap!" she exhaled, letting her head fall back. "They're not going to be able to do the rehearsal dinner for us if the pipe isn't fixed by then. What if it's not fixed by Saturday? We can't have our wedding there with no running water and broken pipes!"

"Deep breaths, Lace," I reminded her. "It will all come together."

I felt her relax as I squeezed her hand and prayed that I wasn't lying.

We got into her car and headed over to The Vine to see if we could help the guys pack stuff up and take it back to the house.

"Are you okay?" Lacey asked me randomly, looking over at me before turning her attention back to the road.

"Yeah, I'm fine. Why?"

"Because I know you better than that," she said softly.

"Everyone is moving forward with their lives, and I'm stuck in this rut," I sighed, looking out the window. "It's not even a rut, per se. It's like I'm moving backward. I have no job, no money, and I'm moving back in with my parents, who are busy traveling the world and enjoying retirement. Everyone is finding their way, and I'm drowning in the deep end."

"What do you mean you don't have a job?" Lacey asked as she turned into the parking lot of The Vine.

"I haven't been able to get any business for the past three weeks. I don't have any clients lined up, and people would rather go two towns over for service than to come to a shop where someone died."

"That wasn't your fault," Lacey said, putting the car in park and turning to look at me. I had told her in very vague detail about what had happened with Mateo. Not what *really* happened, just what the police had said happened.

"You know as well as I do that it doesn't matter in small towns. They weren't that impressed with a female mechanic, to begin with, this just gave them another excuse to go elsewhere."

"Okay, so how do we find new clients? Can you run a special in the paper?"

I loved where her heart was, and I almost hated breaking the news to her. She was one of the few people who had ever believed in me and pushed me to go after my dreams.

"It's not that easy." I paused and forced out the breath that I had been holding. "I signed the paperwork to sell it this morning. I am officially jobless as of February 1st."

"Kayce, I'm so sorry. I can talk to Grant and see if we can loan you—"

I put my hand up to stop her.

"No, but thank you." I pulled my shoulders back and tried to find the confidence that I needed. "I'll be fine. I just have to find my way."

She smiled warmly at me, making me believe that I meant what I had said. The back door of The Vine opened, and Wyatt walked out. My heart skipped a beat when he looked over and locked eyes with me. It was at that moment that I knew that finding my way wasn't going to include him, and that broke my heart.

Forty

Wyatt

"Is that it?" I called over my shoulder while pushing the stack of boxes as far over as I could. There was barely enough room to move without knocking something over, and I wondered how Kayce was supposed to sleep in here tonight.

"Yeah, that was it," Grant confirmed from the hallway.

I carefully backed up and made sure not to bump anything on my way out of the room.

"I thought you guys were having a small wedding," I noted, scratching at the scruff on my chin. "That's not what a small wedding looks like."

"Tell that to Lacey," he laughed and leaned back against the wall. He slid down it and sat on the plush carpet. Tired from moving boxes around all day, I did the same.

"What time do Liam and Annie get home from school today?" I asked, wondering when the house would get back to the loud, somewhat chaotic state that I missed.

"They're actually going to moms for a sleepover. She and Buck went to pick them up from school, and then they were going to the store to get snacks for the movie marathon tonight."

"They really do love movie night, don't they?" I smiled as I remembered doing something similar with my parents and brothers when we were growing up. I tried not to talk much about our childhood because it had never been easy to open up about what happened when my dad died. Even though they had never said it, I always felt like Chase and Grant had looked down on me and blamed me for his death. *If I were older, I would have known what to do. Had they been there, they would have known what to do. Dad might still be alive.*

"Honestly, I think it's Buck more than the kids. Mom doesn't keep a lot of sweets in the house, so he uses it as an excuse to buy stuff for root beer floats and sundaes. On top of all of the candy that the kids insist that they need. I think they're all in on it together."

"I'm glad that mom has Buck in her life. I haven't seen her this happy since...."

My voice trailed off as I fought the urge to talk about what was weighing so heavily on my mind.

"Since dad died," Grant finished for me.

I gave him a sad smile, feeling bad for bringing him up right before his wedding. I was the worst at bringing everyone down with me, and this was just another example of that.

"Dad would be happy," Grant said, catching me off guard. I tilted my head in confusion.

"About mom finding someone to spend the rest of her life with. He'd be really happy about that."

I nodded in agreement, knowing that he was right. My dad was a wonderful man, and he loved my mom more than anything. He didn't have to tell us, we could just see it.

"He'd be happy for you too," he added, tapping my leg with his boot. "You're going after your dreams and what makes you happy. He would be proud of you for being so strong and independent."

His words clutched at my heart and squeezed hard around it.

"I don't know that I'm even happy," I muttered, scrubbing a hand down my face. I felt the prickle of hair and made note that I needed to shave and clean up before the rehearsal dinner tomorrow night. Not only did I want to look nice for their wedding photos, but I also found that I wanted to impress Kayce, as useless as it might be.

"Why not?"

Grant was never one to push or prod me, which I have always appreciated. I always imagined that he would be closer to Chase because they were closer in age than we were, but surprisingly, our relationship seemed to be the strongest. I was there for him when his wife, Renee, lost her battle with cancer. He was there for me when I battled deep depression after hearing the doctors say that I would likely never play baseball again after several intensive surgeries to save my life.

"I don't know," I sighed, cracking my knuckles. "How does anyone even know if they're happy? Maybe we just pretend to be happy, but we're all secretly dead inside and can't feel a thing."

"Well, that's a little deep," he chuckled. "And pretty dark."

I looked up at him, my face stoic. His smile faded, and he nodded.

"Happiness isn't some elusive thing that you have to chase after or wonder if it's real. You know when you've found it."

I quirked a brow and studied him. He had to be shitting me with this so-called advice.

"Do you know how you can tell whether or not you've found it?"

I waited for a minute before I decided to humor him.

"How?"

"You're miserable when it's gone."

His eyes softened as he smiled, knowing that his words had struck a chord with me.

"What am I supposed to do? I can't ask her to pack up and leave her life behind to follow me. And I don't know that I could live with myself if I didn't take this job. I've had a hard enough time accepting that my career is over. I don't know that I'm ready to walk away from baseball altogether."

"Maybe I should have taken your advice from the start and stayed away from her," I sighed heavily, knowing that I wouldn't have been able to do that, even if I tried.

"Or maybe *I* was the one who was wrong. It seems you're both falling pretty hard for each other." He paused to stand up. "Who am I to get in the way of true love?"

He smiled and walked off down the hall, leaving me to sit and ponder whether or not he was right. I knew that I had fallen for her—and hard. But there was no way that it could be true love because a guy like me didn't deserve a woman like her.

Forty One

Kayce

I felt sore and achy from moving boxes, even though the guys handled most of it. I tried to help as much as I could while also keeping Lacey distracted so she would sit down at rest. Finally, around six o'clock, the guys were almost done getting the rest of the boxes loaded in the guestroom while Lacey and I went to pick up dinner.

The line at Paul's Pizza was long, but Lacey assured me that this was *the place* to go for pizza. She swore that it was the best pizza that she had ever had, and I found myself remembering my conversation with Wyatt about how Easterville had the best breakfast burritos. Maybe it was just something people did in small towns—brag about the best food they had.

The smell of the pizza floated out of the lid of the box as it sat on my lap the drive back to Lacey's house. I wasn't sure if Wyatt would still be there when we got back or if he needed to get home to finish packing. I hated that I cringed every time someone mentioned it, but it was a sore spot for me, and each mention of it only reminded me that he was leaving and I wouldn't see him again.

I felt like Sandy from Grease, crying over a boy who I had a minor fling with. But in the movie, she was desperately in love with him, and he loved her too. So much so that he was willing to change for her, even though he was ridiculed by his friends. In the end, she was the one who made the change to be with him, and they lived happily ever after. Or so you thought. Who knew what really happened after that.

The problem was that this was real life and not some made-up fantasy from a movie. One of my favorite movies—but still, a movie.

We pulled into the driveway and waited for the garage door to open before Lacey pulled inside. I hated that I had butterflies in my stomach, secretly hoping that he would still be here. It wasn't fair that I had no way of knowing for sure, because it wasn't like I could look to see if his truck was still here. The damn thing was still sitting in my garage, serving as a constant reminder of the devilish man that drove it.

Once the car was parked, I unbuckled and got out, making sure not to drop the pizzas. I waited for Lacey to press the button to close the garage door before coming around to open the door to go inside. I could have opened it myself, but it felt weird to just make myself at home when I didn't live here. *You don't even have a place of your own anymore,* I thought sourly.

We went into the kitchen, and I set the boxes down on the island. Lacey grabbed some paper plates and napkins from the pantry and set them beside it.

"Pizza is here," she called loudly into the living room, not sure where the guys were. "What do you want to drink?" she asked, opening the fridge.

"Water is fine, thanks."

"We have beer and wine if you want some," she offered, leaning against the open door.

I felt the energy around me change as I looked up and saw Wyatt walk into the room.

"I'll have some wine," I said quickly, walking over to help her. Or maybe I was just trying to put some distance between him and me so I could try to think clearly.

"Do you guys want a beer?" Lacey asked as they pulled out their chairs and sat down at the table. Grant had moved the pizza box over and promptly jumped up to move it back when Lacey gave him a look. He grinned sheepishly as he took a bite of pizza and winked at her.

"Boys," she muttered under her breath.

"Yes or no on the beer?" she asked once more.

"Yes, please," Wyatt said, getting up to come get it himself. She smiled up at him as she handed him a cold bottle from the fridge.

"Here's two. Make sure you share," she teased and handed him another bottle.

"Yes, ma'am," he joked, making me smile.

I hated how much I missed him and seeing his stupid smile with those damn dimples.

A few minutes later, I had the bottle of wine open and was pouring myself a glass before joining everyone else at the table. The only spot available was between Grant and Wyatt. A Walker cookie if you thought about it, which I tried not to because it was wildly inappropriate. Not that I had any attraction whatsoever to Grant, I just couldn't figure out how to keep my legs closed around Wyatt.

We talked as we ate, the mood light and fun. I wondered what it would be like to live in Haven Brook and do this more often? How amazing it would be to see Lacey as we talked daily instead of just hearing her voice on the phone. Or watching Annie and Liam grow up while getting to know the new babies. When I stopped and thought about it, I didn't have anything waiting for me when I went back to Easterville. Everything that was important to me was sitting right here, at this table.

By the time dinner was over, my heart felt as full as my stomach. It was the perfect ending to an emotionally charged day. There were so many ups and downs throughout it that I wondered if we were on a roller coaster and when it would be over.

I helped clean up the kitchen as Lacey yawned. I could see that she was exhausted and needed to rest.

"I'll finish cleaning up. Why don't you go upstairs and rest?" I offered, gently rubbing her back.

The guys had run over to their mom's house to take Annie her pillow that she had left behind and couldn't sleep without.

"It's okay, I can help," she countered stubbornly.

I tilted my head to the side and put my hand on my hip.

"Okay, fine." She yawned again before hugging me and heading upstairs for bed.

I wiped down the table and island, then ran the empty pizza box out to the garage. I was trying to break down the box to get it to fix when the garage door opened, and Grant pulled in. The headlights were too bright for me to see if he was by himself or if he had already dropped Wyatt off at home. I turned my attention back to the box and pushed it down with all of my might as I tried to get it to fit inside the cramped bin.

"Do you need help?" Wyatt asked with a chuckle, walking up beside me.

I stepped to the side to let him have a try at it.

In one quick movement, he pushed the box down, forcing it to fit.

"I could've done that," I mumbled grumpily, folding my arms over my chest.

"I know," he said, humoring me.

Grant had already walked inside, leaving us behind in the garage. We walked side by side the short distance to the door.

"I thought Grant took you home," I blurted out randomly without thinking before I said it.

"Nope, I'm still here," he laughed.

My skin prickled from the heat as the blush spread across my chest and up my neck.

"I can see that."

"Did you want me to go home?" he asked, standing in front of the door but not bothering to open it.

I was reluctant to look up at him, afraid that if I did, the walls that I had been working so hard to build up would suddenly crumble.

He reached over and gently tipped my chin up with his finger. That single touch was all that it took to undo me.

I leaped forward, practically jumping in his arms like a crazed monkey as he wrapped them around me and lifted me to his hips. My heart was racing as I kissed him, my hands desperately pulling him closer as I needed more.

His back hit the door of the garage before he turned and pressed my body against it as I continued to straddle his hips. I could feel his erection pressing into me as he pinned me in place and ran a hand up my side. He slowly kissed my neck as he pushed my hair to the side.

"You look fucking gorgeous with the new hair," he growled in my ear, nipping it before he went back to planting kisses down my neck. "I want to take you home and fuck you so bad."

"Do it," I panted, my nails scratching down his back. "Take me home. Just one night—as friends saying goodbye or whatever. Just one last night," I begged. I didn't care how desperate I sounded right now. This was what I needed—what both of us needed. One night of pretending that things between us weren't about to get a whole lot more complicated.

Forty Two

Wyatt

I didn't bother going inside to look for Grant before I practically yanked Kayce out of the house and took her back to my place. He knew me well enough to know that when we didn't come inside after the first five minutes of being alone, we weren't coming in anytime soon.

I was thankful that Kayce had her truck because I was thinking with my dick right now, and unfortunately, he didn't know how to drive a car.

A few minutes later, we were inside my house, flinging pieces of clothes off left and right. There was something about her that I couldn't stay away from, and I could tell that she felt the same desperate energy that I did. I wanted to touch her and feel her body against mine, but I also knew that I needed to slow down and enjoy this night with her. I needed to treat it as if it was the only night we would ever get with each other because it likely was.

She reached forward to unbuckle my belt, and I reached down and grabbed her hand to stop her. Her head jerked up to look at me, confusion flashing across her beautiful face. Her hair looked darker in the dim light of my bedroom, making her look even sexier. I swallowed hard then licked my lips, ready to make love to her the way she deserved.

"What's wrong?" Her voice was so quiet that I barely heard her.

"Nothing," I assured her, rubbing my thumb across her hand as she continued to hold onto my belt buckle. "I don't want to rush tonight—even though I want nothing more than to be inside of you right now. I want to take my time and make love to you this time."

Her chest rose and fell heavily as she pulled her bottom lip in between her teeth.

"Okay," she agreed, slowly stepping away, closer to the bed.

I undid my belt and pulled it through the loops of my jeans while her eyes focused on every movement. I tossed it to the side, then kicked off my boots and stepped out of them. She was standing in front of my bed, wearing nothing but her black lace bra with matching panties. She looked like a fucking goddess, and I was ready to make a sacrifice.

I walked over to her, wearing nothing but my boxers, and wrapped a hand around her waist. I loved the sound of the gasp she made before I leaned down and kissed her. Gently, I lifted her ass, and she wrapped her legs around me without breaking the kiss.

Our bodies felt like they were made to fit as we moved fluidly around each other. I laid her on her back on the bed, my body pressed against hers. Her legs wrapped tighter around my waist as she tried to pull my pelvis closer to hers. I chuckled lightly, happy to see that I wasn't the only one who wanted this so badly.

I pulled away and rolled off of her. My fingers trailed across her stomach, then along her hips, before dipping into her panties. I felt my dick twitch when my fingers slid inside easily, knowing that she was wet and ready for me. She tilted her head back and moaned as I worked two fingers inside of her.

"You're so fucking wet, baby," I groaned, feeling her pussy tighten around my fingers. Fuck, I wanted it to be my cock right now. I felt ready to explode, the tension mounting.

"I want you, Wyatt," she said in a whisper. "Please, please. Fuck me, Wyatt," she begged as my fingers fucked her harder.

I couldn't take it anymore as I pulled my fingers out and stripped off my boxers. I bent over to reach into my nightstand for a condom when I remembered that I was completely out.

"Fuck!" I growled, startling her.

"What's wrong?"

"I don't have a condom," I muttered with disappointment.

She propped herself up on her elbows, blowing a piece of hair out of her face.

"It's fine," she said, shaking her head and laying back down. "I'm on the pill."

"Kayce, we don't have to do this if you don't want to. I can get condoms in the morning, before—"

"Wyatt, I want to do this. I haven't been with anyone else, and I get tested every year when I go for my annual check-up. Unless you don't want to."

"No, I want to," I rushed before she could get the wrong idea. "I just don't want to fuck this up tonight. I know how important it is to be safe, and I don't want to make you uncomfortable by doing something that you might regret in the morning."

"I appreciate that. But what I really want right now—is that." She looked down at my dick, and a mischievous smile spread across her face.

I made my way back over to her and laid next to her, giving her a chance to change her mind. This wasn't some random girl that I was hooking up with. She was way more than that, and I needed to make sure that she was fully comfortable with what we were doing.

She reached up and wrapped her hands around my neck, pulling me on top of her. Her tongue parted my lips and dipped inside as she arched her back and pressed her breasts against me. I reached down and pulled her panties over her hips and down her legs before tossing them to the floor. I could feel her nails scratching at my back as she anxiously waited.

Slowly, I slid inside of her, closing my eyes as the warmth and wetness of her pussy wrapped around my throbbing cock. I could honestly say that I had never had sex without a condom before, and now that I had been with Kayce without one, I felt even more addicted to her. I thrust harder, her legs spreading open to allow me to go deeper. Everything felt so fucking good and more intense without the barrier that I found myself struggling not to come right away.

She laid underneath me, her golden-brown eyes darkening as they locked onto mine. Her short hair fanned out across my pillow as her breasts bounced beautifully in her face as I drove harder inside of her. Everything about her was perfect, and I wanted to watch that gorgeous face as she came hard on my dick.

I reached down between us and started rubbing her clit with my middle finger, working it in a frenzy as I circled the swollen bud over and over again. I could feel her body responding, her back arching as her legs tightened around me.

"Come for me, Kayce," I coaxed, rubbing harder as I continued to thrust harder. I was close to a release and wanted to make sure she got hers first.

She whimpered and closed her eyes as she panted heavily before her pussy spasmed against my dick, my finger feeling the ripple of her orgasm.

"Fuck!" I growled as I pumped faster inside of her, my orgasm coming right on the heels of hers.

My chest was heaving as I laid on top of her, soaking up every second of being inside of her before it was gone.

Forty Three

Kayce

I laid in Wyatt's arms, resting my head against his chest. My fingers trailed lightly across his chest, tracing over the scars from when he was stabbed and the handful of surgeries that it took to save his life.

"I know that you must hate them, but I love these," I said sleepily, continuing in a circular pattern around them.

"My nipples?" he asked with a laugh, rubbing a hand down my naked back. I still had my bra on because I was in too big of a hurry to take it off.

"Your scar, silly," I giggled. "But I like your nipples too."

"I think yours are better," he teased, making me blush. "Why do you love my scars?"

I thought for a moment of what the best way would be to answer that question. There were so many reasons, and I wasn't sure that I wanted to confess all of them right now.

"Because these scars are the result of the selfless sacrifice that you made to save Lacey," I paused and pulled in a deep breath, trying to find the courage to say what my heart needed me to say. "And, because they are proof that your life was worth saving, even if it took the doctors several tries. They never gave up, and these scars should always be a constant reminder that you were meant to be here. To do great things and live the life after getting a second chance."

He said nothing, just pulled me closer to him, and kissed the top of my head. It was starting to get cold in the room, and I shivered against his body. He reached over and pulled the blankets on top of us. I felt completely relaxed as I quickly fell asleep next to him.

Between it being a long day and the emotional roller coaster that I had been on, I was dead asleep when Wyatt's screams woke me. I jumped up, clutching the sheets against my chest as I looked around for the source of danger. My heart was pounding, my pulse racing. I looked over and found him still asleep, his face tight in anger as he mumbled about saving someone.

"HELP!!! PLEASE, SOMEONE!! HELP MY DAD!!"

I felt my heart sink as I realized that he was having a nightmare about his dad. I didn't know what to do; I felt completely helpless. Lacey used to have bad dreams when she was a kid, and I learned the hard way not to wake her up in the middle of one. It seemed stupid because why would anyone want to stay stuck in a bad dream, but after my black eye from her accidentally punching me, I didn't question it again.

I waited for a few minutes until he seemed calmer. I was about to rub his shoulder to try to wake him when I saw the tears running down his face. My heart broke even harder when I realized how much pain he was still in after losing his dad. I gave it a few more minutes, and then I gently nudged him until he woke up.

"Hey," he croaked out tiredly. "Are you okay?" He rubbed his eyes and looked around the room, confused.

"You were having a bad dream," I said softly, brushing my thumb across his cheek to wipe the tear away.

"Sorry," he apologized, his shoulders tightening with tension again.

"Don't be. I'm sorry that you were having such a bad dream."

"It wasn't a dream," he said, then pulled his lips into a thin line. "I was watching my dad die again. It happens often, like a video that someone plays on repeat. I haven't found a way to stop it, but I hate when it happens."

"That's terrible. I can't imagine having to go through that over and over again."

I still felt just as helpless as I had a few minutes ago, only now, he was awake, and I had no idea what to say or do. I wanted to make him feel better or offer him comfort of some sort, but there was nothing that I could do to take this pain away, and I knew that.

"Is there anything that I can do for you?" I asked anyway.

"Just lay with me," he said with a cheeky grin as he lifted the blanket for me to climb back under next to him. "I like how it feels having your body against mine."

I laid down and curled up next to him, wrapping my legs around his as I rested my arm across his stomach. I had seen him naked a handful of times now, but I had never stopped to admire this heavenly body that was capable of magic. And just like that, within a matter of minutes, we both had fallen asleep in each other's arms.

Morning came too quickly, and I groaned when my phone rang on the nightstand beside me. I was surprised that it hadn't died, given that I hadn't bothered to find a charger last night. Needless to say, my phone wasn't a priority of any sort last night.

I picked it up and swiped the button to answer it.

"Hello," I groaned sleepily, propping myself up on one elbow while holding the sheet against my body. I could feel Wyatt beside me as he reached over and pulled me back over to him.

"Do I even want to know where you are right now?" Lacey asked coyly.

"Umm. Yeah. About that…" I trailed off and didn't bother to complete my sentence when I heard her burst into laughter on the other line.

"I knew it," she teased. "I bet Grant twenty dollars last night that we would wake up and find you at Wyatt's house this morning."

"Now you're making money off of me?" I groaned, covering my face with my hand.

"Only twenty bucks. But if you can get your butt up and ready this morning, I'll use it to buy you breakfast."

My stomach growled loudly as if it heard the invite. Wyatt laughed and rubbed a hand over it. For a moment, I wondered what it would be like if we were to settle down. Would he want to have kids? Would he still be lying next to me in bed, rubbing my pregnant stomach the way I had seen Grant do to Lacey's?

"How long do I have?"

"Forty-five minutes. A minute later, and I will eat your head for breakfast."

I laughed at the thought, wondering if she was serious given that she hadn't laughed herself.

"Fine. I'll be there in forty-five minutes," I laughed and hung up.

"I have to get up and go meet Lacey for breakfast," I said, rolling over to look at him.

"I heard you have forty-five minutes," he said as he raised a brow. "How long do you need to get ready?" He licked his lips and reached down to grab a handful of my ass.

"Twenty? Twenty-five tops," I mumbled as he leaned over and kissed my neck.

"Good, then I'll have time for breakfast before you go."

In one quick movement, the sheet and blankets flew up, and he dove under them, spreading my legs apart before nestling himself in between. I never got around to putting my panties back on, even after I had gotten up to use the restroom a few hours ago. His hands gripped my thighs as his tongue went straight to work, licking my slit before parting my lips and dipping inside. My back arched as I enjoyed every second of it, wanting more from this perfect man.

He continued his delicious torture of licking and sucking, building the perfect rhythm that brought me to the verge of orgasm. I could feel the tension building, the need for him getting stronger as I got closer. I reached down and grabbed the back of his head, pushing it harder against me as he sucked my clit until I came. My thighs clenched around him as my body hummed in pleasure.

He chuckled and came up for air, pushing the blankets off of us.

"What do you know? You *are* the breakfast of champions. Better than a bacon burrito from Jumping Joe's." He winked and smiled his half-smile that I loved so much.

"Now that's just blasphemy," I gasped, acting appalled. "Jumping Joe's is perfection."

"No, Kayce," he said, his tone turning serious. "*You* are perfection."

I felt my heart flutter as I listened to his words, the look on his face confirming that he meant it. I pulled my lower lip in between my teeth, unsure of what to say. I didn't want to mess up this moment between us by saying the wrong thing.

"You better go jump in the shower, or you're going to be late," he warned, moving over so I could get up.

I looked over and saw his cock, hard and waiting for me. Suddenly, I didn't care about breakfast or whether I got there on time.

"I know something else that would be perfect," I said seductively, turning onto my hands and knees as I popped my ass up in the air. His eyebrows shot up high on his forehead as he got my message, loud and clear.

He climbed over and swatted my ass cheek before sliding into me. I rolled my head back in response, loving the feel of his cock deep inside of me. His hands gripped my hips as he slowly started to pump. I spread my legs to let him in, moaning as I reached down to touch myself.

I had no idea how it was possible to be ready for another orgasm so soon, but the harder I rubbed, the closer I got. He felt so good as he thrust harder, forcing my breasts in my face as they bounced in response. I felt him unhook my bra in the back before pushing it down my arm. I slid out of it, making sure not to lose my balance as I held myself up while we continued.

He reached forward and rubbed my nipple between his fingers before moving to the other side. I was right on the verge of climax, and the extra stimulation was about to send me over the edge. I panted heavily as I held myself up with one hand and rubbed my clit with the other. He pounded harder and quicker, and I knew he was close. I waited as long as I could before I gave in and let my orgasm consume me.

It was the most intense feeling that I had ever felt, and every nerve ending in my body was on fire. I screamed his name as I came, feeling his body stiffen right behind me as he climaxed. We were both panting and sweating when we were done. I blew a strand of hair out of my face, knowing that I would definitely have to shower and clean up before I could go see Lacey.

"You're right," he said as he gently pulled out. "That was perfection."

I laughed and looked over my shoulder at him. When our eyes locked, I felt something that I had never felt before now, and it scared the shit out of me.

Forty Four

Wyatt

I had been wearing a shit-eating grin the majority of the day, and no matter how hard I tried, I couldn't get rid of it. Kayce and I had taken a quick shower before she rushed off to go meet Lacey for breakfast, and I had spent the day with Grant, Chase, and Noah for the so-called bachelor party.

I wasn't sure why we were calling it that, especially since it was the middle of the day, and there was little drinking and zero strippers. But either way, I tried to focus on spending time with the guys before I left because I didn't know when I would be able to come back again. I was going to miss this, but more importantly, I was going to miss them.

The day flew by rather quickly, and before I knew it, we were lining up along the wall at The Vine as the minister went over what everyone was supposed to do tomorrow. Thankfully, Grant and Lacey had a smaller wedding party, and since I was the best man, that meant that I got to walk Kayce down the aisle since she was the maid of honor. I tried to keep my attention on what was being said, but I was distracted by her every movement.

Finally, after rehearsing it a few times, we were good to go, and everyone scattered about to set up for the big day. My mom and Buck had been there since this afternoon, getting everything ready, but there was still a lot left to do. Noah ordered some pizzas and offered everyone beer for helping out. The night passed by in a flash, but by the time we were done, everything looked perfect, and Lacey had tears of happiness when she left.

I wanted Kayce to stay around so we could talk, but she left with Lacey and Grant, giving me a quick wave on her way out. It wasn't like she needed a place to stay now that the guest room was cleared out. I knew that my time with her was limited and that I would have to make every minute of it count tomorrow.

I felt like my life was an hourglass, and the end was coming soon.

When I got home, I was too restless to go to sleep, so I stayed up late packing up more of my stuff to move to Phoenix. It was amazing the amount of crap we accumulated without even realizing it. I had started a box for donations, and that seemed to be filling up faster than the boxes that I would be taking with me. Maybe it was better to travel lighter and not have as much baggage to unpack when I got there.

By two in the morning, I was yawning every few minutes, and my body was begging for sleep. I gave in and laid down, smelling Kayce's perfume on my pillow from last night and this morning. While I would have imagined that it would have been some sort of trigger that kept me up even longer and kept me from sleeping, it surprisingly had the opposite effect. Something about feeling like she was there with me was so soothing that I fell asleep almost immediately.

I woke up the next morning feeling rested, even though I had barely gotten five hours of sleep—at most. I guess the difference was getting a solid five hours of sleep compared to getting a full night's sleep that was constantly interrupted by tossing and turning.

I cleaned up and jumped in the shower, ready to take on the day. Okay, so maybe not ready for the day, but ready to see Kayce again. I had been thinking about her nonstop, and even though she had insisted that the other night was just a one-time thing, I couldn't help wondering what it would be like if it were more.

The heavenly aroma of coffee floated through the living room while I gathered the stuff I needed and waited for Chase to come pick me up. I really hated not having my truck and having to have everyone drive me around, but there was nothing that I could do about it, so it was pointless to complain. I filled my travel mug with coffee and made sure the lid was on tight before I rushed out the door to the sound of Chase honking.

I raised an eyebrow as I swung my duffle bag over my shoulder and held my coffee in one hand while locking the door with the other. I jumped in the back seat, behind Noah, and buckled up as Chase started driving. I knew that we were heading to The Vine to finish setting up for the wedding, but I hated how long it would be before I would get to see Kayce. It was like sitting on pins and needles.

"You look bright-eyed and bushy-tailed this morning," Noah commented, turning to look over his shoulder at me.

"I slept good last night." I shrugged and looked out the window to avoid the knowing look that he was giving me.

"Must be nice," they both muttered, and I tried to hold back a laugh.

"Well, I don't have small children to keep me up at night," I added with a wink.

"Just give it time, then you'll be in our club of sleepless nights, and it won't be the kind you're used to," Chase warned playfully.

"Nah, that life isn't for me," I lied, remembering the feeling that I had when I was touching Kayce's stomach yesterday morning. It was so cute to hear it growl so loudly, making it known that she was hungry. But I couldn't help but think about what it would be like if she were pregnant with my baby, and that thought was seeping deeper and deeper into the back of my brain.

I had felt my voice crack and knew that they heard it when they smirked at each other but said nothing. We pulled into the parking lot a few minutes later, which meant that I was free from having to have this conversation with them. There was plenty of work to be done, and that meant no time to talk.

The hours flew by, and before I knew it, it was already three o'clock, and we were being told to get ready. Everything looked perfect, and my mom raved about how wonderful it was that everything had been pulled together at the last minute with all of the unexpected changes. The ceremony was at four, which meant that I only had an hour longer before I would get to see Kayce.

The guys got ready in the back room since the floors were still a little wet and everything was drying out from the broken pipe. Originally, the girls were supposed to get ready back here, but that had been another last-minute change. I got dressed in the bathroom and made sure to fix my tie before putting on my vest and jacket. The suit was classic black and white with a champagne-colored solid tie that matched the girls' dresses.

I was hanging out up front with my mom and Buck when I heard the front door open and froze, wondering if the girls were here early. It was only three-thirty, but I knew that they would be here at any minute to get ready and wait in Chase's office until the ceremony started. A few guests had already started to show up, so I knew that it could easily be another guest. But that didn't keep my heart from getting overly excited at the possibility.

I could feel my mom's eyes on me, watching intently, but I didn't care. My body felt the electricity that radiated between us the moment she walked through the door. It was as if nothing else mattered and no one else was there. I felt my heart skip a beat when I saw her and wondered if this was the feeling that grooms claimed to experience when they saw their bride walking down the aisle to them.

Her hair was pulled up on her head, piled loosely with a few curls that hung perfectly around her face. I loved that her makeup was minimal, giving her a soft romantic look that I loved on her. She looked gorgeous, and the shimmery material of her dress caught the light perfectly, making it look like she belonged in a damn fairytale. Aside from the fact that the dress fit her body perfectly and wrapped tightly around her hips and ass in a way that had me wanting to rip that damn thing off of her with my teeth.

She gave me a flirty smile before walking down the hallway with the other girls. It wasn't lost on me that Mia and Jade had seen how Kayce and I were looking at each other, and I knew that I would be hearing about it from Chase and Noah as soon as the girls had a moment alone with them to gossip. But in all honesty, I didn't care. The whole world could watch me stare at her right now, and I wouldn't bother to look away.

A few minutes later, Annie came in, announcing that Lacey would be coming in a few minutes and that we all needed to clear the room because no one was allowed to see the bride yet. I laughed at how demanding she was for such a little girl, but wandered outside onto the patio with the guys to allow Lacey to come in unseen.

It was almost time, and the seats were filling up fast inside. In all of the years that I had been coming to The Vine, I had never imagined that I would see my brother get married here. It was Chase's baby, so to speak, but it had been something that had become part of our entire family. His dream was something that held us all together and gave us a place to call home when we needed it.

By three forty-five, the men were taken back to where the girls were waiting, while Chase stood up front next to the minister. Everything looked perfect, and we had succeeded in turning their brewery into a beautiful wedding venue at the last minute. I felt my hands start to sweat as I looked for Kayce so we could line up the way we had last night during the rehearsal.

A few minutes later, she walked up behind me and wrapped her arm in mine as we got ready to go.

"You look great," she said, leaning in close to me. We were at the back of the line, behind the groomsmen and bridesmaids, which gave us a small amount of privacy—aside from Lacey, who was standing right behind us with Buck.

"Thank you." I leaned closer to her, getting a whiff of the vanilla in her conditioner that I loved so much. "You look absolutely stunning, Kayce."

She smiled as the blush flashed across her face. I didn't have time to say any of the other things that I wanted to before we were being led down the hall and out into the lobby.

I walked proudly with Kayce on my arm, ignoring the looks of everyone as we passed down the aisle. For once in my life, I didn't notice anyone other than her. The world could explode around us, and I would still be oblivious to anything but her.

When we reached the alter, I stopped and gave her a quick kiss on her cheek before she walked over to stand in front of Mia. I took my spot next to Grant and heard the chuckle escape Chase's throat behind me.

A few minutes later, everyone oohed and ahhed as Liam and Annie walked down the aisle. If ever there was an adorable ring bearer and flower girl, it was these two. They were totally hamming it up for the guests, making everyone laugh, including Lacey. She looked beautiful as she walked down the aisle with Buck, wearing her mother's wedding dress.

Her blonde hair was pulled back, out of her face, as the soft curls hung down her shoulders and back. Her stomach pulled the fabric of the dress tight against her bump, making her look even more beautiful if that was possible. I felt the tears sting my eyes and looked away, scolding myself for being such a pussy. I wasn't the kind of guy that cried at weddings—I was the kind of guy that avoided weddings like the damn plague.

I tried to keep myself focused on the wedding and being present in the moment. But no matter how hard I tried, I couldn't stop thinking about Kayce. I had to force myself to look down at the floor to avoid looking like some sort of creep that couldn't keep his eyes off of her.

After the ceremony was over and Grant and Lacey shared their first kiss, everyone applauded, and the wedding party made our way back to the back while my mom helped set everything up for the reception. It was hard having everything all in one spot, but if anyone could pull it off—it was my mom. And thankfully, they had a rather small wedding with guests that were happy to jump right in and help out.

It was noisy in the hallway as everyone crowded around Grant and Lacey to congratulate them. I waited my turn before squeezing in to hug Lacey.

"You look beautiful," I said while hugging her. "I'm so happy for you guys."

"Thank you," she replied sweetly. "I can't wait to do this again!'

"You're already planning your next wedding?" I asked, one brow raised. "I don't wanna sound like a dick, but maybe give it more than a few minutes before you decide it's not gonna work with my brother."

She laughed and rolled her eyes, swatting me on the chest.

"Not *me!*" she joked, still laughing. "I meant that I can't wait to do this again when *you* get married."

"Me?" I said, acting appalled that she would even consider such a thing. "Nah, weddings aren't my thing. I don't see myself settling down, and…" my words trailed off as Kayce came into view, standing off to the side as she looked down to talk to Annie.

Whatever Annie said to her had her laughing. She threw her head back, her eyes lighting up the way they did when she was truly happy. At that moment, I realized that I would never be able to do that for her. I was the darkness that would forever dim the light that deserved to shine within her.

Forty Five

Kayce

By the end of the night, I had twisted and shouted so much that my body was aching in protest. My heels had been thrown off at one point, and my bare feet were now black from dancing all night. Several times I had tried to pull Wyatt out on the dance floor, but something in him had changed after he talked to Lacey, and I couldn't figure out what. The playful, flirty Wyatt that I had loved being around the past few days was gone. In his place was grumpy, depressed Wyatt that wanted to sit in the corner and drink beer with a frown on his face.

The night wrapped up relatively early, per Lacey's request. They had rented a hotel room for the night, and the kids were staying the night at his mom's house, which left me by myself at their house. I wanted to ask Wyatt if he wanted to stay with me, but every time I worked up the courage, something would happen to stop me.

By the time I finished helping clean up, almost everyone had left, including Wyatt. I made my way back to their house and took a quick shower before turning in for the night. The next morning, I got my stuff together and left Lacey a quick note to let her know that I had gone back to Easterville. I wanted them to have time to themselves, and I had things that I needed to handle.

The drive back would have been quick, however, I decided to take the long way and stopped by the shed. I looked around to make sure no one was nearby before I parked my truck behind the shed and got out. The snow had melted quite a bit over the last few weeks, and I knew that if I had any chance of finding my gun before someone else did, I had to do it now. I tried to remember the area that I had been walking when Mike had found me, hoping that I was close.

I kicked the snow around in the spots where it hadn't yet melted, hoping to find it. After twenty minutes, I was just about to give up hope when I rubbed my foot over something hard. I bent down and pushed the snow out of the way, feeling relief as I found my gun. I picked it up and brushed the snow off of it before tucking it in the back of my jeans.

I should have gotten back in my truck and got the hell out of there, but the curiosity in me was too strong to walk away. Checking again to make sure no one was coming, I walked along the side of the shed and stopped at the window. There were black marks on the wood from where the fire had spread, however, the majority of it was still standing. Likely because the weather was so shitty, and there was so much moisture from the snow.

I sucked in a breath and held it as I turned and looked in the window. The blood was rushing in my ears, making it hard to hear if any cars were coming. I blinked my eyes and tried to focus, unable to believe that the horror scene that I had remembered so vividly before was now gone. Obviously, the police had already been here and collected the bodies, given that it was on the news. I guess I just didn't expect the blood and everything else to be gone as well.

Feeling somewhat relieved, I turned and walked back to my truck, satisfied that I had dealt with at least one of my demons.

When I got back into town, it was already one o'clock. There was plenty to do at home with getting my stuff packed up and moved to my parent's house, but I felt the need to go back to my shop before I did anything else. This weekend had been a nice escape from reality, but it was only temporary. I still had things that I had to take care of if I wanted to move forward with my life.

I pulled into the parking lot and felt the anxiety prickle at the back of my neck. No matter how much I had tried to convince myself that I wanted to keep this shop open and try to make it as the only mechanic in town, part of me desperately wanted to walk away from this chapter in my life. Maybe it was because it was now tainted with images of Mateo's dead body, but either way, I couldn't find my peace there anymore.

THREE STRIKES, YOU'RE GONE

The window was still boarded up, but this time with a bigger piece of wood that covered the entire area. I hadn't bothered buying a new window because I couldn't afford it. I also found that I just didn't care. The drive and determination that I used to have died the day that I murdered Mateo.

I had to constantly remind myself of that gruesome fact. *I MURDERED someone.* It wasn't an accident—I couldn't play that card if I wanted to. It was very deliberate and on purpose. I guess you could say that it was self-defense, given that he had just tried to strangle me a few minutes before. I liked to think that anyone who had been in my situation would have done the same, but I wasn't so sure. Maybe other people would have called the cops and been lucky that they showed up on time. I wasn't one of those people.

I knew what it was like to call them and not have them come on time. To have to think on your toes because some asshole thinks that he can force himself on you and assumes that you're too weak to do anything about it.

The tears stung my cheeks as they spilled over and down my face as that night replayed in my head. While I had been drunk enough to block most of the details of that night out, I vividly remembered Mateo following me to the bathroom at the bar and pinning me against the sink as he tried to rape me. I screamed as loud as I could as I fought him off, but he was stronger than I was and covered my mouth with one hand while undoing his pants with the other. I sobered up immediately as the fear pulsed through me. There was an empty beer bottle next to the sink beside me that ended up being my saving grace. I couldn't remember a more satisfying feeling than the sound of the glass breaking before I took the broken bottle and sliced it down his face.

I shook my head and tried to clear away the thoughts, feeling more at peace for what I had done as I went to my office to finish the paperwork to sell my shop. I spent the afternoon packing up the items in my office and loading them into my truck. On my way home, I stopped by my parent's house and loaded them into the garage.

There was a lot of change surrounding me, but I kept trying to remind myself that it was good change and that I needed to embrace it instead of fight it. I grabbed a quick bite to eat as I headed back to my apartment to pack some more.

The days seemed to blur together when all I was doing was packing.

Between my shop and my apartment, there was no normal for me anymore. My parents would be coming back from their trip to the Grand Canyon this weekend but were planning to leave again the following weekend. I couldn't keep up with their new travel schedule, so I stopped trying.

I sat at my desk and stared at the calendar that had the days crossed through that had already passed. Both my shop and my apartment's lease were up on February 1st, which was coming up on Monday. I had three days left in both and no motivation to do anything before I was officially kicked out.

My phone rang, vibrating across my empty desk.

"Hey," I said, answering Lacey's call. "What's up, *Mrs. Walker*?"

"Hi! It still sounds so strange to hear people call me that."

"Why? Did you keep your name instead of taking his?" I asked, wondering if I had just assumed that she would take his.

"No," she laughed. "I took his name, I just haven't gotten used to people calling me by it yet."

"Oh," I giggled, feeling silly.

"So, I was calling to see if Grant and I can come down this weekend to pick up Wyatt's truck?"

Her question was completely innocent, however, I felt it pierce straight through to my heart. I hadn't talked to Wyatt since the wedding last weekend and had contemplated asking him to come to get his truck because I was closing the shop. I had held off for as long as possible because I didn't want to admit my failure to him. It also stung that he wasn't bothering to come back for it himself, and I wondered if it was because he was avoiding seeing me before he moved to Arizona on Monday.

"Sure," I said, swallowing hard to get past the lump in my throat.

"Thanks. We're heading out tomorrow and leaving on Sunday."

"You're staying the night in Easterville?" I asked, surprised.

"Yeah, we're treating it like a mini honeymoon since we didn't take a real one. Grant is going to take me shopping in Glenview, so we're staying in Easterville. We'll grab the truck on Sunday when we head back if that's okay?"

"Yeah, that's fine." I let out the breath that I had been holding and wrapped up the call with Lacey. It wasn't that I didn't want to talk to her; I just couldn't do it with Wyatt stuck in my head.

THREE STRIKES, YOU'RE GONE

Forty Six

Wyatt

"This feels like a terrible idea," I muttered from the back seat as I saw the sign for Easterville.

"It's not a terrible idea," Lacey countered. "It's a wonderful idea!"

"You're only saying that because it was YOUR idea," Grant laughed as he reached across the console to hold her hand.

"So are you saying that it's a terrible idea?" she scoffed, squeezing his hand.

"I wouldn't say terrible... but..."

"You're such a grumpus! You just can't stand the thought that your baby brother is finally in love and ready to settle down."

"I never said anything about love or settling down," I said with an edge to my tone. But just because I hadn't said it out loud didn't mean that it wasn't true. I was just scared shitless and refused to admit it as we pulled off the highway and headed to Kayce's shop.

"You Walker boys are so stubborn," she sighed. "But it's okay. That's what I'm here for."

"And what's that?" Grant asked with a smile.

Lacey looked out the passenger window for a moment as she thought about it.

"I'm here to make them realize how much they love each other and to make sure they don't make the same mistake I almost made when I thought about running from you."

"You definitely were a runner," he laughed, turning onto the street where Kayce's shop was. "I still check our credit cards every now and then, just to make sure you haven't booked a room somewhere."

"I did," she said as he put the truck in park. "I have a room to myself this weekend, so I can rest and relax and get all of the room service I want."

She winked before she got out of the truck and closed the door before he could say anything.

"Women," he muttered to me before we got out.

I stood next to his truck, looking at the shop and the boarded-up window that still hadn't been fixed, almost a month later.

"You ready?" Lacey asked cheerfully.

Just as I was about to say something stupid, my phone rang. I pulled it out of my pocket and looked at the caller ID.

"Go ahead without me. I've gotta take this call."

She folded her arms over her chest and cocked a brow at me.

"I'll be in as soon as I'm done, but I've gotta take this." I gave her my best *I'm not lying* smile and turned away to answer the call.

I glanced over my shoulder and saw them walking inside as I slid my finger across the screen to answer it.

"Hey, Julian," I said as calmly as I could. "How are things in Phoenix?"

"Warming up, which is a nice change from the cooler temps we've had lately. Though I'm sure it's nothing compared to the storms you guys have had recently," he laughed.

I felt a knot in the pit of my stomach as I talked to him. I was standing in the parking lot of Kayce's shop, talking to the man who held my career in his hands, and all that I could think about was the feisty girl inside who I couldn't get off my mind.

"The reason for my call," he said to clear the silence between us. "Is to confirm what time your flight comes in on Monday."

He continued talking about the rest of the details, but I couldn't focus on what he was saying. I didn't care about my apartment or when the moving vans got there. All I cared about was Kayce, and I realized that I didn't want to do any of this without her.

"I can't do this," I blurted out, scrubbing a hand down my face in frustration. The panic bells were ringing in my head, telling me to shut the fuck up before I ruined everything.

"I'm sorry, I don't understand. Do what?"

"I can't take the job. I'm sorry. I just can't move to Phoenix right now."

The silence on the other end felt thick around me. It was too late to take it back and tell him that I didn't mean it. In one moment of fear, I singlehandedly crushed my dream and everything I had worked so hard for.

"Okay," he said with a heavy sigh. "I'm sorry to hear that you've changed your mind."

"I—" The words caught in my throat.

"I wish you the best in your future endeavors."

That was it. It was over. He wasn't going to beg me to change my mind or ask me what happened. I was easily replaceable, and they would likely have someone by the end of the week who wanted the job and would drop everything to take it.

"Thanks," I mumbled before hanging up.

I chewed the inside of my cheek, frustrated by what I had just done. While I had given up on one dream, maybe it was because I was ready to go after another. Lacey was right; I had to stop running from what I wanted, which meant that I needed to talk to Kayce and tell her how I felt.

I went inside, stopping when I heard voices down the hallway in her office. I headed that way, unsure of whether she knew that I was here or not. Knowing Lacey, she would want it to be a surprise, though I wasn't sure that Kayce would think it was a good one.

"So, is he already gone?" Kayce asked. I could hear the vulnerability in her voice. She didn't want to ask, but she needed to know. "Is that why he didn't come back for his truck himself?"

"We were planning to come through here anyway, so we offered to help out," Lacey said softly.

"Well, it's perfect timing since I'm outta here on Sunday night."

"I'm sorry, Kayce. I know how hard this is for you." Lacey sounded sad, and I wondered what was going on. Where was Kayce going? Why hadn't I heard about her plans to leave?

"It's okay," she sighed heavily. "It's time to say goodbye to the old and make some big changes in my life. I guess I just wish that I would've gotten to say goodbye to him one last time."

I shook my hands a few times, trying to force away the nervousness that was washing over me. I couldn't just lurk in the hallway and eavesdrop all day. I needed to man up and go in there.

"I know, honey," Lacey started to say as I rounded the corner and stood in the doorway.

Kayce's eyes went wide when she saw me. She was sitting at her desk with her hair pulled into the messy bun that I loved when I first met her. Her hair was still the beautiful brown color from the wedding. The memories of that weekend had been tormenting me this week as I yearned for more.

"Hey," I said quietly, leaning against the door frame.

"Hey."

The world felt like it stopped moving as we stayed staring at each other. Grant and Lacey were sitting across from her, looking back and forth between us as they waited for one of us to say something.

"Well, now that you're here, I'll get the keys for you. I can pull the truck up front, then you should be ready to go."

She opened the desk drawer beside her and pulled out the keys. I could tell that she was feeling as uncertain about me being here as I was. The thing that I hated was that she didn't look happy to see me. She almost seemed pissed off.

"I'm not ready to go," I said dumbly, desperate to stop her from moving the truck. It felt like once she did, everything between us would be over. I would have my truck, and everything between us would be done.

"Well, I'm sure you remember the way to the gas station. Mrs. Ashby should be working today, so you can probably grab a room if you take enough candy."

"You know damn well that I'm not here to rent a room." My tone changed as my frustration seeped out.

"Then what are you here for?" she demanded with her hand on her hip.

I looked at Grant and Lacey, suddenly wishing that they weren't sitting there, watching this.

"We should give them some privacy," Grant said quietly to Lacey, bending to stand up before she reached over and swatted his hand.

"No, I'm staying until the end, and so are you," she hissed. "I didn't come all this way to miss the big moment." She was grinning so hard that I worried her cheeks were going to hurt.

"I'm waiting," Kayce said, pulling my attention back to her.

"I'm here for you." I shrugged as if that simple sentence should tell her the words that were wrapped so tightly around my heart that I couldn't say them.

She didn't speak, just stood there staring at me with her hand still planted firmly in her hip. It was apparent that she was going to make me work hard for this.

"I can't eat. I can't sleep. I lay down at night, and I smell the vanilla from your conditioner on my pillow. That's the only thing that calms me. But then I remember that you're not there with me, and I feel this sense of panic that I can't get rid of."

I pushed out a shaky breath, hating that I was having to bare my soul in front of everyone. But if it meant that she gave me another chance, I would strip down naked and bare it all.

"Kayce, we've been through some crazy shit in the little time that we've known each other. I know that you were worried that what you were feeling then was just a coping response to what had happened, but it's not that for me. I've been head over fucking heels in love with you from the very first night when you let me eat your cobbler."

I watched as her cheeks turned scarlet, and Lacey's jaw dropped. I couldn't help the cheeky grin that was spreading across my face as I raised a brow and challenged her to say something about it without further embarrassing herself.

She pressed her lips together and shook her head. Deep down, I could see that I was getting through to her by the way her lips twitched as she tried to hide her smile.

"By the way," I said, turning to Grant. "You guys need to get some barbecue from The Tasty Pig before you head back. And be sure to get the peach cobbler— it's to die for."

"Are you in love with me, or the cobbler?" Kayce asked, folding her arms over her chest.

"Both." I pushed off from the doorway and took a few steps closer to where she was standing. "And if you give me a chance, I'll prove it to you every day. Even if that means that we eat cobbler every night."

"That sounds like a promise you can't keep," she said warily. "It'll be a little hard to share cobbler when you're in Phoenix, and I'm here."

Her face fell as she said it, and I could see the sadness clouding her eyes.

"I'm not going to Phoenix."

I heard the gasp from Lacey and the curse word that flew out of Grant's mouth, but I kept my attention on Kayce as I took a few more steps toward her.

"What do you mean you're not going?" She took a step back as I came behind the desk and stood next to her. She pulled her shoulders back and refused to let her guard down just yet.

"I got a call from the team's manager, confirming what time my flight on Monday. I told him that I couldn't take the job."

"Why on earth would you do that?" Kayce asked, her eyes as big as saucers.

"Because baseball has always been my one true love, and until recently, I thought that was what my life was about. And then I met this beautiful, incredible woman, who I found I couldn't live without. It turns out that *you're* my one true love. Without you, nothing else matters."

She closed her eyes, and the room went silent. A few moments later, she opened her eyes and shook her head.

"Boys are so stupid," she sighed.

"Umm, thanks?" I furrowed my brow.

"You need to call them back and tell them that you made a mistake. A HUGE mistake. Then beg for your job back and let them know that you'll be there Monday morning."

"It's not that easy," I argued, feeling frustrated that this wasn't going the way that I wanted.

"Kayce, I love you, and I can't live without you. So that means that I'm giving up the job so I can stay here to be with you. Unless you don't want me to?"

I felt the panic start to rise inside as I took a step back. Was that what this was all about? Did she want me to go because she didn't feel the same way? Was I head over heels in love with someone who didn't love me back?

"No, I don't want you to do that," she said softly, lowering her voice.

"Got it," I snapped, running my hand through my hair as I looked over at Lacey and Grant. They were looking away from us, trying to give us privacy now that they saw the direction this was going.

Grant looked up and saw the look on my face. He gave me a subtle nod and leaned in to whisper something to Lacey before they stood up and walked out, closing the door behind them.

"I'm sorry, I shouldn't have come here and done this—" I apologized.

"Stop," she interrupted, reaching over to grab my arm as she pulled it away from my hair.

"I'm saying that you shouldn't have given up your dream job to stay here for me. Now that my shop is closing, I don't have anything holding me here. And not that you asked me to, but I would be willing to go with you to Phoenix... if you wanted me to."

I pulled back and studied her, waiting for her to tell me it was a mean joke. Instead, the grin on her face spread quickly as she waited for me to realize that she was being honest. She was willing to pack up her life and go with me.

"You know that I will have to travel—a lot, and that I'll probably be working a lot of weekends?"

She nodded her head yes.

"And it gets hot in Arizona. Like really, really hot."

"I get tired of the cold anyway," she laughed.

"Maybe you could travel with me when I go? And then we can explore whatever city I'm in when I'm done?"

"I would love to travel and explore with you, Wyatt."

I felt the calmness that I had been missing without her and knew that this was where I was meant to be.

"Now get on the phone and tell them that you want your job back," she said as she poked me in the chest with her finger. "I want to be nice and tanned this summer, so maybe we can find a place with a pool?"

I laughed and realized that I hadn't even told her that everything was already set up and ready to go for me.

"I think we can arrange that," I chuckled with a wink.

"Well, I guess I should get started on looking for jobs there right away. I'll have a little bit of money to help with rent for a few months from selling Wrenched, but I don't want you to worry about me not carrying my weight."

"Kayce, I'll take care of you. You don't have to worry about that." My heart swelled as I said it, knowing that I had never spoken truer words in my life.

"I would never ask that of you, and I really do like being able to take care of myself."

"I know you do. But from here on out, we're a team. We're going to tackle things together and celebrate all of the wins as they come."

"Starting with this one," she squealed as she reached up and kissed me.

<u>Epilogue- Nine Months Later</u>

Wyatt

"Hurry up! They're going to be here soon," Kayce squealed as she walked by and pounded on the bathroom door as I finished brushing my teeth.

I put my toothbrush away and rinsed my mouth. It was a huge day for us, and I loved the excitement that Kayce was feeling about it. I opened the door and caught her fluffing the pillows on the couch for the fifteenth time that morning.

"I think they're fluffy," I laughed, walking over and wrapping my arms around her waist. Her hair was shorter than before and colored dark red, matching the Arizona Rattlers jersey that she was wearing.

"I just want everything to be perfect," she said as she laid her head against my chest. Nine months of living together, and I still hadn't had my fill of her yet. I could feel my dick hardening against her ass, wondering if we had time for a quickie before everyone got there.

"Everything is perfect," I murmured against her ear as I ran my tongue up her neck.

"Your mom is going to be here in any minute now, so you better put that thing away," she teased as she bumped me with her butt, not helping my erection go down.

Just then, the doorbell rang, and Kayce took off running to answer it.

After I got up the nerve to call Julian back and beg for my job, he threw another curveball at me and offered me the head coach position instead of the recruiting one I had been initially offered. It turned out that the owner had heard about me from the Colorado Cougars and was impressed with my skills as a player. Given how long I had been playing and my love for the sport, he decided he wanted me to take over when the head coach decided to move to another team in March. With the higher salary and Kayce's new job as a mechanic at the best automotive shop in Phoenix, we decided to forgo the apartment and bought a house with a massive pool in the back. That was probably the single best investment I had made in my life when I found out how much she enjoyed skinny dipping.

"I can't believe you're here!" Kayce beamed as she wrapped Lacey in a hug as they came inside. Grant held two car seats on each arm as Annie and Liam waited their turn to hug Kayce.

"Here, let me help you," I offered, reaching over to take one of the car seats from him.

"Thanks, they get heavy quickly," he laughed, following me inside and leaving the girls to linger in the doorway.

"Hello, princess," I cooed as I set the car seat down on the floor and pulled the blanket back to look at my niece. "Daisy Mae, you just get more beautiful every time I see you."

She smiled up at me and giggled as I tickled her foot. It was hard to believe that the twins were already going on four months old and getting bigger by the minute.

I turned to the other car seat that Grant set down beside her. I felt my grin pull across my face as I looked down at the matching outfits they were wearing. Daisy was wearing an Arizona Rattlers onesie with a fluffy red skirt, and Jackson had the same onesie with red sweat pants. It made me beam with pride when I felt how supportive my family was.

"Future MVP right here," I said as I leaned over and tickled Jackson's toes.

"How was the drive out here?" I asked, looking up at Grant as I sat on the floor with the babies.

"It was good. The new Excursion made it easier," he laughed.

"I can imagine, that's a beast of a vehicle." They definitely needed the room with six of them, including the two car seats, double stroller, and all of their luggage. It was probably the best investment that he had made in his life.

A few minutes later, the girls came over to join us. Kayce stood over my shoulder, looking at the babies as she squealed over how cute they were. I got up and moved out of the way so Lacey could get them out of their car seats as Kayce waited impatiently to hold them.

The doorbell rang again, so I rushed over to answer it.

"Hey!" I stepped back and held the door open for my mom and Buck to come in. Right behind them was Chase, Mia, and the girls. I knew that Noah and Jade wouldn't be too far behind them.

The house was quickly filling with noise as everyone moved about, hugging each other and saying hi. Finally, the entire family was back together, and it felt like home again. Only it was pushing ninety degrees here, and Haven Brook had a severe snowstorm warning back home. There were some things that I didn't miss.

I helped Grant and Lacey get set up in two of the guest rooms while Kayce showed my mom and Buck to the other one. Chase and Noah had rented a house close by for their families, knowing that we all wouldn't fit under one roof for the week. It was hard to believe that they were here for a whole week! I wished that I was on vacation with them, but if anything, I was going to be working overtime since it was the World Series and the Rattlers were in it.

Everyone came out to watch a few games and to have a much-needed vacation. Kayce had taken the week off to entertain everyone and had already planned out the things that she wanted to do, including an all-day trip to the zoo and a girl's day shopping at Scottsdale Fashion Square.

But today, today was a day for all of us to spend together. I didn't have to go in to work, and no one had anything pressing to do. The pool was ready and filled with plenty of giant rafts that Kayce insisted that we needed. We had plenty of food to barbecue and snacks to munch on throughout the day. One thing that I had learned about Kayce was that when she did something- she put everything she had into it. So we weren't just having a pool party and a barbecue. We were having the ULTIMATE pool party and an epic barbecue that would put The Tasty Pig to shame.

THREE STRIKES, YOU'RE GONE

I thought that my life would always be plagued by the nightmares that haunted me for so long after my dad died. It turned out that I just needed a little bit of light in my life to lift some of the darkness. And that light was about to get a whole lot brighter when I asked Kayce to marry me.

Other Books By Samantha Baca

The Haven Brook Series

(small-town romantic suspense):

'Til Death Do Us Part (Haven Brook Book 1)

https://books2read.com/u/m2RJNR

The Cradle Will Fall (Haven Brook Book 2)

https://books2read.com/u/b6O0QE

The Ties That Bind (Haven Brook Book 3)

https://books2read.com/u/mqgoz8

A Very Haven Christmas (Haven Brook Book 4- Novella)

https://books2read.com/u/mvqGjj

Three Strikes, You're Gone (Haven Brook Book 5)

https://books2read.com/u/mvqL2z

The Dark Shadows Trilogy

(romantic suspense)

Five Steps Ahead (Dark Shadows Book 1)

https://books2read.com/u/38Q0gO

Ten Seconds Too Late (Dark Shadows Book 2)

https://books2read.com/u/3JRgVB

Against The Clock (Dark Shadows Book 3)

https://books2read.com/u/m2YwoR

<u>The Stone Creek Series</u>

<u>(small-town- novellas)</u>

Chocolate Covered Mistletoe (Stone Creek Book 1)

https://books2read.com/u/3LRk9N

Candy Coated Promises (Stone Creek Book 2)

https://books2read.com/u/mldP5Y

Pumpkin Spiced Possibilities (Stone Creek Book 3)

https://books2read.com/u/bojdwV

<u>Beaumont Creek Series</u>

<u>(small town)</u>

Just One Time (Beaumont Creek Book 1)

https://books2read.com/u/3G52zK

Second Chances (Beaumont Creek Book 2)

https://books2read.com/u/4Aj6Z0

Third Time's The Charm (Beaumont Creek Book 3)

https://books2read.com/u/b5lEyG

Four-ever Single (Beaumont Creek Book 4)

https://books2read.com/u/4j5jMX

Fifth Wheel (Beaumont Creek Book 5)

https://books2read.com/u/4XwKwa

THREE STRIKES, YOU'RE GONE

Whiskey Mountain Series

(small-town- novellas)

Something To Talk About

https://books2read.com/u/4X62ag

Something To Think About

https://books2read.com/u/3GWAan

Something To Believe In

https://books2read.com/u/3yVzgB

Something To Live For

https://books2read.com/u/mllEOP

Sugarplum Falls Series

(Holiday Novellas- can be read as standalone)

Blame It On The Mistletoe

https://books2read.com/u/bw1rqe

Blame It On The Eggnog

https://books2read.com/u/38PPY6

Blame It On The Candy Canes

https://books2read.com/u/31DNo7

Blame It On The Blizzard

https://books2read.com/u/b6z6XE

<u>Standalone Books</u>

One Last Wish

https://books2read.com/u/mqg7D9

Finding Love In Apartment 2C (novella)

https://books2read.com/u/bze9aZ

Cocky Counsel: A Hero Club Novel

https://books2read.com/u/31Kzkn

All Is Fair In Food And War (novella)

https://books2read.com/u/bp8qjX

<u>Holiday Books</u>

<u>(novellas)</u>

Snow Place To Go

https://books2read.com/u/4A560N

A Christmas Wish

https://books2read.com/u/4EKXpE

Holiday Hijinks

https://books2read.com/u/4DP6Ze

About the Author

Samantha lives in the southwest with her husband and two small children after abandoning her childhood dream of living in a cabin in Colorado when she found that she couldn't afford to live there and was deathly allergic to the woods. When she's not writing, she's usually spouting off sarcastic remarks while drinking wine out of a coffee mug to look like a functional adult while chasing down her toddlers. She enjoys spending time with her family, watching reruns of Friends, and the 24/7 flow of coffee that can be found in her veins. Be sure to follow her on social media for updates on what she's working on.

You can find her here:

Facebook: https://www.facebook.com/AuthorSamanthaBaca

Instagram: https://instagram.com/author_samantha_baca

Goodreads: http://www.goodreads.com/authorsamanthabaca

Facebook Reader Group:
https://www.facebook.com/groups/2945710968775398/

Webpage: https://authorsamanthabaca.wordpress.com

Newsletter: http://eepurl.com/g0NcSj

www.ingramcontent.com/pod-product-compliance
Lightning Source LLC
Chambersburg PA
CBHW021409010826
48972CB00014B/961